"Fans of Jones's bestselling Charley Davidson series and Janet Evanovich's romps will devour this steamy series launch, which introduces both an irresistible pair of crime-busting Gilmore Girls and a quirky, mysterious setting."       —*Booklist*

"Compelling characters and a sexy, angst-filled bunch of mysteries add up to a winning series debut."       —*Kirkus Reviews*

"*A Bad Day for Sunshine* is everything you want from Darynda Jones . . . and more! Laugh-out-loud funny, intensely suspenseful, page-turning fun with a sassy new heroine you will love. Prepare to be hooked by this witty, sexy, and thrilling new series from one of my favorite authors!"

—Allison Brennan, *New York Times* bestselling author

"Swoon-worthy heroes, quirky characters, and a page-turning mystery. Move over, Stephanie Plum; Sunshine Vicram has arrived. Prepare yourself. This book is a keeper!"

—Christie Craig, *New York Times* bestselling author

"Darynda Jones has done it again. With trademark humor, eccentric yet relatable characters, and masterful storytelling, she takes us on a journey we don't want to end. *A Bad Day for Sunshine* is a great day for readers!"       —Tracy Brogan, #1 bestselling author

"Smart, sexy, and outrageously funny. Jones masterfully balances heartwarming comedy and bone-chilling suspense."

—Marina Adair, #1 national bestselling
author of *Summer in Napa*

"From the creative genius who brought you Charley Davidson comes your newest obsession: Sunshine Vicram. Mother. Sheriff. Warden of weird."

—Susan Donovan, *New York Times* bestselling author

"Darynda Jones is always on my MUST-READ list! No one can pull you in to a book like she can!"

—Donna Grant, *New York Times* and *USA Today* bestselling author

"All the snarky humor and engaging writing you've come to expect from master storyteller Darynda Jones. I would read her if she scribbled on a napkin. Luckily, her new story has more than just lipstick and a number. Prepare to get sucked in. Her writing is like a vortex; you can't get out until you're done and sobbing for more."

—Eve Langlais, *New York Times* and *USA Today* bestselling author

"A new town, new characters to become friends with, same snort-in-public humor . . . You're going to love this story!"

—Laura Drake, award-winning author

"*A Bad Day for Sunshine* is deliciously witty, fast-paced, and filled with laugh-out-loud dialogue. Darynda Jones knocks it out of the park with this delightful new series!"

—Robyn Peterman, *New York Times* bestselling author

"Darynda delivers again! *A Bad Day for Sunshine* tugs at your heartstrings and tickles your funny bone. From gut-wrenching heartbreak to full-abdominal belly laughs, *Sunshine* is a literary workout for your core. Another unique read from a stellar story-teller!"

—Diane Kelly, award-winning author of the House-Flipper Mystery series

"Smart, sexy, clever . . . and so many laughs! Darynda Jones brings her trademark wit and charm in *A Bad Day for Sunshine*. I couldn't get enough!"

—Kim Law, award-winning and bestselling author of *Montana Cherries*

## ALSO BY DARYNDA JONES

### Sunshine Vicram

*A Bad Day for Sunshine*

*A Good Day for Chardonnay*

### Charley Davidson

*Summoned to Thirteenth Grave*

*The Trouble with Twelfth Grave*

*Eleventh Grave in Moonlight*

*The Curse of Tenth Grave*

*The Dirt on Ninth Grave*

*Eighth Grave After Dark*

*Seventh Grave and No Body*

*Sixth Grave on the Edge*

*Fifth Grave Past the Light*

*Fourth Grave Beneath My Feet*

*Third Grave Dead Ahead*

*Second Grave on the Left*

*First Grave on the Right*

### Darklight

*Death and the Girl He Loves*

*Death, Doom, and Detention*

*Death and the Girl Next Door*

# A HARD DAY FOR A HANGOVER

## A NOVEL

*Darynda Jones*

ST. MARTIN'S GRIFFIN
NEW YORK

Published in the United States by St. Martin's Griffin, an imprint of St. Martin's Publishing Group

A HARD DAY FOR A HANGOVER. Copyright © 2022 by Darynda Jones. All rights reserved. Printed in the United States of America. For information, address St. Martin's Publishing Group, 120 Broadway, New York, NY 10271.

www.stmartins.com

Designed by Omar Chapa

The Library of Congress has cataloged the hardcover edition as follows:

Names: Jones, Darynda, author.
Title: A hard day for a hangover : a novel / Darynda Jones.
Description: First edition. | New York : St. Martin's Press, 2022. |
    Series: Sunshine Vicram series ; 3
Identifiers: LCCN 2022035061 | ISBN 9781250233141 (hardcover) |
    ISBN 9781250266972 (ebook)
Subjects: LCGFT: Detective and mystery fiction. | Novels.
Classification: LCC PS3610.O6236 H37 2022 | DDC 813/.6—
    dc23/eng/20220721
LC record available at https://lccn.loc.gov/2022035061

ISBN 978-1-250-26696-5 (trade paperback)

Our books may be purchased in bulk for promotional, educational, or business use. Please contact your local bookseller or the Macmillan Corporate and Premium Sales Department at 1-800-221-7945, extension 5442, or by email at MacmillanSpecialMarkets@macmillan.com.

First St. Martin's Griffin Edition: 2023

10  9  8  7  6  5  4  3  2  1

*For first responders everywhere
—thank you for helping those who cannot help themselves—
and for the loved ones who pray for your safe return*

# 1

*When life hands you lemons, hand them back.*
*You deserve chocolate.*

—SIGN AT THE SUGAR SHACK

Normally, Sheriff Sunshine Vicram would've been alarmed at the sight of a knitting needle sticking out of a guy's neck. At the very least, she would've been concerned for the horrified man's well-being. Yet, there she stood. Unmoved. Unshaken. Unstirred. Much like the forgotten bottle of dirty martini mix in the back of her cabinet. At the tender age of early-thirty-something, Sun realized she had seen it all. The world held no more surprises. No more magic. It just was.

"Stop it," the man standing beside her said.

She turned to her chief deputy, the blond bank vault door known as Quincy Cooper, and asked, "Stop what?"

"That." He circled an index finger, outlining her in midair. "That thing you keep doing."

"I have no idea what you're talking about." She crossed her arms over her uniformed chest and went back to staring at the knitting needle and the impaled man behind it.

"You know exactly what I'm talking about. You're pining."

"I'm not pining."

"You're pining." He leaned closer and lowered his voice.

"Worse, you're pining for a man who clearly doesn't want to talk to you."

The accuracy of his words stung like lemon juice on a paper cut, and she had to give it to her bestie. He never missed an opportunity to be brutally honest. "Please," she said, lifting her chin and forcing her poker face to hold fast under fire. "You've been pining after that same man's sister for months. You have no room to talk."

"Touché."

"Besides, it's not that. It's just . . ."

Wait. What was it? The pit of despair she'd fallen into? The black hole of melancholy to which she'd succumbed? The bottle of Patrón she'd finished off at two that morning?

"It's just?" Quincy prodded.

She rubbed her temple. She always forgot how horribly tequila affected her until the morning after, then it all came rushing back. And up. She wrapped a protective arm around her queasy stomach, squishing her memo pad in the process. "It's just . . . this has been a really long week."

He checked his watch. "It's eight thirty-seven—a.m."

A questioning brow rose of its own volition as she looked up at him.

"On Monday."

"Your point being?"

He lifted a heavy shoulder, giving in. "They say the first five days after the weekend are the hardest. Hang in there, cupcake." He nudged her with his elbow.

She nudged back, then returned her attention to one of Vlad's distant cousins, Doug the Impaled.

Their assault victim, an older man wrapped neck-to-kneecaps in a trench coat, lay on a gurney, cradling his neck with both hands. He stared up at them, panic rounding his lids, but he didn't dare speak. Probably because of the knitting needle protruding from one side of said neck. Doug, their resident flasher, had apparently flashed the wrong person and ended up in the emergency room as a result.

"My first question," Quincy said, tilting his head for a better view, "is how did someone get the capped end of a knitting needle so far into his neck like that?"

"Right?" Sun grimaced at the metallic object. "The pointy end is sticking out."

"Maybe both ends are pointy?" he guessed. "Do they make knitting needles with dual pointy ends?"

"Maybe." Sun tilted her head, too. "That makes so much more sense than what I was thinking. Wouldn't it have hurt the assailant's hand, though? To jam it in there like that?" She made a stabbing gesture with her pen, trying to imagine the scene in her head. The needle had been embedded far enough to remain stationary when Doug breathed. Undoubtedly a good four inches, if not more.

Quincy tossed a questioning gaze to the nurse. "Any hand injuries today?"

The nurse, a pretty brunette who looked like she'd graduated from nursing school thirty seconds before walking in the door, shook her head. "Not that I know of." She scanned the area, worry scoring lines into her forehead. "The doctor should be here any minute."

Sun leaned closer to Doug and said loudly, "Do you know who did this?"

Doug glared at her, then shook his head. Just barely, obviously afraid to move.

Quincy cleared his throat from behind her. "Yeah, I don't think Doug's hard of hearing."

"Right." She straightened. "My bad."

She was off her game. She'd been off her game since she told Levi Ravinder—aka, the man she'd been in love with since conception—they had a lot more in common than he might think. They both liked pepperoni pizza. They both loved sunsets and long walks on the beach. They both had a fifteen-year-old daughter named Auri.

Weird.

"You know Auri is yours," she'd said to him, sitting in the back of Quincy's cruiser. Well, Levi was sitting, handcuffed and more than a little miffed. Sun was straddling. Not miffed in the least.

He'd stilled at her words, his inscrutable and impossibly handsome face even harder to read than normal. And she was an above-average reader.

Instead of joy or amazement or elation at finding out he had a daughter he never knew about—all the emotions she'd naïvely hoped for—he just sat there, staring at her, his expression guarded. Cautious. Almost calculating.

Sadly, before Sun could ferret out what lay hidden beneath his stoicism, she got called to the scene of a traffic accident, and the first chance he got, Levi ditched the protective custody she'd forcefully placed him into. He vanished, and in the process, he'd stolen Quincy's cruiser.

Sun understood. Not the car-theft thing but the running thing. It was a lot to lay on a guy. Especially since, five minutes earlier, she and her deputies had also informed Levi that his uncle Clay was trying to kill him—hence the protective custody—and take over his very successful distillery.

She'd blindsided the poor man with those five words, sent him running, and now she could concentrate on little else. They'd found the stolen cruiser at his house an hour later, as was his intention, but no Levi. And, possibly even more concerning, no Uncle Clay.

In her dreams, the scene in the back of Quincy's cruiser had gone very differently. She'd imagined Levi's expression morphing into one of shocked happiness when he learned the truth about their daughter. She'd imagined his mouth covering hers, grateful and eager. Kissing her until her toes curled. Until the oxygen fled her lungs.

"Who'd you piss off, Pettyfer?"

Sun blinked up at Quince, snapping back to the present, and nodded. "Right?" she said, recovering quickly. She had to get a grip or Levi Ravinder was going to cost her more than just her ability to drink in moderation. He was going to cost Del Sol's newest sheriff her job. "Who *did* you piss off? Knitters are usually so laid back."

"Exactly," Quince agreed, making the word sound like an accusation as he stared Doug down. "They hardly ever stab people. Statistically speaking."

The nurse managed to pry Doug's hands off his throat for a better look, but she was afraid to touch anything. "I don't think your windpipe has been punctured, Mr. Pettyfer."

"So, he *can* talk?" Quincy asked.

She offered a noncommittal shrug. "He can try. I guess. I don't know." She bit her lip and glanced up between the two of them. "Wh-what do you think?" Poor girl. She didn't look much older than Auri.

After a quick glance at the girl's name tag, Sun said softly, "Wendy, you're doing great. Doug is just an ass."

He glared at her.

She glared back. The man had refused to reply to their first round of questions, pointing at the knitting needle to justify his silence. She had two missing persons to find. She didn't have time for this. "Cut the crap, Doug. What happened?"

"I'm the victim here," he said, his voice a little hoarse but no worse for the wear. "They tried to kill me."

Quincy shifted his weight and released a long, irritated sigh.

Sun fought the urge to do the same. Doug created more drama than Hollywood during sweeps week. So far, he'd caused a pileup on Main Street, set a woman's hair on fire—long story—and gave Sun a concussion trying to save his ass after he'd flashed Mrs. Papadeaux only to have her chase him under the Cargita Bridge with a melon baller. Sun shuddered to think what the woman would've done with the baller given more time.

"They?" Quince asked, his voice sharp enough to slice through her fuzzy musings once again.

Doug nodded at Quincy's inquiry and instantly regretted it, making a face only a mother could love.

"Did Mrs. Papadeaux finally exact her revenge?" Sun asked. She'd barely been on the job four months, but even she'd had enough of the man.

"Mrs. Papadeaux?" Doug asked, appalled. He had slick, sun-damaged skin, the leathery folds creasing as he frowned at her. "I was jumped. By a gang."

"A gang of knitters?"

He turned an orangish shade of red. Salmon perhaps. Or coral. Why he needed people to see his penis was beyond her. She thought about asking a psychologist, then realized she didn't care.

"How should I know what gang members do in their spare time?" Doug asked. "I was just walking down Main—"

"Wearing a trench coat," Quincy added.

"—minding my own business."

"Doubtful."

"—when out of nowhere, a street gang attacked me."

"Because we have so many of those running around Del Sol." Sun let her doubt manifest into a frown. A frownier frown than she'd previously been wearing. A scowl, if you will.

As a small New Mexico tourist town in the middle of the Sangre de Cristo Mountains, Del Sol just didn't attract many gangs.

Though she hated to admit it, Doug did look pretty beat up. Bruises and scrapes peppered his face and hands, and his left eye was swelling alarmingly fast.

"And all of this happened at the corner of broad and daylight?" Quince asked.

"No. I told you, Main."

"With no witnesses?"

He tested the knitting needle with his left hand before shuddering and dropping it. "I don't know. I don't remember seeing anyone. It . . . it all happened so fast."

Quince wasn't buying it. "I guess I could canvass the area. See if anyone saw anything."

"Oh, you don't have to do that." Doug tried to sit up and immediately regretted it. He lay back with a wince and said, "I can't imagine anyone saw. We were in a pretty secluded spot."

Quince took a step forward, his patience gossamer thin, and said from between gritted teeth, "You just said you were on Main."

"Yeah, but they jumped me right as I turned down that alley between the Sugar Shack and Bernadette's?"

"Of course they did." Sun's chief deputy seemed to be hovering on the same precarious edge she was on. The one called I've Had Just About Enough of You, Mister Man. He crossed his arms over his chest and leaned closer to her. "I say we push the needle the rest of the way in and call it a day."

So tempting. "I hear you, but then we'd have to get rid of Wendy, too, and she seems really nice."

Wendy's startled gaze landed on them. Sun winked at her, and for the first time since they'd arrived, the girl seemed to relax. She hid a grin and said, "I'll see what's keeping the doctor," before sliding the curtain closed around them and heading down the hall.

"I'm going to ask one more time, Doug, then you're on your own." But before Sun could make good on her promise, her phone rang. She answered the call from her new lieutenant, Tricia Salazar, only to be yelled at.

"He's gone!"

Odd way to start a conversation, but okay. She'd play along. "You didn't chain him to the radiator?"

"What? No. Why would I chain him to the radiator?"

"The filing cabinet?"

"No."

"The coffee maker?"

"Is that even possible?"

"Perhaps if I knew who we were talking about, I could answer that question."

"Oh, sorry, boss. Randy escaped again and I panicked."

Sun let the tension drain from her shoulders with a relieved sigh. Just the raccoon. A raccoon that was going to be the death of her. Or Quincy. Probably Quincy. "We should've named him Houdini."

"What should I do?"

Sun cupped a hand over the phone and stage-whispered, "Whatever you do, don't tell Quincy."

Salazar laughed softly into the phone, but Quincy scowled at Sun when realization dawned. He bit down and turned away, anger tightening his jaw.

"How's Doug?" Salazar asked.

"He'll live."

"Oh," she said, not bothering to hide her disappointment.

Sun swallowed a bark of laughter. Salazar didn't *really* want Doug to die, but a more debilitating injury would've made all their lives easier. At least for a little while. "Call me if you find the you-know-what."

"Will do, boss."

She hung up and slid her phone into its case on her belt.

Quincy scrubbed his face and said from behind his hands, "He got out again, didn't he?"

"It's your own fault."

He lowered his hands and scowled at her. Again. "How the hell is it my fault?"

"I have no idea, but I'll think of something."

"That thing is a menace."

"Yeah, yeah." Sun may not know a lot about raccoons, but she knew a ton about her best friend, and no matter how much he grumbled and protested and complained, he admired the clever creature. The fact that it was on a mission to make Quincy's life as miserable as raccoonly possible seemed moot. If Sun didn't know better—and she really didn't—she would swear it was targeting her chief deputy. "We need to move the cage out of the locker room and into the bullpen at night so the cameras can record how he's getting out."

"Yeah, if I don't kill him first."

All talk, this one. "You're just mad because he ate your Twizzlers."

He pressed his lips into a straight line. "Can we finish up so I can go arrest the love of your life?"

Ever since Levi escaped—like, two days ago—Quince had been dead set on arresting him. Like oddly obsessed. As though

Levi stealing—no, borrowing—his cruiser had somehow assaulted his manhood.

"Not yet," Sun said.

"Why not? He stole my cruiser. Stealing is illegal. Arresting him is kind of our job."

"First, he *borrowed* your cruiser."

"Seriously?"

"We found it an hour later." Quince opened his mouth to protest again, but Sun cut him off. "And second, we have something else to do first."

He rubbed the line between his brows. "And that would be?"

She released a withering sigh, hardly able to believe what she was about to say, but it had hit her about three shots past midnight. She steeled herself and said, "We have to find Clay Ravinder before Levi does and put *him* into protective custody before Levi kills him."

Quincy's jaw literally dropped open. After a few blinks of astonished disbelief, he said, "And you want to prevent that from happening why?"

She shrugged. "Apparently that's part of my job."

"Oh, right. The sheriff thing. Still, that's a big ask."

"Quince, if Levi finds him first, he'll make the man rue the day he was ever hatched."

"And that's bad because?"

"Because I don't want Auri visiting her father in prison."

That sobered him. He bit down, his jaw working hard under the stress, then lowered his head. "Does she know yet? The bean sprout?"

A wave of anguish washed over Sun and settled beside the last remnants of tequila souring in the pit of her stomach. How would she tell her daughter who her real father was? How would Auri take the news that he'd been right in front of her this whole time and no one, not even Sun, knew?

She couldn't think about that just yet. She had far too many irons in the fire at the moment, one of them being protecting the most hated man in town from one of the most beloved. Levi was nothing short of a folk hero to the citizens of Del Sol. Putting him in prison for premeditated murder would not sit well with them.

"No," Sun fairly whispered, "she doesn't know yet."

He nodded in thought. "Are you going to tell her?"

Sun's gaze snapped to his profile. "Of course."

"Because no one would blame you if—"

"Quincy," she said, interrupting before he could even finish the sentiment, "just because you never liked the guy—"

"Who says I never liked him?" When Sun's expression flatlined, he lifted a shoulder in defense. "I just think you can do better."

He'd said that very thing many times over the years, but they were no longer talking about the man she'd simply been crushing on since the first time she'd laid eyes on him. Levi was the father of her child. And he was a good man. He'd risen above his family's illicit activities and created a legitimate, thriving business. One that employed half the people in the county, not to mention every member of the Ravinder clan. And keeping that group employed could not be easy.

"Quince, is there something more to your dislike of Levi?"

"More?"

"Something you've never told me?"

"There's plenty I've never told you."

"Really? Like what?"

"You put too much cilantro in your pico."

"Quince, I'm serious. You've never . . . Wait." She had to take a step back, she was so appalled. "I have never put too much cilantro in my pico de gallo."

He snorted. "Please."

"I don't even put cilantro in my pico de gallo."

"Yes, you do. Cilantro is like the brussels sprouts of Mexican cuisine. I can smell it from a mile away."

"Cannot."

"Can too. And you put too much."

"Since when?"

"Since always."

She would not take this lying down. Or standing up. Either way. "Fine." She stepped closer and poked him in the chest. "But just remember, you started this."

He leaned down until they were nose-to-nose. "Oh, don't you worry. I will." After a long pause, he asked, "What'd I start?"

"Cook-off, mister. You. Me. Diced tomatoes. It's time to put your money where your mouth is."

"You cook your pico de gallo? Because that would explain a lot."

"What? No." She turned away from him so he couldn't see the guilt lining her face. It was only once, for heaven's sake. She'd been young. Naïve. Unaccustomed to the nuances of Mexican cuisine. "Levi," she said, getting back to the business at hand.

His gaze volleyed to Doug, then back again, before he replied. "Later. I need to go check on the kid." The kid he referred to was none other than Cruz De los Santos, a high school freshman whose father—one of Quincy's best friends—had recently died, leaving Cruz an orphan and Quincy a first-time guardian. Which was just scary. "What about this guy?" Quince hitched a thumb over a massive shoulder.

"Yeah," Doug said. "What about me?"

Sun closed the memo pad she had yet to write in and stuffed it into her front pocket. "We have your statement, Mr. Pettyfer. We'll be in touch."

No longer the center of attention, Doug's face fell. Honestly, if all the women he flashed would simply point and laugh instead of shrieking with indignant shock, Doug would eventually stop his shenanigans. Sun made a mental note to offer a class on how to handle flashers.

Wendy rushed in with the doctor at last. Because God forbid Doug suffer any longer than necessary.

"If he flashes either of you," she said, glaring at their patient, "call the men in white coats to come get him. I'm done."

To Sun's surprise, the blood drained from Doug's orange

complexion. Interesting. His reaction gave her all the ammunition she needed to get a handle on the man. If she'd known he was so afraid of a stint in the psych ward, she would've threatened him with that months ago. She walked to the parking lot with a renewed bounce in her step.

"I won't be long," Quincy said as he climbed into his cruiser. It was like shoving a stuffed animal into a tin can.

"Give Cruz a hug for me."

Quince shifted his cruiser into reverse, shook his head, and said, "Yeah, not happening," as he backed out of his parking space.

Five minutes later, Sun was still thinking about Cruz when she pushed through the two security doors at the sheriff's station and wound her way through the bullpen toward her admin's office. It still boggled her mind. Cruz, a fifteen-year-old kid, fought off a thirty-year-old with a good fifty pounds on him to save her daughter. She owed him everything.

Her phone rang again just as she got to her admin's desk. Anita Escobar's dark blond ponytail was even frizzier than usual, a sure sign she'd woken up late that morning. An even bigger sign was the fact that her official polo shirt was inside out. A white patch of backing material with chaotic black-and-gold stitching where the embroidered badge would be kept tugging at Sun's gaze. She could hardly blame Anita, though. They'd had a rough few days.

Anita smiled up at her.

Sun smiled back as she answered the second call that day from her lieutenant. "That was fast," she said, looking around for Salazar. "I'm here at the station. Did you catch the mongrel?"

"No," she said breathlessly. "Sorry, boss. I must've just missed you. I'm headed to Copper Canyon. Drew Essary was out hunting this morning. He called in a few minutes ago. He . . . he thinks he found a body."

Sun had been rifling through a stack of messages Anita had on her desk. She stopped and gave Salazar her complete attention. "He doesn't know for sure?"

"He couldn't tell. He only saw it through his binoculars. Said it's on an incline pretty deep in the canyon and hidden under some brush. He wanted to let us know before he tries to go down to check. He will likely lose cell service."

"Good thinking on his part." Sun had known Drew her whole life. An old cowboy, cantankerous through and through, yet razor sharp. He didn't miss much, but a body? Had Levi done something desperate? Had he fought with his uncle Clay? Killed him? Or maybe Clay somehow got the upper hand and finally accomplished his goal of getting Levi out of the way? Sun fought the darkness tightening the edges of her vision. "Where is he exactly? Copper Canyon is a big area."

"I'll text you his directions. I just wanted to get the area cordoned off for you. He said you'll need rappelling gear to get down there. He only has a rope, but he's going to give it a shot."

Sun headed for her office to drop off her things. "Okay. Text me those directions. I'll get the gear and meet you there."

"Should I radio for a bus just in case?"

Sun paused to think about that, then said, "Not yet. Let's make sure Drew is right before calling in the cavalry." She couldn't believe Drew would call them if he weren't seriously concerned, but he could still be mistaken. He could be seeing a pair of pants someone threw out. Or an animal. Or, hell, even a mannequin. No need to call an ambulance just yet.

"You got it, boss."

They hung up and she called Quincy. "Possible DB at Copper Canyon," she said when he picked up. "We need the climbing gear."

"It's at my house."

"Quincy," she whispered, panic closing her throat.

"Don't even think that," he said, reading her mind. "I'll be there in five."

# 2

*Carry binoculars when hiking so when you make frequent
stops, it looks like you're appreciating nature and not fighting
for air.*

—PRO TIP FROM DEL SOL SPORTING GOODS

"I just don't understand why we can't raise penguins."

Auri's grandma gave her a patient look, her silvery blond hair
perfectly coiffed, her pink lipstick expertly applied. As always.

"We have, like, a thousand acres of land behind the house,"
she added, strengthening her argument tenfold.

"We have half an acre."

"Penguins are small."

"And it's illegal to keep a penguin as a pet. Your mother would
have to arrest you."

There was that. "I guess," she said, not convinced in the least.
This called for some serious research on penguin laws. Maybe they
could call it a sanctuary. Or a penguin reserve. Did they have those
in New Mexico? She leaned over and gave her favorite—and only—
grandmother a kiss on the cheek. "Thanks for dropping me off,
Grandma."

"Have a good day, hon."

"I'll try but it's hard when all of your hopes and dreams have
been dashed."

"I think you'll survive."

"Let's hope so." She waved goodbye and closed the door.

Her grandma brought her to school because her mother, the infamous Sunshine Vicram, had been called in to a possible assault. The price of being sheriff, she supposed. But it had always been like that. When her mom became a detective for Santa Fe PD, her hours went from long to endless. Auri would end up at her grandparents' house every time a big case hit, which was more often than not, and her mom had to work for days on end.

Strange thing was, Auri didn't mind. She never minded. Her mom did important stuff and her grandparents spoiled her to the point of obscenity. Win-win.

But Auri was worried about the woman who birthed her. She'd been depressed since Levi escaped. Like, more depressed than usual. So depressed she'd turned to her archnemesis last night: tequila. Never a good sign, so it was up to Auri to hunt Levi down and keep him from killing his uncle.

Auri tossed another wave over her shoulder as her grandmother pulled out of the drop-off area. She then waved at a trio of elementary school boys, the same ones who greeted her every morning while waiting for their bus, before walking toward her first class. She walked until the Buick Encore drove out of sight, then she hooked a left at the ag building and headed toward the tree line that surrounded the high school. Auri had promised to stop sneaking out of the house. She'd said nothing about sneaking out of school.

Skipping a class or two, especially now, was not going to hurt anything. It was a short week and the last week of school. Finals were over and Auri had taken all of her makeup exams that weekend online, save one. In lieu of Mr. Torres's Terrible Test of Torment, she'd opted to write a paper. Because she could. Because she'd been in the hospital. Because his final was only whispered about in the halls of Del Sol High. No one spoke openly about it lest they invoke the demon Mr. Torres had clearly consulted when constructing said test.

Who knew this school would be so much fun? And openminded? Not all school districts would put up with demonconsulting as a side hobby for their teachers.

She hiked uphill far longer than she'd prepared her lungs for, causing her fingers to seek out the inhaler she kept in her jeans pocket. She brushed her fingertips across it, more as a soothing mechanism than a need. She just wanted to know it was there. Her inhaler. An inanimate object, but one she could count on. If everything else fell apart, at least she knew she'd be able to breathe.

Two long, stressful years later, with her lungs screaming for more oxygen, she crested a landform that was apparently only seven inches shorter than Mount Everest and started down the other side toward the Pecos River. More importantly, toward Quincy Cooper's cabin. And even *more* importantly, toward the hottie ensconced inside.

Cruz De los Santos had just gotten out of the hospital and had been ordered to stay home. His injuries were much more extensive than her silly submissive hemogoblin had been. Cruz had been stabbed. Three times. Saving her.

Guilt cinched the vise around her chest tighter, and Auri checked for her inhaler yet again as she stumbled along the uneven ground. She finally hit the row of cabins where Quincy—and now Cruz—lived. Having been part of a river campground before the owners called it quits and sold them off as permanent housing, the cabins all looked the same, so she strolled around a line of piñon trees until she spotted Quincy's lawn chairs and fishing gear on one of the front porches. She'd always loved the area. The river. The trees. The boy looking at her from under the doorframe, his arms crossed over his chest as he leaned against it.

"You're upright!" she said, taking the steps two at a time.

"I am."

She fell to her knees in front of him, lifted his shirt—which was not her usual M.O.—and checked the bandages underneath. No idea why. It's not like she'd know what to do if anything were amiss. "You ripped your stitches. Should you be upright?"

He spread his arms as she examined him and watched her from underneath those impossibly thick lashes. She knew this because she made the mistake of looking up. She stopped assaulting him and took a moment to appreciate what stood before her. His rich gaze sparkled with humor, and he looked much better than he had just last night. The paleness that had plagued him since the incident had disappeared to reveal the bronze skin and smooth features she'd grown so fond of. Even the peach fuzz framing his jaw looked darker, his sculpted mouth somehow fuller.

He reached down and picked up the braid that had fallen over her shoulder. "I like this."

"Oh, thanks." She stood, suddenly embarrassed that she'd been caught, yet again, ogling him. "It's French."

"Ah," he said, fighting a grin.

It happened to him a lot. The ogling. Everywhere they went, gazes tended to wander his way. But he and Auri had been hanging out for months now. She had to get over it. He would eventually grow tired of her constant fawning. Her incessant need to be near him. The tiny hearts bursting out of her eyes every time she looked at him.

The problem lay in the fact that this was Cruz De los Santos. The same Cruz De los Santos who wrote poetry and built computers and modified carburetors. Whatever a carburetor was. He was such an enigma. Quiet and reserved and full of mystery. His dad had died and no one knew for weeks. He'd kept it locked inside him, afraid if anyone knew, he'd be sent away. Away from Del Sol. Away from her.

Auri's heart ached as she studied her shoes. The planks in the porch. The black beetle carrying a leaf four times its size. Anything but him. She could only hope her flushed face didn't match the bright red of her hair.

She cleared her throat and picked up where they'd left off in their texts that morning. "No."

"Umm, yes?"

She looked up at him. "You can't come."

He recrossed his arms over his chest, catching on. "I can, actually."

"No, you can't." She stepped closer. "The doctor said. It's a field trip in the mountains. Too much walking. Too much hiking over uneven terrain."

"It's been almost a week. I'm as good as new."

"Really?" she challenged, then she did something she never thought herself capable of. She poked his abdomen. Hard. Purposely hurting him.

He winced and curled into himself. Covering his midsection with both arms, he actually had the gall to say, "That doesn't mean anything. If I poked you like that, it would hurt, too."

He had a point. "I'm just worried about your innards. What if you rip your stitches again?"

"The only way my stitches will rip is if you keep poking them. Sadist." He rubbed his stomach, then picked up her braid again and ran his thumb over the thick weave. "Is that why you're here and not at school? To poke me?"

"No," she said, her insecurities skyrocketing. But why? She'd never been insecure about anything. Why now? What was it about Cruz De los Santos that made her feel insecure when he was the most respectful guy she'd ever met? She forced a smile. "I'm done with finals. This last week is fluff. Movies and games and popcorn."

He dropped her hair but still didn't look at her. "Which is why you should be there."

And there it was. That feeling. That fluttering of insecurity that had steadily been gaining momentum over the last few days. In hindsight, it began when she almost got him killed. "Yeah, well, my submissive hemogoblin would beg to differ. Some of the kids get pretty rowdy."

During the attack, the one where Cruz had saved not only her life but Mrs. Fairborn's as well, Auri had been thrown across the kitchen floor. She'd hit her head on the corner of a hutch and got a killer percussion. Or, as the doctor had called it, a submissive hemogoblin. She'd lost consciousness soon after. Not soon enough, however. She'd stayed lucid just long enough to see a knife slide into Cruz's abdomen. Three times. One horrifying violation after another. She'd been having nightmares about it ever since.

He straightened in alarm at her confession. "Does it hurt?" He tilted his head to look at the side of hers. The shaved and stitched side she'd carefully covered with the French braid. When he reached up and took her chin in his hand to angle her head for a better look, the warmth of his fingers sent electricity shooting through her body.

"N-no, it doesn't hurt. Not much anyway. I just wanted to check on you. See if you need anything."

"Besides you?" he asked softly, lifting one of the plaits of hair to check her stitches.

She stilled. She'd never wanted to *be* with a guy. Not in that way. Not until Cruz. He was proving the exception to every rule she'd ever created. Not to mention a few her mother had composed. Namely, *Thou shalt not have sex until thou art thirty-two.* Her mom took her duties very seriously, but Auri's body turned to lava every time she was around this guy.

Apparently satisfied, Cruz eased his hold, though his fingers lingered and his bronze gaze locked onto hers for a solid minute.

She took an involuntary step closer. Wanting his mouth on hers. Wanting his arms around her. His hips pressed into her abdomen. But she couldn't bring herself to initiate. Instead, she dropped her gaze and asked, "You said in your text you had something to tell me? Something important?"

He dropped his hand, stuffed it into his front pocket, and looked across the river flowing a few yards away. "I do, but I want you to know I'm saying it with the utmost respect."

Her stomach clenched so hard she almost doubled over. Here it comes. He was breaking up with her even though they'd never been exclusive. Not officially. "Oh. Okay."

"I didn't want to be the one to tell you this, but you're saying it wrong."

She blinked up at him and felt her brows inch together. "I'm sorry?"

He turned back to her, his expression severe if not for the slight crinkling at the corners of his eyes. "Hemogoblin." If she didn't know better, and she really didn't, she'd swear he was on the verge of laughing. "That's not a real word."

She stepped back, appalled. "It most certainly is."

"Wanna bet?"

She didn't dare. "No. But it is."

"Well, *hemoglobin* is a word, but I'm pretty sure it doesn't mean what you think it does."

"Hemoglobin?"

"Yes."

"Glow?"

"Yes."

"And it doesn't mean—?"

"No."

She crossed her arms over her chest. "Then what does it mean, Mr. Smarty Pants?"

"It's a protein in your red blood cells that carries oxygen to your organs. Among other things."

"What?" She took another step back. "It's not a head wound?"

"Not that I know of."

"Oh." Stunned, she walked to one of the chairs on the porch and sank onto it, the wood slats creaking against her weight. "I was wondering why swelling in the brain would be named after a goblin. I just thought it was left over from medieval times or something. Like when they would use a drill on someone's skull to release the evil spirits."

"Ah."

"So, I don't have a submissive hemo-*glow*-bin?"

He sat in the chair beside her. "I don't think that's a real thing."

"Why didn't my mother tell me?"

"I can't imagine," he said, trying to hide his nuclear smile behind a fist.

She studied it, that smile, for a few seconds. "If I didn't know better—" she began, but the sound of a vehicle pulling into the drive stopped her mid-sentence.

Both heads snapped toward the sound.

"Quincy!" she whispered. No clue why. She jumped to her feet. "I can't be here. He'll tell my mom, then my mom'll call my grandma, and my grandma'll tell my grandpa, and they'll send out the National Guard and the CIA because my grandpa was in military intelligence and he has connections, and then I'll be grounded for the rest of my natural-born life. Or all summer. Whichever ends first." She said all of this while searching frantically for a place to hide. Without thought, she rushed inside the cabin and wedged herself between a wall and a pile of—thankfully—clean laundry, praying he hadn't come home to change his clothes.

"Hey, kid," she heard Quincy say. A car door closed and footsteps sounded as Quincy's heavy boots trod up the steps.

"Hey," Cruz said.

Quincy stopped just outside the door. "You okay?"

"Peachy."

Auri almost giggled. Not many boys her age would willingly use the word *peachy*.

"Are you heating the entire neighborhood?" He must've noticed the wide-open front door. It was hard to miss.

"Heater's off."

"Right. Right, I know." He shuffled his feet. Kicked at something. "I just figure I should say shit like that, me being your guardian and all."

"I appreciate it."

Auri could hear the humor in Cruz's voice.

"Okay, well, carry on," Quincy said before stepping into the cabin and walking to what sounded like a metal cabinet not three feet from her head.

She froze, praying she'd managed to get her shoes all the way under the clothes.

"Ten-four," Cruz said, following him in, his footsteps much lighter than Quincy's. Only the creaks of the floorboards gave away his position.

She still couldn't believe Cruz was living with Quincy. At least for now. And they worked well together. Auri would've appreciated that fact more if she weren't on the verge of being discovered by her mother's BFF. She squeezed her eyes shut, afraid to breathe even though his laundry smelled lovely.

She heard metal scraping along a shelf as Quincy drug something out of the cabinet.

"Cool climbing gear," Cruz said as he nudged the bottom of her right foot.

She panicked and tried to pull her knee to her chest without disturbing the mountain of clothes on top of her. The act proved impossible, so she stopped and prayed he wouldn't notice a random foot sticking out from under his laundry.

"I may or may not have been using county gear for a trip to Mexico a few months ago, but we need it now. Official business."

"Going undercover as a submissive?"

"Rappelling down the side of a mountain."

"*So close,*" he whispered loudly, and Auri had to suppress a giggle.

Quincy walked to the door but stopped long enough to say, "By the way, if that juvenile delinquent isn't out of this house in two minutes, I'm siccing her mother on her."

Auri rose up from the laundry like a phoenix rising from the ashes, only not nearly as majestically. "Juvenile delinquent?"

"Two minutes," Quincy said with a soft laugh before closing the door behind him.

She gaped at Cruz, but before she could say anything, Quincy's phone rang from outside a window near her head. Worried it was her mother, Auri scrambled to her feet to peek through the pane.

Quincy had stopped on the porch to stuff the gear into a canvas duffel bag. Fumbling to get his phone out of the case at his belt, he half dropped it onto the side table between the two patio chairs and put it on speaker as he continued his mission packing ropes, harnesses, and rings of those metal clasps into the bag.

"Hey, Drew. We're on our way."

"You . . . to hurry," the caller said. The spotty connection cut out every few words. "I'm at . . . Injured female. Teen. Maybe early twenties."

Quincy stopped packing and stared at the phone. "Holy shit."

"I don't . . . how long . . . down here."

"You're in the canyon with her now? How do you have cell reception?"

"Yeah, she's . . . so not far down. Bitch to get here, though. She's . . . of an incline. Hurt pretty bad. She . . ."

"You're cutting out, Drew. Can you repeat the last?"

"Hold on." After a minute of grunts and heavy breathing, he came back on the line. "Had to climb up a little. Can you hear me?"

"I can. What's up?"

"I don't have a good foothold, but I wanted you to know. She woke up just long enough to beg me not to tell the sheriff I found her."

Quincy's gaze shot to Auri's, the hazy pane distorting his worried expression. "What do you mean?"

"She lost consciousness again before she could explain. The kid's beat to hell, Quincy. Someone got the better of her, and for some reason she doesn't want the sheriff to know."

# 3

*Sometimes, someone unexpected comes into your life out of no-
where, makes your heart race, and changes you forever.
Those people are called cops.*

—SIGN AT QUINCY'S DESK

"He didn't recognize her?" Sun tightened her grip on the steering
wheel as she took a curve up the narrow highway a tad too fast. It
didn't help that the early morning sun was in her face.

Quincy tensed, not daring to take his eyes off the road despite
the blinding sun. "No. He kept cutting out. She's young, though."

Sun spotted an ambulance in her rearview about a mile behind them, lights blazing and siren blaring, a split second before
the mountain separated them again. And behind the ambulance, she'd spotted one of her deputies' cruisers. Probably Rojas
since he'd responded to her call first. "How do you know she's
young?"

"He called her a kid."

Sun glanced at him long enough for him to gesture toward the
winding road ahead of them with a quick nod. She turned back
and took another turn faster than a sheriff had a right to. "Have
you heard any chatter? Anyone missing?"

"Not a damned thing." He looked over his shoulder at the
steep drop barely two feet from him. He'd never been a fan of
heights, but he seemed more uncomfortable than usual.

"What?" she asked him.

He glanced back at her. "What what?"

"What aren't you telling me?"

He shook his head and studied the road again. "We've known each other way too long."

"True, and you're the richer for it. What's going on?"

He bit down, his jaw muscle jumping at the pressure he exerted on it before answering. "She spoke to him. Only a few seconds before losing consciousness again."

Sun swerved to miss a boulder on the side of the mountain that protruded onto the road. She'd been complaining about the safety hazard for years and was finally in a position to do something about it, but it had yet to climb to the top of her to-do list. Cases had been flying at her left and right since she'd taken office, and now this. "And?"

After Quincy took a calming breath, he explained. "For some reason, she doesn't want you to know Essary found her."

She stared at him, spurring him to gesture toward the road again. "What's that supposed to mean?"

"No idea, boss. Apparently, she begged him not to tell the sheriff he'd found her."

Sun frowned and thought back. She hadn't arrested any young females lately. Or older ones. Who would be afraid of her?

"Want to talk about Clay?" he asked her.

Sun winced. "Why on planet Earth would I want to talk about Levi's uncle?"

"I don't know. You're the one who wants to put him into protective custody."

"I don't *want* to," Sun argued, feeling the need to justify her actions. It was a hard pill to swallow even for her. "I have to if I want to keep my daughter's father out of prison."

Quince didn't reply, which meant he didn't entirely disagree with her, and it irked him. He studied the horizon in thought, and Sun could almost hear the wheels in his head spinning.

"You agree with me?" she asked, spurring him for his thoughts.

He snapped out of it and released a breathy sigh. "I don't really have a choice, do I?"

She snorted. "Since when did that stop you?"

"No time like the present. There's Salazar." He pointed to her lieutenant's cruiser, changing the subject.

With her emergency lights on, Salazar had parked and barricaded the road down to one lane. Thankfully, this wasn't a busy highway. Mostly locals with an occasional tourist or hunter. But Salazar knew enough not to park on the dirt pull-off which would hopefully be teeming with evidence.

What surprised Sun most about the scene, however, was the fact that Levi's truck was parked on the other side of the pull-off, hugging the face of the mountain as much as possible. Salazar had cordoned off his pickup as though he were a part of the first response team, and for some bizarre reason, that warmed Sun's heart. Not that he didn't deserve it. He'd helped with several cases. He'd saved her life. He'd earned the right to be cordoned.

Sun pulled in behind Salazar and turned on her emergency lights. Anyone coming around the mountain should have enough time to slow down, provided they weren't driving fast enough to break the sound barrier. Rojas could take the other end of the roadblock when he got there to keep traffic flowing.

She looked up and saw Levi grabbing some gear out of the back of his truck.

Quincy put a hand on her arm to stay her before she could get out, his expression serious when he asked, "Can I arrest him now?"

"No."

She got out and started to close her door when she heard him whisper, "I never get to have any fun."

"Hey, boss," Salazar said as she motioned for a motorist to go around.

"Hey, Lieutenant. What do we have?"

"Essary is down there about a hundred feet." She gestured toward the guardrail, then pointed to the dirt near it. "There are some tire tracks there. And a pretty good footprint there. It looks like someone pulled over and threw the victim over the side of the guardrail after the rain."

"Is that blood?"

Salazar nodded. "Looks like it. I've already called for a forensics team."

"Thank you, Lieutenant."

"Sure thing, boss."

Quincy knelt down to survey the area from a different angle. "There's some hair and possible fibers underneath that rail there." He gestured toward the possible evidence, then stood.

Salazar bent at the waist for a better view. "You're right. I'll point that out to forensics when they get here."

Sun nodded and watched as nonchalantly as possible, doing everything in her power to slow her heart rate when Levi walked up to them, his smooth gait that of a predator. Sadly, she didn't do nonchalant well. She was much more of a *chalant* girl.

"How was my cruiser?" Quincy asked him, a sharp edge to his voice.

The smirk that overtook Levi's features caused Sun's stomach to clench. "Drives great. Thanks for asking."

Quincy stepped closer to him but Levi simply graced him with a bored expression. While their lofty heights were almost a perfect match, Quincy was bigger than Levi. His arms more muscular. His shoulders ever-so-slightly wider.

But Levi's lean frame suited him. He was strong, wiry, and fast. His whiskey-colored irises glistened with humor, but Sun could see the lines of fatigue and worry etched into his handsome face. At least two days' worth of stubble framed a mouth she'd been in love with since childhood. Though still clearly visible, the bruise he'd received a few days prior, along with a subconjunctival hemorrhage in his left eye, was finally beginning to fade. Hopefully he'd learned a valuable lesson about trying to stop a truck with his body. Those altercations never ended well.

"Why don't you get the gear?" Sun said to Quince. He wouldn't really start anything, but she figured she'd give him an excuse to back down either way.

After another testosterone-infused moment of dick measuring, Quincy walked to the back of the cruiser to grab their climbing gear.

"How'd you beat us here?" she asked Levi.

He carried climbing gear like he was going to join them. "I was on my way to Taos when I heard the call." He gestured north as evidence, but Sun doubted his explanation. One could certainly get to Taos, New Mexico, from this road, but it would take at least an hour longer than the traditional route. Why come this way?

Levi had a knack for disappearing. For falling off the grid. And once he did, finding him was damn near impossible. If Levi Ravinder didn't want to be found, he wouldn't be found. Simple as that.

Sun had always wondered where he went. Was his hideout nearby? Did he have a cabin up here somewhere?

She made a mental note to check out all the homesteads in the area before turning back to him. "And you thought you'd tag along?" she asked as she grabbed an emergency backpack out of her cruiser.

The stoic look he gave her revealed nothing. He only tightened his grip on the rope he had slung over his shoulder. The wide shoulder with an impossibly long arm attached to it, all muscle and sinew. The long-sleeved shirt he wore could not disguise the pristine physique of his arms.

He pressed his mouth together as though waiting for a follow-up. She wanted nothing more than to throw in the towel and just ask him. Was he mad at her for trying to put him into protective custody? Was he upset that his own uncle was trying to kill him? Which, who wouldn't be? Or was it simpler than that? Was he mad about being a father? Maybe he was one of those men who vowed never to have kids, and Sun had thrown a wrench into those plans. If so, sucked to be him. It took two to make a baby. He should've thought about that before seducing her. At least, she assumed that's what happened. The details of that night were still a little sketchy. Either way, now was not the time to bring it up. Not when a woman's life hung in the balance.

She took a rope and harness from Quincy and walked around to the edge of the guardrail. Trying to preserve the scene as much as possible, she stepped to where the guardrail met the mountain. There was just enough space to squeeze between them, but not much of a rim beyond that.

She leaned over and spotted Drew Essary. He sat on the incline in full hunting regalia, one foot braced against a branch, holding the unconscious girl's hand.

From what Sun could see, the girl wore a bra, only. At least on her upper half. Lacy and bright pink. The bottom half of her body was covered in leaves and brush, and Sun wondered if the girl had done that in an effort to stay warm or if Drew had done it. Her hair, recently dyed purple, obscured most of her face, but the small portion Sun could see was swollen beyond recognition. Identifying her could be difficult.

Quincy and Levi both looked over her shoulder.

"Mr. Essary," Sun called down.

He looked up, visibly relaxed, waved. "I'm glad you're here."

"Me too. We're coming down."

He nodded, then shifted his weight for a better position as though beginning to cramp. It was still early enough in the high canyon to be chilly. Their breaths fogged the air as she built her anchor using a wood post of the guardrail. Once built, she strapped on her harness, knotted both ends of her rope and clipped it to the anchor, then started over the side.

Her newest deputy, Poetry Rojas, pulled up to the scene, the ambulance right behind him. Trusting her lieutenant to figure out how best to preserve the area, she began her descent. Quincy used the post next to hers, careful to disturb the dirt as little as possible, while Levi used the guardrail itself as an anchor. A fact she was not fond of. The edge his rope would travel on was dangerously sharp, but she understood his reasoning. If he'd used the next post, he'd be getting too close to their active crime scene.

It took less than sixty seconds to get down to Drew and their victim. Sun arrived with a few scrapes from random branches and a lock of blond hair tugged loose from her French braid, but no worse for the wear. She didn't want to disturb the scene, but there was no help for it.

"I'm sure glad you're here, Sheriff," Drew said, keeping the girl's small hand enveloped in his own. The older man wore khaki coveralls, his scruffy beard matching perfectly.

"Mr. Essary, why are you out here hunting alone?"

"Please. I been hunting this land since I could walk. And I was there the day you were born, Sunny Girl. Call me Drew."

Sun smiled but kept her gaze on the girl. Keeping a tight grip on her rope with one hand, she took off the glove of the other to check the girl's pulse. She was like ice, her pulse weak, and Sun knew she would never have survived another night in the canyon. "Thank you for doing this, Drew."

"Couldn't leave her here to die. I'm just glad I seen her." He pointed to the canyon floor. "I was hunting over there by the pass when I saw her."

Sun realized how fortunate their Jane Doe was. "How on earth did you see her from there?"

"Binoculars. Seen a foot first." He pointed. "Purple sock. Went from there."

The girl's left foot was indeed visible through the leaves, the purple sock hanging halfway off her tiny foot, bright against the fallen brown leaves and brush that surrounded it. But the odds of him seeing even that were fairly astronomical.

Levi wedged himself beside Sun and took the blanket out of her backpack. After handing it to her, he rezipped the canvas bag and surveyed the area while Sun pretended not to be flustered by his nearness.

"Any thoughts on how to get her up?" Quincy asked as he

rappelled to the girl's other side and helped Sun cover her with the blanket.

"It would be easier to go down," Levi said.

Sun looked over her shoulder and followed his line of sight. "I agree. There." She gestured toward a small clearing, the frigid waters of the Gallinas River trickling beside it. "We can call in a helicopter."

"This isn't going to be easy either way," Quince said, taking in the distance. They were halfway up the incline, about a hundred feet before hitting the floor.

"I'm game if you are," Levi said, a challenge settling on his face. A gorgeous challenge. A provocative one.

Sun was so hyperaware of every aspect of Levi Ravinder—his nearness, the heat wafting off him, the darkness lying just beneath the glint of humor in his eyes—it was a wonder she could think straight at all.

Quincy shrugged, rising nonchalantly to the challenge, and began preparations by tying a second rope onto his first. She loved these two men so much. One like a brother. The other not even remotely brotherly like. Unless one were into that sort of thing.

"Sunshine," Drew said, his graveness slingshotting her attention back to him.

She leaned in and asked softly, "What is it?"

He cleared his throat, glanced at her cohorts, then said softly, "I—I touched her."

Normally in a situation like that, warning bells would have been ringing off every corner of her brain, but she'd known Drew a long time. Apparently since the day she was born.

"She was . . . exposed." He shifted, unable to look Sun in the eye. "I—I moved her bra a bit. You know, to cover her."

Sun nodded and put her free hand on his arm. "It's okay. I'll tell forensics when we get her to the hospital. You might have to give them a DNA sample to rule yours out."

His gaze shot to hers. "Absolutely. Anything you need, Sunny."

"Did you move these leaves on top of her?"

"No, ma'am. Those were like that when I got here. I wanted to take off my coveralls and put them on her, but I didn't think I could get them off without tumbling down this damn mountain, probably breaking my neck in the process. And I wasn't sure I should move her."

Sun reached over and brushed a strand of the girl's purple hair aside. The right half of her face was the most swollen, her eye a mere slit in a sea of blue-and-yellow puffiness, which meant her assailant was a lefty. Her lips didn't fare much better. A vertical crack split the right corner of her lips. And her small nose sat crooked on what promised to have been a beautiful face. But with all the swelling and bruises, even with the girl's light skin tone, Sun couldn't be certain of her ethnicity.

She turned back to him. "You were right to leave her as you found her and call us. We don't know the extent of her injuries. I'd bet my last nickel that you saved her life."

He acknowledged her praise with a stoic nod, then returned his gaze to the girl. "Poor little thing. She's just a kid."

"I think your initial assessment of late teens or very early twenty-something was correct."

"Who would do this?"

"I don't know, but we'll damned sure find out." Sun squeezed his arm reassuringly, then reached for the mic on her shoulder. "Salazar, we need a neck brace, a stretcher, and a helicopter. We're taking her down."

"I agree, boss. That seems like the least dangerous route and the canyon walls are plenty wide for a chopper."

"Roger that." She heard Salazar call out for a stretcher as she studied her team. "This isn't going to be easy."

"Nothing worth it ever is," Quincy said.

# 4

*If your coffee was so dark a demon mistook it
for a portal to hell, you will need three things:
a new mug, a mop, and an exorcism.*

—SIGN AT CAFFEINE-WAH

Auri couldn't hear anything else after Quincy took his phone off speaker. And he'd walked off the porch after spotting her. Even his side of the conversation had been muffled. He'd ended the call, threw his truck into gear, and took off, tearing out of his drive with lights blazing before Auri could ask him anything.

Cruz brought her back to school in his late father's red Dodge. They'd pulled up just as first period was ending, so Auri wouldn't have to enter a classroom late without an excuse.

She looked over at him.

"Why would that girl say that about my mom?"

"I don't know." He got out and went around the other side to open the door for her. How many guys did that nowadays?

"Who would be afraid of my mom?" she asked when he opened the door. "It doesn't make any sense."

"I don't know. I'm a little afraid of your mom."

"Yeah, in a mom way. Not in a sheriff way."

"I'm not sure I see the distinction."

"Well, there is one. A big one."

He held out his arms as though to help her down. It was quite a leap, but she slapped his hands away. "That's just what we need. For you to rip your stitches helping me down."

He chuckled and helped her anyway despite her protests.

She fell against him, her body sliding over his until her toes touched the ground. It was startlingly nice, and she gazed up at him like a lovesick puppy. Again. Apparently, she did that a lot. Too often, most likely. She recovered and stepped back. "I'm pretty sure you're not supposed to drive in your condition."

He closed the door behind her. "I'm pretty sure you're not supposed to skip school in any condition."

Touché.

"Hey, Cruz."

A group of kids spotted them and walked over.

"You back?" a boy named Fernando asked.

"No. The doctors are making me stay home the rest of the week."

"What?" A pretty girl with thick black hair sulked gorgeously. "What about the field trip?"

Cruz shrugged an apology as the other kids greeted him by clasping hands and leaning in to softly bump shoulders.

Auri probably should've been jealous at all the attention, but she wasn't. Not in the least. To say that Cruz was well-liked would be a massive understatement. Popularity had been thrust upon him. Along with greatness. And hotness. A whole lot of hotness. But he didn't seem to care. Had never seemed to care.

It fascinated Auri, and she had been contemplating that very thing when something Mr. Essary had said over the phone call with Quincy tugged her thoughts in a different direction. A teen girl? Maybe early twenties? A thought hit her. Before she could be certain, though, she had to find her archnemesis, Lynelle Amaia.

"Okay, well bye!" She tiptoed to press her lips to his cheek.

He bent obligingly and gave her a crooked smile.

She stopped for half a second to admire it before snapping back to the present. She had stuff to do. "Get some rest," she said before whirling around to hunt down Lynelle.

She was stopped dead in her tracks, however, when Cruz barked a sharp, "Vicram!"

She froze. Time stood still as she turned on her heels toward him, mortification exploding inside her. The sea of kids that had been hurrying to class around them stopped mid-journey as well. They looked at Cruz, then at her, then back again before parting obligingly so she could have a clear view of her opponent.

And what a view it was. Suspicion narrowed his eyes. Knitted his brow. Thinned his lips. He recrossed his arms over his chest and waited.

She shrugged in question, the sharp action conveying just how mortified she was.

Then a dimple appeared on one corner of his mouth. "Where are you going?" he asked, his tone suddenly as pure and innocent as the freshly driven snow.

The sea of heads that had swiveled toward him swiveled back again, waiting for her response.

She offered a tight smile and said from between clenched teeth, "I'm going to class."

"No, you're not."

How could he possibly know that? She blinked and raised her chin a visible notch. "I most certainly am."

"I know that look."

"What look?"

"That look." He drew a circle in the air indicating her . . . look. "The one you're wearing right now."

She crossed her arms over her chest, mimicking him with a huff of indignation. "I'm not wearing anything."

"You weren't wearing anything in my dreams last night."

While the kids around them snorted at his confession, a shot of electricity rushed through Auri's body, making her skin tingle.

"But here in the present," he added, lowering his head to study her from underneath his lashes, "you are most definitely wearing a look."

The other kids started scattering since the tardy bell was about to ring. Judging by their expressions, they did so reluctantly, still hoping for an argument to gossip about later.

Once they were alone, Auri walked back to Cruz, trying to ignore the warmth stirring in her abdomen. "Cruz De los Santos, I have no idea what you're talking about."

"Yes, you do." It was like he didn't trust her at all. The nerve. "What are you up to?"

"I just remembered something about Lynelle."

"And that would be?"

The bell rang a split second later, dashing her dreams of forgoing a trip to the office for a tardy slip.

Giving up, she dropped her backpack on the ground and leaned against his truck. "I was in the bathroom the other day with Lynelle and her minions. I mean, they didn't know I was in there. I was in a stall, but she was saying something about how her cousin, a freshman at UNM, was supposed to come stay with her after her last final on Thursday but she never showed up."

"Really? Did they call her parents?"

"I don't know, but Bonnie reminded Lynelle about what a spaz her cousin is. How she was always changing her plans last minute and canceling on them. Lynelle agreed and dropped it. But she's the right age, Cruz."

"The right age for?"

"The girl in the canyon. The one Mr. Essary found."

He leaned against his truck, too. "Holy shit, you think it's her?"

"I don't know. I was going to ask Lynelle if her cousin ever showed up."

"She's not at school today."

A-a-a-and, there it was. That spark of jealousy that occasionally managed to wriggle its way into her skull. Right beneath her submissive hemoglobin. "How do you know?"

"She posted something on Snapchat."

"Oh? You're friends with Lynelle on Snapchat?"

He grinned. "I'm friends with lots of people on Snapchat. She stayed home with a sick friend."

"Ah," she said, bouncing back into investigative mode. "Maybe it's her cousin. Maybe that's why she was so late." She grabbed her backpack and took out her phone.

"Maybe. Who you calling?"

"My mom." She hit the CALL button but got her automated message. "Dang it. It's not going through. She must be at the canyon already. I wonder if—"

An urgent whisper interrupted her mid-sentence, echoing off the buildings around them. "Auri!"

She looked around for the speaker and saw a piece of notebook paper flying frantically from an open classroom window. She tilted her head for a better view.

"Auri, run!" the speaker said, her whisper not unlike the mating call of a screech owl.

She pushed off the truck and straightened. "Sybil?"

"Run! Coach Love spotted you. He's . . ." The hand disappeared just as Coach Love cornered the building and walked toward them.

Auri hitched her backpack over a shoulder and prepared to run, but the coach was way faster than he looked. He was on them in three strides. There was no escape now. She looked over and saw Sybil's head half out of the window, craning her neck for a better view, and tried not to giggle despite her dire circumstances.

"Ms. Vicram," the coach said as he came to a stop in front of them. "Mr. De los Santos."

"Coach," they replied in unison.

"I haven't seen you since everything happened, Cruz. I just . . . I wanted to . . ." He lowered his head and stuffed his hands in his pockets. "I'm very sorry about your father."

"Oh." Cruz cast Auri a surprised glance before turning back to him. "Thanks, Coach."

The coach reached out his hand and took Cruz's in a firm shake. "And, despite everything you've been through, I hope you'll stay in Del Sol. The football team won't be the same without you, son."

Auri had heard Cruz was quite the quarterback and destined

to be first string for varsity next year even though he would only be a sophomore. Having started at Del Sol High after the winter break, she'd missed the entire season.

"And, well, I hope you'll consider us part of your family." When Cruz hesitated, he quickly added, "No one can replace your dad, of course. I'm not suggesting that. Just, you know, like long-lost aunts and uncles and cousins and such. Either way, we're here if you need anything."

"I second that."

They turned to see Principal Jacobs come out of the front offices. Auri tried not to groan. He was super tight with her mom. Called her Little Miss Sunshine, which was horrifying on so many levels.

"Anything you need, Cruz," the principal said, "just call my cell."

Cruz had the principal's contact info? "Hey, Mr. Jacobs," Auri said a little too perkily.

"Auri," he replied, swinging his attention her way. Slowly. Purposefully. "Is there a reason you're not in class?"

"It's my fault, Mr. Jacobs." Cruz grabbed his midsection and only then did Auri see the spots of blood on the front of his white T-shirt.

"Cruz!" She knew it. Helping her down had been a bad idea.

"I asked her to come out here. I think I ripped my stitches."

"Oh, son," Mr. Jacobs said, lunging forward, clearly shaken. "Let's get you to the nurse's office."

"Okay, thanks." Cruz put an arm around Auri's shoulders, cast her a single, conspiratorial wink, and made a show of limping inside the building.

She could have kissed him for saving her. Or punched him for ripping his stitches. It was a fine line.

Not thirty seconds after Sun had asked her newest deputy for a neck brace and stretcher from the ambulance that had shown up, Rojas was lowering the requested items over the guardrail, clearly two steps ahead of her. They went to work, first securing their Jane

Doe's neck, then easing her onto the stretcher while balancing their own weight against the sharp incline.

There would be time later to assess girl's wounds. She had deep gashes on her abdomen and thighs. None were bleeding or seemed life-threatening at the moment, but the fact that they'd clearly been put there on purpose—almost painstakingly so—was troublesome.

Rojas came over the radio. "Tie the rope onto the head of the stretcher, boss."

Another of her deputies, Azaria Bell—aka, Zee—came on the radio. "We don't have any more anchors, boss, but Rojas and I will keep her from getting away from you."

Sun glanced up to see Del Sol County's official sniper peering down at them from over the guardrail. Rojas looked on from beside her, a place he liked to be. He'd been pining over the woman for weeks. Sun could hardly blame him. The dark-skinned beauty had mad skills and could pad her résumé with accolades like a stellar military service record, two years with Albuquerque PD, and multiple competition wins. She'd been with the APD SWAT team when Sun lured her away with promises of slow, stress-free days and high pay, neither of which she actually delivered on. Yet there Zee was. Watching over her from above. Thankfully it wasn't through a scope. Sun didn't miss the fact that Rojas stole glances at the sniper every few seconds.

"Thanks, Zee," she said into her mic. She took a deep breath and returned her attention to Quince and Levi. "Are we ready?"

They both nodded, Quincy studying their path and Levi tying the rope onto the head end of the stretcher before checking Sun's harness yet again. He tugged at her ties and tested the knots at her carabiner while Sun tried to ignore what his ministrations were doing to her insides. And not just the lower parts, either. Her chest tightened with his attention to detail on her behalf.

"What can I do?" Drew asked.

Sun considered where best to use him. "Maybe go ahead of us. If we lose control . . ."

"Got it." He started down the mountain and barely managed to stop when he hit a particularly slippery spot, the moisture beneath the leaves proving hazardous.

"Take hold of my rope if you need to, Drew."

"Will do."

Once he had a strong foothold, Levi and Quince nodded to each other and started down as Sun took hold of the stretcher, hoping to bear some of the weight.

Drew tried to help keep it steady, but he ended up sliding down the incline with almost every step. If not for the rappelling gear, Sun would've done the same. As Rojas and Zee fed them rope, they slowly picked their way down the steep incline. Which didn't look that steep from up top. She'd never look at the Sangre de Cristos the same way again.

By the time they got to the bottom, Sun's hands ached with effort, but she never lost her grip, even when Quincy slid into a muddy indentation and dropped his side, jostling their victim. Levi and Sun kept hold until he righted himself, straining under the weight despite the fact that their Jane was little more than a toothpick. But having to keep both themselves and their victim from sliding on the muddy pass was proving far more difficult than she'd imagined.

What amazed Sun, however, was how well Quincy and Levi worked together to get their victim to safety. They grunted and swore under their breaths, but they kept the lines of communication open all the way down.

"I've got her," Levi would say, his muscles bunching with effort when Quincy needed some leeway to adjust his footing.

"I'll take the weight until you stabilize," Quince said, giving Levi the chance to steady himself against a tree before releasing the tension on his rope.

They worked in unison, as though the entire event had been choreographed, and Sun couldn't have been prouder. Or she would've been if she weren't dying. She kept a grip on the top of the stretcher, near their Jane's head, worried they'd all slip and the girl would go tumbling down the side of the mountain.

By the time they got to the bottom, Sun's arms were shaking. She had to pry her fingers off the stretcher and from around her rope, and that tequila that had been souring in the pit of her stomach was bubbling up her esophagus like hot acid.

Guilt assailed her. She had literally put this woman's life in danger by showing up to work with a hangover like a college kid showing up for her shift at Walmart after a night of debauchery. Humiliation and disappointment surged through her with every crisp breath she took. What a role model for her daughter she made.

Drew helped once they got to the bottom, tucking the blanket around the girl and checking her pulse, and Sun remembered he'd done a stint in the military. He must've picked up a few skills.

As Sun brushed herself off, Levi reached over and pulled a twig out of her hair. A simple gesture, but she reveled in the fact that he'd cared enough to do it. That he'd checked her gear. That he'd caught her once when her foot slipped out from under her, his strong arm steadying her until she could get a foothold. Maybe he didn't hate her.

"Her pulse is really weak," Drew said.

Quince checked it and spoke into his mic. "How long until the chopper gets here?"

"Two minutes," Salazar said. "Is she going to be okay?"

Quince's gaze locked with Sun's, doubt evident in every line on his face. "It's too early to tell."

"Ten-four," Salazar said, her voice no longer full of hope.

"Drew," Sun said now that they had a minute to catch their breaths, "any idea why she didn't want you to contact me?"

Drew pressed his mouth together and shook his head. "I'm sorry I didn't call you first, Sunny. She was just so scared and . . . well, I didn't know what to do."

"No, that's okay. You did everything right here today, Drew Essary."

He lifted an unconvinced shoulder.

"Did she say anything else?"

"Not a word. She could barely get her eyes open. I tried to tell her to hang in there, I was getting help, but something came over her. She started trembling, grabbed my arm, and begged me not to call you."

"That doesn't make any sense," Quincy said, frustrated.

Sun agreed, but she hadn't been there. "What exactly did she say?"

"'Please don't call the sheriff,'" he said matter-of-fact. "Just like that. Then she passed out again."

Sun wracked her brain but not for long. They heard the medevac a few seconds before they saw it, its blades beating the air into submission as it whirled over the mountain into sight. The leaves that had fallen months ago rose into the air, a flurry of vegetation as they picked up their charge and rushed her to the clearing.

An EMT jumped out of the helicopter, emergency kit in hand, and hurried toward them, ducking against the strong force of the blades. Another followed him, and before Sun knew it, their Jane Doe had been secured on board and was being lifted into the air.

"They're taking her to Pres in Santa Fe," Quincy said, referring to a hospital there. He turned to the mountain. "The question is, which route are we taking back?"

Sun turned to look at the foreboding trek ahead, not sure she had it in her to climb up the sheer incline again. Her arms and legs felt like a Jell-O mold, only not as stable. But if she had her deputies come around and down the pass to pick them up, it would take almost an hour for them to get there. Then another hour to get up top. Too long. She needed to get back to that crime scene.

She cupped a hand over her brow and saw a couple of state uniforms at the top. "Staties are here. Maybe they could winch us up?"

"Nah," Levi said, stepping out of his harness. "Our ride should be here any minute."

She and Quincy turned to him.

"Our ride?" she asked.

He gestured toward the pass with a nod. A black-and-tan four-seated utility vehicle sped toward them, creating its own road as its right tires splashed along the edge of the river.

"How did you call for a ride?" Quincy asked.

"No," Sun said. "*When* did you call for a ride?"

Levi smirked as he folded his gear. "Before we descended. I don't know about you, but I'm not in the mood to climb back up."

He had a point. Sun's only concern had been the unidentified victim. She needed to think ahead more often. Formulate step-by-step plans of action. Shit like that. She'd put that on her to-do list as soon as she created one.

The UTV rushed toward them, bumping and bouncing along the nonexistent path. Thanks to a fallen tree, it came to a stop about fifty yards away.

Sun squinted, trying to identify their chauffeur as they walked toward the idling vehicle. They were in the backwoods, after all, the area a little too *Deliverance* for her comfort.

"I need to get my gear out of the blind," Drew said, scratching his scruffy beard. "And I have an ATV a few yards out. Should I come by the station later?"

She stopped and turned to him. "Please. I should be there this afternoon, but you can give your statement to any of my deputies."

The man smiled sadly. "Will do, Sunny Girl."

"Thank you again, Drew. You're a hero."

"I don't know about that." Refusing to accept his new title, he turned and headed for his hunting blind as though it were just another day.

Sun walked to the waiting UTV, shocked to see the man in the driver's seat.

Keith Seabright flashed her a smile as big as the state of her shock. Freshly shaven, dark hair still a little wet, he looked a thousand times better than when last she'd seen him. In his defense, most people looked bad lying in a hospital bed with multiple stab wounds. It was probably the lighting.

As a former major in the special forces, Keith Seabright had proven himself nigh indestructible when he was drugged and attacked by three knife-wielding hitmen. Thanks to the quick actions of his bestie, aka Levi Ravinder, Seabright survived. But it was his dedication to the boy he'd been protecting that convinced Sun he would make a fantastic law enforcement officer, so she was in the midst of blackmailing him into joining her gang. Fingers crossed.

"You're out of the hospital," she said, surprise evident in her voice. "And driving. Should you be driving? Especially a UTV?" Not many people she knew had been drugged and then stabbed multiple times in a bar fight only to go four-wheeling a week later. Her concern was warranted.

The same went for Levi. When he'd jumped in to save his friend, he ended up trying to stop a truck with his body. Thus he sported his own set of bruises to both face and pride. And yet here they both were. Rappelling. Carrying victims across rough terrain. Swooping in out of nowhere to save the day. Wasn't there a word for people like that?

Seabright offered her a two-fingered salute. "Deputy Seabright, reporting for duty, Sheriff."

"It's about time," she said, turning away to put on her sunglasses lest he see her poker face slip. Was he serious? Would he really join her ragtag team of crime-fighters? She'd only issued her idle threat—become one of her deputies or go to prison for kidnapping—two days ago. She figured he would call her on her bluff and go about his merry way, but here he was reporting for duty. In a sense.

She should probably feel guilty about pressing him into service, but he'd been one of the culprits behind an elaborate ruse that had haunted her for years. Her first case as a detective in Santa Fe PD involved a missing boy, Elliot Kent, and had gone unsolved for five years. She thought she'd failed until she spotted Elliot in some security footage at a local convenience store, alive and well. Turns out, Elliot's parents had faked his kidnapping to keep him safe from a criminal organization his abusive father had become entangled with, and his mother had recruited Seabright to keep

Elliot hidden. Five years later, the case came to a head, and they all almost lost their lives. If not for Levi and her expert team, they likely would have. The fact that Seabright fell in love with Elliot's mother while his father stewed in prison was a plus. Seabright now had a ready-made family who adored him waiting in the wings and, thanks to Sun, a shiny new job to boot.

She was happy for him. And herself. The forty-year-old just got better looking every time she saw him. It could've been the glistening dark hair and silvery-blue eyes, but Sun figured it was more the strong jaw and the fact that he could kill a man with a Tic Tac. He would make a great sergeant.

She walked around and took the front passenger's seat, which both Levi and Quince had left for her. After she clicked her racer-like seat belt and settled into the seat, she asked him, "But for reals, should you be driving? Especially here? Don't you still have stitches to contend with?"

He had one long arm draped over the steering wheel, the other on the gear shift. "My stitches and I have come to an arrangement." He put the UTV in reverse and proceeded to do a rumbling three-pointer.

"And what's that?" she asked over the noise.

"They don't rip me. I don't rip them."

"Sounds legit. Did you rent the house on Apollo?" She'd strongly encouraged her newest extortion-recruited deputy to rent one of the houses in town and move his new family into it as soon as possible. Apparently, he was much better at following orders than her daughter.

"Yes, ma'am. They're packing as we speak."

"And the wedding?" she asked, unable to keep the hope out of her voice.

He smirked at her. "She has to get divorced from her criminally insane husband first."

Her shoulders deflated. "Good point. At least you're on the right track."

"I like to think I am."

Sun nodded her approval. The logistics of how he was going about it all. She looked in the rearview that, from her vantage, just happened to be perfectly focused on the man of her dreams.

He sat staring right back at her.

"So, is your uncle still alive?" she asked as they bounced and splashed through the canyon.

"Two of them are. At least as far as I know. You'll have to be more specific."

She turned in her seat to face him—not an easy feat in a four-point harness—and didn't miss the wince from their driver when he drove over a small boulder. "Clay."

Levi lifted a perfectly sculpted shoulder. "Maybe. Haven't seen him for days."

She could play cat and mouse with him for hours, mostly because she enjoyed it more than breathing, but her worry was too great to be squelched for long. "So, you didn't kill him?"

He kept his gaze steady under her scrutiny a long moment before answering. "You must think that's all we Ravinders do. Make moonshine and kill each other."

In her defense, they did do a lot of both. "Your uncle started it," she said, defending both him and her thought process at the same time. Word on the street was that Clay wanted nothing more than to kill his nephew, take over the distillery, and reestablish ties with his Southern Mafia connections. She could hardly blame Levi for taking matters into his own hands, but she'd certainly prefer he didn't.

"Maybe," he said.

She leaned her chin on the back of her seat. "He didn't start it?"

One corner of Levi's mouth rose ever so slightly. Ever so sexily. "It's a gray area."

"Ah." A man with more mysteries than a library. She couldn't help but notice he sat with his knees far apart, most likely to annoy the other passenger who was also manspreading to assert his dominance, to claim the most territory in the cramped space, their knees almost touching but not daring to. Because guys. "Either way, that doesn't answer my question."

Levi looked out the nonexistent window and released a heavy sigh before saying, "If he is dead, I didn't do it."

Relief eased the tension in her neck. It wasn't a 100 percent guarantee that the man was still alive, but she'd take it. She looked over the seat at her chief deputy. "Okay, he's a lefty, knows the area, and drives a pickup with aftermarket tires."

Quincy nodded, easily catching onto the fact that she'd changed the subject rather abruptly. "That's a lot more to go on than I'd anticipated."

"I agree. Anyone come to mind?"

"No. But only because I'm having a hard time getting past the fact that I'm starving."

As though on cue, her stomach growled and gurgled in agony, the humiliating sounds heard over the roar of the engine. She couldn't decide if she was hungry or nauseous. Probably a little of both.

"Me too, apparently. I want another look at the crime scene before we head back, though."

"Okay, but if I pass out from malnutrition, you're carrying me into my house."

# 5

Forty minutes. Auri had forty minutes for lunch before the bell rang for fifth period. That gave her ten minutes to walk home and get her bike, ten to ride to Lynelle's house, ten to talk to Lynelle if she didn't immediately slam the door in her face, and ten to ride back to school. It didn't give her a lot wiggle room, but she'd risk it. And if she were tardy to fifth, what would they do to her? It was the last week of school. Even if she were sent to detention, how long could it last?

That morning, she'd made a quick inquiry with a couple of side characters from Lynelle's posse and learned that her cousin never showed up. Could the woman they found in the canyon really be Lynelle's cousin? Auri needed to know for certain the girl didn't show and, if she didn't, whether Lynelle had heard from her. Auri's mother had enough to deal with without her daughter sending her on a wild-goose chase.

Thus, after taking a hit of her inhaler, Auri hustled home, snuck around back to get her bike without disturbing—aka, alerting—her grandparents to her presence, and hurried to Lynelle's.

The only reason she knew where Lynelle lived was because her house sat three houses beyond Sybil's in the rich part of town, otherwise known as The Hills. Unfortunately, the properties were in the more mountainous region of Del Sol, which meant a lot of uphill pedaling. Auri began struggling about a mile into her trek, realizing it could take longer than expected. She checked her watch. Already two minutes behind schedule. She pumped harder, her legs burning under the strain as she came to a horrifying realization. Lynelle's house may have sat near Sybil's, but all the houses in the area were a quarter mile or more apart. How had she not noticed that before? She passed Sybil's and still had half a mile's worth of uphill climb.

Once there, she hopped off her bike and ran to the porch. With no time to catch her breath, she knocked on the front door.

Lynelle answered, her expression one of mild curiosity until her gaze landed on Auri. With her long dark hair pulled into a ponytail, she looked like she was going for a casual look, but her makeup, which had been applied with razor-sharp precision, suggested otherwise.

"Hey, Lynelle," Auri said, gasping for air.

The girl's face morphed into one of disgust complete with a baring of her teeth and a wrinkling of her nose.

Auri understood. She was an acquired taste. "I was just wondering," she began, stopping to inhale again, "if your cousin ever showed up."

After a rather long moment of stupefied astonishment, Lynelle finally spoke. "What the fuck?"

Auri braced a hand against the doorframe, filled her lungs, and said, "Your cousin. You said she was supposed to be here Thursday but she never showed up. I was wondering if she ever made it."

Lynelle turned to look over her shoulder, and Auri realized there was a boy in her house. Maybe the sick friend she'd posted about on Snapchat?

The kid walked up, his expression as hard as Lynelle's was astonished, but what caught Auri by complete surprise were the bruises that colored the entire right side of his face. So much so, his right eye was swollen almost completely shut.

"What happened to you?" Auri asked, the words leaving her mouth before she had time to run them through her nonexistent sensitivity filter.

Incredibly, his expression hardened even further before a glint of curiosity raced across his features. Features that were normally quite handsome. "You're the new sheriff's kid."

Auri straightened. She'd never met the former sheriff's son, Tim Redding, but he was by far the most popular boy in school. Then again, Cruz was only a freshman. Give that kid another year, and he would easily lay claim to that title.

"I am," she said, adjusting the backpack she still wore. Since her mom had basically stolen his dad's job, this could prove really awkward, but he seemed okay with it.

"She's cool," he said, reaching up to sweep his fingers through his dark blond hair like a movie star. Even bruised and swollen, the slick golden boy of Del Sol High was handsome. He had pretty brown eyes, when one wasn't swollen shut, and enough height to have to duck for ill-placed light fixtures every once in a while. "She pulled me over one day. Forty-seven in a thirty-five, but she let me off with a warning."

Auri grinned. "You must've charmed her."

One corner of his mouth rose, but the blistering heat from Lynelle's glare dragged Auri's gaze off it.

"What do you want?" she asked.

"Lynn," he said, putting a hand on her shoulder, "you have to learn to be nice to people."

She looked over her shoulder at him. "She's not people."

He only chuckled, and asked, "You wanna come in? I promise her bark is worse than her bite."

The look of utter astonishment on Lynelle's face had Auri fighting a wicked grin. "No, thank you. I have to get back to school. I just wanted to know about *Lynn*'s cousin."

The murderous glare Lynelle shot her was definitely worth the jab. She would probably pay in some dire way, but for now, the glittering hatred was a reward unto itself. "Do you know her?"

"No."

"Then what the fuck do you care?"

"Lynn," Tim said, his voice a little sharper than before. He turned back to Auri. "She texted and said she went skiing with some friends instead of coming to spend time with her cousin. Which boggles the mind, right?"

The bark of laughter that escaped Auri before she could stop it was immediately met with a slammed door in her face. She figured that would happen. She was just surprised it took as long as it did. But when she turned to leave, the door opened again.

Tim stood there alone, a half smile on his face. "Hey, give me your phone."

Auri had just pulled it out to try to call her mom again. She'd left her quite a message. But it would seem the girl in the canyon was not Lynelle's cousin after all. She should probably mention that. She frowned at Tim and pulled it against her chest. "I love this phone. Get your own."

He laughed and just held out his hand.

She decided not to push the whole beaten-to-a-pulp thing and complied, handing it over when a thought hit her. "So, she texted Lynelle? She didn't call?"

"Whitney?" he asked, busy typing. "Yeah. She texted to tell her she went skiing somewhere in Colorado with some friends from college." He handed the phone back, then narrowed his lids on her. "Why? What's this about?"

She took the phone. "Oh, nothing. I just wanted to talk to her about . . . UNM. I'm thinking about going. You know, if I can manage to make it past high school." Coming up with excuses under pressure was clearly not her strong suit.

"For reals? I just got a football scholarship. I start in September."

"Wow, congratulations." She knew that, of course. Everyone in Del Sol knew that, and she'd been a tad envious when she heard. While other people dreamed of Harvard and Yale, Auri dreamed of the adobe halls of the University of New Mexico in Albuquerque.

She wanted nothing more than to follow in her mother's footsteps. "That's an amazing accomplishment."

He shook off her compliment by lifting a bashful shoulder, then glanced up at her from underneath some pretty thick lashes. "We could visit the campus together sometime. If you want."

It took a moment for his words to sink in. For Auri to realize he was flirting with her. *Her.* A mere freshman and the daughter of his father's enemy. "Oh, yeah," she said, backing off the porch. "That would be cool." It was a lie, but her ten-minute time limit was fast approaching.

He did the *call me* sign and winked at her before closing the door. An admirable feat considering the state of his eyes, but worry gnawed at her stomach. Well, worry and hunger, but the hunger could wait. The more important question at the moment was who hit him. Repeatedly. And with much enthusiasm. Not that he seemed terribly worried about it, but Auri certainly was.

She threw a leg over her bike before checking her phone. He'd added himself to her contacts, putting a heart between the names Tim and Redding. A heart! She barely knew the guy. Maybe that was how older boys flirted. Still . . .

She edited the contact info, deleting the heart, before heading back into town. As flattering as his attention was, her heart was already taken. And it just so happened, the cabin in which the thief of hearts currently resided was on her way. After the situation with Lynelle, she needed a Cruz break, but she only had five minutes to get back to school if she was going to beat the tardy bell. She weighed her options. She had already missed first period. What was one more? It's not like she would miss a lecture. They were scheduled to watch a film on World War II. And knowing her granddad, the war buff probably had a copy of it in his library.

In the end, Cruz won out. He often did. She glided downhill almost the entire way into town, took a right at the Pecos, and pedaled to Quincy's cabin, dodging to miss an occasional tree branch and a rampaging squirrel. The nurse had sent him home after a quick check. He hadn't ripped any stitches loose, but he did pull at them hard enough to cause some minor bleeding. She'd sterilized the area, applied surgical tape to hopefully avoid that in the future, then kicked him off campus, insisting he go home and get some rest. The look on Cruz's face told Auri he was getting tired of hearing those words, but that's what he got for getting stabbed saving her.

Cruz's big red truck was there, but Cruz was not. She checked the cabin, marveling at all the gifts the town had sent him. Besides the usual flowers of condolence and get-well cards was a plethora of clothes, jackets, shoes, and food. Mostly food. Banana bread, cakes, and fruit baskets lined the kitchen counter while Auri knew the fridge was stuffed with fried chicken and lasagna. He and Quincy had been living off the town's generosity for two days. It thrilled Auri that the citizens of Del Sol had rallied around one of its own like they had.

Hiking down to the river, she finally spotted him on a rock about waist high, his back against a jagged cliff. She walked closer and realized, much to her surprise, that he was asleep. He had an arm draped over one knee. The other leg stretched out over the boulder, a journal on his lap with a limp hand barely holding down the pages in the breeze. His profile struck her yet again. The perfect lines. The well-proportioned dimensions. His hair ruffled in the breeze and his lashes created shadows across his cheeks.

She watched him a moment before tiptoeing closer and doing something she should've probably been ashamed of. Perhaps she would later, but for now, she eased onto the boulder next to him and pressed down the page he'd been writing on so she could read it. The pen hung loosely in his hand, threatening to fall as she leaned over and studied his work.

It was only a few lines, but they struck her so hard she felt the breath leave her lungs. She blinked in astonishment and read them again.

*I think I'll be happy once I give in to the black. Once I succumb. Once it swallows me. Devours me. Bites through my bones and drowns me in my blood. With the coldness will come the numb, and the molecules in my body will finally stop screaming. It's a heavy price to pay, but freedom, as they say, is never really free.*

Auri stared at the page, her heart threatening to break under the stress of the tightening cage around it. The page blurred as tears gathered between her lashes.

"It's just a poem."

She jumped and scrambled back, her shock impossible to hide when she met his gaze.

He casually closed the book, like it was just any other book. Like he hadn't written his intentions in it. "It's just a poem."

Shaking her head, she slid off the rock. "That wasn't just a poem, Cruz."

He turned away and looked out onto the Pecos, the water flowing cool and bright under the warm New Mexico sun. "I'm not going to take my own life, Auri. I thought you knew me better than that." Her doubt must've shown when he looked back at her, because he reiterated, "It's just a poem."

She didn't argue with him. There was no need. She'd been there once, too. In that dark place. He could pretend all he wanted, but she knew that place better than most.

He stuffed the book into his back pocket, stood on the boulder, and held out his hand to her. "What are you doing here anyway?" he asked, that lopsided tilt back in his grin.

She backed away. "I have to get to class."

"Auri, wait."

She turned and hurried to her bike before her tears betrayed her, as they were wont to do. Instead of going back to school, she rode straight home, heedless of the time.

"Hey, pumpkin," her grandfather said when she burst into the house. He went back to pouring his coffee. "Aren't you supposed to be at—"

She tackle-hugged him before he could finish his statement.

"Oh. All right, then." He sat the coffeepot and his cup down and wrapped her in his arms, his embrace warm and soothing. Just what she needed, because she had been where Cruz was now. She had been in that dark place. And she knew exactly what came next.

Seabright pulled the UTV to a stop behind Levi's truck at the top of the pass. Sun got out and turned back to her newest recruit. "The next academy doesn't start for a few weeks. That'll give you some time to recuperate, then I can hire you in a probationary capacity until the class starts."

He smirked at her. "So, I'll be on probation?"

"Yes. No fraternizing with criminals." She wagged a finger at him in warning.

He looked over his shoulder as Levi closed his door. "I guess this is the end of our bromance, dude."

Levi frowned as he grabbed the climbing gear someone had rolled up for him and put beside his truck. "Last time I checked, you were the sketchy one, what with you kidnapping children and living off-grid like the Unabomber."

"At least I don't make moonshine in my daddy's shed."

Sun almost laughed. That *shed* was a sixty-thousand-square-foot, state-of-the-art distillery, the floors of which she could eat off of, and Levi's father had nothing to do with its creation.

She glanced around, realizing what they were on—a state highway—and what Seabright was driving—a utility vehicle created for off-roading. "Is this thing street legal?"

Seabright reared back, clearly affronted. "Are you questioning my dedication to the law already?"

"Go," she said, pointing into the distance. "Rest. Get better. Give your new family a hug for me and call me in a few days."

"You got it, boss." He gave her another salute, lifted his chin in goodbye to Levi, and performed an illegal U-turn before heading out.

She shook her head, then watched as Levi tossed his gear into an aluminum toolbox in the back of his truck, still wearing his harness, the same harness that framed his steely buttocks to perfection.

He unbuckled the straps and stepped out of it before stowing it in the toolbox as well.

After studying him another moment, she folded her arms on the tailgate and rested her chin on them. "So, you just happened to be heading to Taos—taking the long route, no less—with climbing gear at the ready, when you heard the call?"

He didn't answer at first, and when he did, he didn't look at her, but that was okay. It was hard to beat a profile like his. Studying it was hardly a chore. "Something like that," he said at last. He walked around to the back of the truck, and she turned to face him when he stopped directly in front of her, but he glanced at something in the bed of his truck.

While a thousand questions danced on the tip of her tongue, mostly questions about his sentiments now that he knew he had a daughter, she veered toward safer ground instead. "Do you have a cabin up here somewhere? Is this where you hide out?"

He still refused to make eye contact. Instead, he reached over her shoulder, the act bringing him so close he pressed into her. His sculpted mouth almost brushed across hers and she felt his breath fan across her face as he lifted out a bottle of water from a cooler. He opened it, the plastic sound crackling in the still air, then braced his free hand on the tailgate beside her and finally captured her gaze with his, the bronze depths ensnaring her in their trap.

After an eternity of will he or won't he, he let his gaze drop to her mouth and linger there a long moment before it sank lower, and only then did she realize her top two buttons had come undone during the rescue. Before she could see to them, he handed her the water, tilting it toward her lips, and buttoned them for her as she drank from both the water and him.

The backs of his fingers slid across her skin as he worked, causing a ripple of pleasure she couldn't have tamped down if she'd wanted to. Then, without another word, he tugged her shirt to straighten it, strolled to the driver's-side door, and left her standing there. Standing there, wondering if she'd made any progress. Only realizing after he'd left she didn't get a chance to talk to him about anything. About Clay. About Auri. About his new title. Aka, Dad. The suspense was driving her crazy, which was probably his point entirely.

"Boss?"

She took another swig, then turned to her new lieutenant.

"Sorry, boss," Salazar said as she motioned another motorist through. Her shoulders were tight, her round face taut with concern.

"What's up?" Sun asked her, heading to help Quincy with the gear.

Salazar followed, still motioning to the occasional vehicle. Zee had taken the south end of the scene while Rojas took the north. They coordinated via radio on when to release vehicles. Salazar's role was superfluous at the moment, but it never hurt to have an extra set of eyes.

"When you were down in the canyon," Salazar said almost reluctantly, "Redding showed up asking a lot of odd questions."

In the middle of rolling up her gear, Sun stopped and looked at her lieutenant. The adrenaline her nervous system dumped into her body raced across her skin like an electrical current. Her predecessor, former sheriff Baldwin Redding, was not a fan of Sun's. He'd been doing everything in his power to get his old job back since she took office. Not to mention the fact that he was in cahoots with Levi's uncle Clay. In what capacity, no one really knew, but she'd been handed intel from her spy, aka Hailey Ravinder, that they were working together on something big.

She handed Quincy her climbing gear as he gave Salazar his attention. "What kinds of questions?"

"About our Jane Doe mostly."

Quincy's lashes narrowed on Sun before saying, "Can you be more specific?"

"Just the usual stuff, Chief. Who found her. How long she'd been down there. Did we have an ID. How old she was. I guess as a former sheriff his curiosity was piqued?"

The hairs on the back of Sun's neck stood up as her Spidey senses kicked in. "Maybe."

Quincy shook his head at her, not buying it for a minute, then threw the bag of climbing gear in the back of her cruiser.

"Odd thing, though," Salazar added. "I had to ask him three times to stay away from the pull-off. He kept inching closer to the north side of the guardrail for a peek at what you guys were doing."

"That's interesting." Especially considering the fact that the tire tracks and their one and only footprint were on that side.

"Maybe we need to pay him a visit," Quincy suggested.

"Nah. No need to tip our hand just yet." She nodded to Salazar. "Thanks for that."

"Of course, boss."

Salazar had been recruited by Redding. It was nice to know Sun could count on her allegiance despite that fact.

"What did you want a second look at?" Quince asked her.

"That hair you spotted." She pulled on a pair of latex gloves and slipped disposable covers over her boots before picking her way across the dirt pull-off to where Quince had seen the hair on the guardrail.

"Wrong color," he said from the side of the road. "Could be months old."

"It's strange, though, don't you think?"

"This whole situation is strange. Do you think it's from the assailant?"

She knelt down and tilted her head to look under the guardrail. The clump of hair had wedged itself between the wood post and the metal rail. Almost as though someone caught their hair on it only to have it violently ripped out. At least ten strands from the same head of hair flew in the soft breeze, many with the roots still attached.

"This is definitely from a woman," she said, tilting her head the other direction. "The bottom half was dyed blond and the tips have a tinge of pink."

"Men dye their hair, too," Quince said.

"Do they also wear glitter?"

He made a shrugging sound in thought. "Maybe on special occasions."

Sun carefully took the hair in her gloved hand and leaned forward to try to get a hint of any scent wafting off it.

When she stood, Quince questioned her with a raised brow.

She shook her head. "It's been out here too long, but someone really liked shimmering hair care products."

"Who doesn't?"

"Forensics will be here in thirty," Salazar said, securing her phone.

"Great. I'm going to check a couple of places for Clay Ravinder before heading to Santa Fe for an update on our victim." She wanted to get a look at the minuscule amount of clothes their Jane was wearing, but she needed to get something in her stomach first. "You got this, Lieutenant?"

"Course, boss."

She took off the shoe covers and put them into an evidence bag that Salazar held open for her. "Good work today."

Salazar smiled, the act emphasizing the roundness of her cheeks. "Thank you. I'll keep you updated."

Sun checked on her other two deputies, Zee and Rojas, before gathering her BFF and heading toward the Ravinder compound. She could lie to herself all day and pretend she really was there to check on Clay Ravinder. To make sure he hadn't been beaten to death by his nephew. But deep down she wanted to confront said nephew in a less crime-scene-esque area. And with fewer witnesses. Of course, Levi wouldn't open up in front of all of her deputies, but would he open up when they were alone?

She pulled her cruiser close to the gorgeous mansion Levi had built for his family a few years prior. A far cry from the dilapidated structures that had littered the Ravinder land for years, metal and heavy woods framed every wall inside and out, and huge plate glass windows reflected the blue skyline and the surrounding trees like paintings. She could only imagine the thought Levi put into the place. The care he took choosing each grain of wood. Each sheet of metal.

She knew that Levi, his sister Hailey, her son Jimmy, and Clay lived there, but she wondered if a couple of his cousins didn't live there as well. They were a pretty tight-knit brood and Levi tended to keep his top employees close.

"Do you think Hailey is here?" she asked Quincy, who'd recently fallen for the woman. Hard. A match she wouldn't have seen coming with the Hubble telescope.

"She had to go to Santa Fe. If Ravinder is here," he said, referring to Levi, "can I finally arrest him?" While the whole clan carried the last name of Ravinder, as head of the household, only Levi went by their given name. According to her source, aka Hailey, it was a sign of respect by the rest of the family.

"I told you, Levi didn't steal your cruiser. He borrowed it."

He released a melodramatic sigh, then pleaded with her. "Fine. Just let me arrest him a little."

She felt her mouth crinkle at the corners and turned away to hide that fact. "How do you arrest someone a little?"

"You know. Throw him against the cruiser, rough him up a bit, and call it a day. Bam, bitch," he said, throwing signs.

"No."

"What?"

"No bamming."

"Why?"

"This is a bam-free zone. And what are we in? A seventies action movie? You can't *rough him up.*"

"Sure, I can. A couple of quick shots to the kidneys . . ." He threw a few jabs at the dashboard to demonstrate, then held up his fists for her to inspect. "Three seconds with these babies and he'll think twice next time he needs a ride. Call an Uber, pal." He snorted and pretended to jab her arm. "Am I right?"

"Absolutely not," she said, growing more concerned.

Quince dropped the fists of fury with a loud sigh. "We've been through a lot together, right, Sunburn?"

"Yes. And most of it was your fault."

"But you still always take his side."

"Not always," she argued. Shifting her cruiser into park and killing the engine, she turned and gave him her full attention. "Remember that time we were getting ice cream, and you ordered a scoop of chocolate mint and a scoop of rainbow sherbert in the same cone, and we didn't realize Levi and his cousin Joshua were behind us, and Joshua said you were weird, and Levi laughed in agreement?" Her delicate heart had fluttered like a sparrow caught in a glass jar when she saw Levi standing behind them, shirtless with faded jeans, his sun-kissed skin slick from riding his bike into town. Every time she saw that boy, she became a jellyfish with legs. And that day, the sun had been hot enough to cause wisps of dark auburn hair to stick to his dampened face. "I turned and told them you weren't weird. That you just had demanding taste buds." Sun would never forget the way Levi's gaze had locked onto her. Even when she'd turned around, she could see him eyeing her in the mirror behind the counter. She'd never been the same.

"That was in the third grade," he said, unimpressed.

"And I had your back."

"I guess. Let's get this over with. I'm nigh skin and bone."

She studied his bodybuilder frame with a smirk. "Think you'll survive long enough to make it to Tía Juana's?" Even under the constant threat of nausea, she craved that woman's green chile enchiladas like there was no tomorrow. Who needed a stomach lining, anyway?

"Fingers crossed," he said, exiting her cruiser.

When they walked up to the massive wood door, Quincy took up a tactical position a few feet on her right, out of view of whoever might open said door. Whether he wanted to get a jump on Levi now that they didn't need him for a rescue or simply wanted to have her back should Clay actually answer, Sun couldn't say.

She tossed him a warning glare either way, then knocked, ignoring the butterflies in her stomach. The hungover ones slamming into each other and souring her innards. The last three times she'd knocked on that door, no one answered. This time, the knob turned. She straightened in surprise and prepared herself for a confrontation.

The door swung wide to reveal the weathered face of Clay Ravinder. His graying brown hair hadn't been washed in a few days, his jaw was scruffier than usual, and a thick layer of dust covered the shoulders of his plaid shirt. But at least he was alive, for better or worse.

"Clay," she said, greeting him with a stiff nod. "Have you seen your nephew around?"

He popped the top off a can of cheap beer and took a sip before obliging. "Which one?" he asked, the question quickly followed by a belch.

"The smart one," she answered, unable to resist the jab.

He took another sip, then stepped closer to her as though readying to share a secret. "He ain't quite as smart as you might think."

"I'm pretty sure he is. Have you seen him? Perhaps from across the barrel of a rifle?"

"I haven't pointed my rifle at no one in a long time."

"I meant his rifle." She raised her hands and pantomimed Levi raising his rifle on his uncle. "Pointed at you."

"Is that supposed to scare me?"

Dropping her arms, she said, "Not at all. It's just a question. But you might want to remember something before you make a mistake you can't come back from."

"And what would that be?"

She took her turn and leaned into him, lowering her voice as she said, "You should never wound what you can't kill."

His muddy eyes fairly sparkled with intrigue. "I never do."

"In case you haven't caught on, this is me warning you your nephew knows what you've been up to."

"I highly doubt that, missy."

"I have to ask if you'd like to be put into protective custody. For your own safety, of course."

The humor that flashed across his face spoke volumes. He tilted his head to let his gaze travel the length of her. Because her uniform was so flattering. "It's funny," he said, leaning close again, "you coming out here to see Levi all on your pretty lonesome."

"That would be funny if it were true." She tilted her head to the right and Clay finally noticed the massive deputy standing not ten feet from them.

Quincy tipped an invisible hat.

Clay clamped his jaw shut before speaking from between clenched teeth. "I ain't seen him. And whatever lies you been spreading better end if you know what's good for you."

"That sounds like a threat to me," Quincy said.

"It does to me, too." She narrowed her gaze on the odious man. "Mr. Ravinder, are you threatening an officer of the law?"

"Why, Miss Sunshine, I'd never." He stepped back and slammed the door shut.

# 6

*If you like your whiskey like you like your men,*
*twice your age and from Scotland,*
*we've got you covered.*

—SIGN AT THE ROADHOUSE

Sun turned to Quincy after Clay slammed the door in her face. "We might want to reconsider our crushes."

"What do you mean?" he asked as he followed her to the cruiser.

She got in and waited for him to shut his door before continuing. "We're both in love with Ravinders."

"And?"

"And Ravinders come with all kinds of baggage. Namely their extended family."

"I know. I've considered that. Can you imagine holidays?"

"Yikes." She made a face as an image of chaos and violence surfaced.

"There are some good ones, though," he said, brightening with the thought.

"Holidays?"

"Extended family members."

She pulled out of the drive and started for town. First, sustenance. Second, Santa Fe to check on their victim. "Like?"

Quince smiled as he looked out the window. "Jimmy's pretty great."

He was right. Hailey's autistic son Jimmy was one of Auri's best friends, and Sun loved him almost as much as Auri did. "I agree."

"And there are a couple of cousins I can tolerate."

"The question is," she said, unable to resist the opportunity he'd practically handed her on a silver platter, "will they be able to tolerate you?"

He lifted a heavy shoulder. "I am a bit of an acquired taste."

Her phone rang before they got back to town, and she almost didn't answer the unrecognized number. Tía Juana's was calling her name and her mouth watered as visions of Mexican cuisine danced through her head.

"Are you going to get that?" Quincy asked, charging into her daydream like a hangry bull.

"I just want to eat." She pressed the green button only to be surprised when her mother came on the line.

"Where are you?"

Alarm shot through her. "Mom? I'm on my way back. What'd she do now?"

"Who, sweetheart?"

It was sad that every time her parents called her anymore, Sun's first thought slingshot to Auri. Or, more accurately, to what trouble Auri had gotten herself into. "Never mind. Whose phone are you using?"

"Wanda's. Mine jumped out of my hands and fell in the toilet."

Of course it did. "Wanda is with you?" She grinned at her side-kick, who scrubbed his forehead, keeping up the act. He loved the old girl and he would never convince Sun otherwise.

"Yes. I have you on speakerphone. Everyone's here waiting."

When she questioned Quincy with a raised brow, he just shrugged. "First, who's everyone? Second, why are you at the station?"

The sauciness of her mother's voice when she answered came through in glaring Technicolor. "Well, if you don't know why we're here, how do you know we're at the station?"

"Because I can hear Darlene talking to my administrative assistant."

"Oh," she said, clearly impressed. "You're good."

"That's why they pay me the big bucks."

Her mother snorted. "We were supposed to come in today? Crime? Research? Ringing any bells?"

"Not any familiar ones."

"That's okay. I know Drew found a woman in the canyon."

Freaking small towns.

"How is she? Will she be okay? Do I know her?"

"Mom, you know I can't give out any info yet."

"But I'm your mother."

Sun took a left onto Highway 50. "I'll be there in five. You don't happen to have any taquitos, do you?"

"Not on me. But Ruby did bake some muffins. We brought a basket over."

That woman and her muffins. "That's probably why this poor girl got hurt in the canyon."

"Sun, you can't honestly believe Ruby's muffins are cursed."

She pressed the phone to her chest and said to Quincy, "I'm beginning to wonder."

"I tried to tell you."

She nodded and put the phone back to her ear.

"Did you find Levi?" a young girl asked. A girl with a startlingly familiar voice.

"Auri? Why are you at the station? Why aren't you in school?"

"I'm going back now. I kind of accidentally missed fifth period. And possibly first."

"Aurora Dawn Vicram."

"I'm sorry, Mom. I thought I might know who that girl is, but I was wrong."

Sun struggled for patience. "Mother, can you take me off speaker for a minute?"

"Why?" Auri asked. "Did you find Levi? What happened?"

"This isn't about Levi, bug. I'll see you in a bit."

"Okay then," she said, her voice deflating. "Love you."

"I love you, too."

"Okay, you're off speaker," her mom said, whispering into the phone. God, she loved these people. "What's up?"

Since she had her on the phone, maybe she knew something about Sun's first victim of the day. "Any thoughts on who might have stabbed Doug in the neck with a knitting needle?"

Auri chimed in once again. "Doug was stabbed in the neck with a knitting needle?"

"Mother," Sun said, aghast.

"Sorry. I pushed the button, I swear."

Sun could hear her mother literally stabbing her phone. "Okay. It's okay, Mom. She knows now." How the sheriff's office managed to keep any secrets in this town was the biggest mystery of all.

"Why would you keep that from me?" Auri asked.

"Sweetheart, you've had enough violence in your life lately, don't you think?"

"I guess. He's a little creepy but he seems nice. Who would stab him?"

Sun stilled at the thought of Doug flashing her daughter. She would kill him. A plethora of charges ran through her mind—indecent exposure, public nuisance, assault with a limp noodle. "Auri, has he ever flashed you?"

"No. Gross, Mom. I'm just a kid."

Relief flooded every cell in her body. "What about you, Mother?"

"No, Sunshine. I've told you before, he only flashes women he can get a rise out of. The first and only time he tried to flash me, I giggled."

"I knew it! Everyone just needs to laugh at him. He'll stop."

"Well, I'm fairly certain your father paid him a visit later that day. That probably helped, too."

She was right. That would certainly do the trick.

"Hey, Sunny," her dad said.

He was at the station, too? Was it a block party and she hadn't been invited? "Dad, did you threaten Doug?"

"Sure did. With a mallet and a chisel, if I recall correctly."

Sounded about right.

"Why does he flash people, Mom?" Auri asked. "It's disgusting."

"We can discuss it later. For now, you stay away from that man, okay?"

"Aye-aye, Cap'n."

She grinned. "Have you been sneaking my pirate romances again?"

"No," she said with only a slight hesitation.

Sun rolled her eyes. She needed a better hiding spot. "So, Mom, Dad, any thoughts on who could've done it?"

"I've considered it," her mom said. "Only I'd aim a little lower."

"Yeah, well, you have a pretty solid alibi. Anyone else you can think of? He swears he was attacked by a gang."

"A gang of knitters?"

"Exactly! If you hear anything, will you let me know?"

"Will do, hon."

"I'm taking the kid back to school," her dad said.

"Thanks, Dad. Can you make sure she stays this time?"

"No idea how to do that other than implanting a tracking chip under her skin."

"Can you get your hands on one?"

"No," Auri said. "That sounds painful."

"So does a life of solitary confinement in your room. Get your ass to school and keep it there. You can tell me about your suspicions later."

"All right."

"Bye, pumpkin," Sun heard her mom say, followed by kissy sounds. "Okay, I'm back. Where are you?"

"Pulling up now. Any idea why my daughter has been crying?" She could hear the stuffiness of her nose in her voice, and she'd learned long ago the difference between allergies and sorrow.

"No. She wouldn't tell us, but I have my suspicions."

"And?"

"It's nothing I can elaborate on at the moment."

"Talk in a sec." She hung up and put the cruiser in park.

"Ten minutes, then I'm doing the thing," Quincy said, referring to their everlasting plan to break away from work when they were hungry. The plan was also ever-evolving, so there was no telling what Quince would come up with.

Sun grabbed her stomach as it gurgled yet again. "Make it five."

He gave her a thumbs-up. They walked into the station to see the group of women, otherwise known as the Book Babes, in the lobby. Before Anita could let them into the bullpen, they came to the security door en masse and stood at the glass like desperate shoppers waiting for the doors to open on Black Friday.

"I'll let them in," Quince said, walking to the door.

Sun headed to her office for a quick pick-me-up in the form of a steaming cup of java. Once there, she scrounged for the energy bar she'd stashed only to realize what Quincy meant earlier. He'd taken the last one. Or, well, *borrowed* it, though she could say in all honesty she didn't want it back. She sank into her chair, disappointment and day-old tequila gnawing a hole into her stomach.

After a fierce membership drive, the Book Babes had recently upped their numbers from six to seven, but only four showed up at her office. They spilled inside, thanking Quincy—some more profusely than others—and chittering amongst themselves as they stopped in front of her desk. After they formed a straight line, Darlene Tapia put the basket of muffins on her desk, then greeted her with a solemn, "Sheriff."

Sun scooted up in the chair and eyed them suspiciously. The women and the muffins. Hunger won out. She scooped one up and started peeling off the plastic wrap. "What's up?"

Apparently having been appointed their spokeswoman, Darlene, a curvy Latina with more salt than pepper, cleared her throat and said, "We're here on official business."

Here we go. Sun rubbed her forehead, then tucked a strand of blond hair that had fallen from her French braid behind her ear. "Did you guys attack Doug and stab him in the neck with a knitting needle?"

They turned and questioned each other for a split second before three of their gazes landed on the spitfire known as Wanda Stephanopoulos.

Wanda stood a head shorter than the others, her frame rail thin but strong, her silver pixie tipped with hot pink. She gaped at her friends who were currently throwing her under a bus. "What? I didn't stab Doug this time. I swear."

"This time?" Sun asked before realizing she didn't want to know. She raised a palm to thwart any explanation coming her way. "Look, Doug is sitting in urgent care with a knitting needle sticking out of his neck. Or at least he was a few hours ago. He said a gang attacked him."

"A gang of knitters?" Darlene asked.

"Right?" Feeling strangely vindicated for the shade she'd thrown Doug, Sun nodded in agreement at her mother's oldest and dearest. She rarely shared information about an ongoing case, but if anyone knew who might stab a man with a knitting needle in this town, it was one of the four women standing before her. "Any thoughts on who could've done it?"

Three of them glanced at each other again and shrugged, but the fourth dropped her gaze to study the dark blue carpet beneath her feet.

So easy.

Sun didn't know Karen Oxley as well as she knew the others. She'd grown up surrounded by her mother's friends, but Karen had moved to Del Sol after Sun had moved away. Karen, the youngest in the group, was the football coach's wife and seemed to be well-liked. Maybe she had a dark side nobody knew about. Rather like the toast her daughter had tried to pawn off on her the other day. The toast she'd served smothered in butter, beige-side up.

After a quick bite, Sun had gagged and lifted it to look at the solid black underside. "How did you only burn one side?" she had asked the copper-headed fruit of her loins.

Her daughter leaned toward her over the counter and gave her a saucy wink before saying, "Skill, baby. Pure skill."

"Mrs. Oxley?" Sun nudged, suppressing a grin at the memory.

The other three women turned their heads to stare at their spiky-haired friend. "Karen?" Darlene said. "Did you stab Doug in the neck with your knitting needle?"

"What, no!" Her gaze flew to Sun's. "No, Sunshine, I didn't. I would never. But I may have overheard someone the other day say something . . . oddly specific to what you've described."

Now they were getting somewhere. Sun sank back into her chair. "And who would that someone be?"

"Well, I'm not sure . . . I mean . . ." Karen hedged, shifting from one foot to the other like a second-grader in the principal's office. "I don't want to get anyone into trouble."

Sun swallowed the bite she took before asking, "Okay, then how about what you overheard?"

"Oh, of course. I was at Bernadette's getting my lowlights done and I heard Mrs. . . . one of Del Sol's most upstanding citizens, state that if Doug flashes her again, she was going to stab him in the throat with her favorite knitting needle."

"Wow. That *is* oddly specific."

"Yes. Bernadette asked why not his penis, and she said she wouldn't touch that old thing with a ten-foot pole, much less her favorite knitting needle."

Sun fought a grin. "If it helps," she said, trying to coax more out of her, "I'm fairly certain it was self-defense. I doubt the perpetrator will even be arrested." Unless, of course, it was premeditated. That could wrinkle a few collars.

"In that case . . ." Karen paused as though considering her options, then barreled ahead with, "Mrs. Fairborn." She dropped her head in shame as everyone gaped at her. "It was Mrs. Fairborn."

"Karen," Wanda said, "you can't honestly suggest that Mrs. Fairborn—"

"No. Not at all. I mean, she couldn't, right?" Her gaze darted back to Sun. "She's too small. Too frail. Too . . ."

"Too eighty-something?" Darlene asked.

"Yes."

After getting to know Mrs. Fairborn on a more personal level recently, Sun figured she could do anything she set her mind to, but even Sun doubted the woman capable of sinking a knitting needle with two pointy ends four inches into Doug's sun-dried neck. "I highly doubt Mrs. Fairborn could manage to stab Doug with a knitting needle, but I'll check into it, hon."

Karen pressed her mouth together and nodded, clearly guilt-ridden for ratting out her friend.

"So, what's this official business?" Sun asked, leaning forward onto her elbows and clasping her fingers together.

Darlene took the lead again. "If you'll remember, we've decided to write a book."

Sun nodded. "Oh, right." It was all coming back to her.

"A mystery," Karen added.

"Gotcha." Sun knew where this was headed, but her mind had stalled on the image of seven women—women who could bicker for hours about the pros and cons of pleated drapes—struggling to write a book together.

"And," Helen Maez said, having yet to chime in, "we want to go on some ride-alongs to get a feel for what it's like to be in law enforcement." Almost as vertically challenged as Wanda, Helen had corkscrew curls, rich and tawny, that brushed the tops of her shoulders when she talked.

"Maybe with Quincy?" Wanda suggested, craning her neck to see him through the glass wall of Sun's office. The woman had always had a thing for Quince. A dark thing. A disturbing thing.

"We can't do this today, but maybe we can work something out." Quince would kill her. The mere thought made her giddy.

Karen stepped forward. "I'd like to ride with Zee, if I can. She's a sniper." Her gaze slid past Sun. "I've always wondered what it would be like to kill people from a distance." She snapped back when she realized what she'd said. "Bad guys. I mean, what it would be like to kill bad guys from a distance."

Sun understood that temptation all too well. She took out a notepad to jot down their preferences. Odds were, nothing would ever come of this. Their interest would probably wane once they actually tried to sit down and write together. If not, she would have to get her deputies' permissions first. Except for Quince. She'd surprise him.

Darlene pointed to the notes. "Can you put me down for Poetry?"

Sun paused. Darlene had practically raised her newest deputy, Poetry Rojas. The odds were astronomical, but if he got into a life-threatening situation with her in the vehicle, Darlene could put both of their lives at risk.

"Unless you think I would embarrass him," she added when Sun hesitated.

"Darlene," Sun said, putting the pen aside, "I have seen him bask in the glory of your attention when you smoothed his hair with your own spit. He adores you. You would never be an embarrassment to him. I'm just worried what would happen if things went south."

Darlene's brows slid together. "Like if we had to chase a bad guy into Mexico?"

Sun coughed softly to camouflage a chuckle. "Not that far south."

"I would like to go with Poetry, too," Helen said, her curls practically vibrating with excitement at the thought of the ride-alongs. "I could keep an eye on this one." She hitched a thumb toward Darlene. "Make sure she doesn't try to be a hero."

Darlene frowned at her. "What if my baby gets into trouble?"

Exactly. "I'll tell you what," Sun said, entering into negotiation mode. "You guys write the first chapter of your book and then we'll talk ride-alongs."

All but one seemed to deflate. Wanda scratched her chin in thought, and said, "I still think it should be about a group of older women who go around killing murderers and rapists and people who talk in theaters, and the hot FBI agent who hunts them down. One-by-one. And arrests them. With handcuffs." Her expression turned dreamy, and Sun rubbed her forehead again to hide her grin.

"That sounds fantastic," she said. "When I see chapter one, we'll talk."

"Should we carry guns?" Wanda asked. "In case we run into trouble?"

"No." But Wanda's question opened up the floor for them to fire questions at Sun with speed of an Uzi. Apparently, they'd reached the lightning round.

"Can we arrest people?" one of them asked.

"No."

"Can we have badges?" another asked.

"No."

"Can we give sobriety tests?" And yet another.

"No."

"Can we read someone their rights?"

"Can we take a Taser for a spin?"

"What if we have to test a sample of cocaine? Is there a class for that?"

This was clearly going to take a while, and Quince had yet to save her. She held up a hand to stop them as the hangries took over. Her stomach growled in testament. "Guys, if you want to do a ride-along, you have to abide by the rules. You are to observe only. You cannot interact with anyone but the deputies, and only when they are not engaged in official business."

The four women shrank in disappointment but acquiesced with a reluctant nod.

Darlene recovered first. She stepped forward and took Sun's hand, then turned back to the troops. "Okay, girls, let's do this."

The *girls* high-fived each other while a notion niggled at the back of Sun's neck. What if they actually pulled it off? What if they actually quit bickering long enough to get a chapter written? Then what? How would she convince her deputies to let her mother's book club do ride-alongs? Bribery, yes, but with what? Money? Food? Beer?

Probably beer.

"Thanks, Sun," Karen said as they headed out.

But a thought hit Sun. "Who else was there?"

She turned back. "Pardon?"

"When Mrs. Fairborn said that about the knitting needle, who else was there?"

"Oh, just me, Mrs. Fairborn, Bernadette, and Dusty. It was a slow day, so the other girl took off."

Sun nodded and waved at them. "Thanks. You guys stay out of trouble."

Darlene snorted and they all laughed before thanking her with a wave and leaving.

All except Wanda. "I'll meet you guys at Caffeine-Wah," she said to her friends.

So close. Sun made eye contact with Quincy and shrugged a question, wondering where his big plan to get them out of there was.

He held up his phone as Wanda sank into a chair across from Sun's desk, a grave expression on her face. This must be serious.

Honestly, if Wanda tried to convince Sun to invest in a strip club one more time, she was going to kill her. Sun didn't have time for—

"I was robbed."

Sun's gaze snapped back to Wanda's, and she abandoned her muffin. "What? When?"

Wanda drew in a deep breath, clearly distressed. "Last night. I think."

"You think?" Sun stood and walked around the desk to take the chair next to her. She leaned close. "Wanda, did someone break into your house?"

She nodded and dropped her gaze to her shaking hands. This had been weighing on her, yet she'd acted completely nonchalant while the other women were there. She had some major acting chops, but why would she want to keep this from her best friends?

Sun would get to that later. "You didn't call it in?"

"No." Her voice cracked. There was clearly more to this than a simple break-in.

She put a hand on the older woman's shoulder. "Wanda, were you there when it happened? Did they hurt you?"

Zee walked into the station then and tossed Sun a questioning gaze through the blinds. Sun held up a finger, telling Zee to give her a minute. The deputy nodded and walked to her desk in the bullpen.

After a moment, Wanda swallowed hard and said, "I don't know if I was there or not. They could've broken in while I was sleeping." She clasped her hands together. "Do you think they would do that?"

A woman living alone being broken into? She had to feel utterly violated and vulnerable. "Hold on, hon. Let's start from the beginning. When did you notice your house had been broken into?"

"This morning. I woke up and realized the place had been ransacked."

"So, it hadn't been ransacked before you went to bed?"

She pressed one side of her mouth together as though reluctant to answer. After a moment, she said, "I don't know. I was a little . . . tipsy when I got home."

"Wanda, did you drink and drive?" How else would the woman not know if her place had been ransacked when she got home?

"What? No," she said, appalled. "My date drove me home."

"And had he been drinking?"

"I don't know. He may have had one or two."

So, yes. "Okay, hon. Let's back up. Where were you last night?"

"On a date with a man I met in Santa Fe. He seemed okay."

"I'll need his name and contact info."

Her gaze flew to Sun's. "Why? He didn't have anything to do with this and nothing of value is missing anyway. Well, maybe a couple of old coins, but I don't care about them."

"You've gone through everything?"

"Yes. Mostly. Other than the coins, I didn't really have anything of value. What little jewelry I had is gone but it wasn't worth much."

Sun looked up to get Zee's attention. "I'm going to bring Zee in, okay? She'll help with the investigation."

Again, her gaze flew to Sun's and she clutched at her arm. "No! You can't! No one can know. This has to stay between you and me, Sunshine. No deputies. No official report. Nothing."

More confused than ever, Sun took Wanda's hand into hers, peeling her claws out of her skin first. She patted her hand and asked, "Bottom line, Wanda. What's going on?"

Wanda nodded, resigned to her fate, and started over. "Okay, I went on a date last night. When I left, my house was a disaster."

"So they broke in during the day yesterday?"

She waved a dismissive hand. "Oh, no. My house is always a disaster."

Why didn't that surprise her?

"What I'm saying is, maybe I just didn't notice it when I got home." She hit Sun with a look of hope, desperately wanting to believe that she hadn't been broken into while she was there. Sun understood that feeling of vulnerability all too well.

"Maybe," she offered to console her. "Did your date go in?"

"No. He was quite the gentleman. He kissed me goodbye at the door and left."

The thought of Wanda, who was sixty-five if she was a day, getting kissed on her doorstep after a first date was all kinds of adorable. "Then?"

"Then I went to bed. I didn't notice anything out of the ordinary until this morning."

"And what did you see?"

"My clothes." She stood and looked out the window to the street beyond. "My clothes were strewn all over my room. They'd gone through my drawers. Through my closet." Her hands began shaking again as she covered her eyes.

Sun stood beside her. "And?"

"And I don't care about any of that. I only care about one thing." She turned to Sun, the desperation back tenfold. "My sewing tin."

Sun blinked, letting that sink in. "Your sewing tin?"

"Yes. Or, more to the point," she said, leaning closer and dropping her voice to a whisper, "what's in my sewing tin."

Sun nodded as understanding dawned. "I'm guessing it's not sewing needles."

"Not even close."

"Then what?"

"Oh." She straightened. "I can't tell you."

"Why not?"

"Be . . . cause?"

"Yeah, that's not a good reason."

"Sunshine, you have to find that tin. You can't ask me why. You can't ask me what's inside. And you have to keep it off the books. Especially from . . . Never mind."

"Especially from who?" Sun prompted.

"That doesn't matter. I'll pay you."

"That's called accepting a bribe and is, in fact, frowned upon in most law enforcement offices."

"No, not like that." She patted Sun's arm. "Silly rabbit. You know, like a reward." She tilted her head and winked. Three times. Because the first wink wasn't obvious enough.

Sun pinched the bridge of her nose, begging the powers that be for patience. She looked over and motioned Zee to come to her office. "Wanda, I'm going to have Zee take you home and get a look at your locks."

"Sunshine," she started to protest, but Sun held up a hand.

"I won't tell her everything, but we do need to take a look, hon. You could've been hurt."

"You won't tell her about the tin?"

She raised three fingers on one hand and pressed the other to her heart. "Scout's honor."

Wanda narrowed her lashes on her. "Were you really a scout?"

"No, but I went steady with one in the third grade."

"Well, all right then."

Sun hid a grin and explained the situation to Zee as succinctly as possible, then sent her home with Wanda to check out the scene. Innate curiosity burned in her chest, rather like heartburn. It was probably the cursed muffin. Still, what was inside that tin? What could be that important and yet keep Wanda so secretive? She said it was nothing of value. She meant it was nothing of value to anyone besides herself.

Sun went over what she knew about Wanda as she gathered her things, readying to head to Santa Fe. But first, she opened her office door and threw a muffin at her chief deputy, nailing him on the back of the head. He spun around in his chair and gaped at her.

"That could've been a grenade," she said, shaking her head at him.

He ended his call and stood to follow her out. "Why would someone throw a grenade inside the station?"

"No idea, but you have to stay vigilant and alert at all times. If that had been a real grenade, we would never make it to Tía Juana's in time for fresh sopas."

# 7

Her mother had been dodging her calls all afternoon. Sun left three messages and sent a dozen texts. The last one, the one that read *Call me with an update or you'll never see your turquoise earrings again,* did not live up to her expectations. Her mother loved those earrings. Instead of an update or an explanation as to why Auri had been crying earlier, her mother simply texted her back with *Call your daughter.* Which, duh. Sun already knew that. She just wanted a heads-up as to what was going on underneath that submissive hemogoblin of hers. Auri had a way of catching her off guard.

With no other choice, she tapped Auri's name on her phone as she and Quincy sat at Presbyterian in Santa Fe, waiting for the doctor. Their Jane Doe was in critical, but she was alive. For now, that was enough. Zee and Salazar were checking missing persons reports while Rojas checked for witnesses at the houses nearest the canyon.

"Hey, Mom," Auri said just as an ambulance brought in a heart attack victim.

The EMTs rushed the man past her and Quincy, and Sun couldn't help but notice he'd been handcuffed to the gurney.

"Hey, bug. Whatcha doing?"

"Reflecting on how badly I want to be Beth Dutton when I grow up."

"Beth Dutton? I thought Lisbeth Salander was your hero."

"Oh, she is. But Beth is my kindred spirit. I'm thinking about combining the two of them, sprinkling in a little Ellen Ripley, and morphing into a badass. But I need more real-world experience if I'm going to rise to Beth's level of quick comebacks. I wonder if there's a class I could take."

"Perhaps, but for now I think we should hold off on some of her more colorful phrases until you're older."

"I guess. So what's up?"

"Do you want to tell me why you were upset today?"

"I wasn't . . . How did you know?"

"Bug, I can always tell when you've been crying."

"Is that like a sheriff thing?"

"No, it's like a mom thing. What gives?"

"I wasn't going to tell you until you got home."

"I could be late with this case."

"Oh, the case. So, I thought the girl Mr. Essary found might be Lynelle's cousin who never showed up after her finals, but then Whitney texted Lynelle and said she'd gone skiing in Colorado with some friends. What's wrong with that picture?"

Sun almost laughed as a couple of cops hurried past, following the gurney. Clearly her daughter was picking up a lot from her. "Well, first it was a text and not an actual phone call."

"Exactly. Anyone could have sent it. And two?"

"It's a little late in the season to go snow skiing. Even in Colorado."

"Bingo. It just seems really suspish."

"I agree." Her daughter could be onto something. Then again, she usually was. "How do you know Lynelle's cousin never showed up and then texted her? Are you guys talking now?"

"Not hardly," she said with a snort. "I overheard a conversation last week before . . . before everything happened." Before she and Cruz walked in on a robbery and almost died. "I tried to talk to Lynelle at school, but she'd stayed home to take care of a sick friend, so I went by her house during lunch."

"Who was the friend?"

"Tim Redding."

"The former sheriff's son?"

"Yes. Only he wasn't sick, Mom. He was covered in bruises and his right eye was swollen almost shut. Like someone hit him."

Alarm bells once again rang in her ears as she and Quince locked gazes. "You're sure it was his right eye?"

"Yes. If someone did hit him, he was a southpaw."

Holy crap, Sun was going to have to be more careful. The kid didn't miss a thing. But what were the odds of two lefties beating up two kids in her county around the same time?

"That would narrow it down, right? If he was a southpaw?"

"It would. I'll check into it."

"You can't tell Tim I told you, though. I don't want him to think I betrayed a secret."

"Of course not."

"Thanks, Mom."

"Is that why you were upset today? Because of Tim?"

"What? Oh, no, it's not. I just . . . I mean, I feel bad for him. Don't get me wrong. But I'm mostly worried about Cruz."

"Cruz? Did something happen?"

"He wrote a poem."

She released a breath she hadn't realized she'd been holding. "Isn't that his thing?"

"Not like this. Not . . . It came from a very dark place."

Sun's chest tightened around her heart.

"It came from *that* dark place."

Sun nodded and stared pointedly at Quince. "We'll check into it, bug. We'll get him help. I promise."

"Okay. Granddad went to check on him for now and Sybil is coming over so we can do some research."

"For school?"

Auri snorted, reminding Sun who she was talking to. "Not

even. I'll find a pic of Lynelle's cousin Whitney and shoot it to you. Just in case. And we're going to check all the ski lodges. See if any of them are still open."

"All right, but no more interviews, hear me? I'll follow up."

"Aye-aye, Cap'n."

"And stay out of my pirate romances."

"Mom, I tore through your collection two years ago. I've been raiding Grandma's stash."

"Grandma has a stash of pirate romances?"

"And cowboys and vampires and there's this one series about a female grim reaper who's in love with the son of—"

"Wait a minute. How spicy are these books?"

"If they were green chile, they would've been harvested during a drought." The drier the season, the hotter the chile.

"Auri, you are too young for books like that."

"Grandma already told me how old you were when you started sneaking her romance novels."

Damn it. That woman was going to give her a bad rep. "That's hardly the point."

"It's entirely the point. And it's a really sharp one, too."

"How's your submissive hemogoblin?"

"Mom," Auri said, her voice irritated. Like from drain cleaner. Or battery acid.

"Auri," Sun countered.

"I know."

"You know what?"

"I know that's not what it's called. It's not a submissive he-mogoblin. It's a submissive hemo-*glow*-bin. *Glow.* I've been saying it wrong this whole time."

"Really?" Sun asked, infusing her voice with as much surprise as possible.

"You know I have. And it's not even really called that."

"Oh, yeah? What's it called then?"

"Well, I don't know but not that. And you never told me. What if I'd gone to medical school? I would've been a laughing stock."

Kid had a point. She and Quincy both fought a grin as she said, "I'm sorry, hon."

"I can hear the laughter in your voice, Mom."

"What?"

"Are you laughing, too, Quincy?"

He sobered instantly. "No way, kiddo. I'm on your side. Your mom is a sadist."

"Thank you. From now on I'm just calling it what it is. A percussion."

"Actually," Quincy began, but Sun slammed a hand over his mouth and pressed the phone to her chest.

After taking a moment to glare at him, she whispered, "Don't you dare take this from me." She grabbed his collar and shook him. Or tried to. If he weren't made of rebar and concrete, she would've succeeded. "I demand to be entertained."

"You are pure evil," he whispered back.

"What did I say wrong this time?" Auri said, still on speakerphone.

"Nothing sweetheart."

"Mom."

"Oh, look. The doctor is here. Talk to you later, hon."

"Mothe—"

Sun hung up before her daughter could finish the threat, then said to Quince, "Where do you think she gets her sass from?"

"I can't imagine." He slid down in his chair, staring off into space.

"We'll talk to him," Sun said.

Quince nodded, unconvinced. "I shouldn't have taken him in. He just lost his dad. He was almost killed. He saw the girl he loves get attacked. He needs someone who knows what the fuck they're doing, Sun. I could barely keep my goldfish alive."

"Quince." Sun sank farther into her chair and wrapped her arms around one of his. "You could never keep your goldfish alive. Your mother kept replacing it every time it died. And Cruz needs someone in his life right now who loved his dad as much as he did. You're the closest thing to an uncle he has."

"And look where that's gotten him."

Before Sun could argue, a doctor really did walk up to them, a round elderly woman with a soft Middle Eastern accent. "Are you Sheriff Vicram?"

"I am." They both stood and Sun held out her hand. "We were wanting an update on the unidentified female brought in earlier today."

Two corrections officers ran past them, almost knocking the doctor to the ground.

Quince grabbed her, then glared after the COs from the state pen on the outskirts of town.

"Thank you," she said, righting herself and brushing off her white coat. "I'm Dr. Habib." She looked around as an alarm sounded down the hall. "She's still unconscious."

"How is it looking?"

"She does have some significant swelling. Despite this, she has good brain activity. We're keeping her sedated for now, but her prognosis is promising."

"That's fantastic. And her ribs?" Sun had noticed a lot of scrapes and bruising along her rib cage.

"A couple of broken ribs, her occipital lobe was shattered and she has a fractured wrist. But there were some other abnormalities that I wanted to talk to you about."

"What do you mean?" Quince asked, angling for a peek at the Jane's chart. The doctor could've refused. HIPAA laws were pretty straightforward. Without a warrant or a written declaration of their intentions as to the investigation, she could've chosen not to show them the girl's chart. But she obliged anyway by holding it out for him.

He flipped through the pages as she asked, "Did you see the lacerations on her legs when you found her?"

"I did notice some cuts," Sun said, reading what she could as

Quincy flipped. "But we didn't get a good look. We were just try-ing to get her off that mountain." She stopped Quince by putting her finger on one particular line in the doctor's statement. "What's this?"

The doctor tilted her head to see what Sun was pointing at. "Yes. It looks like she was . . . mutilated, for lack of a better word. We did an assault kit on her, of course. We found spermicide but no sperm."

"So, he used a condom."

"Most likely, but the investigator is hoping they got some peripheral DNA."

"Was she raped?" Quince asked.

The doctor nodded. "There was significant tearing and bruis-ing. The investigator believes she was sexually assaulted. But there were also deliberate mutilations on and around her genitalia. Mostly on her inner thighs and lower abdomen."

"What kind of mutilations?"

"Bite marks. And many of them. That's where we're betting to get a viable DNA sample."

"Are you telling me someone bit her before . . ."

"Or after," she said. "We can't be certain of a timeline. Per-haps when she regains consciousness, she can answer a few of your questions, but with her subdural hematoma, there are no guaran-tees she'll be able to recall what happened immediately."

"So, she never woke up?" Sun asked. Despite the odds, she'd been hoping for an ID on this poor girl.

"No. But, again, we had to take her into surgery immediately to relieve the swelling in her brain and she's been out ever since."

Sun nodded her understanding.

"Can I get a copy of these?"

"I'll have the nurse make you one."

"Thank you." Sun took a card out of her pocket. "Doctor, can you call me directly if she wakes up? Or if there is any change at all?"

"Of course," she said right as another officer ran past.

Sun and Quince looked at a commotion down the hall.

"I'm going to request a police guard," Sun said, wanting to make sure the doctor understood. "Until then, her life could very much be in danger."

The doctor tore her gaze away and pointed at the nurses' station. "That's why she's right here by the station. We're keeping an eye on this room, but a guard would be nice."

"What the hell is going on?" Quincy asked as two police officers ran past them in the other direction.

"I don't know." The doctor craned her neck. "They brought in a prisoner. Heart attack, I believe."

"This is not happening," a corrections officer said to his partner as they ran past like they were in pursuit.

Realization hit Sun and Quincy at the exact same moment. They turned and gaped at each other.

"Did he escape?" Sun asked Quince.

"That's what I'm thinking." He turned to the doctor. "Do you know who it was?"

A nurse had walked up, straining to see as well, when she said, "I just admitted him. His name is Wynn Ravinder."

"What did your mom say?" Auri asked Sybil when she knocked on her front door.

The girl rushed inside, a metaphorical wind whirling around her like a mini-tornado. It suited her new BFF. "I told her we were assigned this project and if we didn't do it together, we'd both get a zero."

Auri laughed as she closed the door. "And she believed you?"

"She takes my GPA very seriously. She has no idea we've already finished all of our finals." She dropped her backpack on the couch and headed for the kitchen where the freshly delivered pizza sat. "This smells divine."

"It is." Auri sat down and took a bite out of the piece she'd grabbed before Sybil got there. "I'm sorry your mom doesn't want us hanging anymore."

"She'll get over it. Once things get back to normal and you stop skipping school, breaking into houses, and almost getting killed, she'll let me come over more."

"In my defense, I thought Mrs. Fairborn was a serial killer."

"I know. I tried to explain that. Sadly, the fact that you tried to find a serial killer on your own didn't help." Sybil opened the box, took out a piece, and claimed a bite twice the size of her mouth like she'd been part of a starvation experiment. She moaned in ecstasy.

Auri giggled.

"My mom doesn't let me eat pizza anymore," she said between chews. "I'm in hell."

"She just cares about your health. And salt intake. And the fact that you're lactose intolerant. Are you sure you're going to be okay?"

"Oh, yeah. I took a Lactaid when she wasn't looking." She pushed her round glasses up her nose, piled three pieces of pizza on a plate, then came back to the couch. "Thanks for letting me come over."

"Please, I wish you lived here."

"Yeah, if only you'd stop almost getting killed."

Auri gaped at her. "You started it."

"I know, right? My mom still hasn't gotten over that whole kidnapping-and-almost-dying thing."

"I can't imagine why," she said, taking a sip of her soda.

Sybil's face lit up. "Is that Dr Pepper?"

"There's more in the fridge. So what did you find out?"

"Oh, heck no." Sybil jumped up, grabbed a soda out of the fridge, and hurried back. "I need more. I need all the deets. The dirt. The skinny. The 4–1–1. The lowdown."

Auri loved it when Sybil morphed into a thesaurus. She brought out her phone to show her. "Right there. He just put it in. Himself. With Lynelle almost nearby."

Sybil took her phone, then pressed it to her chest and fell back. "Do you know what this means?"

"Tim Redding is insanely brave?"

"It means the most popular boy in school likes you so much he put his number in your phone. Do you understand how amazing that is?"

"Not really since, you know, I'm saving myself for a better offer."

Sybil's dreamy gaze landed on her again. "Have you and Cruz . . . you know . . . ?"

"Had sex?"

Sybil went ramrod straight. "What? No. Wait." She leaned in and whispered, "Have you?"

"No. Not even. I mean, I did see his butt that one time."

"Oh, my god, that is the best story ever. Tell me again." She sat expectantly, waiting for Auri to tell her the towel story for the thousandth time.

"I am not telling you again. We have work to do."

"Right." She took a sip to wash down her pizza, then took out her laptop. "I'm on it." She opened it up and angled it toward Auri. "From what I can tell after scouring Lynelle's social accounts, she has seven cousins."

Auri deflated. "Seven?"

"Don't get your panties in a wad. Only three of them are girls."

"My panties?"

"And of the three girls, only one goes to UNM." She pointed to a girl on her screen. "Whitney Amaia." The girl Sybil pointed to, a freshman at UNM, looked nothing like Lynelle, but they were only cousins. Whitney defined perky with blond hair, a button nose, and a sparkling smile. Lynelle was tall and slim with eyes like a bobcat. They were both supermodel material, just in very different ways. "But, and this is odd considering how kids are these days, she has yet to check in on any of her social accounts. Or share any pictures of her and her friends skiing."

"That's very odd."

"Right? What did you get?"

"Okay." Auri opened her laptop, too. "I looked it up and there actually is one ski resort in Colorado that is still open. The Arapahoe Basin. It's open for another week so, I mean, it's plausible."

"Weird." Sybil took another bite and chewed in thoughtful repose.

"Sybil, can I ask you something strange?"

"Are you kidding?" She dropped her pizza onto her plate and refocused on Auri. "You know me. I live for the strange."

Auri scooted closer and lowered her voice. No clue why. "If someone you knew, someone you loved with all of your heart and soul, was considering taking their own life, what would you do?"

Caught off guard, Sybil sat a moment, then put her plate on the coffee table in front of them and turned toward Auri, an expression of absolute understanding and compassion on her freckled face. "He's been through a lot, Auri."

Auri pulled her bottom lip between her teeth and lowered her gaze.

Sybil put her hand on her arm and squeezed. "I would do everything in my power to let him know how loved he is. How adored. How . . . un-alone. And I would beg him to use a semicolon. Not a period."

It took Auri a minute to get her meaning, but it was beyond perfect. Pause. Don't end. Suddenly the whole semicolon movement made so much more sense. "Would you rat him out? Would you try to get him help? Because, I kind of did that very thing."

Sybil frowned in thought, but she didn't answer because her attention had been hijacked by something at the back of the house. Her gaze had strolled past Auri toward the kitchen window.

Auri looked over her shoulder. "What is it?"

Sybil pointed, the blood draining from her face. "Someone's outside."

"Cruz?" She started to jump up, but Sybil grabbed her arm and pulled her back down. "No. Not Cruz."

Auri stilled and tried desperately to see past the blackness of night. "Sybil, you're scaring me."

"I'm scaring me, too," she whispered.

"Was it one of my grandparents?" Although why they would be at the back of the house in the dark she couldn't fathom.

Unable to take her eyes off the window, Sybil simply shook her head.

"Jimmy Ravinder?" Auri asked hopefully. Surely it was Jimmy. He came over all the time and knocked on her bedroom window instead of the door, but again Sybil shook her head.

"Older. Bigger. Dark hair and beady eyes."

Goose bumps raced across Auri's skin as her brain shifted into overdrive. "Okay." She clasped Sybil's face and turned her gaze toward hers. It took some doing, but she finally got Sybil to quit looking at the window and focus on her. "Here's what we're going to do. I'm going to call 9–1–1 and we are going to make a run for it."

Sybil's already huge eyes went even larger, the outline as round as the wire frames on her glasses. "We're going to run for it?"

"Yes."

"Run for what?" she screeched, panic kicking in.

"Sybil," Auri whispered harshly to get her attention. "For my grandparents' house. It's, like, twelve feet away."

"It's at least a hundred."

"Okay, it's thirty."

"Thirty feet is plenty of room to kill and dismember someone." Sybil's voice grew louder with each word.

Auri rolled her eyes. They'd both seen the harsh uncertainties life had to offer, and the fear leaching into every molecule in Auri's body proved she clearly had a touch of PTSD because of it. "Okay, whoever he is, he's at the back of the house. If we run out the front door . . ."

"That's exactly what killers want!" She shook Auri's shoulders, trying to get her to understand. "They want us outside where we're vulnerable. Have you never seen a slasher film?"

"You're right," Auri said, trying not to hyperventilate even knowing in the back of her mind Sybil could've seen an owl or a wolf or even a mountain lion. They lived in the wilds of New Mexico, after all. But for some reason, the thought of a man being outside her house scared her a lot more than a mountain lion. "I'll call my granddad to come get us, okay?"

Sybil nodded with renewed vigor. "Yes. Yes. Good idea."

"In the meantime . . ."

"Where are you going?" Sybil hissed.

"I need to lock the door and grab a weapon."

"You're just going to leave me?"

"I'm right here."

"I'm going with you." She clutched Auri's arm, her nails digging into the tender flesh underneath, but Auri didn't mind. She was freaking, too.

She dialed her granddad before getting up to lock the door, but before it rang, the front door opened. Both of them clawed at each other and screamed bloody murder for thirty seconds before realizing it was the very man she was trying to call.

He watched them a moment before answering his phone with absolute calmness. "Auri?" he asked, even though she stood right in front of him. "Are you okay?"

Her brain having turned to mush, she put her phone to her ear to answer before realizing she didn't need to. She pointed sheepishly toward the kitchen window. "There's someone outside."

He didn't hesitate. He closed and locked the door, then keyed in the code to her mother's safe to grab her extra sidearm, a black 9 mm with inferiority issues, according to her mom. Then he turned out the lights so he could see outside, only Sybil had not been expecting the lights to go out and the shriek that erupted out of her lungs would've rivaled that of a velociraptor.

When she was finished, Auri's grandpa asked, "Are you okay, sweetheart?"

The nightlight from the kitchen was enough to see Sybil nod, but she didn't dare let go of her lifeline. Aka, Auri.

"You two sit down and stay here."

"Okay," Sybil squeaked, sinking onto the couch and dragging Auri with her.

As much as Auri wanted to follow her grandfather, she couldn't leave Sybil alone. She'd never seen her in such a state of panic. Not even after her ordeal with a kidnapper.

"I don't see anyone," he said before checking the other windows. "What exactly did you see?"

He was asking Auri, who was beginning to feel more than a little sheepish. "I didn't see anything. Sybil saw a man outside."

"Dark hair. Beady eyes. He practically screamed serial killer."

Her granddad's brows slid together. He grabbed the flashlight her mom always kept in the kitchen. "I'll check outside. Lock the door behind me."

Auri nodded. "Thanks, Grandpa." Thankfully, Sybil let her up long enough to lock the door behind her grandfather.

Sybil clamped onto her arm again and whispered, "This is so going into my super-secret project."

Auri watched the flashlight bounce around as he circled the house. She glanced over her shoulder. "You have a super-secret project? What is it?"

Sybil pursed her lips, clearly disappointed in her bestie. "It's super secret."

"Right," she said, turning away so Sybil wouldn't see her grin. "Sorry."

After a quick trek out to his storage shed and checking the lock there, her grandpa walked back. She let him in and waited for the verdict.

"I didn't see anyone, but the ground below the window has been disturbed. You two get your things and come to the house."

"I should probably get home," Sybil said, clearly feeling she was no longer safe.

Auri understood. She grabbed the extra set of keys to her grandma's Buick her mom kept on a hook next to the safe. "I'll drive you home," she said, putting an arm around her friend's shoulders.

"Nice try, peanut." He took the keys from her and waited for them to gather their things.

"Oh, how was Cruz?" Auri asked as they followed him to his truck.

"Fast asleep."

"So . . . he was breathing? You checked?"

"Effortlessly." He squeezed her shoulders as he opened the door for them. "He's okay for now, hon."

"Thank you for doing that, Grandpa."

"Of course." He closed the door behind them and walked around as Auri's heart leapt into her chest. A car drove past the house and the light from its headlamps illuminated a figure in the trees across the street. She didn't want to say anything. Sybil was already on her last thread of sanity. But if she didn't know better, she would've sworn it was the former sheriff of Del Sol, Tim Redding's father.

# 8

*Driver stated there was no reason to tailgate her when she was doing 50 in a 35. And the flashing lights on top of my car look ridiculous.*

—POLICE BLOTTER: DEPUTY ROJAS

"You did this on purpose so you could see me again." Sun looked up as US Marshal Vincent Deleon strolled into the hospital like he owned the place. She'd been briefing the state police officers on what she knew, which was next to nothing, and hoping to get a briefing in return. Mainly, how the hell Wynn Ravinder set up a prison break right under her nose.

"You think I'd stage a prison break just to see you?"

He lifted a shoulder, as though it were the only logical explanation. Sun had met Marshal Deleon when she'd first taken office. There had been a prison break then, too, and Sun was beginning to question the prison's hiring standards.

"You look good," she said, his skin rich and dark, his eyes as full of mischief as the first time she met him.

"You look like you've missed a few nights' sleep."

"Thanks." She walked to a row of chairs in the hall and sat beside Quincy, who was talking to one of his cop friends in Albuquerque, "Where's your partner?"

Deleon sat beside her. "Vacation in Hawaii."

"Lucky."

"Right? How'd you end up in the middle of this?"

The smile she let slide across her face held little humor. "I know how this looks, Deleon."

She and Quince had been at the hospital for three hours and had already been fielding questions about her involvement. Because it was Sun who had him transferred from Arizona State Prison to the state pen in Santa Fe.

"Do you?"

She let out a long breath. "What do you need to know?"

"We could start with why you had him transferred in the first place. Guy's been here less than a week and he's already out?"

"It was for another case we're working on. He offered to give testimony and produce a weapon in exchange for a transfer."

"So, he said jump and you said how high?"

"No." She stood and started pacing again. "He's helping with another case as well. One that involves a threat to a local businessman." She'd tried to call that businessman, to let Levi know what was going on with his uncle, but naturally he didn't pick up. She left a message for him to call her immediately. Police business. Maybe that would work.

"Ah, yes." Deleon opened a file he'd been carrying. "I see on your transfer request he was going to help you close a decades-old murder and help you with an ongoing investigation."

"Yes."

"And you just happened to be at the very hospital he vanished from." He glanced up at her. "Bit of a big coincidence pill to swallow, if you ask me."

She stopped in front of him. "Are you accusing me of something, Deleon?"

He snorted. "Please. I've seen your record." He stood, forcing her to back up. "All I'm saying is, it looks suspicious. You need to understand, there could be an official inquiry."

"Great." She whirled around and started pacing again.

"Of course, it all hinges on my report."

She turned to him. Slowly. Methodically. "And what are you putting in your report?"

"The truth, but I could sugarcoat the hell out of it if I were offered something in return."

Quincy didn't bat a lash when she looked at him, his face buried in his phone, but she knew he was listening to every word. "And what would that be?"

One corner of Deleon's mouth lifted playfully. "If I thought I had a snowball's chance in hell, I'd make you have dinner with me."

She crossed her arms over her chest. "That is wrong on so many levels. Not to mention illegal."

"Thus my abstinence," he said, holding up his hands in surrender. "We could just agree that you owe me one."

That was easy. "Okay."

"But, and I say this with the utmost respect, I'd sure put my house in order if I were you. Just in case the higher-ups catch wind of this and the proverbial shit hits the fan."

"I will. But, and I say this with the utmost respect, you need to find Wynn before I do."

He laughed softly. "And why is that?"

"Because if I find him first, I'm going to kill him."

Before he could respond, a man in a suit walked up to them. "Marshal," he said with a nod to Deleon. He turned to Sun. "Sheriff, I found the footage if you'd like to follow me to my office."

"What did you see?" Sun asked as she, Quincy, and Deleon followed the hospital's head of security to their control room.

"In a word," he said over his shoulder, "he had help."

Of course he did. Wynn was too much like his nephew, Levi. Or vice versa. Either way, he probably did nothing without a plan. And sure enough, five minutes later, Sun stood in absolute awe as they watched the footage in the control room a second time.

"Could he have faked a heart attack?" the state police captain asked as he leaned closer to the grainy feed. The large man with graying black hair and a clean-shaven jaw had joined them in the cramped space a few moments earlier, his presence depleting the oxygen supply even faster, so Sun tried to take shallow breaths.

Deleon shrugged. "Heart attacks can absolutely be faked."

"But he had that enzyme," Sun argued, probably sounding like an idiot. She should have paid more attention when the doctor was talking to her about Wynn's cardiac event. "That enzyme that shows up when you have a heart attack. A real one."

The head of security, a man named Johnston if his ID was to be believed, had come in on his day off just for this. He explained. "There are drugs that can induce a heart attack."

It was Quincy's turn to be astonished. "You mean, he took a drug that brought on a real heart attack?"

"Looks like it." Deleon handed him a chart with the readings on it. Because that would help.

Sun and Quince glanced at the test results and decided to take his word for it. If only she'd gone to medical school in her free time.

"Okay, here," Johnston said. He pointed to one of the monitors. "A nurse closes the curtains around his bed in the ER and then nothing. Not until another nurse walks up and realizes he's gone."

"With the curtain closed like that, you can hardly see the other beds." Like most emergency rooms, the area housed a row of beds separated only by curtains, but the angle of the camera didn't allow a clear shot of the other beds, especially with the curtains partially closed. "Go back a little farther." Johnston rewound the feed until she said, "Stop. There." She pointed at the top corner of the screen. "It's the same nurse a few minutes earlier. She's closing the curtains, purposely blocking the camera."

"Son of a bitch," Deleon said. "That was before Wynn Ravinder even arrived. This whole thing was planned."

"Sure looks that way," the captain said.

"That's how they got past the corrections officers," Quincy said. "They could have skirted around the other beds and gone out a side door."

"Exactly." Sun squinted as she studied the screen.

The guard sped up the tape until after the nurse had closed the curtain, then focused on cameras out in the hallway.

"Is that you?" Deleon asked.

Sun froze, humiliation surging through her. Just as she'd feared, Wynn and his accomplice had walked right past her and Quincy as they were talking to the doctor, seconds before the cops started running up and down the halls. "How did I not recognize him?" she asked with a groan, swearing off tequila right then and there. She leaned in for another look and eyed the screen suspiciously. "Would you say that nurse is more of a dirty blond or a strawberry?"

Quincy gave her a knowing look. "You know who that is."

"I have an inkling." And she was going to kill her. If Sun wasn't mistaken, her best friend in Santa Fe, Nancy Danforth, just broke a convicted killer out of prison.

"Care to share your inkling with the rest of the class?" Deleon asked nonchalantly, while the captain looked on expectantly. But what if she was wrong? This a barrel she wanted to get to the bottom of herself before spilling its contents to the rest of the world.

"I have an inkling. I'll check it out and get back to you."

The captain glared at her. "Sheriff, if you know something, you—"

Her phone rang before he could finish. When she held up a finger to put him on pause, he turned the funniest shade of purple she'd ever seen. "Hey, Dad," she said, throwing as much perk into her inflection as possible just to fuck with the captain. She'd had enough of the boy's-club mentality when she was with Santa Fe PD.

"How's it going?" her dad asked.

"Great. My victim is still unconscious, Doug got stabbed in the neck with a knitting needle, and a prisoner I had transferred to the state pen from Arizona just escaped right under our noses. What's up?"

"Well, not to add fuel to the fire, but someone was outside your house. Scared the bejesus out of your daughter and Sybil."

"A creeping tom?" she asked in alarm. "Did you see anyone?"

"I did not."

"Are the girls okay?"

"Yeah. A little shaken."

"Not stirred?" she teased. It was the way of her people.

"Mom!" Auri said in the background. "We could've been killed."

She was right. Especially with her track record of late. "I'll be there in thirty."

"You don't have to rush home, hon."

"I'm done here anyway. We can study the footage at the station."

"Okay. Drive safe."

She handed the security guard her card with her email address. "Can I get a copy of all of this? Even the parking lots? We'll try to get a make on their vehicle."

"I'll send it immediately."

She turned to the marshal and offered him a curt not. "Thanks, Deleon."

He tipped an invisible hat. "Vicram. If you do get a make—"

"I'll call."

She started to leave but the captain stepped in her path. She gaped up at him dramatically, to convey her astonishment at the size of the guy's cojones. "Do you mind?"

"Not at all, as soon as you give me that name."

"Oh, right." She snapped her fingers. "I almost forgot. Buffy Summers."

He took out a notepad and wrote down the name as Deleon fought a grin tooth and nail. Quincy turned away, unable to rein his in. It always was a recalcitrant thing.

The captain closed the pad, proud of himself. "Was that so hard?"

She raised her brows and gestured toward the door. "Do you mind?"

He stepped aside and offered her a sweep of his hand.

"Thanks for your help," she said to the security guard.

He nodded, clearly in on the joke.

A big fan of the honey-draws-more-flies method, she showed

the captain her very best smile, then strolled past him. At least she wasn't showing her age too terribly if everyone but the captain got her Buffy reference. She dialed Nancy's number as she and Quince strode toward the exit, but got her voicemail. "Hey, girlfriend," she said, reinstating the perky bit. "Broke any felons out of prison lately? How about you give me a call when you get a chance?" She lowered her voice, and added, "And you tell that son of a bitch he's a dead man," before hanging up, wishing she could've slammed down the phone to emphasize her statement, but that never ended well anymore. She set her jaw and turned to Quincy. "They set me up."

"You really think that was your friend?"

"I can't be certain, but it makes sense. They've been in contact for years. She's done . . . questionable things for him." Nancy had manipulated a DNA test they'd done on the foreign blood found on Kubrick Ravinder's body. She'd used it to clear Levi's name and implicate Wynn on Wynn's orders. The way he explained it to Sun, he was already doing a double life sentence for a crime he didn't commit. He may as well take the fall for his nephew who killed Kubrick saving Sunshine.

All of these were facts she had yet to share with her chief deputy. If they turned Nancy in, every case she'd ever processed would be questioned. Guilty people would go free for crimes they committed. Even knowing this, Sun found herself struggling with the decision to keep quiet. She would talk with Quincy about it, just not today.

"In what way?" he asked, suspicion knitting his brow.

"For one, she's been in love with Wynn since they first met. She's too naïve to realize Wynn is using her."

"Or she doesn't care."

"True. Either way, I can't be a hundred percent sure it was her, which is why I didn't divulge her name."

"Gotcha. Honestly, though, who doesn't know Buffy?"

"And you saw him?" Sun asked, marveling at the turn of events. She sat at her parents' kitchen table with Quincy, Auri, and the aforementioned parents.

"Auri," her dad said, putting a hand over hers, "why didn't you say anything?"

This would mark the second time that day former sheriff Baldwin Redding crossed their afore-agreed-upon boundaries and entered Sun's orbit. She could be optimistic and try to believe he only wanted to talk about the unidentified woman found in the canyon, to see if he could be of any assistance, but she knew better. He'd burn in hell before assisting her on a case.

"I don't know," Auri said, lifting a slim shoulder self-consciously. "I mean, it looked like him, but I don't want to get anyone in trouble."

Auri had French braided her coppery hair that morning, but long, delicate strands had shaken loose throughout the day to frame her angelic face in dancing flames of red. Sun had hoped she would eventually get over how beautiful the fruit of her loins was. The girl had mesmerized her from the moment she was born, like a glistening fairy made of earth and sea and fire, and Auri used that fact strategically any time she got into trouble. So, often.

"Are you okay, bug?"

Auri nodded. "Yeah. I think Sybil got me worked up over nothing."

Sun wasn't so sure, but she went along with her daughter's assessment for her sake. "I understand. Quincy does that to me sometimes, too."

Quince gaped at her, feigning insult and succeeded in making Auri giggle.

"Oh," Auri said, opening her laptop and angling it toward them. "This is Lynelle's cousin Whitney. What do you think?"

Sun leaned in to get a better look at the girl in the picture. "I just don't know, bug. Our Jane Doe was so bruised and swollen, it's hard to say if this is the same girl."

"And our Jane's hair was dyed purple," Quince said.

Auri gasped softly. She punched a few keys to bring up all the photos on Whitney's timeline and pointed. "Look at her clothes. Purple is her favorite color."

It was true. She wore purple in almost every picture, but her hair had never been dyed that color.

"What color were her clothes when you found her?" Auri asked.

Sun cast a quick glance at her parents before saying, "She wasn't, hon. She only had a bra and it was pink."

"Oh," Auri said, surprised. Sun could see her mind racing a thousand miles an hour. "That poor girl."

"She's alive, sweetheart. That's what we need to focus on right now."

"And this is a huge help," Quince added. "Which picture is Whitney's most recent?"

Auri scrolled back to the top. "She posted this one after her last final." She pointed out a pic of Whiney throwing papers into the air, a huge smile on her face. "And these were taken about a couple of days before that, when she was studying." She gestured toward a pic of Whitney sprawled out on a bed in a dorm room, book in one hand, pizza in the other. Though her hair was blond and longer than their Jane's, she could've gotten a new do before leaving Albuquerque or soon afterward.

Sun pressed the PRINT button on one of the more recent photos and waited for her parents' printer to kick in before saying, "We'll get on this, bug."

Her mother stood to get the printout.

"You need to look at her phone log, too," Auri offered. "She hasn't checked in since getting to the ski resort, which is very unusual, but maybe they don't have service there?"

"Maybe not on the mountain," Quince said, continuing to scroll. "But you know the resort will. She should've posted something."

"Right? She never goes for more than a day or two without posting."

"Have you seen anything we could use to identify her?" Sun asked. "A birthmark or a tattoo?"

Auri deflated and shook her head. "No. She said somewhere that she wants a tattoo but she's afraid of needles. Wait, what about her eye color? Whitney's eyes are blue."

Quince nodded. "Our Jane's are blue, too, but—"

"That doesn't prove it's her, I know. Still . . ."

Quince stopped scrolling and grinned at her, telling Sun, "If I ever go missing, boss, I want your daughter leading the investigation."

The blinding smile that widened across Auri's face caused Sun's insides to warm.

"Thanks, Mom," Sun said when her mother handed her the printout. She refocused on Auri. "We're going to head back to the station if you're okay, hon?"

"Of course," she said. "I'm sorry you hurried back from Santa Fe because of this."

"No worries," Quince said, standing. "We needed to get back anyway."

Her dad stood and slapped Quince on the back. "Let us know if you kids need anything."

Her mom was clanging dishes in the kitchen. "Dinner's not quite ready, but I can bring you two a plate later."

The bashful grin that commandeered Quincy's face had Sun fighting a giggle. "That would be amazing, Mrs. Freyr." When would that man get over his crush on her mother?

Sun gave Auri a hug. "No more investigating, okay? We're on this."

"But, Mom, what if I have an epiphany that could break the case wide open?"

"Then you call me and I'll look into it."

She frowned and crossed her arms over her chest. "So you can take the credit for my genius?"

"Yes," Sun said, deadpanning her. "That is exactly why you should call me. I could not possibly do this job without your genius insights into the criminal mind."

"I figured as much."

She laughed and gave her another hug. "See you guys later," she said to her parents.

They waved as Sun and Quince walked to the front door.

Sun glanced up at her bestie. "I want to get back out to Copper Canyon tomorrow."

"Did you see something in the photos?"

"Maybe. I just want to make sure forensics didn't miss anything."

"Like?"

"Did you notice the necklace Whitney had on in almost every picture?"

"The one our Jane Doe wasn't wearing when we found her? I did. You think it's really her?"

"I don't know. I just want to double check."

"You got it, boss."

Auri had started for her room when she heard her mom and Quincy talking as they left. She had somehow missed the fact that the girl who may or may not be Lynelle's cousin had been found at Copper Canyon. It rang a bell, but she couldn't remember why.

She hurried to her room and called Sybil.

"Hey, Auri," Sybil said, her voice almost despondent.

"Hey, Syb. Are you okay?"

"Yes, I'm fine. It's just, I'm so sorry, Auri."

Auri sat at her desk and opened her laptop. "What? Why?"

"I freaked out and my freak-out freaked you out."

"So, lots of freaking out."

"They're infectious. Like herpes. Or Ebola. You never freak out, Auri. You're so calm under fire, you're like ice. You can handle anything, and then I come along and . . . I wish I were more like you."

"Sybil St. Aubin, stop that right now. You are amazing and you've survived a horrible situation against terrible odds. It's natural for you to be hyperaware of your environment for at least the next thirty years."

"I guess. But I feel like I'm dragging you down with me."

"Actually, I think you're a good influence. Maybe I'd stay out of trouble if I were more hyperaware."

"Really?"

"Really."

"Gracias."

"De nada. Hey, do you remember hearing something about Copper Canyon?"

"Yes. They found that girl there this morning."

"Right, but I mean before that." Auri chewed her bottom lip in thought, trying to remember. "I feel like something happened there. Something really strange."

"Oh! Oh, my god, yes!" She could hear Sybil tearing through paper or pages of some kind. Maybe a journal? "What was it? Wait. I'll find it."

"You wrote it down?"

"Are you kidding? I write everything down. Every word is going in my tell-all. People need to know about the crazy stuff that happens in this town."

"Your tell-all? Is that the super-secret project you were talking about?"

"Oops. Yes, it is. I'm so bad at keeping secrets."

"No, this is cool. I had no idea you were writing a book. Wait." The reality of how a memoir about their antics in Del Sol could go horribly wrong hit her. "You can't publish anything until we're, like, really old. In our thirties, maybe. Or even our forties, if we live that long. Then we can't get into trouble for anything we *allegedly* did in our youth."

"That's a good point. Okay. How about thirty-five-ish? That should give me a couple of years to enjoy my fame before I'm old and decrepit."

"That'll work. Did you find anything?"

"Yes. Wait a minute . . . Blah, blah, blah. Oh, right. Wow, Auri."

"Yes?" she said from her throne of pins and needles.

"This can't be a coincidence."

"Sybil," she said, her patience waning. "What is it?"

"It was from a conversation some kids were having at lunch. Remember? They were talking about a girl who was taken to the ER last year with head trauma and a broken arm."

Auri snapped. She knew she'd heard something. "I do remember. A driver found her on the side of the road leading up to the pass over Copper Canyon. Said she was really disoriented."

"Yes, she told the doctors she couldn't remember what happened."

It was all coming back to her. "Right. I can see why you wrote that down. You didn't happen to get her name, did you?"

"I don't think they ever said, and we certainly didn't ask."

"Why?"

Sybil dropped her voice to a whisper, "Because we were eavesdropping on Lynelle and her super psycho friends, trying to get dirt on her for the *Del Sol Inquisitor*."

Lynelle again. "Oh, right. We were going to start a gossip rag, but other than this story, we couldn't find any good gossip. Makes sense why we didn't ask."

"Exactly."

Auri's brain raced with how best to find the girl. Sybil was right. No way was this a coincidence, but she couldn't tell her mom just yet. She'd promised no more investigating. "Okay, thanks, Sybil."

"Hold on. Are you about to do what I think you're about to do?"

"No. Possibly. Why?"

"Because I want in."

"I don't know, Sybil."

"I promise not to freak out. I'm good now."

"Okay, tomorrow we ride."

"Where?"

"No, it's just a saying. Never mind. Tomorrow we hack into the sheriff's database and find that girl. There has to be a report."

Sybil clapped into the phone, her excitement infectious.

# 9

*If you sometimes look at people and think,*
*"Really? That's the sperm that won?"*
*we have a whiskey sour with your name on it.*

—SIGN AT THE ROADHOUSE

Quincy stomped into Sun's office, his face redder than usual, his chest heaving. She'd been poring over the security footage from the hospital, trying to figure out what vehicle Wynn and his accomplice got into, but nothing was coming up. Either they'd changed into a disguise somewhere along their route, or they never left the hospital.

"How's Cruz?" she asked before he could vent.

He pointed toward the locker room and said from between clenched teeth, "He took the extra shirt I had hanging outside my locker."

"Cruz?" she asked, teasing him. She knew full well he was referring to a certain adorable masked bandit named Randy. At the moment, the shirt interested her more.

"What? No. Cruz is good. He's asleep."

"Okay, then why was your shirt hanging outside your locker?"

"It was drying. I swerved to avoid a squirrel this morning and had a run-in with a mocha latte. I had to change into my spare before we went to see Doug."

Sun shook her head and tsk-tsked her chief deputy. "Raccoons. Squirrels. Mocha lattes. Is there anything you haven't pissed off?"

"Whatever. Why would he take my shirt?"

"Maybe because it tasted like a mocha latte."

He let out an aggravated breath. "Okay, *where* would he take my shirt? Where is that little shit?"

"Well, the last time Randy and I sat down for a one-on-one—"

"Never mind." He started to stomp off, but Sun called out to him.

"Sit down, Chief," she said, adding an edge to her voice. Not a particularly sharp one, but it worked.

Quincy walked back and took a seat across from her desk, slumping down like a kid in the principal's office. Not that Sun would know anything about that. "What is going on with you?"

He edged up in the chair. "What do you mean?"

"You've been in a mood for three days. I know it can't be about Levi stealing your cruiser."

"So, you admit he stole it," he said, his face practically screaming *Gotcha*.

Damn it. "No. And you're deflecting."

"Am not."

"Are too."

"Am not."

She grabbed her letter opener to threaten him, but was interrupted. Probably for the best.

"Boss?"

They both looked over to see Poetry Rojas standing in the doorway.

"I hate to interrupt this stimulating conversation."

"It's okay." She waved him in with the letter opener. "Why are you still here?"

"Trying to make a good impression."

"Well, you are succeeding, mister." She looked at Quincy and hooked a thumb toward Rojas, impressed.

"Also, Tía Darlene keeps trying to set me up with the new waitress at the diner, so I'm avoiding going home."

"Figures. What's up?"

He walked in and handed her a printout. "This is how you create a heart attack."

She scanned the article he'd hunted down on a type of drug called digitalis. Rojas had been in prison, doing time in his twin brother's stead after the authorities had accidentally arrested him. He knew how things worked at the big house, and anytime she needed info on the goings-on behind bars, for better or for worse, she went to him.

"So, heart attacks *can* be faked."

"Not so much faked as induced," he said. "According to his records, he did have a cardiac event. He had a specific enzyme in his blood that only occurs with a real heart attack."

She gaped up at him. "You mean he gave himself a real heart attack?"

"I can't say for certain, but I had a cellmate that did it once knowing he was on the Aryans' hit list. Not to mention the precision in how the escape was coordinated, it just seems like a lot to organize at the last minute. How would he get word to his accomplice that quickly?"

"This is crazy," she said, now angry at Wynn Ravinder. She hated to admit a fondness for the guy, but he was actively trying to take the blame for a death Levi caused, even though it was in self-defense while saving her seventeen-year-old ass. An ass she would kill for now that she'd gotten older.

"But how would he get his hands on this kind of medication?" Quincy asked, taking the printout she handed him.

"Clearly, you've never been to prison."

"And neither have you," Sun said, giving Rojas a conspiratorial wink. "On that note, however, you're saying he could've gotten this drug somehow?"

"Rather easily. Smugglers can get almost anything into a prison. They're very creative."

"Wonderful." She knew prisons were notorious for all kinds of contraband, but a drug that induces heart attacks?

"Thank you for this."

"Sure thing."

Someone rang at the security door. "Your dad," he said. "I'll let him in."

"Sweet," Quincy said. "Dinner."

Sun pointed the letter opener at him. "Hold up there, Mr. Cooper."

"Mr. Cooper? What'd I do now?"

"You have thirty seconds. What's up?"

He sank down in the chair again, like a schoolboy being chastised. "I don't want to talk about it."

"Oh, my god, this must be good." She leaned forward, so full of anticipation her stomach fluttered.

"Sun—"

"Don't even." She waved the letter opener in negation. "What's bothering you?"

He sank even further into the chair and scrubbed his face. "I can't talk about it here."

This must be serious. "Does this have anything to do with the fact that one of your best friends died and you are now the caretaker for his teenaged son?"

"No." He stood and started pacing. "Maybe a little. I don't know."

"Wait. Is this about Hailey Ravinder?"

"No. Not really. I don't know. It's just . . . It's everything."

"Quincy, if you are rethinking Cruz living with you—"

"No!" he said, turning toward her. "Not at all. That kid is amazing."

"I agree, but it's still a lot to take on."

"I know. That's not the issue."

"Well, you've been out of sorts since before we found out about the poem he wrote, so I don't think it's that."

"It's not. It's just . . ."

"Hey, Sunny." Her dad walked in with an insulated bag. "Your mother sent over some vittles for you two. But there's plenty if Deputy Rojas wants some."

"Thanks, Dad. Why don't you take that to the break room, Quince, while I have a word with my father. I'll be there in a sec."

"Sure thing," he said, a curious glint in his eyes.

Her dad, Cyrus Freyr, took Quincy's chair, his brows raised.

Since they'd been talking about prisons, she decided to broach her new favorite subject: the fact that Rojas, who had an uncanny ability to tell when someone had done hard time, swore that her father had been to prison. Not jail. Prison. The big house. The slammer.

"Turkey," she said, narrowing her gaze at him. "You were busted trying to smuggle opium out of the country and sent to a Turkish prison where you got in a fight with the head bad guy and bit his tongue off."

"Sunny, you gotta give this up. I have never been to prison."

She leaned back in her chair and crossed her arms over her chest. "Not under your own name. I checked. But identifying people who have been to prison is kind of like Poetry's superpower, and he says you've been to prison."

"You checked?"

"Is Cyrus Freyr even your real name?"

"Yes."

"Did you rat on a cellmate, so they put you in WITSEC in exchange for your testimony?"

"Not that I know of."

"Did you use a drug to induce a heart attack so you could escape, and now you're having to go by an assumed identity?"

He scratched his jaw. "Not recently."

"Did you—"

"Sunshine," he said, using her real name. Something he rarely did. "I have never been to prison." He leaned forward and lowered his voice. "As far as you or anybody else knows." Then he winked at her and stood to leave.

"Rojas knows," she said, following him. "Is he in danger?"

"Only from his *tía* Darlene if she finds out he's avoiding her."

"Siberia!" she shouted. "You were in military intelligence and got busted in Siberia. That's where you did your time."

He turned and shook his head sadly. "So close and yet so far away."

When she gasped softly, he chuckled and left before she could ask anything else. *So close and yet so far away.* There had to be a clue in there somewhere.

As the three of them sat eating her mother's famous lasagna, also known as Stouffer's, Sun went over her day, trying to decide which aspects to prioritize and which ones to hand off to her very capable deputies. First Doug. Then their Jane Doe. Redding showing up not only to the crime scene at Copper Canyon but creeping around her house. Cruz's mental health. The possible abuse of Tim Redding. The possible disappearance of Whitney Amaia. Wynn Ravinder essentially escaping from prison via the Presbyterian hospital in Santa Fe. And finally Wanda Stephanopoulos's break-in and subsequent missing tin.

There was only so much she could do at that hour. It was getting late, but most people were still up at nine p.m. She could at least check out Wanda's story. "I'm going to go knock on a few doors."

"What doors?"

She started to explain, then remembered she hadn't told either of them about Wanda's situation since she'd been sworn to secrecy. She figured as long as she didn't tell anyone about the tin, she was good. "Wanda thinks she was broken into last night."

Quincy's gaze shot to hers. "I didn't see that report."

"She didn't want to file one. Not officially. She's not absolutely sure she was broken into. I'm just going to check on a few things."

He wiped his mouth and started to stand. "I'll come with."

"No, that's okay. Zee's on it. I just want to make sure Wanda's okay."

He stood anyway. "Is she hurt? Was anything taken?"

Sun knew Quince had a soft spot for the woman he'd dubbed the town menace. How Wanda beat out Doug was beyond her, but she found his concern endearing.

"No, I need you to get what you can on Whitney Amaia, just in case. And call that ski resort."

The suspicion on his face was impossible to miss, but that is exactly what Sun pretended to do.

"I'm going to check on Wanda, then probably head home. I suggest you do the same."

She found Zee sitting outside Wanda's house in her cruiser. She pulled in behind her and walked to her window.

"Hey, boss," Zee said, rolling down her window.

Sun swallowed the two ibuprofen she'd popped into her mouth with a sip of water before asking, "What are you doing out here?"

"Waiting for Billy Harmon."

"The lock guy?"

"The one and only."

She looked over Zee's hood at Wanda's humble abode. It was a white narrow Victorian complete with a bay window and decorative cornice in desperate need of a paint job. "So she was definitely broken into?"

"Hard to say. Her locks are fine, but I want her to get new ones, just in case someone swiped a key. She's really shaken up."

She looked around the cozy neighborhood. "Did anyone see anything?"

"Not a soul, but I noticed two of her neighbors have security cameras." She pointed to two of the houses. "I doubt they had a good view of Wanda's house from their front porch, but you never know. They could have caught someone sneaking around."

"Good job, Zee."

"Thanks. They both said they'd check their footage and get back with me. Who knows if they will?"

"Well then," Sun said, rubbing her hands together, "maybe I can encourage them. When is Billy supposed to be here?"

"About eight."

Sun checked her watch. "It's almost nine."

"Oh, sorry, boss. I meant eight in the morning."

"Zee," Sun said in surprise, "you do not have to stay here all night."

"Are you kidding? Wanda's making me strawberry tarts."

"Seriously? I've had her strawberry tarts. Maybe I should stay out here with you."

Zee laughed. "I'm good, boss."

"Fine. At least save me one."

"Not likely, but I'll think about you while I'm eating them."

"That's so sweet. I'm going to talk to homeowners."

"I'll be here."

Unfortunately, the first homeowner Sun visited confessed that his camera was just for show. It was the one Sun was excited about. Professionally installed. High tech. And as fake as the orgasm she had when she and Tab Villanueva got drunk in college and tried to *do it* in his mother's laundry room. It did not turn out well for either of them.

She hit paydirt with the second homeowner. Kind of.

"It picked up something off in the distance," Principal Jacobs said, "but I can't tell what. If my cat hadn't triggered the camera, it wouldn't even have picked up that much."

Sun leaned closer to his phone. "What time was this?"

"About nine last night. See?" He pointed to a dark spot in the background. "It looks like someone is lurking. There's just not enough light to see who. I can send you the footage, though. Maybe your tech guy can clean it up?"

If only she had a tech guy. Still . . . "Rojas is pretty good at this stuff." So was her daughter, but she didn't mention that to him. "Send it over. You never know."

"Sure thing, Sunshine. How's every little thing?" He touched his nose secret-signal-like.

She'd known Mr. Jacobs since she was in high school when everyone called him Coach J. He was now Auri's principal and a bona fide member of her new club of Dangerous Daughters and

Sinister Sons, an organization that secretly ran the town. This town belonged in Ripley's Believe It or Not. "It's going okay. I didn't realize you lived here."

"Yep. Been here for years. That Wanda is a hoot."

"She is at that."

He leaned in and elbowed her playfully. "She throws some wild parties."

There were just some things she didn't need to know. "I can only imagine. Can you email me those videos?"

"I may have to drop them into the cloud, but I'll get 'em to you, Little Miss Sunshine."

She knew he couldn't make it through a whole conversation without mentioning the nickname he'd given her in high school.

"That never gets old," he said with a chuckle before going back inside. At least he was happy.

Her phone rang before she got off the porch. She swiped right. "Hey, Lieutenant."

"Hey, boss. Just wanted to give you an update."

"I'm all ears."

"No one fitting our Jane Doe's description has been reported missing in the last couple of weeks. Tomorrow I'll broaden the search to outside of New Mexico unless you think we should focus on Whitney Amaia."

"Not just yet. I'm going to do some recon tomorrow, but I want you to stick to the missing persons reports for now."

"You got it. Talk tomorrow?"

"Trish," she said though she rarely used Salazar's first name, "when Redding came to the crime scene today, did you happen to notice his hands?"

The question threw her. Sun could tell. She hesitated before answering, "Nothing stood out, boss. I'm sorry I didn't pay closer attention, but if I remember correctly, he never took off his gloves." She lowered her voice. "What are you thinking?"

"I have it on good authority his son took a pretty serious beating.

I was just wondering if you saw any signs of abuse while Redding was sheriff."

"The opposite, actually," Salazar said. "If anything, Tim had his dad wrapped around his finger. Like to an odd degree."

She stopped halfway to her cruiser. "Really? In what way?"

"Besides the usual, like Redding keeping Tim's name out of a couple of altercations he was involved in—"

"Typical abuse of power."

"Exactly. Their relationship always struck me as strange. Almost in the opposite way that you're thinking."

"Opposite of what?"

"This is going to sound weird."

"I'm all for weird."

"There were a couple of instances where it almost seemed like Redding was being bullied by his son. I don't know how to explain it. Like he was afraid of him, only he wasn't. I mean, he ran the roost with an iron fist and yet . . . I'm sorry, I don't know how to describe it. Maybe the chief can explain it better."

Sun waved to Zee as she strode past and climbed into her cruiser. "I'll talk to him. Thanks, Lieutenant."

"Sorry I couldn't be of more help."

"No, this is great."

Since she was about sixty seconds away from Quincy's cabin, she drove by. His cruiser sat out front and the porch light was on. She knocked softly on his front door, hoping she wouldn't disturb Cruz.

Quince opened the door and frowned at her. "Didn't I see you, like, five minutes ago?"

"Is your former boss left-handed?"

He leaned against the doorframe and took a sip of beer in thought. "He wore his duty weapon on his right hip, but he wrote with his left hand, so maybe." He widened the door and held up his beer bottle, offering to get her one of her very own.

"No, thanks." She stepped inside. "I've had enough alcohol to last me the rest of the month. Is Cruz up?"

"Nah. Out like a light."

"Good. He needs the rest. Trish told me something tonight I thought I'd run past you."

He gestured toward his couch as he took the recliner. "Shoot."

Sun explained what Salazar had told her as Quincy nursed his beer. "Have you ever seen anything like that? Like Tim bullying his father?"

Quince shook his head. "Tim's a cocky little fuck, don't get me wrong, but I can't see Redding being afraid of him. But that's the thing. Salazar sees things the rest of us don't. It's like she's psychic or something."

"Or just very intuitive," Sun said, which was why she was so glad to have the lieutenant on her team. "Okay, then. I'm heading home the second you tell me what's been bothering you."

"Shit." He stood to get another beer. "I knew I shouldn't have answered the door."

Sun pointed to his front door, the one with the half-moon window in it. "I would've seen you sitting here watching TV either way."

He twisted the cap off and took a healthy swig. "Well, I can't say anything here. Not in front of the kid."

"The one that's out like a light?"

"Damn it, Sunburn." He fell into the recliner, once again reminding Sun of a kid in trouble with the principal. "I don't know. It's just a lot of things."

She took a throw pillow, put it on her lap, and started playing with the fringed threads. "Quince, I know you're hurting over Cruz's dad. I just need to make sure there's not something more to this."

"Like what?"

"Like . . . are you okay?"

He leaned forward and put his elbows on his knees. "I'm fine. Or at least I was until you got here."

"So, this isn't about Cruz or Levi or even Hailey?"

There it was. He flinched when she said Hailey and Sun stared at him in surprise.

"What?" he asked.

"Hailey." She pointed at his face. "You flinched."

He tsked and sat back. "I didn't flinch."

"You flinched."

Frustrated that she wasn't giving up, he stood and walked to the door. "Freaking chicks. You're all psychic, I swear."

"Again, we're intuitive." She walked over to him and looked out at the Pecos, listening to the sound of rushing water. "What's going on?"

"I can't tell you without lowering your opinion of me."

She curled an arm around his and squeezed. "Quince, it really can't get much lower than it already is."

"I guess," he said, but he still hesitated. After a deep moment of contemplation, he finally admitted, "She wants to go all the way."

Sun stilled, forcing herself not to giggle. But it was hard and soon tears formed between her lashes. She had to press her mouth shut and look away.

He let out a long sigh, then said, "Go ahead. Get it out of your system."

She did. A bubble of laughter rose out of her, but she kept it in check for the most part. "What happened to the man who could open up the heavens and make the angels sing?"

"Normally I can, but this is Hailey and . . . I can't fuck it up. I think she's the one."

"Wow." That sobered her like a splash of cold water to her face. "Then what's the problem?"

"Remember Vicki Hughes in ninth grade?"

"Oh, yeah," she said, thinking back. "She was cute."

"I really, really liked her."

She nodded. "I remember."

"And we did it."

Sun sucked in a breath for so long, even she marveled at her lung capacity. "You did it with Vicki Hughes?" she whispered. No idea why.

"Yes."

She socked him on the arm. Hard. "And you didn't tell me?"

He rubbed his biceps for her benefit. She doubted he felt it. "Like you tell me everything."

"True. Where are you going with this?"

"Well, after we did it, I never heard from her again."

She blinked at him in disbelief before commenting. "Quincy, she moved to France."

"And they don't have phones in France?"

"So, you think if you and Hailey hook up, you'll lose her?"

"I'm not finished," he said, getting defensive.

"Oh, sorry. Kind of a font of information once you get started, huh?"

"Remember Stacy Ortecho?"

"No." Sun stood gaping at him for a solid minute, then snatched the beer out of his hands and downed half of it. "You and Stacy?" she asked, wiping her mouth on her sleeve. "She was a senior when we were freshman and, like, a supermodel."

"She is a supermodel. And she never called me again."

"I can't believe this." Shock was slowly taking hold, numbing her from the top of her scalp to the tips of her toes. "You and Stacy Ortecho?"

"There's more."

She eased closer. "Who else? Because right now, I'm freaking out over both of those women. Not that they're out of your league," she added when he glared at her. "But Stacy Ortecho?" She shook her head. "Just wow. I don't think you can top that."

"You know that country singer, Rae Dawn McVey?"

"Shut the fuck up," she whispered, but it came out more like a muffled screech. When he just gave her a sideways look, she took another drink. "It's like I don't even know you."

"One night of fiery passion and then nothing."

"Holy shit." She fell back against the doorjamb in thought, and then realized he was very serious. And about to make a huge mistake if he thought he ran those women off somehow. She reached up and put her arm around his shoulders. Well, most of them. He was quite tall and they were quite wide. "All right, Quince. I know you've been with your fair share of women over the years. You've told me about all of them. Well, except those three. You know how things work. You used to study female anatomy for that very reason. Do you think you did something wrong to run them off?"

"I never told you about those three because I really liked them. I mean, I really, really liked them. And then they just fell off the face of the earth." He looked over his shoulder to make sure they were not being eavesdropped upon. Even so, he lowered his voice when he added, "You know, after. I had to have done something wrong."

"Quincy," she said, leading him to the couch. She pushed him down and sat beside him. "Let's think about this. When did you hook up with Vicki?"

"The night before her family moved to France."

"Okay, I think that's a pretty big clue as to why she didn't call."

He lifted an unconvinced shoulder.

"What about Stacy?"

"The night she graduated high school. She went to Los Angeles the next day with a modeling contract."

"And you don't think that had anything to do with her not calling?"

"Because they don't have phones in California, either?"

"Fine. What about Rae Dawn?"

"On her tour bus when she gave a concert in Albuquerque."

"You mean the one night she was in town and hasn't been back since?"

"You're missing the point."

"No, you are. Quince," she said, putting her hand on his cheek, "you are a catch and a half. And I happen to know that Hailey is crazy about you. Also, as far as I know, she's not leaving town anytime soon, so you totally have a chance of keeping this one." She couldn't help a chuckle when he glared at her.

"I just don't want to fuck it up."

"Quincy Lynn Cooper, every girl deserves the right to have the heavens open up and the angels sing at least once in her life. Hailey definitely does."

He sank back into the couch. "It's so weird that you guys are friends after all those years of blind hatred."

She sank back beside him and rested her head on his shoulder. "You know what's weirder?"

"I'm sure you're going to tell me."

"The thought of you having sex with her."

He eased away from her. "Why would you even think about that?"

"Just don't run her out of town. I really like her."

"I can't make any promises."

# 10

*Do you suffer from shyness?*
*Do you sometimes wish you were more assertive?*
*Ask your doctor about tequila.*

—SIGN AT THE ROADHOUSE

That night, Sun dreamed once again of a long-forgotten time. Of kissing a boy in a pickup. Of fogged windows and soft music. Of Levi's hands on her breasts and his mouth at her ear. He said something important, something she needed to remember, but before she could figure out what it was, someone began banging on the window.

She startled awake and almost fell out of bed, her legs were so twisted in her sheets, but the banging continued. She kicked until the sheets came loose, then scrambled to pull on a pair of sweats, vowing to kill whoever was at her door.

"I'll get it," Auri said, practically floating toward the front door.

"Aurora Dawn!" Sun yelled.

Auri jumped and turned to her. "What? Someone's at the door."

"At three in the morning." She rushed to her and took her by the shoulders. "You never answer the door to someone pounding on it at three in the morning. Especially after what happened last night."

"Oh, yeah." She rubbed her eyes. "But he won't shut up."

"I know." Sun opened her safe and took out her duty weapon before calling out to the intruder. "Who is it?"

"It's me. He's gone."

Sun's and Auri's shocked gazes met for a split second before she opened the door to Quincy Cooper. "What do you mean, he's gone?"

Quincy barreled past her and looked around like a wild bear who'd lost her cub. "Cruz. He's not in his bed."

"Mom," Auri said, fear rounding her lids.

"We can't jump to conclusions, bug. Quincy," she said, sharpening her tone, "when did you see him last?"

"I went to bed right after you left. I thought he was sound asleep. I got up to go to the restroom and decided to check on him. He'd been asleep for a while. But he wasn't there." Quincy whirled around the room. "He stuffed his bed with pillows. I have no idea how long he's been gone." He ran to Auri's room to check and then to Sun's.

"Quince, he's not here. Let me get dressed—"

"Wait," Auri said. She hurried to her window. "I could've sworn I heard something last night." She struggled to lift her window.

Sun helped, and they looked over the edge to see a sleeping boy propped up against the garden supply box.

Auri didn't hesitate. She turned to Quincy, then rushed past him outside. He followed her, Sun on his heels.

"Cruz!" she said, sliding to a stop beside him.

He was dressed in a thin T-shirt and jeans. Even in May the mountains got chilly at night.

"Quincy, get a blanket," Sun said.

With a worried nod, he rushed back in.

"Cruz," Auri said, patting his face softly. "Cruz, wake up."

When he didn't wake up fast enough for her daughter, Auri patted harder until he caught her hand in his to stop the attack. "Please, stop hitting me."

Auri released a sigh of relief and took his hand into both of hers. "Sorry. I panicked."

Sun knelt beside them and draped the blanket over him. He was so disoriented, Sun began to worry. "Cruz, sweetheart, did you take something?"

"Only the painkillers the doctor gave me," he said, slurring his words.

"And how many did you take?"

He tried to hold up two fingers but couldn't quite manage it.

"We need to get him to the hospital."

"No, no, no," he said, trying to push the blanket off him. "I'm a really heavy sleeper. I'm okay."

"He is," Auri said, nodding in agreement.

"And just how would you know that, young lady?"

"We were in the hospital together for days, Mom."

"Right," she said, narrowing her eyes in suspicion.

Cruz managed to hold up two fingers at last. "I've only had two painkillers all day today. I took the second one right before bed, but then I heard the call on the radio."

"What call?" Quincy asked, helping him to his feet.

He shook his head to clear the cobwebs. "The one about some guy looking in the window."

"You came here to keep watch?" Auri asked, and Sun could've sworn she saw tiny hearts burst out of her daughter's eyes.

"I got here late and didn't want to scare you."

"Where's your truck?" Sun asked.

Quincy answered. "It's still at the house. Was that to trick me?"

"Trick you?"

They walked inside, and Quincy helped Cruz to a chair at the kitchen table as Sun got him some water. Auri sat next to him, keeping her arm around his.

"I didn't trick you," he said to Quince. "I didn't want to drive after taking a painkiller, so I walked."

This kid never ceased to amaze Sun.

"What about the pillows in the bed to make it look like you were asleep?"

"I sleep with pillows beside me. It helps support my stomach. It's still a little sore." He grabbed his side in explanation.

Quincy sank into the chair next to him. "Son of a bitch. I thought . . ."

"What?" Cruz asked after gulping down half the glass.

Quince glanced at Auri before answering. "I was just worried about you."

Cruz glanced at her, too, then rubbed his forehead. "The poem."

"I'm sorry, Cruz." She dropped her gaze. "I had no right to tell anyone."

He turned to her. "Yes, you did." When she refocused on him, he continued. "You did the right thing, Auri. Any time you think a friend is headed down that path, it's your responsibility to talk to someone. But I promise you, I'm not. It really was just a poem."

Sun sat across from him, and said softly, "I'm going to say something that you're not going to like, sweetheart."

He eyed her, but didn't protest.

"Whether you had written that poem or not, we were going to get you into counseling. We talked about it even before all of this."

He shifted self-consciously. "I'm fine, Sheriff. I promise."

"I know you are, but you have been through hell and back, all in a matter of weeks. If it were one of my deputies, I wouldn't give them a choice. So this isn't me picking on you, Cruz. It's me doing my duty to you and Quincy and Auri and everyone in this town who loves you."

He studied the glass in front of him, his lids growing heavy as they spoke. Those must be some powerful painkillers.

"How about you sleep here tonight?" she said, surprising Auri and Quincy. But he was absolutely wasted. What could he do? "You can sleep on the couch."

"I'll sleep in the chair," Auri offered. "You know, to make sure he's okay."

He cast her the sweetest smile Sun had ever seen. One that reminded her so much of Levi. Her daughter was in so much trouble.

"Okay, you can sleep with Auri, one on top of the covers and one underneath."

"Deal!" Auri said before her mother changed her mind. She stood and helped Cruz to her room.

"I can take him home," Quincy said, seemingly offended.

Sun stood to follow the kids into the room. She turned back to him. "I'm not questioning your capabilities as a guardian, Quince. I just want someone to watch over him while we go to Albuquerque tomorrow.

"I thought we were going back to the canyon."

"We are, but first I want to talk to Whitney's roommate. And with Cruz already here—"

"Your parents can keep an eye on him."

"Precisely." She made a mental note to request pancakes first thing in the morning and explain the situation to her mom.

By the time Sun got to Auri's room, Cruz was already curled up next to Auri asleep. Auri pulled the blanket off the foot of her bed and covered him with it. He woke up for just a moment and gazed into her eyes, his own glazed over, leaving Sun to wonder what the hell the doctors gave him.

Auri laughed softly. "No more painkillers for you, mister."

"Did you know I don't have a single family member left?" he said, slurring his words sleepily.

Auri leaned closer and whispered, "Yes, you do, handsome," before kissing him on the nose and snuggling closer.

Sun was in so much trouble.

"Thanks for doing this, Mom." Sun washed down a bite of banana pancake with coffee as Auri walked in, dressed for school. "Is he still asleep?"

"Yes. He had a rough night."

"In what way?" Sun asked in alarm.

"He—he was having nightmares. He tossed and turned a lot."

Sun nodded. "I'm sorry, hon. I thought he'd sleep through the night."

"Thank you for letting him stay, Mom. I'm glad I could be here for him."

"I think we need to look at the painkillers the doctors gave him."

"He flushed them down the toilet at about five this morning. Said they are not worth the weird dreams they give him."

"He had weird dreams, too, huh?" Sun turned to her mother. "I have ibuprofen and Tylenol."

"I know, hon. We'll be fine."

Auri ran over for a hug. "Thanks, again, Grandma. And thanks for the pancakes."

"You are very welcome. Have a good day."

After sliding her backpack over her favorite peach sweater, she shrugged resentfully. "We aren't even doing anything."

"But these are the days you'll remember most," her mother told her. "The school parties and the movies and the joking around. It's like a week of unwinding."

"I guess. I'd rather stay with Cruz."

"I know, bug." Sun gestured her toward the door. "Couple more days and you'll have over two months of fun."

Sun opened the door to find Wanda Stephanopoulos readying to knock. "Sunshine," she said, just as surprised as Sun.

"Wanda, how are you?"

"Oh, you know. Hi, Auri."

"Hey, Wanda."

"I'll meet you at the car, bug."

"Okay."

She watched as her daughter traipsed off with more attitude than a teenager had a right to before turning back to Wanda. "I have some footage that I'm hoping will be useful and we are getting new locks today. Is everything okay?"

"Oh, yes. It's fine. I just wanted to check in."

"Wanda?"

They turned as her mom walked out.

"What are you doing here?"

Wanda's expression went from hand-in-the-cookie-jar to just-out-for-a-stroll. "I'm here to see you. Thought you might want to grab some coffee."

"Come in, come in," she said, shooing her good friend inside. "I have to stick around here for a bit, but I made pancakes."

"You drive a hard bargain, woman."

Her mom laughed. "I really do."

Sun watched them go inside, then drove Auri to school, wondering how to broach the subject at hand. How does one broach such a subject, after all? Sure, they'd had the talk. On numerous occasions, just to make sure Auri understood, but her daughter was falling hard and fast for Cruz, and as much as Sun adored him, he was still a guy. With guy parts. And a guy brain.

Ignoring the fact that Auri was just as much of a girl, with girl parts, a girl brain, and a girl *heart*, she pulled up to the drop-off and put her cruiser in park.

Auri turned a worried expression on her. "Why did you do that?"

"I just thought we could have a talk."

"Oh, my god, not again."

"It's not that bad. I just feel like it's been a while since we reviewed the facts of life."

"I know the facts of life better than most girls my age. And probably better than most girls your age."

Such a kidder, this one. "Okay, so we girls have this little thing I like to call 'the sin cave.'"

"The what?" she asked, especially horrified, so Sun knew she was doing her job and doing it well.

"Now, there are many men out there who like to spelunk."

"Oh, my god." She sank down in her seat. Like that would help.

"And they like spelunking nowhere better than in the sin cave."

"This is so wrong, Mom."

"Now, I know you are very fond of Cruz, but guess what his one goal in life is?"

"I'm calling social services," she said, taking out her phone.

"That's right. To spelunk your sin cave."

"He has never tried to spelunk my sin cave, Mom."

Sun chastised herself for not recording this conversation, wondering how she could get her to say those exact words again into a recorder. "But he will, bug. At some point in their little lives, all boys yearn to become spelunkers in one way or another."

"What do you mean, in one way or another?"

"You know, they either spelunk for the joy of it or the bragging rights."

"Oh. Yeah, I guess you're right."

"Of course I am. And it's our jobs to protect our sin cave above all other caves by sabotaging their ropes so they fall and splat onto—"

"Mom, it's not Whitney." She held out her phone.

"What?" Sun took it and scrolled through the new pics Whitney put up that morning.

"She posted new pics of her skiing. It's not . . . I'm sorry. I thought it might have been her. I made such a big deal."

"I don't know, bug." Sun zoomed in on some of the images. "I'm not ruling this out completely, but I do hope it's her skiing and she's okay."

"Me too, but I feel bad now. What if you had called her mom and worried her for nothing?"

"Which is why I didn't call her yet."

"I just wanted to help."

Sun tilted her head and studied her daughter. "Can I ask why?"

Auri looked at her in surprise. "What do you mean?"

"I understand wanting to help, believe you me, but do you know why you want to help?"

"I don't know. I never thought about it." She tore at a piece of paper sticking out of her chem book. "I guess I just like helping people. Like you do."

"And that's noble, Auri. I can't tell you how proud I am of that fact, but I don't want you putting yourself in harm's way to help someone else."

"But that's what you do, right?"

"Not if I can help it," she said with a laugh. "And even if I do, it's my job, bug."

"Well, I've made a decision."

"Oh, yeah?" She crossed her arms over her chest. "This should be good."

"I want to go into the FBI."

That one shocked her. For the most part, the FBI was safe enough and had some incredible opportunities, but it would most likely mean her getting sent to an office far away. Still, if it was what she wanted . . . "In that case, I need to tell you something."

"Okay," Auri said hesitantly.

"To get into the FBI, you have to have an excellent vocabulary, top-notch mathematical skills, and an analytical brain. And you have to have the ability to thrive under pressure."

"You don't think I can do it?"

"Not at all. I know you can do it, but you need to know, just in case you are ever asked, it's not a percussion. It's a concussion. And you didn't have a submissive hemogoblin. You have a subdural hematoma."

"Oh."

"Otherwise, I have to say, you have an excellent vocabulary. But there is one more thing you need to get into the FBI."

"What's that?"

"Your virginity."

Her daughter had the nerve to deadpan her. "Aren't you the one who told me virginity is a social construct aimed to shame and oppress women? That there's no such thing?"

Sun thought back. "I don't remember telling you that."

"Really? Because it was, like, two weeks ago."

"Weird, but okay, you're right. It is a social construct. A social one *and* an FBI one. They check. Trust me. You do not want to get through the whole process only to be rejected because you allowed your sin cave to be spelunked prematurely."

She grabbed her phone back and picked up her backpack. "I am so out of here."

"'Kay. Make good choices!" she yelled as Auri got out of the cruiser.

Three kids had been standing around waiting for her to get out. Young kids dressed like tiny rappers.

"Yo, Ariana," one of them said.

Auri laughed. "My real name is actually Aurora," she said before closing the door.

These kids were no more than nine or ten, but Auri treated them with such kindness. She stood and talked to them as they waited for their bus. If Sun hadn't been in labor for thirty-two hours and then given birth to a copper-headed wailing bowling ball, she would've sworn her daughter was an alien from another planet. They were only a few hours from Roswell. It could happen.

She pulled out of the drop-off area and called Quince.

"How's the kid?" he asked in lieu of saying hello.

"Well, we talked about her sin cave and how boys were only out to spelunk it."

"You did not."

"Did too."

"I meant Cruz, but thanks for that update."

"Oh, he's still asleep. He tossed and turned all night. What the hell did that doctor give him?"

"Vicodin."

"Holy cow. No wonder he could barely walk last night. Auri said he flushed the rest and my mom is staying with him today, just to make sure he doesn't have any side effects."

"Your mom? Maybe I should go over, too."

"Nice try, Romeo. I need you to check Whitney's socials. She posted pics from her trip. I'll be there in five."

"You got it."

By the time she walked into the station, latte from Caffeine-Wah in hand, Quincy was already shaking his head.

"What? How I teach my daughter about the facts of life is my business. You need to think about having a talk with that little spelunker before—"

"No, the new pics on Whitney Amaia's Insta," he said, cutting off my rant. "They're from a year ago."

Sun stashed her bag in her office and hurried to his desk.

"That was my first clue," he said, pointing to a sign in the background that read SKI APACHE. "That's near Ruidoso. Nowhere near the Arapahoe resort."

"And it's closed," she added.

"Yep, so I did some scrolling. Some of the pics have never been on any of her socials before, but this one has." He stopped at a pic of Whitney eating a snow cone on a mountain top. "And look at her hair. These are from different years."

"So, someone has her phone. We need to ping it."

"Already on it, boss," Rojas said. "It's been turned off. Whoever's doing this could have her laptop, as well, but I did find out Whitney Amaia's college roommate stayed on over the summer break as an RA, so she's still there."

"Nice," she said, giving him a thumbs-up. "Find out where those pics came from." She looked at Quince. "We're going to talk to the roommate."

Quince stood, but before they could head out, Anita let a ruffian into the bullpen. Sun looked up and watched Keith Seabright walk in.

"You here to start already?"

He laughed. "I'm here to see how serious you are."

"Dead."

"Okay, then. Rojas is going to give me the lowdown on the

academy and Anita is going to give me the paperwork to fill out. I start classes next month."

Quincy walked over and took the man's hand in a firm shake. "Good to have you on board. Have you seen Ravinder lately? I still need to arrest him."

Seabright laughed. "Not today."

Sun perked up. "But you know where he's staying?"

He shook his head. "Sorry, Sheriff."

"Is this a bros-before-hos thing?"

"No," he said, flashing her a wickedly handsome grin. "This is an I-don't-know-where-his-secret-hideout-is thing."

"Figures. Are you going to be ready for the academy that soon?" She gestured toward his torso. The same torso that had been stabbed multiple times. It had been a strange couple of weeks.

"I will be if it means a job."

She stepped closer and looked up at him, only just realizing he was almost as tall as Levi. "Don't push yourself. We can hold off on the academy and put you behind a desk until you're able to go."

"Do I look like a desk kind of guy?" As a former Army Ranger, he really didn't.

"Okay, then. You guys have fun."

"Will do, boss," Rojas said, suddenly frowning at his computer. She walked over to him. "What's up?"

He shook his head, then leaned closer to his screen. "Have you been cloned, by chance?"

"Not that I know of, but the way my tenure as sheriff has been going, I wouldn't be surprised. Why do you ask?"

"I could be wrong, but it looks like someone may have stolen your identity."

# 11

*Help! I live in a house where my mother*
*takes breathing hard as backtalk.*

—JOURNAL ENTRY: AURORA VICRAM

Auri tugged Sybil's braid as she sat behind her in second period. They
were scheduled to watch a riveting documentary on the emotional
impact of social media platforms, but Auri asked if she could work
on her laptop instead. Coach Love agreed and that was how Aurora
Dawn Vicram got arrested hacking into the sheriff's database.

But before that, she and Sybil sat against a wall, close to an outlet
for her charger, and typed in her mother's username and password.

"Are you sure this is okay?" Sybil asked, her round glasses
sliding down her nose.

"Are you kidding? I do it all the time."

"Yes, at home. Where your mom's IP address will show up. But
you're using a VPN. Won't they know the access is unauthorized?"

"What's the worst that can happen?" she asked.

"You know, every time you say that, something horrible
happens."

Auri winced. "You're right. I'll stop. But look. We can access
all the reports that were filed. You said the girl who was found
wounded near Copper Canyon was wearing a prom dress?"

"That's what I have in my notes."

"Okay, if she goes to Del Sol, then prom was April twenty-second."

She scrolled through the police reports until she came to April of last year. "Here we go. April twenty-second. An unidentified female was brought into urgent care with a head injury and a broken arm. She was found by a passing motorist on Canyon Highway just before the pass."

"That's it." Sybil scooted closer. "Does it give her name?"

"Not in this report, because they didn't know it yet. Let me see . . ." She found a second report and clicked on it. "What?" she asked aloud, disappointed. "It just says she was flown to Albuquerque."

"No name?"

"No. What the heck?"

"Maybe your mom can pull it up?"

"Maybe. I kind of promised her I'd quit investigating."

"This case?"

She shrugged. "Pretty much any case."

"Oh. Darn."

"Yeah, but don't you think this is kind of strange? I mean, there are no follow-up reports with this case number. It's almost like they didn't even investigate it."

"Wait," Sybil said, leaning closer, "what's that?"

Auri clicked on the image of an eye and they both froze. A picture of an injured girl popped onto the screen. She lay unconscious on a gurney in a neck brace, a mass of dark hair framing a pretty face with a few scrapes and bruises. But the pièce de résistance was the swollen knot on the left side of her forehead.

"That poor girl," Sybil said.

"Sybil," Auri whispered, somehow afraid to say it out loud, "I know who that is."

Sybil turned to her. "Who?"

It took her a moment, but she recognized the girl who'd come to her aid when Auri was a kid. All she remembered was a baseball slamming into the side of her head and then a girl a few years older than her helping her to a park bench. She even offered Auri a piece of grape bubblegum and sat with her until her grandparents showed up. Auri had never forgotten the beauty with the long dark hair and huge brown eyes or her kindness. "That's Chloe Farr."

"The senior?" she asked, leaning in for a closer look.

"Yes."

"Are you sure?"

"Yes."

"How do you know?"

"She helped me once when I was a kid. I'll never forget that face."

"Wait," Sybil said, easing back. "You know Chloe Farr? *The* Chloe Farr? The same Chloe Farr that was homecoming queen, prom queen, and Little Miss New Mexico? *That* Chloe Farr?"

Auri snapped out of her reverie and shook her head. "No. Not really. It's a long story. The good news is, we can search her name for more information."

"Or," a man said from close by, "someone with actual clearance can."

Auri's lungs froze as her gaze spotted a black tactical boot, traveled up a pair of black police-issue pants to a holstered sidearm, up further to a black button-down, to finally land on the irritated and slightly disappointed face of Poetry Rojas.

She scrambled to her feet, upending her laptop in the process. "Poetry," she started, then rethought her tack. "Deputy Rojas, what are you doing here?"

"Catching a hacker."

"Really?" She looked around, the picture of innocence. "Who would do such a thing?"

Poetry pressed his mouth together and motioned for her to turn around, saying, "Aurora Vicram—"

Auri slammed her eyes shut. This was not happening.

"—you are under arrest for cybercrimes under the Computer Fraud and Abuse Act. Turn around and put your hands behind your back."

"Hold that thought," Sun said to Quince, interrupting his soliloquy on the intricacies of knife-making.

"Okay, but it's really heavy."

They'd left Rojas to check into her identity crisis and stopped by the hospital in Santa Fe, but their Jane Doe hadn't regained consciousness yet. She talked to the state police officer set to watch her to make sure there hadn't been any unusual activity.

"You mean besides the jailbreak yesterday? No."

She thanked him and promised the nurse who'd given them the update they'd be back that afternoon. She left yet another card, hoping she would get a call if their Jane's status changed even a smidge.

They were headed for UNM, halfway between Santa Fe and Albuquerque, when her phone rang from a number in Farmington.

She winked at Quince and put the phone on speaker. "Sheriff Vicram."

A man came on the line. "Hey, Sheriff. My name is Brandt Medina. I'm—"

"The chief of police in Farmington."

"My reputation precedes me." She could hear the smile in his voice.

"We met a few years ago when I was a detective in Santa Fe."

"Oh, dang. I knew I recognized your name. Congrats on the successful bid for sheriff. That's a tough county."

"Thanks. I didn't do much," she said, giving her BFF the side-eye.

"I had nothing to do with that," he whispered.

"Well, you did good. I heard you have an unidentified female on your hands."

She perked up. "We do. You wouldn't happen to have an ID on her?"

"Sorry. It just reminded me to circle back to see if there have been any developments on the Sandoval case."

"The Sandoval case?" She looked at Quince. He shrugged.

"Missing nineteen-year-old female from Farmington. Misty Sandoval. You don't know it?"

"No, and I studied all the active cases when I took office. I don't remember that name."

"Well, damn. I spoke to your former sheriff about it months ago. Sent him copies of the entire file."

"Really?" she asked. Two questions popped into her mind simultaneously. One, why had Chief Medina been so intent on getting the file to Redding? And two, what happened to it? "Can you give me the highlights?"

"She was last seen on her way to Del Sol to spend the weekend with her new boyfriend. The sheriff was going to look into it."

"If he did, he never filed a report."

"I remember seeing an Amber Alert on the girl," Quincy said. "But I don't remember anything about Del Sol."

"We kept it out of the news because we didn't know how accurate that information was."

"Who was she supposed to meet?"

"No clue. He used a burner phone. With the internet, it could've been anyone. Her best friend only saw one picture of the guy, but her description wasn't much to go on. And who knows if it was really him?"

"Chief, if our Jane Doe is who we think she is, these cases sound eerily familiar. A female in her late teens comes to Del Sol from out of town and goes missing."

"That can't be a coincidence."

"No, sir, it cannot. I'll get back with you when we know more. In the meantime, can you send over those files again?"

"Consider it done. Thanks so much, Sheriff. I'd love to give this family some closure."

"I would, too. Let me know if you have any developments." She hung up and turned to Quince. "Now, what are the odds of that?"

He turned and looked out the window.

"What?" she asked.

"Why didn't I hear about Chief Medina's inquiry? Redding said nothing to us." He looked back at her, astonished. "You don't think he purposely suppressed—"

"I don't think anything yet." She wasn't quite ready to burn

Redding at the stake. They needed a lot more evidence, but first they needed to identify their Jane Doe.

They parked in a near-empty garage beside the university's theater, Popejoy Hall.

"I feel like we would get further if we weren't in uniform," Quince said as they walked toward the dorms.

"You want to go undercover just to interview a few college students?"

"Yeah. You know. Put them at ease." He waved to a kid on a bike who was using the empty campus to his advantage. The kid eyed him suspiciously.

"See?" he said, the kid clearly proving his point. "We need to get to know them. Become a part of their pack. First, we share a couple of beers, then we ask about Whitney."

"That would imply they had something to hide."

"Don't we all?"

She couldn't argue that. "And Whitney's roommate is a freshman, just like her. I don't see how encouraging underaged drinking would benefit our cause."

"Clearly you don't understand college culture."

"Oh, I understand it just fine. And I understand where the line is when interviewing potential witnesses. We may as well offer them some pot."

They found the dorm and headed to the second floor.

Quince shook his head. "That would never work. Your inexperience would blow our cover. Have you even ever rolled a joint?"

"I rolled my ankle joint once."

"Can I help you?" A young woman in a robe and carrying a bathroom caddy stepped out of the very room they were headed for, apparently headed for the showers.

"Hey, we're looking for the RA?"

"My name is Heather. I'm the temporary RA."

"Just the girl we're looking for," Quincy said, not sounding creepy at all.

The girl took a wary step back and closed the top of her robe self-consciously.

"Sorry," Sun said, "he was raised in a barn. I'm Sheriff Vicram and this is Chief Deputy Cooper. We're from Del Sol County and wanted to ask you a couple of questions about your roommate."

She blinked, completely thrown. "Whitney? Did something happen?"

"That's what we're trying to find out. Have you spoken to her since she left?"

"Yeah." She lifted a shoulder, unconcerned. "I mean, she texted me a couple of times. Which is weird, but okay."

"Why is that weird?" Quince asked.

"Well, I mean, we were roommates but it's not like we were besties. She had her crowd and I had mine."

"Were?"

"Yeah. Next year we'll get new roommates. That's just kind of how it works. Don't get me wrong. I like Whitney a lot, but we didn't keep tabs on each other. And we certainly didn't hang."

"Gotcha," Sun said, taking out her notepad, just in case. "Do you know who she did hang with?"

She pressed her lips together in thought. "Not really. I might recognize a couple of her friends if you showed me a picture, but Whitney was super popular. I'm more of a band geek."

"Ah. So her texting you was odd."

"Very."

"Did Whitney dye her hair before she left after finals?" Quince asked.

"Whitney? No way." She shook her head, her dark curls bouncing around her head. "She loved her blond hair."

"Even if she really liked purple? Would she have dyed it maybe just for summer break?"

"She definitely loved purple, but . . . I just don't know. Anything is possible, I guess. She was under a lot of stress with her anthropology final and she ended up acing it. So, maybe?"

"What about her underwear?" Quincy asked as he jotted down some notes. "Do you know what color underwear she was wearing when she left?"

Sun was going to kill him. Especially when Heather closed her robe again and eyed him with a mixture of horror and revulsion.

Quincy finally noticed. He lowered the notepad. "Sorry. This isn't as creepy as it sounds. It's for an ongoing investigation."

"Oh. Well, like I said, we weren't that close and we damned sure weren't sharing-underwear close."

Sun stepped in. "Heather, this is really important. This is still all very up in the air, but Whitney could be in trouble."

"Oh." She dropped her hands. "I'm sorry."

"It's okay. I know these are odd questions, but do you know if Whitney had any bright pink underwear?"

"Yeah, but so does every other girl in this dorm."

She had a point.

"She left a few things, though, if you want to take a look. She knew I'd be here for a few more weeks so, there ya go. Leave your crap with the lesser being."

"Not that you're bitter," Sun said, grinning warmly at her.

She ducked to hide a sheepish smile. "Sorry, Whitney's really nice to me. I shouldn't be so harsh." She opened the door to let them in. "Her stuff is in that wardrobe."

They walked over to a freestanding wardrobe and opened it only to be met with a purple laundry basket stacked high with odds and ends on top of a few articles of clothing.

Sun knelt to go through it. She hit gold immediately. A brush Whitney must've left behind.

"Is this Whitney's?" she asked, double checking.

"Yeah. Weird that she'd forget it."

Quince brought out an evidence bag and Sun dropped it in. "Do you know who she was going to see in Del Sol?" Maybe going to see her cousin was simply a cover story for Whitney and she was actually meeting someone. Like a new boyfriend similar to the missing woman from Farmington.

"Yeah, her cousin. I met her once." She snorted as she scrolled through her phone. "So not impressed."

As Sun rummaged through the clothes, hoping to find the matching underwear to their Jane Doe's bra, she touched something cold. She wrapped her fingers around it and pulled out a necklace with the name Whitney written in cursive. It was the same necklace Whitney wore in almost every pic they saw of her.

She held it up to Heather. "Did Whitney leave this in the basket?"

"Oh, no, I found that on the floor. I was surprised. Whitney never went anywhere without that necklace."

"So, you put it in this basket?"

"Y-yeah." She looked between the two of them. "Is that okay?"

"It's fine."

Quincy took out an evidence bag as she held it up. She dropped it in, then bent for a better look at the carpet. "Was there anything else out of place?"

She looked around as though double checking. "Not really. I had to vacuum her side of the room, but that's about it."

Sun sat back on her heels. "Did you actually see her leave the building, Heather?"

Heather sank onto her bed. "No. She was gone when I got back. Do you think . . . ? Did something happen here?"

"I rather doubt it," Sun assured her. "Before I ask for a forensics team, are there security cameras in the dorm?"

"On every floor," she said. "But I don't know where the control room is."

"I'll find it. I just want to make sure Whitney walked out of this dorm on her own."

After taking one last look around the room, they left Heather to find the security office. Two hours later, with the help of campus police, they found the footage of Whitney leaving her dorm room. They tracked her carrying two boxes and a stuffed zebra until she got to her car and left the parking garage.

"Well, she wasn't attacked here." She turned to Quince and added, "If our Jane Doe is even her."

"I'm wondering, too. With Whitney seemingly so proud of her blond hair, it's hard to believe she'd dye it."

"People do strange things when finals are over, though," Quincy pointed out. "It's like being released from prison. They go crazy."

"True. I hate to say this, but it's time. We need to talk to Whitney's parents even if we're wrong."

"I hate to agree with you, but I do."

Cold metal encircled her wrists as every kid in class watched Auri's downfall. Some watched with glee. Others with unabated shock. She would never live this down. She could only imagine what a kick Lynelle would get out of this.

"You have the right to remain silent," Poetry said softly. "I suggest you exercise it."

Auri looked at Sybil, who only gaped up at her, her mouth opening and closing like a goldfish struggling to breathe. Her reaction only amplified Auri's desire for the earth to open up and swallow her whole as the deputy read her the Miranda rights. He needn't have bothered. She'd been so fascinated with her mother's job, she'd memorized them when she was four. Other than the fact that she thought they were called *banana rights*, she'd nailed it and repeated them every night in her prayers for good measure.

When he finished, he turned her to face him and put his fingers underneath her chin to reestablish eye contact. Then he winked at her and said softly, "If you want to get out of this relatively unscathed, play along."

She blinked in confusion. "What?"

He cracked up as though he couldn't keep his composure and looked around at all the astonished students. "Good one, Ms. Vicram," he said, before turning her back around and unlocking her new fashion accessory. Once the cuffs were off, he gestured toward her and clapped. "Auri Vicram, ladies and gentlemen. She'll be here all week." Then, in a hushed voice meant only for her ears, he added, "If she knows what's good for her." And with that, he threw an arm over her shoulders and hugged her playfully.

Auri laughed, hesitantly at first, but she caught on quickly and joined the game. Soon the entire class was laughing with them.

"You got me," a kid named Chance said, clapping and pointing at her. "And no one gets me."

A couple more classmates came up and shook her hand, saying things like, "Way to go, Vicram," and "That was awesome."

After Coach Love got the class to settle down, he walked up to them. "I thought for sure you were a goner, Ms. Vicram, because your mother would kill you if you were really arrested."

"You're not kidding," she said, forcing a breathy chuckle.

Poetry gestured toward the door and she followed, her head hung low. He turned to her before leaving the classroom. "I want you to remember the feeling of me putting cuffs on you in front of all your friends next time you decide to hack a government website."

"I doubt I could forget that if I tried." She put a hand to her face, the heat still radiating off it, and she could only imagine how red she'd gotten. Mortification was not her best color.

After a quick glance at the coach to get his approval, they stepped outside the classroom and into the hall. "How did you know I'd hacked into the database?"

"Because you used your mother's log-in info while she was standing right in front of me. You know, not logging in."

"So you just assumed it was me without giving me the benefit of the doubt?"

His snort of laughter was answer enough.

"I'm sorry," she said with head bowed. "I was just trying to help with the investigation."

"You're just sorry you got caught, gingersnap. What were you looking for?"

"We heard about another girl who was found hurt on the highway going up to Copper Canyon."

"We?"

"Me and Sybil, but that can't be a coincidence, right? Two girls hurt on the same road? It has to mean something."

Poetry bent his head in thought. "What'd you find?"

"There's an initial report that doesn't mention her name because they didn't know it yet, but there's a picture and I recognized her from when I was a kid. She's a student here."

"Go on."

"That's just it. After that, there's nothing. There's no follow-up. Don't you find that strange?"

"Not necessarily. Another agency could've taken over the case."

"I wondered about that, too." She chewed her lower lip before asking, "Are you going to tell my mom?"

He scoffed. "And give up my only leverage? Never. Blackmail is a beautiful thing."

The relief that flooded her body must've shown on her face because he laughed again, albeit softly and almost sympathetically.

"How about you come to me next time? Just don't get me in trouble with your mom."

"Okay, thanks, Poetry. Deputy Rojas."

"Poetry is fine. Get back to class."

She nodded and watched as he took out his phone and strolled down the hall, then she turned tail and ran to the bathroom. The feeling of nausea she got when she was being cuffed had yet to wane.

Standing over the sink, she checked her reflection to make sure she wasn't glowing a bright red. Nope, just her usual orange. She splashed cold water on her face just as the bell rang, then groaned.

Hurrying to dry her face as kids came into her sanctuary, she went to throw away the paper towel only to come face-to-face with a miffed Lynelle. Then again, when wasn't she miffed?

"Why did you come to my house yesterday?"

"I told you. To check on your cousin."

"I texted her. She's fine. And she doesn't know you, so I'll ask again. Why did you come to my house?"

"Look, I heard she never showed up and the cops found a girl in Copper Canyon yesterday. I was worried it might be her."

"Why would you even think that?" Lynelle asked, eyeing her like she had two heads.

Auri looked from Lynelle to her two friends, then back again. "I have to get my things from Coach Love's. Can we talk about this later?"

"I want an answer, freak. You're as bad as your mom, nosing around everyone's business."

"Yeah, that's kinda her job."

"Whatever, just stay away from me."

"That's exactly what I'm trying to do."

The sea parted and the girls who were pretending not to pay attention to the conversation dispersed.

Auri slid past them and hurried to Coach Love's just in time to see Sybil rushing toward her, Auri's backpack in tow. "I just saw her," she said, breathless with anticipation. "Also, you almost got arrested."

"Don't remind me." She took her backpack and hooked it over her shoulder. "You just saw who."

"Chloe Farr. Look." She pointed down the hall to a girl going into the same bathroom Auri had just come out of. A tall girl with long dark hair pushed her way inside.

"Perfect," Auri said. "We need to talk to her."

"But we'll be late for third."

She turned to take in Sybil's rounded eyes. She couldn't get her friend into any more trouble. "You're right. You get to class and I'll see you at lunch."

"Okay. Are you going to talk to her?"

"Yes, but it's okay. You go."

She pushed her glasses up her nose. "Are you sure?"

"Positive. What's the worst that could happen?"

"Auri," Sybil said, her voice a harsh whisper, "you have got to quit saying that."

Sybil was right. Again. But seriously, she'd simply be tardy to her next class. What could possibly go wrong?

She hurried back to the bathroom before Chloe exited. Thankfully it had cleared out and Chloe was at the sink, fluffing her long dark hair.

Auri eased up to her and cleared her throat.

Chloe raised a brow at her in the mirror.

"Um, you're Chloe Farr, right?"

One corner of her mouth rose. "Who wants to know?"

"Oh, I'm Auri." She stepped forward and offered her hand.

Chloe took it. "I know who you are. You're the sheriff's daughter."

"I am," Auri said, a little disappointed she didn't remember her from the baseball-to-the-head incident.

"So, sheriff's daughter," she said, grabbing her bag off the floor, "what can I do for you?"

"Well, this is going to sound really strange, but I was wondering what happened to you last year at prom."

Chloe stilled, her expression morphing into disbelief. She clutched her bag tighter and looked at the stalls to make sure no one else was in the room. When she looked back at Auri, gone was the sweet upperclassman who'd greeted her so kindly.

Another girl burst through the door, her short locks a wild mess like she'd narrowly escaped a tornado. "Girl, what are you doing?" she asked Chloe with a giggle right as the tardy bell rang. She looked toward the heavens, her arms open wide as though questioning the universe before throwing a playful glare to Chloe. "A-a-a-and now we're late thanks to you primpers. Come the heck on."

When she turned and left, Chloe looked back at Auri, her gaze boring into her with a combination of fear and guilt.

"I'm sorry, Chloe. I didn't mean to upset—"

"Not here," she said, her voice low and harsh.

"O-okay. Should I—"

Before Auri could finish her question, Chloe strode past her and out the door, tossing one last worried expression over her shoulder.

# 12

*Remember when you were little and you'd fall*
*while on the trampoline and everyone*
*would keep jumping so you couldn't get back up?*
*That's adulthood. Try adding coffee.*

—SIGN AT CAFFEINE-WAH

"What do you think?" Quincy asked Sun as they drove back to Del Sol.

According to a neighbor, they'd missed the Amaias by a few days. They'd gone on a cruise out of Galveston with Mrs. Amaia's mother and would be gone for a couple of weeks.

"I think you should try them again."

That same neighbor had graciously given them both of the Amaias' numbers, which matched the emergency contact info supplied by the UNM campus police. Whitney had also listed her aunt as an emergency contact, Lynelle's mother, Corrine, an admin at the Del Sol High School.

Quince tried both numbers. They went straight to voicemail, which meant they probably didn't accept phone calls from numbers outside their contacts list. "Hi, this is Chief Deputy Cooper from Del Sol again. Please call this number at your earliest convenience." He ended the call and shook his head in frustration.

Sun tapped the steering wheel with her thumbs in thought.

"Two women head to Del Sol. One of them ends up in the hospital and the other one is never heard from again."

"You think our victim is Whitney?"

"I can't say for certain, of course, but I think we need to get back out to that scene. Can you call the canine search and rescue, see if we can get a couple of cadaver dogs over there?"

"Well, I would, but our victim is still alive."

"Right, but what about Misty?"

"You think the person who dumped our Jane Doe at the canyon has done it before and the missing girl from Farmington could be out there?"

"Statistically, it's worth a shot. Familiar ground and all."

"I'm on it."

Sun's phone rang before he could call them, and they exchanged a quick, hopeful glance, but it was only Poetry.

"Hey, Rojas."

"Hey, boss. So, I got a tip that an injured high school girl was found wandering Canyon Highway near the canyon last year by a passing motorist."

"A tip from who?"

"Well, it was anonymous, so . . ."

"Did they call it in to our tip line?"

"Yes. That's exactly what they did."

"We don't have a tip line, Deputy." When Rojas remained silent for a solid thirty seconds, she asked, "Did that little redhead call you?"

"No. No, boss. Your daughter did not call me."

"Then you called her."

"I don't know why you think she had anything to do with—"

"She's involved in this. I can feel it to the marrow of my bones."

After a lengthy sigh, he admitted, "She didn't call me, exactly. Let's just say I happened to be in the neighborhood when she was . . . looking into this case."

Sun pressed the palm of her free hand to her temple. "I'm going to kill her."

"In her defense, boss, it's a really good tip."

Sun had little doubt of that. Her daughter had a knack for ferreting out the most obscure clues and piecing them together like it was an Olympic sport and she was a gold medalist. The problem with that trait lately, however, was the fact that she kept almost getting killed as a result of her prying. Nevertheless, Sun couldn't help but be proud of her daughter's ability to make such solid connections.

She resigned herself to that fact, and asked reluctantly, "Who was the girl?"

"Her name is Chloe Farr."

"Oh," she said in surprise. "Jim Farr's kid. I know her."

"She was lucky that motorist found her."

"Okay, give me the details."

Rojas explained the case and the fact that there was never any follow-up. Just like with Misty Sandoval from Farmington. Redding never even looked into them.

"Either Redding was the worst sheriff in history—"

"Or he's deliberately impeding these investigations," Quince said.

"Just thought you should know, boss."

"Thanks, Rojas. What is it going to take with this kid?" she asked Quince when she hung up.

"Right? Never listens. Does the opposite of what her mother tells her to do. Puts herself in danger to help others."

Sun frowned at him. "You're funny."

"I can't help it if the bean sprout didn't fall far from the tree. Disobedience and rebellion must be genetic traits."

"I was not a rebel."

"Yeah," he scoffed, not bothering to argue. "And this case just gets bigger and bigger."

"It does."

He angled his wide shoulders so he could look at her when he asked, "Do you think we have a serial criminal on our hands?"

"It's sure looking like that could be the case."

"I'll call in the dogs."

An hour later, after checking in once again with their Jane Doe, they pulled into Del Sol right as both of their phones released an alarm similar to an Amber Alert.

"What the hell?" Sun took out her phone and showed Quince the logo plastered on her home screen. He showed her his, a matching set.

"Now?" she asked, astonished the Dangerous Daughters could summon them out of the blue like that. "No one told me we'd be expected to show up for emergency meetings at any time of day or night."

"They did, actually."

"Well, yeah, but I didn't think they'd really do it. Summon us like we're demons from a hell dimension and they found their great-grandmothers' book of shadows."

After he stared at her for a while, he said, "You are an odd person to be around."

"This better be important. We have places to be and people to put behind bars."

"Are you going to ground her?" he asked.

"Bug? Only until she's thirty-five. And to think, every time she promises me something, I believe her. Like I haven't been in law enforcement for the last ten years."

"Yeah, your mom did, too."

She gritted her teeth. Auri caught up to the whole of Sun's rebellious antics years ago and left Sun to breathe the dust in her wake.

They parked behind the Angry Angler, Del Sol's favorite—and only—fishing supply store and took the stairs down to the finished basement. The super-secret basement where all the super-secret planning went down. Sun pushed her sunglasses to the top of her head to let her pupils adjust. Sure enough, the gang was all there. Thirteen of the town's finest, including her parents, the mayor, Mrs. Fairborn, Principal Jacobs, and . . . and Levi.

. Sun stopped short when she saw him, the Sinister Son in all his sinister glory. Mussed mahogany hair, the tips still damp from a recent washing. Shimmering eyes the color of whiskey-filtered sunlight. Powerful shoulders as though sculpted by Michelangelo.

"Sunshine," her mother said, rushing up to her. "I had to leave Cruz at your house."

She tore her gaze off Levi. "It's okay, Mom."

"He was reading when we left," her dad said. "But he did eat a huge plate of pancakes. That many carbs should put him out in no time."

"That's good." Sun couldn't stop her gaze from traveling back to Levi every chance it got.

He sat on a heavy side table in the back of the room, one knee pulled up with an arm thrown over it, and had yet to return the favor. So they were back to ignoring each other. She could deal with that. She could ignore with the best of them. She'd even been called aloof once.

"Sunshine," Mrs. Fairborn said, shuffling up to her and Quincy, "as Dangerous, it's your job to call the meeting to order."

Sun had taken Mrs. Fairborn's place as the leader of the pack, apparently, but hell if she knew what she was doing. Or what any of them did, for that matter. "Okay. Fine." She walked to the podium at the front of the room, her mouth watering at the smell of fresh coffee, and banged the gavel softly. "I hereby call this meeting to order. Now, what the hell are we doing here?"

"I'm not sure that's how it works, Sunshine," Darlene Tapia said. She'd put down her knitting to offer Sun a withering frown.

"Guys, I have a couple of pretty big cases at the moment. Quince and I really need to get back to the office."

"Sordid," Mrs. Fairborn said.

"What? There's nothing sordid about it. We have to do our jobs."

"No, Quincy. In here, he's Sordid. The Son Sordid to be exact."

"Damn straight, I am." He offered Mrs. Fairborn a fist bump. She gladly accepted, closing her frail hand into a fist Quincy could bump as Sun prayed for patience.

Principal Jacobs chimed in with, "We need to know what's going on, Dangerous."

"With what?"

"You can start with that girl Drew found," Mayor Lomas said, looking like a cover model, the tips of her short sandy bob brushing her shoulders as she spoke. Softly. Sensually.

Sun rolled her eyes. She seriously needed to get over her crush on the woman.

She chastised the lot of them with a well-timed glare. "Is that why you brought Quincy and me into the clubhouse? To get the lowdown on our cases?"

The mayor scoffed. "I can get the lowdown any time I want. I'm the mayor. I just thought you could fill in everyone else."

"Look, guys, I can't share the details of active investigations."

"Then just share the highlights," Mrs. Fairborn said. "You know, broad strokes."

Sun filled her lungs and tried to give them just enough information to appease them. "Okay, Drew Essary found an as-yet-unidentified woman in Copper Canyon."

"So, still no ID?" the mayor asked.

"Not a solid one. We're working on it."

The group chatted amongst themselves as Sun's gaze crept toward Levi again. She fought his gravitational force until Mrs. Fairborn spoke again.

"Item two," she said, snapping Sun's attention back to her like a rubber band. "What is your office doing about Clay Ravinder?"

That caught Levi's attention. His head whipped around to the elderly woman, his face full of concern.

"If he's really got our Son Sinister in his crosshairs," she continued, "we need to do something about it."

Everyone agreed, their heads nodding in unison.

"How did you even know about . . . You know what? Never mind. We're very aware that Clay is trying to wrest control of Dark River Shine from"—her gaze locked with Levi's for an eternity—

"Sinister. I'm working with a couple of people to help bring him to justice before anything like that happens."

"And who would those people be?" Levi asked, his voice honed to a glisteningly sharp edge.

"I can't say."

"Can't? Or won't?"

She raised her chin, accepting the challenge. "It's prudent for the lives of my assets that they remain anonymous."

"Speaking of Wynn Ravinder," her mother said, "we want the test to stand. The test Wynn had doctored."

"Mom!"

"Devilish, sweetheart." Her mother leaned closer. "In here, I'm Devilish."

"I just said my assets need to remain anonymous."

"Well, he escaped, so what does it matter now?"

"He escaped?" Levi asked, his face the picture of astonishment. Sun wasn't buying it. For all she knew, he helped, too. "Yes. He escaped yesterday."

"From prison?" he asked, incredulous.

"No. He had a heart attack—one we believe was self-induced—and escaped when they brought him to the hospital in Santa Fe." She crossed her arms over her chest. "You wouldn't know anything about that, would you?"

He huffed out a sound that was part scoff and part laughter, clearly impressed with his uncle. "Not a thing."

"Well, if you happen to see him, would you ask him to give me a call?"

He narrowed his shimmering eyes and nodded. "I'll get right on that. And since your other source is my sister, just how were you planning to protect her when the shit hit the fan?"

"Levi," Sun said, aghast for the second time in five minutes.

"Sinister, sweetheart."

She didn't spare her mother a glance that time. Levi had just outed his own sister, exposing her part in a very dangerous game of cat and mouse. Sun had no idea how invested the Southern Mafia had become with Clay's plans for the distillery. Were they in on the planned coup? According to Hailey, they wanted that business for the profits and the money laundering capabilities, and Clay wanted back inside their organization.

She had yet to figure out how Del Sol's former sheriff, Baldwin Redding, played into it all, but Hailey assured her, they were planning something big together.

"Dangerous," her mother said, drawing her attention away from Levi, "you are not understanding the point of this organization."

"I guess I'm not, Mom."

"Devilish, sweetheart," she said, correcting her yet again.

"Devilish," Sun said, feeling a little ridiculous. "I don't care what the point of this organization is. I can't share sensitive details about a case with you."

"It's okay," Mayor Lomas said. She stood to address the masses. "I didn't understand at first, either, Daughters and Sons. She'll come around."

"I doubt I will. I don't get to break the law because it's inconvenient."

A tiny voice spoke up then, breathy and quivering. Myrtle was quite possibly older than Mrs. Fairborn. "We are the law, Dangerous. At least in this town. And we've been protecting it with our lives for decades."

Sun released a lead-filled sigh. "I understand, but—"

"No," her mother said. She stood and squared off against Sun, her face morphing into a mask of anger. "You don't understand. You weren't here when our fallen Son Savage died protecting a group of churchgoers from a maniacal gunman."

Sun blinked, taken aback. "When the hell did that happen?"

"Or when our fallen Daughter Diabolical was killed trying to stop a fire from spreading into town."

"Mom," Sun whispered.

"Devilish," she said, clearly fed up with her daughter's impertinence. "What happens within these walls stays within these walls. No one talks about anything discussed here outside of this room. Ever. If two members want to discuss anything said here, they come back here to do so. We are Del Sol's protectors. Her heroes. We will fight for her and the people she harbors to the death, and we will do it with or without your help."

Sun forgot how to breathe as she watched her mother through blurred vision, unable to believe she'd just been taken down a visible notch by the woman who birthed her in front of a room chock full of Del Sol patriots.

Her father reached up and took her mother's hand, coaxing her to sit down. She did, but she was not happy about it.

In the awkward silence that followed, Quince stood and walked over to Sun. Taking hold of her shoulders, he turned her to face him, looked into her eyes, and whispered, "I have never been more in love with your mother than I am right now."

Sun almost smiled, which was his point entirely. "Get a grip, *Sordid*," she said under her breath before addressing the room. She put her arm in his, holding him beside her as she spoke. "In response to your point about Wynn Ravinder, the test that implicated him as his brother Kubrick's killer sixteen years ago was doctored."

"It doesn't matter," her father said. "He wants to take the fall, Dangerous. Let him take the fall. The person who really killed Brick did it to save your life. Let the test stand."

It took everything Sun had not to look at Levi, the real person who killed Kubrick. The real person who saved her life all those years ago, only to have her suffer from head trauma and forget the whole thing. Until recently, anyway.

"And my sister?" he asked from the back of the room, but she still didn't look at him.

She had been thoroughly chastised by her mother and few things ripped her flesh open with more vigor. She stood in front of the room like a quivering mass of raw nerve endings, the slightest glance from her audience causing her pain.

"How were you planning on protecting her once you thrust her into Clay's crosshairs?"

She refrained from telling him that it was actually Hailey who came to her. It wouldn't have mattered to him either way. Even Quincy had been angry with her for putting Hailey in harm's way.

Instead of answering, she looked at him at last and said, "I need to know you won't go after Clay. I'm building a case against him."

He scoffed. "Do you honestly think I didn't know what my uncle was up to?"

"You knew?" Of course he knew. Her face burned under his blistering scrutiny.

"He's wanted to take over Dark River for years."

"I'm sure that's true, but it's escalating. From my intel, he has an actual plan in place."

"Your intel being my sister."

Once again, she refrained from answering. Was that the source of his anger? "Your sister's a big girl, Levi. She's worried about you. I guess she shouldn't have bothered, what with you being so informed and all."

He pushed off the table, his turn to be fighting mad.

But Sun wasn't finished. "Is that why you're so angry with me? Or is it something else?" she asked, practically daring to bring up the elephant in the room. The challenge hung heavy in the air. If this group was so open, so trustworthy, then he wouldn't mind if they knew the truth about Auri. About his new status where she was concerned. It's not every day one finds out he's a father, and Levi was not handling it well. Then again, they had more issues than *The Wall Street Journal*. "Maybe you regret saving me all those years ago."

He cast her a rueful smile before turning to leave.

Sun grabbed her nearly empty water bottle and threw it across the room at him.

He caught it with ease, the sound like a slap on the air, before placing it on the table he'd just vacated and walking out.

"Isn't that assault?" Myrtle asked meekly.

It was indeed. Sun couldn't fuck up her life more if someone paid her to do it.

She followed him out. Not to confront him but to get away from the League of Extraordinary Gossips. Mostly her mother. They got what they wanted. Sun's confirmation on several sensitive facts that could get people killed. They wanted details Sun could not legally share, but even if she were willing, she simply wasn't wired that way. Telling her mother and father what she could share was one thing. She trusted them to the depths of her soul. But a room full of Del Sol gossipmongers? No matter what oaths they took, it was going to take some time before she could trust them with the goings-on of her office.

She heard Levi's truck roar to life on a side street and had no desire to look at him at the moment. Except she did, damn it, so she turned the opposite direction and went around to the front of the building.

Quincy jogged up behind her. "Where you headed?"

"Caffeine-Wah."

"Right. You want me to take your cruiser to the station?"

"Sure." It was only a couple of blocks, and she didn't want to take up a spot the Angry Angler might need. Tourists were coming into town by the droves now that schools were letting out for the summer. She handed him the keys, then looked out over Main Street. "Am I wrong, Quince?" When he only shot her a questioning look, she elaborated. "I can't tell a room full of people our business. Loose lips sink ships."

He scratched his chin in thought, then said, "The jury's still out for me. I mean, how cool would it be to have a group like this that not only runs the town but actually has its best interest at heart? No corruption. No hidden agendas."

"There's always corruption," she reminded him. "In any seat of power. There are always hidden agendas."

"But they have safeguards in place to guard against those kinds of things."

"So they say."

"And, if you think about it, the Dangerous Daughters are the best-kept secret since the JFK assassination. Or, you know, the truth about who was behind it."

"You're saying they can keep a secret."

"I'm saying they've done a damn good job of it for the last six decades."

"What is that?" Sun asked, pointing to a store going in across the street from her favorite watering hole, Caffeine-Wah.

Quincy looked over his shoulder and turned toward the new store. "I don't know, but any store called Wine and Shine deserves a second look."

They walked over to the small store wedged between two other businesses. She gestured toward a sign in the window. "The grand opening is in two weeks."

"They would've gotten a liquor license." Quince cupped his hand to look through the dusty plate glass window. "You didn't know about this?"

"Not a thing." The store promised to be all kinds of adorable. White cabinets and lots of glass. Very elegant, especially for Del Sol.

A female voice wafted toward them. "We would only need a license if we didn't already have one."

They turned to see Hailey Ravinder carrying a box. She smiled, her wispy blond hair and gauze tunic draped over her slight build giving her the look of a fairy princess from Middle-earth.

Quincy hurried to her and took the box out of her arms. "Thanks," she said, gazing up at the intrepid deputy like he hung the moon. Or at least claimed he did in one of those land-development schemes. The minute he started selling plots of land on the moon, Sun was locking him away for good.

"Hailey," Sun said, wrapping her arms around her enemy-turned-lover only without the sexy times. "What the heck? You're opening a store?"

She flashed them a blinding smile. "I am." She took out her keys and opened the door, holding it open for them to come in. "At last. I've wanted to do this for years. I finally told Levi and he's all for it." She grinned at Sun. "You're good for him."

Taken aback, Sun shook her head. "Oh, no, hon. That was not me."

"Please. He's been in heaven since you moved back." She pointed to a counter for Quince to set the box down just as Levi walked in carrying another one.

He didn't spare Sun a glance. Instead, he strode past them and told Hailey, "She threw a water bottle at me," before heading to a back room.

Sun stared at him, incredulous. "There was hardly any water in it."

He strode back in and gave his sister the side-eye. "Either way, don't let her near the wine."

Before Hailey could answer, he was out the door again.

Sun's mouth fell open. She turned to Hailey. "He was furious with me five minutes ago."

Hailey offered her an apologetic shrug. "Yes, and I was furious with him five minutes ago, because he can *bite my ass*." She said the last bit loud enough for him to hear.

He'd gone back to his truck to get another box, so Sun wasn't sure he did.

"I'm sorry, Sunshine. He has no right to be mad at you."

"Hailey, it's not your fault."

"It kind of is. If I hadn't started this whole thing with Clay and Redding . . ."

"You didn't start anything. You're simply trying to save your ingrate brother's life."

Levi walked back in and breezed past again, ignoring them completely. Or so it would seem.

"Yeah, he doesn't see it that way. 'Cause he's a guy with a penis and apparently that makes him invincible."

"Where do you guys find these tiny mason jars?" Quincy asked, picking up a shot-sized jar of Dark River Shine fine corn whiskey.

"That's all Levi. He found this great distributor out of Ohio, and you probably don't care," she said, trailing off.

"No, I do." He studied the various types of whiskey they'd already stocked and the décor, which was country chic with original hardwood floors and soft lighting.

"You're going to make this town seem downright elegant if you're not careful," Sun said.

Hailey laughed as Levi brought in another box and disappeared into the back room again. "I'll still be working for Levi, just in another capacity. And I'll have something that's more—"

"Your own."

"Exactly."

Sun turned full circle. "I'm so happy for you, Hailey."

"Up until the moment she gets you killed," Levi said, stopping in front of his sister, which meant turning his back on Sun. Because they were in the second grade. "That's the last for now. Don't let your uncle take any of it." He'd better be referring to Clay.

"It's funny how he's *my* uncle when he's on *your* shit list."

Family.

He lifted a shoulder, unconcerned, and strode out of the shop without so much as a by-your-leave.

When she heard his truck roar to life again, Sun refocused on Hailey. "I suppose you've heard your uncle Wynn escaped yesterday?"

"Levi told me a few minutes ago." She sank onto a stepladder someone had been using to paint. "How crazy is that?"

"The woman who helped him had a slight build and light-colored hair."

Quincy whirled around so fast, it made Sun's head spin.

She stifled a giggle and continued. "Been involved in any prison breaks lately?" If not for the miracle of peripheral vision, Sun would never have seen the glare Quincy hurled at her like a Tomahawk missile.

Hailey skewed her mouth to one side and looked up in thought. "Not that I can recall, unless you count that one time I distracted a deputy by throwing rocks at him so Levi could run away after getting busted shoplifting a G.I. Joe action figure for our cousin Joshua's birthday."

"So, last week or thereabouts?"

"I was eight."

"Now, that is a story I'd like to hear."

"That's odd. It's a story I'd like to tell. Coffee?" she asked, pointing to Caffeine-Wah.

"I thought you'd never ask." They walked out of the store arm-in-arm like they hadn't a care in the world. Sure, she had several cases boiling over on the front burner, but one of those involved Hailey's blood relations and Sun figured it was time for an update. "Coming?" she asked Quince when he just stood there, wondering what to do.

"I'll get your cruiser and meet you there."

"Don't take too long," Hailey said, doing everything to flirt with him except batting her lashes. She let him out, then locked the door before taking Sun's arm again.

The sting of her mother's words lessened with every second that passed. She'd rarely faced her mother's wrath, even when she deserved it. Still, nothing compared to a negative response from her father. If there was one thing Sun could not handle, it was seeing disappointment in her father's eyes.

While it was good to catch up with Hailey, she didn't know any more about Clay and Redding's plans than she had the last time they spoke. Clay was suddenly very evasive and being more careful than usual, which had sharpened Hailey's pins and needles to even finer points.

"I really believe something is going to happen soon, Sunshine. I just don't know what."

"We'll figure it out." This was the first time they were able to meet in public. They usually met in the back room of Caffeine-Wah, as it was owned by two of Sun's besties whom she trusted with her life. But with the cat out of the bag about their friendship, there was no reason to hide anymore. Sun's skin still prickled with worry, however. If Clay found out Hailey had been keeping tabs on him, informing on him, her life could very well be in danger.

She sat like a third wheel as Quincy and Hailey tried desperately not to flirt with each other, and Sun suddenly saw the problem. They liked to flirt as long as they didn't get too close. As long as it didn't get either of their hearts broken.

Sun's phone rang before she could suggest they just have sex and get it over with. Probably a good thing. "Hey, Anita," she said to her admin.

"Hey, boss. There is someone here to see you. She says it's urgent."

"Is it Wanda again?" Her and that tin.

"No, it's a Nancy Danforth? She says you know her."

# 13

*If you want to be spiritually evolved but beat people up, too, we can help!*

—SIGN AT DEL SOL MIXED MARTIAL ARTS
AND DANCE STUDIO

Auri and Sybil found Chloe in the parking lot at lunch, heading for her car. They hurried to catch her before she got in, but Chloe saw Auri and shook her head, much like she'd done in the bathroom. As kids took off toward town for lunch, radios blaring, Chloe took out her notebook, wrote in it, then tore out the page, folded it, and threw it on the ground.

Auri looked around, wondering who could be watching them that would make Chloe so nervous. By the time Chloe got into her car, most of the students with vehicles had cleared out. Those left behind, the carless kids like Sybil and Auri, stood around chatting and eating whatever they had on hand for lunch. These were the kids too cool to eat at the school cafeteria. Thankfully, Auri had never been that cool. Probably never would be. She liked food far too much.

"Hey, guys!"

Auri turned to see Chastity Bertram walking up to them.

"Hey, Chastity," Sybil said. "What's up?"

"Absolutely nothing. Are you guys skipping again?"

"What? We never skip." Auri walked to the middle of the

parking lot and spotted the paper Chloe had dropped, but did she dare pick it up? She risked another glance around, worried about who could be watching. Would picking it up put Chloe in some kind of danger? She was scared and Auri didn't know why.

Before she could make a decision on what to do, Sybil plowed into her, dropping her backpack. Half the contents spilled out as she stood there gaping at Auri. "I am so sorry. I tripped."

Chastity giggled behind them. "You two are so odd."

"You're one to talk," Sybil said, kneeling down to grab her things before they blew away.

Auri knelt to help her, accepting the paper Chloe had dropped in the process.

"Thanks," Sybil said, zipping her backpack and standing. "I'm such a klutz."

Auri stood and whispered, "I could kiss you right now."

"Okay, but that's the only base you're getting to. I'm saving myself for true love."

"Oh, me, too," Chastity said as Auri opened the note as nonchalantly as possible. "I believe there is someone out there just for me, and he's waiting for me just like I'm waiting for him, and our eyes will meet from across a crowded room, and the air around us will go still; we'll just know, and then we'll get married and have two-point-five kids that we'll lug around in our own tour bus because we don't want the other band members cussing and smoking and drinking in front of our children, who will be raised Wiccan and ethically vegan."

"The other band members?" Sybil asked as they started back to the cafeteria.

"Did I not mention he's a rock star who's signed on to be the next Marvel superhero?"

Auri laughed even with the twinge of disappointment nagging at her. Chloe wrote down a time and place for them to meet, but it wasn't until the next morning. Fortunately, it was at her favorite place on earth, Caffeine-Wah. With that appointment set in her mind, she had something else to do. "Hey, I need to run home and check on Cruz."

"You are skipping! Wait, Cruz is at your house?" Chastity's face was positively aglow with adoration.

"Yeah, it's a long story. I'll let Sybil tell you."

Sybil nodded. "Want anything from the cafeteria?"

"No, thanks. I'll grab something at home." If she hadn't been so focused on Chloe and the note, she may have noticed Principal Jacobs standing in her path, listening to their every word. She stuffed the note in her backpack and plowed into the man, ricocheting off him like a 9 mm. She looked up and lost her voice for a sec. "I'm sorry, Mr. Jacobs," she said when she found it.

"Freshmen can't leave the campus for lunch and I'm pretty sure you know that, Ms. Vicram."

"Really?" She snorted. "That's the first I'm hearing about it."

"Auri," he said in warning.

"I'm sorry," she said, deflating like a balloon with a slow leak. "I just wanted to check on Cruz, sir. He got really sick last night."

Alarm flashed across his face. She'd apparently chosen her words wisely. "Is there anything I can do?"

She looked up at him through her lashes, daring to hope against all odds. "Let me go check on him?"

He let out a heavy sigh, and she knew she'd won before he said anything. "How 'bout I drive you?"

She did not see that coming. "Thanks."

He nodded and they headed toward the faculty parking lot.

She heard Chastity ask Sybil, "How does she do that?"

"It's her superpower."

Auri giggled to herself. "Thanks for doing this, Mr. Jacobs," she said when they got into his white SUV.

"Not a problem. How's he doing?"

She looked out the window as they passed through town. "I don't know," she said, worry gnawing at her stomach.

"Odds are, he'll be fine, Ms. Vicram. It just may take a while for him to get back to a good place."

She nodded, grateful for his concern. "I'll just be a minute. Want to come in?"

"Looks like I have company."

Auri's grandma was already headed out to talk to Mr. Jacobs. "What'd she do now, Steve?"

He laughed. "Nothing we didn't do when we were kids."

"She's in a lot of trouble then."

"Hey, Grandma," Auri said, giving her a hug before hurrying inside. She found Cruz on her bed reading, his long legs crossed at the ankles. "No more painkillers for you, mister."

He put the book down and smiled at her. "Are you skipping again?"

"Yep, only this time I got Principal Jacobs to drive me."

"Holy shit, you're good."

"Right?" She plopped down on the bed next to him.

He'd taken a shower, his hair still damp and glistening in the sunlight streaming in through the window.

"Are you okay?"

He dropped his gaze. "I'm humiliated. Other than that, I'm fine."

"Why are you embarrassed?"

"I'm so stupid. I must've doubled up on the painkillers. They're strong but not that strong. I was just trying to make sure you were okay, and I pass out instead?" He gave her a sideways glance. "You must feel really safe with me around."

She scooted next to him and put her head on his shoulder. "I do. Very safe."

"Your mom is never going to let me see you again."

"No way. She understands, Cruz. But . . ."

"But?" he asked when she didn't continue.

"She's very worried about you."

He lifted a knee and propped an elbow on it. "You told her about the poem."

"Of course I did." She sat on her heels and faced him. "Cruz, you may think you're all alone in the world right now, but you're wrong."

"Auri, it was just . . . a . . . poem."

She pushed his arm off his knee and propped her chin on it to force him to look at her. "I believe that you believe that. I really do. But I think you're wrong."

"Why?"

"Because I've been there."

His eyes shimmered as he studied her. "What do you mean?"

"I've been in that place, Cruz. I've thought something very similar and I was one hundred percent ready to go through with it."

"When you found out how you were conceived," he said, remembering her tale. She'd half hoped he wouldn't.

"Yes."

When he looked away, unconvinced their stories were similar, she asked, "Do you remember what you said to me last night?"

"I hardly remember what I said five minutes ago." He pressed a palm to his forehead. "I am never doing drugs again. Not even legal ones."

She laughed softly. "You told me you don't have a single family member left."

"Oh, that. Was I wrong?"

"Maybe not a blood relative, but you have me and my mom, Cruz. And my grandparents. And Quincy. And pretty much the entire town."

He nodded for her benefit before changing the subject. "You were right, though. I saw that man last night, even in my drug-induced stupor."

"Mr. Redding?"

"Tim's dad?" He shook his head. "No. This guy had blond hair. Why was Tim's dad at your house?"

"I don't know, but I'm more interested in who the blond guy was. Are you sure you weren't seeing things?"

"No," he said with a soft laugh. "But I could've sworn he had on a prison uniform."

Sun could not get to the station fast enough. She and Quince went in the back door and hurried to the front where Nancy sat waiting for her, pretty as you please.

It had only been a few days since she found out Nancy, a tech at the forensics lab in Santa Fe, had altered the DNA test to implicate Wynn Ravinder for Kubrick Ravinder's death. A fact Sun knew to be false, as her memory was slowly returning and she'd recently remembered bits and pieces of that night. Mainly the fact that it was Levi who'd rescued her when Kubrick had kidnapped her. That it was him who'd fought his own uncle to the death. Who'd been stabbed in the process and almost died trying to get Sun to the hospital.

Once she'd been in good hands, he ducked out and his uncle Wynn found him half dead and took him to a hospital in Albuquerque. But no one ever made the connection between Sun and Levi. Until now.

Why Wynn wanted to take the fall for his nephew was a bit of a mystery other than the fact that he loved Levi. And, possibly even more important, he loved his sister-in-law. Aka, Levi's mother.

Nancy admitted to altering the test results on Wynn's orders, but Sun had yet to really understand their connection and why she would risk her career like that. Turns out, she was in love with Wynn. Had been for years.

"Nancy," she said, holding the security door open to let her in.

Nancy hesitated as though worried she wouldn't be allowed to exit once inside. "Hey, Sun," she said, stepping inside at last.

"We can go to my office."

"Okay."

Feeling a bit like a spider luring a fly into her trap, Sun exchanged astonished glances with Quincy. What were the odds that their main suspect in a prison break would knock on their front door? Metaphorically speaking.

Salazar stood, holding a printout up to Sun, but Quincy quickly ran interference. He whispered in her ear and it was Salazar's turn to be astonished.

"Have a seat," Sun said, sinking into the chair behind her desk.

Nancy sat on the edge of the chair across from her, the tension radiating out of her palpable.

"What can I do—"

"I can't . . . I can't lose my job, Sunshine."

Sun sat back and eyed her friend. They'd known each other for so long and, admittedly, the thought of arresting Nancy broke her heart. "You probably should have thought of that before you impeded an investigation."

"Who did I hurt?" she asked, desperation pouring out of her.

"Wynn," she started, then looked around to make sure no one was listening since Sun didn't close the door. "Wynn wanted me to switch out the results to implicate him. The person really responsible for that man's death killed him in self-defense, so it's not like he's going around murdering people."

"And you know that because?"

"Wynn told me."

"Ah. And inmates never lie."

"Sunshine," she said, as though growing frustrated. She tucked a strand of strawberry-blond hair behind an ear and tried again. "I'm asking you who I hurt. And who would be hurt if the real test got out?"

Sun tapped her fingers on her desk. Nancy wasn't wrong, but there was still this little thing Sun liked to call *the law*.

"If you really want the test . . ." She reached into her bag and brought out a manila envelope. She lifted her chin and said softly, "Just know, you'll be signing my death warrant."

Rather than take the envelope from her, Sun let Nancy drop it onto her desk as though it were toxic. It really was in her hands now. She'd insisted the other night that Nancy retire from her position while Sun considered what to do, but Nancy had insisted she couldn't. "Have you filed your resignation letter yet?"

"You don't understand. The man I work for—"

"Is dangerous. I got that before. But you're still compromised."

"Like you're perfect?"

Touché. "Nancy, I've never claimed to be."

"Haven't you?" she asked, her voice an octave higher than usual. "Always a head above the rest. Just a little better. Just a little holier than your colleagues."

She was lashing out. Fighting for survival and taking her anger out on Sun. Even though she knew that, Sun still felt the sting of her words. "I didn't know you felt that way."

"Now you do."

"Now I do," she said, her voice filled with regret. "I don't suppose you've seen him."

Nancy fidgeted with the clasp on her bag. "We never meet in person. I get instructions through an encrypted email account."

"I'm not talking about the man you're really working for. Have you seen Wynn Ravinder?"

She dropped her gaze. "Not since he got transferred to Santa Fe. I didn't know if he'd want to see me."

"What about at the hospital yesterday?"

Her head jerked up. "The hospital? Is he okay?"

"It's hard to say. He escaped about thirty minutes after they brought him in."

Shock seemed to ripple through the woman, starting with a soft gasp escaping through her lips. "E-escaped?"

Either Nancy Danforth was the best actress Sun had ever seen or she really had no idea Wynn had escaped. "Yes, with the help of a slender woman with light-colored hair. Possibly even strawberry blond."

A hand shot to Nancy's mouth and tears threatened to spill over her lashes. "Sunshine, you can't possibly believe I had anything to do with a prison break. I haven't heard from Wynn in weeks. Not since he asked me to alter that test."

"Nancy, if I find out—"

"Sunshine." She stood and took a step back, pressing both hands to her chest. "You can't be serious. I wouldn't know the first thing about breaking someone out of prison. How is something like that even possible?"

"We believe he took digitalis to induce a heart attack so they'd take him to the hospital. A drug a lab tech in forensics could get her hands on given the right motivation."

She sat back down, her expression shifting from shock and denial to concern. "If he took digitalis and then drank lots of coffee, maybe did a lot of push-ups, then he really could have induced a heart attack."

"We believe he did."

She grabbed the decorative tie at her collar and squeezed as though the mere thought caused her pain. "Sun, he could be hurt. Even if drug induced, a heart attack is a heart attack. We have to find him."

"There are a lot of people working on that as we speak."

She sank back into the chair, her mind racing. "Where would he go? Who would help him? Doesn't he have a niece?"

"She was just as shocked to learn of his escape as you are."

"I'm sorry, Sun. I just don't know. But I swear on my mother's life, I had nothing to do with it. You have to believe me."

Unfortunately, she did. And that put her back at square one.

With absolutely nothing to hold Nancy on, Sun had to let her go. Mostly because she got up and walked out when Sun asked her a third time if she'd seen Wynn. The woman was in love with him and he knew it. If Sun's gut was right—and she liked to think it was—he would go to her eventually. Whether love or desperation would be the motivating factor for that visit was still up in the air.

She didn't look at the test results. The ones proving the man of her dreams—literally—had killed his uncle. She stuck the envelope underneath some files in a desk drawer, then walked out to find a US marshal had invaded her turf.

"What's up, Deleon?" she asked, feigning nonchalance as she poured a cup of coffee.

Quincy cast her a frustrated glare. He'd been waiting to find out what Sun learned from Nancy, and now he had to wait longer. His frustration could also be due to the fact that he found his missing shirt. He held it in his hands, the black material shredded like confetti.

That raccoon really had it out for her bestie.

He dumped the shirt in the trash, then went back to his desk.

"Just checking in." Deleon glanced around the station as though searching for something.

"It's not here."

"What's not here?"

"Whatever you're looking for."

"I don't know. I've found some pretty strange things where one would least expect it."

"Like?"

"Like a strawberry blonde resembling the woman in the video in a sheriff's station."

"Really? That is strange. Coffee?"

"Nah. I've had, like, twelve cups today. So, she's a friend of yours?"

Sun took a sip, angling her face away from him so she could roll her eyes. It looked bad. Really bad. First, she gets Wynn transferred from Arizona to Santa Fe. Then he fakes a heart attack and escapes from a hospital she just happens to be at. And last, she was good friends with a woman resembling their suspect. If Sun made it out of this case unscathed, she'd be very surprised.

"Who?" she asked, turning back to him.

"Nancy Danforth. The woman who just left your office."

"Did she?" When he crossed his arms over his chest, she caved, but only because he could haul her in right then and there if he wanted to. "Yes, Nancy is a friend of mine. Yes, I thought she could've been the one who helped Wynn escape. And, no, I no longer believe it was her, but I'm not an idiot, Deleon. I'll check her alibi. If it doesn't pan out, I'll bring her in."

"No, I'll bring her in. You give me a call."

"Fine. But why are you here? Are you staking out my station?"

"Nope. We had a possible sighting."

She stilled with her cup halfway to her mouth. "A possible sighting? Of Wynn Ravinder?"

He nodded.

"Here? In Del Sol?"

Another nod. Sun walked back to her office in a daze, thinking back to everything she knew about the man. And everything he knew about her. "His family is here, so it makes sense, but he's too smart to come back to this area for that very reason."

"I don't know. In my experience convicts aren't all that intelligent."

"Who called it in?"

"Anonymous, but she sounded elderly."

Sun nodded, her mind racing. Wynn knew Auri was Levi's. He'd known for years. And now he was in Del Sol, but why? He had to have a good reason to come back to the area most likely to be searched by hungry dogs.

Levi would help him. No question about it. But Wynn wouldn't put him or Hailey in that kind of danger. Did he come back for Clay? Did he have money stashed somewhere? Or maybe one of Del Sol's finest mistook another man for Wynn.

"Where did the caller see him?"

"It was hard to understand her. Something about a bridge and a convenience store. Thought maybe you could help me out with the search."

"I'd love to, but I need to get another look at a crime scene."

"Need any help?"

She snapped back to the present and shook her head. "Nah, it's probably nothing."

"I don't know, Sheriff. You don't seem like a woman who chases nothing."

"Thanks?"

Deputy Rojas walked in then, and Sun could've fainted. In fact, she would if Deleon got too good a look. She might need a distraction. She tried to get Rojas's attention by pretending to choke on her coffee, but when he looked over at her, Deleon looked, too.

He patted her back. "You should sip it slowly."

"Good tip," she said, straining her voice.

Rojas lifted his chin in greeting right as Deleon followed her line of sight straight to him.

He started to turn back, then did a double take. He blinked. Studied the man in a deputy's uniform. Blinked again.

She knew this day would come. She knew someone at some point would recognize Poetry as Ramses Rojas's twin brother.

Poetry was way too smart not to notice the attention coming his way. He stood and walked back to the locker room holding a file like he didn't even notice a US marshal checking him out.

Deleon turned to her, his jaw slack as he said, "Mind explaining that?"

"What? My deputy? Oh, that's right." She slapped his arm. "His brother was one of the fugitives you were chasing a few months back. Small world, eh?"

"That isn't his brother." He turned toward the locker room. "That's him."

"Deleon," she said, sharpening her voice and her claws, "Ramses Rojas is in prison in Santa Fe, unless they lost him, too. That is his twin brother, Poetry."

"Really?" he asked, unconvinced. He scratched his chin, and said, "You know, there was always something I couldn't quite figure out."

"What's that?"

"How Rojas had a small tattoo on the side of his eye when he escaped that transport van and how it had vanished when he was recaptured a couple of weeks later."

If Deleon looked too closely, he would indeed see a faint scar where Poetry had had that same tattoo removed. "They can do that, you know. They have the technology."

"Right." He turned back to her. "So at some point during his two weeks on the lam, he made an appointment to get a tattoo removed."

She snorted. "Weird, right?"

He narrowed his eyes to study her, and she had to wonder if

he was nearsighted. "I'll see you later," he said at last, his tone exposing the fact that he was so done with her.

She forced a plastic smile. "Not sticking around?"

He didn't answer, and Sun stifled a groan. This day—this month—was turning out to be more trouble than it was worth. She was starting to rethink her strategy of getting out of bed every morning.

Her phone rang before she could follow him out. She put a lid on her coffee, because the two she had at Caffeine-Wah had not been enough, and answered. "Hey, bug."

"Hey, Mom. I'm not skipping."

"Good to know," she said, her voice growing wary.

"Principal Jacobs drove me home so I could check on Cruz."

"Hey, Sunny Girl," he said from a distance.

"We're headed back to school now. Cruz is doing okay, but I think we should tell him you won't let us hang anymore unless he agrees to counseling."

"Because it's true?"

After a very long moment, Auri asked meekly, "Is it true?"

"You must have ESP."

"Mom, would you really—"

"He needs to talk to someone, bug. Just like you needed to talk to someone once, too."

"I agree, but I won't abandon him if he won't go to counseling, Mom."

"We'll cross that bridge should it ever be built. In the meantime, Deputy Rojas called."

After a long moment, she lowered her voice and asked, "Did he?"

"Aurora Dawn—"

"I can explain!" she shouted, suddenly desperate to give her side of the story.

"—what did we literally just talk about?"

"But it was important."

"I know about Chloe."

She released a huff of air. "I can't believe he told you after he swore he wouldn't."

"He didn't. The information is good, but I want you to back off now. I'll take it from here." When she was met with a telltale silence that stretched into eternity, she said, "I will take that fancy laptop your grandfather bought you."

"I still have my old one."

"That's not the point!"

Mr. Jacobs did a fake cough thing to disguise his amusement.

"Okay, I'm sorry, Mom, but can I back off after tomorrow morning?"

"What happens tomorrow morning?"

"I'm meeting Chloe for coffee, and she's scared, Mom. Like, really scared."

"Then this stops now."

"No, Mom! I'm *this* close."

"To getting killed?"

"To finding out who's behind these attacks. She's never told anyone. She's too scared, but she's agreed to meet with me. Alone."

Son of a bitch, the girl was good, but if her suspicions were correct, Baldwin Redding was behind them, and Auri was the last person Sun wanted on Redding's radar. "You're not meeting her alone."

"Mom, I have to."

"Hon, she won't know anyone else is there. Believe it or not, we may be a small county, but we can do our jobs."

"I'm not saying you can't."

"Speaking of jobs, I have one for you. I need you to drag out the video-editing software and log onto Dropbox. I have a video of a possible robbery but it's too dark."

"Oh, my god! I'm so on it. You can count on me. Thanks, Mom."

"Well, now I know what to get you for Christmas."

She hung up and ran through a dozen possible scenarios on how best to handle the meetup. Not only would she have a couple of deputies there in civvies, she'd assign two bulldogs, Richard and Ricky, to keep an eye on Auri. The exuberant owners of Caffeine-Wah would do anything to protect the kid since they thought of her as their own.

Speaking of protectors, Sun wondered how she was going to tell Richard and Ricky about Levi. The part about him being Auri's father. How was she going to tell her parents? How was she going to tell Auri?

Then again, it may not matter. For all she knew, she could be in federal custody before she had to make any decisions if Deleon decided to look closer at the case.

"Well?" Quincy had walked into her office. He gestured toward the front door through which Deleon exited.

"I'm pretty much screwed, but we can worry about that later. You ready to do this?"

"Absolutely. One hundred percent. What are we doing?"

Ten minutes later, they wound their way up the pass toward Copper Canyon for another look-see. They'd called on their Jane Doe. Still no change, for better or worse.

"Fettuccini alfredo?" she asked him. It was her twentieth attempt.

"Nope."

"Deviled eggs?"

"Nope."

"Carrot sticks?"

"How do you make carrot sticks?"

"Fine, what can you make?"

"Faces. Plans." He narrowed his lashes and gave her his best come-hither. "Sweet, sweet love."

"Ew." She backhanded his arm. "Save it for Hailey." She happened to know that Quincy was an incredible cook, but he had yet to cook for the newest member of their circle. Maybe that was the first step. Getting him to cook for her. "You hardly said a word to her at coffee."

"How could I? You did all the talking."

"I did not." She may have. "Call her and ask her to come to dinner."

"You cooking?"

"No. Your fajitas are divine. And your crème brûlée is like a gift from God."

"That wasn't me. I just told you, I can't cook."

"So all those times you had dinner parties and cookouts, you'd secretly had them catered?"

"I had to impress your mom somehow. My cooking damned sure wouldn't do it. Besides, I need to focus on Cruz right now."

"Because you can't do both?"

"Oh, look." He pointed to the pull-off. "Here we are."

"Saved by the crime scene." Since forensics had already come and gone, Sun parked on the pull-off, careful to miss the crime scene tape left behind by the investigators.

"What happened with the hair?"

"I'm trying a new gel." He looked in the mirror and patted the top of his head.

"I meant the hair found on the guardrail."

"Well, you might want to specify those kinds of things sooner next time so I'm not embarrassed. They don't have much yet, but it's definitely from a female who is not our victim. There was some viable DNA, so they are running it now."

They stepped out and looked over the rail at the sheer drop below them.

"What are you thinking?" he asked.

"What if simply throwing our Jane off the side of a mountain wasn't his goal? What if something happened and he had to make a quick decision?"

"Could have, I suppose."

"And if this wasn't his first time . . . Think about it. What if he panicked and had to get her out of his truck sooner than he'd expected?"

"And he was hoping no one would ever find her?"

"That's just it." She pointed at him. "He had to know someone would see her eventually. What if he'd planned to come back and finish the job but it didn't go as planned and Drew Essary beat him to the punch?"

Quincy nodded in thought. "So, he tosses her over the side, and then what? He'd have a hard time finding her at night. And it's not like he could bury her in broad daylight."

"If he got her to a secluded spot, he could." She walked along the guardrail. "Or maybe this was just the fastest way to get her to the bottom." She gestured toward a grouping of bushes and boulders that sat on one side of the canyon floor. "If I tossed you over the side here, you'd tumble all the way to the floor and land in those bushes."

"The odds of anyone seeing me from either the floor or from up here would be slim to none."

"Exactly. But either he got in a hurry, or it was too dark and he missed his mark."

"Or she fought him tooth and nail," Quince offered.

"Good point." She put her arms on his shoulders. "Okay, I'm fighting you and you're pushing me over the side."

"But you're beat to hell," he said, shoving her over the guard-rail. "Grabbing at anything you can get your hands on. Anything to keep you from falling."

"But there is nothing." Sun feigns falling over the side. "There are no trees up here for me to grab. So I . . ." She looked around for something their victim could have used to try to save herself.

"You grab the guardrail and hold on for dear life."

"Of course." She turned to study it again. "But it's rained. The guardrail is slick."

"And you're seriously injured."

"And I can only hold on so long either way."

"Or I force you to lose your grip."

"But somehow I tumble down the wrong direction."

"Ending up over there," he said, looking to where Drew found their Jane. "Maybe he wanted to come back, but he couldn't get to her because she didn't fall all the way down."

"Or he couldn't risk it during the day and was waiting for the cover of night. We don't know for sure that this didn't happen in broad daylight."

"True." Quincy knelt down and studied the area again. "Let's say it wasn't a last-minute decision. Maybe that's his MO. He throws them over the side because it would be too risky to drag them through the canyon. Any one of a dozen people could see him."

"Mostly hunters," Sun said as she studied the guardrail and the posts closer.

"So he gets them to the bottom, their bodies camouflaged by that rocky terrain, and comes back for them later."

"Right, with an ATV or a UTV."

"Or even a dirt bike," he offered.

"Exactly. I don't think a truck could make it all the way down to the floor."

"It can't. Trust me. Redding was furious when I tried in my cruiser. Seven thousand dollars later, I was surprised I still had a job."

"If it was in the line of duty . . ."

He shook his head to stop her. "Not even close."

She didn't want to know. "So, Redding has been down here?"

"He didn't come down that day, but this is a favorite haunt for him and his hunting buddies. Told me this is the lushest part of the entire area. The fauna loves it."

"Interesting." Sun combed through the dirt, worried forensics had missed something since their investigation had been focused on the tracks and the hair. She found an old penny that she vowed to keep forever, a couple of tabs—from beer cans most likely—and a tiny pink barrette. She bagged the barrette just in case, though it looked like a child's.

"Boss," Quince said, gesturing her over. "What's that?"

Something shimmered in the waning sunlight underneath the guardrail about five feet down the side of the canyon wall. It was probably nothing, but they couldn't risk missing a single clue.

"Hold my legs," she said, shimmying under the guardrail.

"Screw that."

"Quince, it's right there."

"Okay, but when you fall to your death, I'm telling everyone at your funeral your last words were *Hold my legs.* Your parents will love that."

"Yeah, well, my mom's pissed at me anyway."

"Hold on." Quince jumped up and ran to the cruiser as Sun lay on her belly overlooking a rather nauseating drop. "Here," he said, handing her a Slim Jim. "There's no way you can reach whatever that is without rappelling."

"Maybe we should. Just to get a better look."

He glanced at his watch, noting the time. "Let's see what we have first. Lift."

She lifted her midsection, and he wrapped a rope around her waist, then tied the other end around his own as a precaution.

"I'm not sure I like this plan," she said. "If I go down, so do you."

"Not when I'm on the other side of the guardrail and you weigh like three pounds."

She gasped and looked over her shoulder at him. "I have never been more in love with you than I am right now."

"Yeah, yeah. Scootch."

She scooted as far down as she could go without falling to her death, and he sat on her legs as ordered.

"I'm so close," she said, straining to hook what looked like a small key ring.

He chuckled. "That's what she said."

"Got it," she said triumphantly. "You can get off me now."

"She said that, too." He pulled her ankles through the guardrail until she could shimmy back under it.

She popped up, covered head to tail in dirt, but she didn't care.

"It's part of a chain," he said when she held it out to him. He opened an evidence bag and she dropped it in.

"It's a charm and part of a charm bracelet."

"You think it's our Jane's?"

"No, I don't." She took the bag and turned it over.

"You're filthy."

"We're not talking about my mind right now, Quince. Do you know what this is?"

"Yes, but only because you told me."

She held it up for him to get a closer look. "It's Shiprock."

"Oh, yeah," he said, tilting his head for a better view. Then what she was hinting at sank in. "Holy shit."

Sun nodded and looked over the edge again. Shiprock was a gorgeous rock formation on the Navajo Nation in the northwestern corner of New Mexico, about an hour from Farmington. The town Misty Sandoval went missing from. She willed her eyes to see past the brush and between the rocks below to no avail. "Quince, we need to coordinate a search immediately."

"I'll call again. We can have the dogs here first thing in the morning."

"And get out the ATV."

"Will do, boss."

Someone had been attacking girls on her watch. That was their first mistake. Their second was to think they could get away with it.

# 14

*Now if you'll excuse me,*
*tonight's bad decision isn't going to make itself.*

—T-SHIRT

Three hours later, Sun and Quince had coordinated with the state police and a certified canine search-and-rescue team. They would be there first thing in the morning, so there was nothing she could do at the moment. She called to check on their Jane. Still critical but stable. Then she called Zee on her way home.

"Hey, Zee. You're not still sitting outside Wanda's house, are you?"

"No."

"Really? Because I'm parked behind you and I'm startlingly close to Wanda's abode."

"Sorry, boss," she said, chuckling sheepishly. "I was just gonna sit here until Wanda went to bed. She's still worried sick. Did you ever get that video footage back from tech?"

"You mean back from my daughter? I'm about to check with her if she isn't in bed yet. Go home. I'll get my mom to stay with her tomorrow. We have a busy day ahead."

"Yeah, I heard about the search. That's crazy."

"It is. Get some rest."

She waved as she drove past her favorite sniper.

By the time she got to her parents' house, Auri was in bed but not asleep. "Hey, Mom. Quincy picked up Cruz a little while ago."

"Really? He doesn't seem like Quince's type."

"Funny. We worked on this footage together. I hope that's okay."

"Sure thing." She sat beside her on the bed as Auri dragged out her laptop. "So, what did these guys do?"

"These guys? There's more than one? And you can see them?" Sun never thought it possible. The footage was way too dark.

"Yep." She hit PLAY on the footage she'd lightened, then pointed as she spoke. "It's super grainy, but you can see two of them here and another one running in the background. See there?"

"I do. Holy cow, good job, bug."

"Thanks. Okay, here." She hit PAUSE. "It looks like they're throwing something in Mr. Jacobs's bushes."

"They are." Surely this wouldn't be that easy. "Can you get a screenshot of their faces?"

"I can do better than that. I know who they are. Kind of."

Sun gaped at her. "Seriously?"

"They say hi to me every morning at the high school while they're waiting for their bus."

"They walk to the high school to catch the bus?"

She nodded. "They must live nearby."

"What are their names?"

"Mom," she said, appalled, "why would I know that? They're kids."

"Oh, okay." Sun didn't realize ageism was so rampant in today's youth. "They're so cute. They're like a tiny boy band."

"Right?"

She leaned back to gaze at her daughter adoringly. "You kicked ass on this, Auri. This is amazing."

She lifted a bashful shoulder. "Cruz helped."

Sun's mother knocked softly before coming in to check on them. They hadn't spoken since the Dangerous Daughters debacle. She cringed inwardly every time she thought about it. Nothing like being taken down a notch by your own mother in front of a room full of people you know and kind of admire.

She turned back to Auri. "I don't know, bug. I think you have a real shot at the FBI as long as you keep a strong hold on that V-card."

"Mother," Auri said, clearly having had enough.

"I just want all of your dreams to come true. Except the one where you and Cruz go all the way on a bearskin rug in a room full of candles."

Auri closed her laptop. "Night, Grandma," she said, holding out her arms for a hug.

Elaine stepped around the bed and gave her favorite grand-daughter a hug.

"She's all yours," she added in her grandma's ear.

Sun glanced at her mom before giving Auri a hug. "Thanks again, bug. Sleep well."

"You, too, Mom. I'd come home, but . . ."

"You're comfy. I get it."

Auri settled under the covers and was breathing evenly before Sun and her mom got out of the room.

"How'd it go?" her mom asked.

"Which part?"

"All of it. You went back to the canyon, right?"

Sun nodded and led her mom to the kitchen. The last thing she needed was Auri finding out about a missing girl and taking up another cause. She was already in too deep for Sun's comfort. "I'm not even going to ask how you knew that," she said.

"We have excellent resources. Are you hungry?"

"No, but I would like to apologize to you."

"To me?" Her mom shook her head.

"I was a bit snobbish to the Sons and Daughters, truth be told."

"No, Sunshine, you weren't." Her father walked up then and stood beside his wife as she continued. "We're the ones who dragged you into this. We got you elected. Uprooted you from the amazing life you built for yourself and Auri. Turned both of your worlds upside down. And then we expected you to accept the statutes of a secret society that you'd known nothing about, and we expected you to do it literally overnight. I should never have spoken to you that way in front of everyone."

Sun produced a half smile. "It's something you're clearly passionate about, Mom. You too, Dad. It'll just take some time to fully understand it all."

"We get that."

"Of course, I'll never be able to face them again."

Her mom giggled. "Sunshine, if you knew half the crap that lot has pulled . . . Trust me, you're going to fit right in."

"Good to know."

She looked at her dad, the one constant in her life. The rock. The stone-faced liar. She wondered yet again about his time in the big house. "You were just a kid when you and your best friend went to Mexico to find work as caballeros. You befriended another boy, who had a horse and a pistol, but he lost them in a storm and you helped him find them, but someone else had taken possession, so the kid stole the horse and pistol back, killing a man in the process, which landed you all in a Mexican prison after you fell in love with a ranch owner's daughter and—"

"Wrong," he said, holding up a hand for her to stop. "How many prison movies have you seen?"

"Oh, I have a crap ton more, and the guesses will continue until you tell me why you were in prison."

"And you're not going to believe that I was never in prison?"

"I told you, ferreting out former inmates is Poetry's superpower."

"Well, I don't know what to tell you, Sunny. He's wrong."

She narrowed her eyes on him, conceding the possibility that she could be placing a little too much faith in Poetry's powers of observation. Still, he'd been quite adamant. "Thanks for watching Cruz today, Mom."

"That boy is such a sweetheart."

"I agree. And, this is neither here nor there, but can you stop by Wanda's tomorrow?"

Her mother gasped softly. "I knew it. I could tell something was bothering her. What is it? What happened?"

"I hate to sound like a broken record, but I can't give you any details. I can tell you that she could use a friend right now."

"I'll go by first thing in the morning. Will we have Cruz again?"

"I don't know. I'll talk to Quince in the A and M. For now, it's bedtime."

She hugged them good night and headed to her humble abode. The one they built when they hatched their evil plan to get her and Auri back to Del Sol. They took their ne'er-do-well responsibilities very seriously.

As a career law enforcement officer, when Sun unlocked and opened her front door, she really should have noticed the man sitting in her living room, pretty as you please. She shouldn't have stowed her duty weapon first. Or kicked off her boots. Or even moseyed over to the refrigerator for a glass of chardonnay. Yesterday, she'd sworn off alcohol for the rest of her life. Today, she'd downgraded to DEFCON 2, deciding to allow the occasional glass of fermented grapes past her rosy lips. Or her pale, chapped ones. Either way.

It was around that moment, the same moment she caught the scent of coffee wafting in the air, that a voice in the darkness said, "I guess I should clear my throat or something to announce my presence."

The wine catapulted from her glass and became airborne, flying free for a glorious two seconds before landing on the tile floor with a splash. She whirled around, holding the glass like a knife, ready to cut a bitch if need be. Or pour another. She wanted to keep her options open.

Levi sat lounging in her favorite chair, a rust-colored wingback with a matching ottoman upon which her feet had been dying to rest. Meanwhile, his feet remained firmly on solid ground, boots and all, his knees spread in a relaxed position like he hadn't a care in the world. He remained expressionless as he looked from her face, to the knife-slash-wineglass, then back to her face. "It's a dream come true to see those catlike reflexes in action."

She put the glass on the counter with a clink and pressed a hand to her heart. "What the fuck, Ravinder?"

"Are we back to last names only?"

"You tell me." She grabbed a towel to sop up the wine. "You're the town Grinch, all grumpy and last-namey."

"I've always seen myself more as a Scrooge on Christmas morning. I used to be grumpy and last-namey, but I turned a corner and have decided to use my powers for good. And to occasionally call people by their first names."

She was reminded of Hailey's nickname for him, *the dark lord*, and wondered if he knew. Laughing to herself, she picked up the towel and tossed it into the sink before fetching the bottle again and pouring herself another. Without offering the dark lord one, she might add. Mostly because he had a cup of coffee perched on his knee, held in place with long, almost elegant fingers.

When he noticed the state of her clothing, he lifted a curious brow. "What happened?"

She took a sip, moaned, then took one more before answering. "You should see the other guy." He didn't need to know she'd been rolling around in the dirt, looking for clues at Copper Canyon. Way less exciting than the thought of her getting into a scuffle and coming out the victor. "How'd you get in here?"

"You have to stop leaving a spare key where anyone can get it."

"I don't."

"Weird." He wore a black, form-fitted T-shirt that had the Dark River Shine logo on the upper left corner.

She'd never wanted to be a T-shirt more in her life. Or a logo, for that matter.

"How did my sister become involved in all of this?"

She sank onto the sofa catty-corner from him and put her feet on the coffee table. Not as soft as the ottoman, but it would do in a pinch. She noticed a folder that hadn't been there before and made a mental note to remind Auri she'd left her schoolwork in the living room before turning her attention back to the intruder. "Hailey was worried about you, so she came to me."

He rested his elbow on the arm of the chair and a large hand at his mouth in thought. The muscle and sinew in his forearm confirmed he worked hard for a living, even as the owner of the business. He clearly didn't sit behind a desk all day. "When was this?"

"Few months ago."

"Months?" he asked, his powerful gaze locking onto hers, his whiskey-colored irises shimmering in the low light, but therein lay the rub. There was still light. It wasn't pitch black in the apartment. How she didn't notice him immediately was beyond her. And a little disturbing. She was becoming too complacent. Too settled.

She nodded in answer. "Before Auri and I moved back. I was still a detective in Santa Fe when she first contacted me, much to my surprise." Sun could see his mind racing as his gaze slid past her again.

"What happened to make her think I was in danger?"

"Clay had been meeting secretly with Redding, and she'd heard talk of a hostile takeover. Hostile, as in, you're dead and Clay takes over the distillery. But you already knew that?"

"Of course." He took a sip of coffee. "Clay has never been one for subtlety. He's wanted the distillery since I got it up and running."

"He wants back in the Southern Mafia."

One corner of his mouth slid into a humorous smirk. "Is that what you kids are calling it these days?"

According to Sun's spy—aka, Hailey Ravinder—Clay had reconnected with his old buddies in the Southern Mafia and made a deal. They get control of the distillery, and he gets his status inside the criminal organization restored. Sun had been working with Hailey for months to get evidence of his illegal activities, but he was proving far more elusive than either of them would've imagined. The only thing they knew for certain was that he would do anything to wrest control of the distillery from Levi's hands, and Sun had an inkling jealousy had more to do with it than pride or greed.

"You know what I mean," she said, tipping the glass at her lips. She swallowed, then added, "He wants to be part of the old gang again, and he plans on buying his way back in by gift wrapping them your business."

"I get all of that," he said, a frown lining his handsome face, "but why you?"

"That's not insulting at all," she said from behind her glass.

"You know what I mean. You guys didn't exactly hang out growing up."

She thought back to the good old days. "I guess I became bitter after she stole my bike right in front of me." \

"I can't imagine why."

Sun bounced back. "Anyway, like I said, I was surprised, too, but she'd heard I was a detective, and it wasn't like she could go to Redding."

"So you thought you'd get another notch in your belt with a big arrest by getting her to spy for you?"

"Really?" she asked, appalled. "Do I strike you as a notch-in-the-belt kind of girl?" When he didn't answer, she elaborated. "Levi, I didn't even have jurisdiction. We were trying to get enough evidence to go to the feds. To turn it all over to them. I would've taken none of the credit. That's not why I was helping her." When he shook his head as though he didn't believe her, she asked, "What do you think happens to Hailey and Jimmy should Clay succeed?"

He met her gaze. "They'll be very well taken care of."

"Really? Are you sure?"

"Very."

"Ah," she said, unconvinced. She took another sip, then asked, "Will that be before or after Clay pushes them out of the business and probably that rustic mansion you've built?"

"You don't understand. I have a contingency plan in place."

"What kind of contingency plan?"

He nodded toward the burgundy folder on the coffee table, the one she had thought was Auri's. With curiosity piqued, she put her wineglass on the table and grabbed the folder.

"Read it," he said when she hesitated.

She opened it to the first page of many, read for a few seconds, then stilled. After a long moment of contemplation, she said, "I don't understand." She looked back at him. "You left a third of the business to Hailey, a third to Auri, and a third to me? Is that what you've been doing the last couple of days?"

"Look at the date."

"Wait," she said, tears stinging the backs of her eyes as reality sank in, "this is dated twelve years ago."

He took another draft of coffee.

She continued reading the minute details of Levant Arun Ravinder's last will and testament. "You've known Auri was yours for twelve years?"

"No," he said, picking at invisible lint on his jeans. "But I've known for a long time now."

"If you didn't know then, why would you leave us . . . Wait." Emotions Sun never knew existed rushed through her like a hurricane. Elation, betrayal, and everything in between. She settled for the moment on betrayal, because it seemed to be the easiest. The most salient. "You let me believe I was . . ." She stopped, not quite able to get the word out.

"What?" he asked, a challenge glittering in his eyes.

She swallowed hard and said, "Violated."

"Hold on." He sat forward, resting his elbows on his knees. "You seem to forget, you were the one going around saying you got married and your husband tragically died in Afghanistan."

"I never said that."

"Yeah, well, your parents did and you never set the record straight. After all, they had to explain away the pregnancy somehow."

"They didn't do it for me," she said, her defenses rising. "They did it because of my abductor. They didn't want him thinking Auri was his. They had no idea he was already dead. And they did it for Auri. They didn't want her growing up thinking she was the product of a rape."

"And yet, how do you think I met her?"

That shut her up. The truth of his statement hit her square in the solar plexus. He'd met Auri when she was seconds away from taking her own life. He'd saved her just like he'd saved Sun. She owed him everything. Absolutely everything. She dropped her gaze and said softly, "I know how you met her, Levi, and I am forever grateful."

"Either way, since it was my uncle who took you, Auri would've been family no matter how you look at it. The fact that copper hair doesn't exactly run in the Ravinder family was a pretty big clue that he wasn't the dad, however."

Sun had heard the rumor that Harlan Ravinder wasn't Levi's real father. That his mother had had an affair with a biracial man from the Mescalero Apache Reservation and he was the result. That she had died because of it at his father's hands, but that could never be proven.

"We hooked up a week before your abduction," he continued. "Auri was born nine months later. You do the math."

A sharp pain dug into her heart like a serrated dagger, and she fought to fill her lungs with air. How could he keep her in the dark about something like this for so long? "Levi, we honestly believed Auri was a result of that horrible week. Whereas, you've known for years and you never told me."

"Like you've ever confided in me. Like you've ever trusted me. And the icing on the cake? You don't even remember our one night together." He turned away from her, but before he did, Sun didn't miss the emotion shimmering between his lashes. The wetness gathering there. "A night, I might add, I've never forgotten, no matter how hard I've tried."

He stood and walked back to the coffeepot to pour another cup as Sun sat stewing in a sea of heartache. For years, she believed the spotty remnants of that night to be a figment of her vivid imagination. She'd wanted it to be true so badly. She'd loved him for so long. To find out it was all real, that she and Levi had really hooked up when she was seventeen, barely a week before her abduction, was almost more surreal than the abduction itself.

"The fact that the pregnancy wasn't terminated," he said from the kitchen, "was nothing short of a miracle. Don't they automatically give the morning-after pill in rape cases?"

She stood and used the pretense of refreshing her glass to shorten the orbital distance between them. "They do. Maybe they realized I wasn't raped and didn't worry about it? I have no clue."

He replaced the carafe and said softly, "Either way, look what we have because of it." He glanced over his shoulder at a picture Sun had of Auri on their mantel. "What the world has."

*What the world has.* He actually said *what the world has.* What an incredible thing to say. To feel. He was clearly as proud of their daughter as she was.

She decided to switch to coffee instead and got a cup out of the cupboard, mostly because it brought her even closer to him. "All of that aside, I still don't quite understand your reaction when I told you Auri was yours."

He took a second to study her mouth before turning and walking back to the chair. His absence left a cavernous schism between them once again. "How would you know what my reaction was? You took off twelve seconds later."

"I got called in," she said, doctoring her coffee, then taking her place on the couch again. "Big difference. Then you steal a cruiser—Quincy's, no less—and disappear like you always do? What the hell?"

"I disappear like I always do?" He sat his cup on the coffee table and scrubbed his face before asking, "Who ran away the minute she graduated high school?"

The barrage of memories from that precarious time stung. She'd been going through a lot, and she'd done it all with a newborn in her arms. If not for the careful ministrations of her parents and teachers, she might not have even graduated high school. She didn't know who'd abducted her. She didn't know if he'd take another stab at it, and she couldn't breathe as a result. "That's not fair."

"Who stayed gone for fifteen years?" he said, unmoved.

Growing resentful, she answered just as coldly, "I was busy."

He picked up his cup again, sat back, and eyed her from behind it a very long moment before saying, "If I *disappear like I always do*, it's because I learned from the best."

He was hurt. He was still hurting, but it was hardly her fault. "Levi, I was . . . I *thought* I'd been violated." She scooted closer to him to make sure he was listening. To make sure he understood. "You will never know that feeling. Ever. I thought I had a child because of that violation. I just needed . . . a change, I guess. I don't know. I was suffocating, not knowing who took me. Who hurt me. And yet believing he was still out there. I didn't remember anything from that night, from the night the two of you fought, until the other day."

He rubbed a finger across his lips in thought.

"Levi, bottom line is, you almost died saving me, and I didn't even know it."

All the emotion swelling inside Sun seemed to sweep into him as well. As though stunned speechless, he released a quick breath and averted his shimmering gaze. Then he frowned as her words sank in. "I get that you remembered a lot from that night, but how do you know I almost died?"

"Wynn," she said, but he frowned as though thinking back.

He shook his head. "How could Wynn possibly know that? I've never told anyone."

"He said you were delirious when he took you to the hospital and on painkillers for days afterward. You must've told him then that we hooked up, too, because when I talked to him in Arizona, he told me you knew about Auri. About the fact that she's yours. How would he know that you'd figured out she's yours if you've never talked to him about her?"

"I can't imagine. I've never . . ." He stopped and closed his eyes as realization dawned. "That man is too smart for his own good."

"It must run in the family after all. What do you mean?"

He laughed softly as he thought back. "He came to town one summer a few years ago and saw me buy Auri an ice cream cone." He looked at her, an astonished smile lifting the corners of his mouth. "He asked me about her in passing, but I played it off. Said she was your kid and that your husband had died in Afghanistan. I didn't realize I'd told him about us. About that night."

"He put two and two together, figured out she was yours, and that you knew," Sun said, almost as astonished as Levi was himself. "And yet, I never figured out either one of those facts." And now here they were, in this ridiculous predicament. She scoffed aloud at her own ineptitude, then glanced at the folder. "I don't expect anything from you, Levi. Especially not this." She pointed at the will with her chin. "I would never. I'm just . . . I'm thankful to you for being in Auri's life. You didn't have to be."

Without looking at her, he said softly, "It's an easy place to be."

She studied him a moment, knowing words could never convey the depths of her gratitude. "Either way, thank you."

A dismissive frown flashed across his face. He stood and walked to the window to look out into the blackness of night, his wide shoulders stiff and unyielding, and that insecure girl from high school came rushing back, knocking her breath away.

When he spoke, he did it so softly, Sun had to strain to hear him. "We can't tell her."

She stood and stepped closer. "What do you mean? We can't tell who?"

"Auri," he said over his shoulder. "We can't tell her the truth."

Sun's mind raced with why that might be, but nothing stood out. "Why can't we tell her?"

"It's like you said. I've known for a long time, and I've never told her. Either of you. What if she can't forgive me? What if she hates me because of it? Or hates the thought of me being her father. Or just hates me altogether?"

"Why would she hate you?"

He laughed softly, the sound reverberating with bitterness. "I'm a Ravinder, Shine."

"Auri doesn't think like that."

"This entire town thinks like that."

She crossed her arms over her chest. His insecurity, his honesty and vulnerability, made Sun love him all the more. But she also realized how beaten down he must've been as a kid. The entire town practically worshiped him now. Did he really not understand that?

"She's all that matters," he said softly. "I don't want to disrupt her life any more than it already has been lately. And I don't expect her to think of me as her father. I would never expect that much, but even telling her puts her in a position where she has to make an unfair decision. That's why I think it would be better if this were just kept between the two of us."

"You mean easier."

"She's been through enough lately."

"Levi." She put her hand on his face and turned it toward her. "I think you are seriously underestimating our daughter. Yes, it will ultimately be her decision, but she has a right to know. And the longer we wait to tell her, the more hurt she'll be."

He studied her, the sparkle in his eyes the most alluring thing she'd seen in decades. "So, we're really doing this?"

Though she kept her expression impassive, elation burst inside her mixed with a healthy dose of disbelief. "Well, maybe not tonight," she said, teasing him. "But yes. Where Auri is concerned, we're really doing this."

He bit down, his shapely jaw working under the strain, and closed what little distance still lay between them. "And you're okay with it all? With me being in your lives?" He lowered his head and looked at her from underneath unfairly thick lashes, and added, "In your life?"

The mere thought caused a warmth to spread in her chest and spill into other parts of her. "Levi, I've wanted you in my life for decades. But we can just be friends for now. Get to really know each other before making any decisions as far as our relationship goes."

He huffed out a quick sigh as though relieved, then wrapped a large hand around her throat and pulled her closer. "You want to be friends?"

She swallowed hard at the intensity of his gaze. "Don't you think we should be?"

Leaning forward until his mouth was at her ear, he whispered, "I don't need a friend, Shine. Not when all I can think about is fucking you every chance I get."

A sensual pressure rose low in her abdomen as he loomed over her, the expanse of his shoulders, the fullness of his mouth muddling her thoughts.

"I have no intention of this thing between us being platonic." He leaned back, his gaze easily penetrating the layers of armor she'd spent her entire life amassing. "Are you okay with that as well?"

"Depends," she said, a little too breathlessly. "Are you still mad?"

He wet his bottom lip and narrowed his eyes on her as he considered his answer. "Do you want me to be?"

A delicious heat coiled between her legs. "Maybe a little."

He lowered his head again and whispered magic words that liquefied the bones in her legs. "You have no idea what I'm capable of when I'm angry."

# 15

Sun had seen what the man was capable of when he wasn't angry. She could only imagine what he was capable of when he was. The mere thought had molten lava pouring into her nether parts.

His shimmering gaze dropped to her collar and lingered there a moment before he placed his hands on the top button to unfasten it.

Ignoring the heat that exploded like a flash grenade inside her, she quirked a brow. "This is a bold move."

He parted the collar and continued to the next button. "Not really. If I've learned one thing from running my own business, it's that the direct approach is always best."

"I like a man who's direct," she said, trembling as the backs of his fingers brushed across her skin. "Straightforward," she added, pretending she wasn't nervous in the least. "Ridiculously sexy."

"Ridiculously?" he asked, impressed. He moved to yet another button, his slightest touch leaving heat trails on her skin. "High praise coming from someone who's hotter than the sun."

Before she could comment, he tugged the shirt up out of her pants, pulled the collar down over her shoulders, and tightened the whole thing around her upper arms, imprisoning her while simultaneously deepening her cleavage. And researchers say men can't multitask. His gaze lingered on the valley between her breasts a long moment before he pulled her closer and put his mouth on hers.

And Sun felt everything at once. She was the girl he kissed at the lake, his mouth tasting like caramel and moonshine. She was the senior when they made love in his truck, rain falling around them as he unbuttoned her jeans and pushed his hand between her legs. She was the victim he carried into the hospital after being stabbed himself, his arms the safest place she'd ever felt in her life. She was the newly elected sheriff standing in front of the station, seeing him, for the first time in years, across the street his mahogany hair disheveled as he tossed supplies into the back of his truck. And then he turned and their eyes met and all the feelings she'd bottled up for years rushed over her in one massive gust, leaving her fighting for air. For the strength not to run to him and throw her arms around his neck right then and there.

She'd always lost all sense of decorum when he was nearby, and now was no exception. Arousal laced up her spine as his tongue dipped inside her mouth, hot and wet and demanding, and all she could think about was how she'd wanted him to be hers—really hers, body and soul—for longer than she could remember. How she'd wanted this for longer than she could remember.

He kept the shirt tight around her torso, pinning her arms at her side, but her hands were still free to stake her claim. She took a page from his playbook, opted for the direct approach, and reached for the button of his jeans.

His flat stomach clenched in response and the outline in his jeans lengthened when she slid the zipper down, the metallic sound drowned out by her labored breathing. One hand traveled north to explore the marble-like terrain of his abs and the other went south to burrow into his jeans and encircle his rock-hard erection. He released a sound somewhere between a groan and a growl and tilted his head to deepen the kiss as he backed her against a wall and pressed into her. His scent, musk and sandalwood, filled the air around them, adding to the turmoil churning inside her.

Releasing her shirt at last, he used one hand to unfasten the front clasp of her bra. Her breasts spilled out and he cupped them in his palms, all the while keeping his mouth locked onto hers. When he brushed his thumbs over her nipples, causing a spike of ecstasy she felt from the top of her head to the tips of her toes, it was almost her undoing.

His hands explored the rest of her, the sensations he stirred making her dizzy. The world tilted a little to the left just as he wrapped his arms around her and pulled her with him toward the bedroom. Unfortunately, they didn't quite make it. He took her as far as the little alcove that led to Sun's room and lifted her onto the edge of the antique marble-top table. The cold stone on her ass caused her breath to catch in her lungs, and she wondered where the hell her pants had gone off to. She could've sworn she was wearing a pair when she walked in.

Figuring all was fair in love and war, she slid his jeans over his steely buttocks, scraping her nails over his cheeks as she went. His cock pressed into her abdomen, and she wrapped her hand around the hardened flesh, eliciting an instant reaction from him. He sucked cool air in between their lips and blood rushed beneath her fingers. She had every intention of ducking down and sliding her lips over his exquisite erection, of tasting every inch of him, but he locked one arm around her to keep her in place and pushed his hips between her knees.

She waited with breathless anticipation, her hunger reaching a fever pitch, but he didn't enter her as she'd hoped. Instead, he lifted two fingers to his mouth, wet them, then dipped them between her parted legs. She almost jumped off the side table when he spread her and circled her clit, his touch featherlight and painstakingly slow.

She clamped both of her arms around him as he worked, but she wanted more. When she tried again to wiggle off the table to drop to her knees, he tightened his grip and issued a soft warning, his deep voice bathing her in a buttery warmth. "Uh-uh," he said as he brushed his tongue over her ear. "Come first. Then I'll let you go."

He was right. She was very close, but he was torturing her. Circling her clit with such meticulous precision, he coaxed her with a skill that bordered on cruel. Even still, she didn't know if she'd be able to—

*A-a-a-and there it was.*

Her climax rose up inside her so hard and so fast, it shook the very foundations of her soul. The quickening, almost violent in its nature, shuddered through her, wave after wave pouring into her abdomen and crashing into her bones, suffusing every cell in her body with light.

Before she could come down, he pulled her even closer, his arms under her knees and his large hands on either side of her hips, and slid into her in one smooth thrust. The sharp delight that followed spiked her orgasm again. She saw stars, quite literally, as he slammed into her over and over. Digging her fingers into his hair, she rode the new high he'd taken her to with astonished abandon, the sweet sting of orgasm seemingly endless.

When his muscles contracted and he spilled into her with a soft groan, she tightened around him again in disbelief. He stilled inside her and rode out his own wave of pleasure, his expression part euphoria and part agony.

After a long moment, he relaxed and braced a hand against the wall behind her as he tried to catch his breath. "Fuck. That didn't go as planned," he said, his voice hoarse. He pulled her to him and held her against him.

"What do you mean?" she asked, panting into the crook of his neck. "I thought it was pretty amazing."

"I wanted this to be romantic."

She did her damnedest not to laugh. Who knew Mr. Gruff would be a romantic at heart? "Oh, trust me, hon, I felt the romance to the deepest depths of my soul."

"That was my cock."

"I felt that, too. But if you really want romance, I have Barry White in my playlist and we have all night."

"True. Maybe we'll actually make it to the bedroom next time."

She laughed as she considered their current furnishing of choice. She'd never loved an antique more. "This has to stay between us," she said, patting the marble top. "If my mother finds out we did it on her favorite table, she'll disown me."

He deflated against her, then leaned back. "I'm sorry, Shine. I really didn't mean to make a pit stop in the alcove. I'll do better."

"Levi," she said, chastising him, "how can you possibly do better? Do you have any idea how many times I came?"

His expression morphed into one of unmitigated surprise. "You came more than once?"

She offered him a sly smile and held up three fingers.

He crossed his arms over his chest and looked away, an adorable pout on his handsome face. "That is so unfair."

"Isn't it, though?" she said with a giggle. She reached up and turned his face toward her again. "Seriously, Levi, this was all kinds of wonderful. And I read that having sex in places other than the bedroom is the secret ingredient to a long and happy relationship." When he narrowed his eyes on her in doubt, she laughed out loud.

He pulled her to him again and started nibbling her ear, sending spasms of delight along her nerve endings.

Before they got too carried away, however, she asked, "What happened to my pants?"

Sun lay staring at the sleeping man she'd been in love with since the beginning of time. She'd recently become convinced her soul had seen his from across a sea of spirits waiting to be assigned a human, and she'd prayed they would end up in the same space. In the same town. And the first time she saw him and fell in love in less time than it took for her heart to beat, her soul had simply recognized his.

She ran a finger over his perfect nose and decided he didn't make sense. How could he be so strangely elegant yet so ruggedly handsome? Arrogant yet humble. Imperious yet, in many ways, shy. He just didn't make sense.

"You're staring," he said, his voice thick and groggy.

"You're supposed to be sleeping."

"I'm trying to but this weird chick keeps staring at me."

"You can't leave me a third of your shit. Leave it all to Hailey and Auri."

He drew in a deep breath and snuggled closer to her. "I left you a third of my shit twelve years ago."

"Why?" She couldn't help herself. She lay a hand on his face, her incessant need to touch him too overwhelming to ignore. "If you didn't know Auri was yours yet, why leave us anything at all?"

He turned into her hand and kissed her palm before answering. "I figured my family owed you. And it's not my fault you're just now figuring all of this out. The will is set in stone now. The statute of limitations has run out."

She snorted softly. "I'm pretty sure that's not a real thing."

"And you call yourself an officer of the law?"

"We're like two ships in the night who keep crossing each other and have a series of near-misses but we just can't seem to find solid ground and . . ."

When she didn't continue, he asked, "And?"

She'd been wanting this for so long. Wanting him for so long. She swallowed hard, and though she meant to sound confident and matter-of-fact, her voice became a breathy whisper. "And will you marry me?"

His eyes flew open at last, a little puffy from sleep and having been beaten to shit only days prior, but the boyish effect was all kinds of adorable.

"You know," she added when he just stared at her. "For Auri." Her heart fought its enclosure as time slipped by. "I think it would make the whole thing easier for her to take if she knew we were engaged and going to be a family. If she knew that we"—she lowered her head—"that we loved each other."

His face remained expressionless and utterly unreadable when he said, "That's a good point, Vicram, but we can't get engaged."

She tried to hide the disappointment that surely flashed across her own face. The one that was most definitely filled with expression and very readable even when she didn't want it to be. She nodded. "I know. It's silly. It was just a thought."

A lopsided grin stole his expression, stopping her heart in its tracks. "We can't get engaged because we already are."

She frowned at him, her brain racing with memories coming at her left and right. "Wait, that's what you said in the truck," she whispered in astonishment. "That night we were together, you said something important but I couldn't remember what it was. You . . ."

"Asked you to marry me? Yes."

"No." Her brows snapped together, then she grinned up at him. "You didn't ask me, so to speak. You suggested it."

He laughed. "Did I?"

"Yes. I remember. You said, and I quote, 'We should get hitched.'"

He tugged on a strand of hair, and Sun could only imagine what it looked like at this point. "And you said?" he asked.

"I said, 'What took you so long?'"

He eased back to study her as though impressed. "You do remember."

"Levi, all the time we wasted, all the moments we missed—"

"We can't think like that. We have the rest of our lives to make up for it, so we'll have to pull a few double shifts. Coordinate our schedules. Auri might have to quit school so we can make up for all the camping trips we've missed. We could be out there a year or more."

"I don't think it works like that. Maybe we should hold off on the whole thing until—"

"Hey," he said, his tone suddenly razor-sharp. "You already asked me."

"Yeah? Well, you asked me first."

"Either way, you can't take it back without looking like a dick."

A surprised giggle bubbled up. "I certainly don't want to look like a dick. Wait, since you left me a third of your shit, does that mean you're rich? If not, I might have to embrace dickdom after all."

A grin as wicked as Levi was beautiful lit his face. "I'm penniless."

She heaved a heavy, weight-of-the-world sigh and sank back against her pillow. "Fine. I'll support us, but you have to do the laundry."

"Done."

"And make me tacos."

"Done."

"And tell me I'm pretty."

"How 'bout I show you?" He dipped under the covers and Sun was sure she'd died and gone to a paradise where money and orgasms grew on trees. Because they do that in paradise.

# 16

"Mom! What are you doing? I have to meet Chloe in ten minutes."

Sun sprang up so fast the room spun. She looked around for Levi but he was gone. Had she dreamed the whole thing? Again?

Then she saw the copy of his will on her nightstand, tucked under her clock radio, and sank back against her pillow. For two point three seconds before another screech echoed through the house.

"Mom!" Auri shouted from the door that was three feet away from her.

"Okay, okay!" They stayed up way too late, she and Levi. And it was all kinds of wonderful. His scent wafted around her, and she was sore in all the right places.

"For real?"

And then there was the gingersnap. She grabbed a pillow, the one that read THE MOM, THE MYTH, THE LEGEND, and threw it at her, rushing her daughter out of her room. Then she pulled on a pair of sweats and some slip-ons. "I'll drop you off and come back to get dressed."

"Wait." Auri appeared at her door again, half dressed with

her hair like something out of a horror movie. "I thought you were going to be there."

"I will be. The second I get dressed. But I'm worried she won't talk to you if she sees me. Don't sweat it. I'm sending in some of my best deputies."

"Deputies?" she called out, having disappeared back into the cave that was her room. "Mom, how many are you sending?"

"All of them, I think. They have to get coffee anyway, right? And this way the county will buy since it's an undercover operation."

Auri burst out of her room, fully dressed at last, and grabbed her backpack. She took one look at Sun and stopped mid-step. "You're going like that?"

"What?" She looked herself up and down. "It's not like anyone's going to see me. I'll drop you off at the corner and hurry back home."

She crossed her arms and thrust out a hip. "Mother, have you even met the people in this town? I'll be surprised if a sheriff in a purple T-shirt that says INSPIRATIONAL QUOTE: DON'T BE A DICK doesn't make the evening news."

"What? It's good advice."

They hopped in the cruiser and took a right on Main to scope out the scene.

"She's already here," Auri said when they drove past Caffeine-Wah. Right before she hit the floorboard.

"What are you doing?"

"I don't want her to see us together."

"Yeah, but she knows you're my daughter, right?"

Auri crawled back into her seat. "Yes, but she doesn't know you dress like a college kid with a fake ID at Daytona Beach."

"I've taught you so well, Padawan." Sun parked next to the station. Caffeine-Wah was right next door. "Okay, Poetry and Zee are already inside. You should be good. You know what to ask Chloe, right?"

"Yes. No. I think so. Crap, I should've made notes."

"Auri, if you want to back out . . ."

"No. I started this, Mom. I need to see it through. I should be able to do at least that much."

"Hey," she said, drawing Auri's attention back to her. "What does that mean?"

"I don't know. I feel like everything I do lately is wrong. Like I only get people hurt because I'm stupid and worthless."

Sun ignored her knee-jerk reaction, took Auri's face into her hands, and said, "Honey, you are not, nor have you ever been, worthless. Your kidneys are worth a fortune on the black market."

"Really?"

"Would I lie to you?"

"I guess not."

"Yeah, let's go with that." She patted her cheek softly. "And we're talking about this tonight."

"I didn't mean it, Mom. I'm fine."

"Says every passive-aggressive human on the planet."

"It's just, I'm the whole reason Cruz had to take painkillers in the first place. It's all my fault."

Ah. It was going to be a take-the-world-upon-my-shoulders kind of day.

Before Sun could think of a smartass remark, Auri filled her lungs, and said, "Okay, wish me all the luck."

"All the luck. And remember, I'll be back in thirty to take you to school, so don't even think about going to check on that boy of yours."

Auri grinned. "You think he's mine?"

"I think you have that poor kid wrapped around your little finger."

With Auri's disposition doing a one-eighty, she hopped out of the cruiser and walked around the station toward Caffeine-Wah. Sun had already warned Richard and Ricky what was going down. Hopefully they wouldn't hinder Auri's interview. They tended to hover when it came to Aurora Dawn.

A soft rap on her window jerked her out of her musings. She turned to see Quince, who was looking spiffy in his crisp new uniform thanks to a certain varmint who shall not be named. "What are you doing here so early?" she asked, rolling down her window.

"Like I'm going to leave the redhead to fend for herself—and what the fuck are you wearing?" He leaned his head in to get a better look at her outfit, if one could call it that with a straight face.

"What? I slept late."

"I can see that. You look like heck. What'd you do last night?" Besides make sweet love to the man of her dreams? "I organized a threesome."

"Without me?"

"There were a couple of no-shows, but I still had fun."

"Nice."

"How's Cruz?"

"Mad that he's missing the field trip."

"I would be, too. What field trip?"

"The one that's scheduled for tomorrow? The one taking a bus full of high school freshmen to the petroglyphs? The one your daughter is going on?" When she only shook her head, he added, "The one you signed the permission slip for?"

"Oh, is that what that was for? I totally misunderstood the whole field-trip thing. Why is he so keen on going?"

"Your daughter is going."

"Right, but he sees her every day regardless."

"Your daughter is going," he repeated like she'd lost her mind.

"Gotcha."

"He wants me to fire his doctor and get a new one."

"Did you tell him we only have the one? We're a small town."

"I did. He's insisting."

"Poor kid. I'll be back in thirty. Don't scare Chloe off by getting too close."

"Okay."

"But don't get so far away you can't see them."

"Gotcha."

"And try to be incognito."

"In my uniform?"

"Do your best."

He nodded. "I'm on it, boss."

"And get me a mocha latte."

"Tyrant."

Auri drew in another deep breath, the mountain air still cool enough to fog when she breathed out. She could do this. And she would do it without getting anyone hurt. Especially Chloe.

She stepped inside and was instantly greeted by two of her favorite people on earth.

"Hey, pumpkin head," they said almost in unison. Richard and Ricky had opened up a Caffeine-Wah shop in Del Sol. They'd opened the first two in Santa Fe, and they were so successful, they'd opened one here. They said because of the tourists coming off I-25, but Auri knew it was because of her and her mom. They were like the impeccably dressed uncles she never had. They pulled her into a huge hug.

"Where's your mom?" Ricky asked, feigning ignorance.

"You do not want her in your store right now. You should see what she's wearing."

Richard made a face, his dark hair glistening with freshly applied gel. "Is it bad?"

"Only if you're not keen on post-apocalyptic attire."

He laughed. "What can I get you, honey?"

"I guess a caramel macchiato?"

"You got it."

She slipped a quick smile to Zee and then to Poetry, who sat at different tables, and gestured a greeting to Chloe, who sat in the farthest corner from the door. This was like a real sting and she was a principal player. She felt giddy. "Hey," she said to Chloe before sitting down.

"Hey." The upperclassman wore a watermelon wraparound shirt that looked amazing with her olive complexion and hot pink sunglasses perched on her head. "First," she said, getting down to business, "how did you know I was the one found on the highway last year?"

And that was the ten-million-dollar question. "I cheated. If it makes you feel better, I almost got arrested because of it."

"Right," Chloe said with a soft scoff. "Because sheriffs' kids are bound by the same laws as the rest of us."

"What does that mean?"

"Is that girl, the one they found at the canyon, is she going to be okay?" she asked, changing the subject.

"They don't know yet."

Ricky set her drink down. "Here you go, love. Enjoy."

"Thanks, Ricky."

"Aren't you going to pay for that?" Chloe asked, her resentment still throwing Auri for a loop. Clearly there was something more behind it.

"They just put it on my tab."

"Is that a sheriff's perk, too?"

"No, it's an *I lived in their garage in Santa Fe for years* perk. They're like family. Even so, my mom insists on paying them every month."

"Oh." She looked down and played with the handle of her mug. "Sorry. I'm a little jaded."

"It's okay." In Chloe's defense, Auri did get that kind of resentment occasionally. Even in Santa Fe, one kid accused her of using her mom's influence to get him kicked out of school. She did, but he was a volatile jerk and should've been locked up, not just expelled.

"Look, I get where you're going with this. You think the girl they found is somehow connected to what happened to me."

Auri took a sip of her macchiato and barely suppressed a moan of ecstasy, feeling it wasn't the time. "Am I wrong?" she asked when the moment passed.

"I don't know. It doesn't matter either way. I can't talk about it."

"Okay," Auri said, her voice soft with understanding. "Can I ask why you agreed to meet with me then?"

"So you wouldn't get me killed."

Auri pressed her mouth together in regret. If there was one thing she was good at, it was putting other people in danger. But since Chloe refused to talk to her at school, that meant she was afraid of a high school student. Or a teacher. Someone who could see them talking and get the wrong idea. Or the right one. "Chloe, my mom can protect you."

A bitter laugh escaped her, and she started to stand. "I'm out of here. You're sweet and all, Auri, but don't try to talk to me again."

Auri followed suit. "Chloe, please. You don't have to give me any details you don't want to give. I just have a couple of questions."

After gritting her teeth, she sat back down. "Does your mom know you're doing this?"

She thought about lying, but that was the last thing Chloe needed right now. "Not at first, but now she does." She didn't miss the infinitesimal widening of Chloe's lids.

"Then why isn't she here instead of you?"

"I was afraid you'd leave if I brought her. Also she was dressed hideously. Can you run through what happened to you that night?"

Chloe rubbed her brow, her gaze darting around the room, and Auri tensed, worried she'd realize they were surrounded by her mother's deputies. "Are you going to tell your mom?"

"Only if it's okay with you." The surprised look Chloe gave her caused hope to well in Auri's chest. "And, for the record, we're safe here, but Richard and Ricky have a really cool back room if you'd feel better talking in complete privacy."

After a quick shake of her head, Chloe said, "No, thanks. I want to see who drives by."

"I understand. Can I ask what you were doing, going up to Copper Canyon, if you were supposed to be on your way to prom?"

Her lips flattened into a sad smile. "That's the question, right? Would I have been found had things gone differently?"

"Chloe, are you telling me the same person who hurt you is the one who hurt the woman they found?"

She shook her head. "No one hurt me, Auri. I jumped out of

that truck all on my lonesome, five-hundred-dollar prom dress and all."

Auri lunged forward. "You jumped?" she asked, her whisper rising an octave. "Wait, your dress cost five hundred dollars?"

Chloe laughed at that. "It did and I did. Have you ever known something was off but you couldn't put your finger on what?"

"Several times."

"Well, there was just something . . . wrong that night. Something I felt like a punch to my gut. He said he wanted to make out before prom, but we were going up to the pass where there was nowhere to park. Not really. When I asked him about it, he got squirrely." Her gaze slid away as she thought back to what had to have been a very traumatic night for her. "When I asked again, he got mad. He did that a lot. But this was different. This was . . . focused. He seemed very determined, like he was in another world. Like . . . like I wasn't a person anymore."

Auri resisted the urge to shiver. "Chloe, who was it?"

She shook her head. "No way am I telling you that, Auri, so you may as well stop while you're ahead. This is all you're getting."

"What happened next?" she asked, taking her advice.

"I asked him to pull over. I told him I was going to be sick, but he wouldn't. He said we were almost there."

"You were almost to the pass."

"Yes," she said with a thoughtful nod. "I just thought, it's now or never. I undid my seat belt and jumped when he had to slow down to take a curve."

"Chloe, those are hundred-foot drops up there."

"Tell me about it," she said with a soft scoff. "But that's how I got away. He thought I went over the side. By the time he got turned around, I'd ripped my dress off and thrown it down to the bottom."

"Even with a broken arm?"

"How did you— Never mind. Yes, I broke my arm. But at least I was alive."

"Chloe, that is the coolest thing I've ever heard in my whole life."

She laughed and shook her head, her dark hair falling forward with the motion. "I was afraid for my life. There was nothing cool about it."

"We are going to have to agree to disagree. You are amazing. I don't think I would've had the guts to do that."

Chloe flashed her a mischievous smile. "No, I think you would've tossed him out and taken the truck back to town without him."

Auri laughed.

"I just can't believe this." She took another sip. "I've never told anyone, Auri. Not a soul. I was too scared it would get back to him."

"Thank you for telling me. You could be saving another girl's life. Maybe lots of girls' lives."

"If I'd come forward in the first place, maybe the girl they found in the canyon would never have been in that situation."

"You can't think like that," Auri said, wanting to take her hand. To reassure her. She held fast. Not everyone appreciated physical contact.

Chloe slipped her a conspiratorial smile. "I'll say this, he was more than a little surprised to see me at school the following Monday."

Auri gasped softly, in absolute awe of the guts this girl had. Since she was on a roll, she decided to go for the gold. She figured she had a 50/50 shot. Chloe could be talking about someone in the office or a counselor or, heck, even a custodian, but she took a chance with, "I bet. So, he's a student?"

Chloe's smile went from conspiratorial to sly. She leaned back and crossed her arms over her chest, eyeing Auri as though she was impressed as well. "Fine. I'll give you that one. Yes, but I'm not saying who."

*Score.* One more piece of the puzzle. "I understand. Thank you for that, but I have to ask. Did he confront you about that night?"

"That's the thing, Auri." She leaned closer again.

Auri followed suit, taking note of the fact that Chloe smelled like Obsession and cherry ChapStick.

"He didn't. He acted like nothing happened. Like we were best friends. It was so weird. No threats. No ultimatums. Just radio silence on the subject for a year."

"That is really strange," Auri said, her brows cinching together.

"Isn't it? But I'm worried with that girl being found up there that—"

"Maybe he'll try to tie up loose ends."

"Yes."

"And that's why you're so jumpy."

"Can you blame me?" she asked, her question sincere.

"Not even a little. Either way, you need to tell your parents."

She shook her head. "No. No way. Don't get me wrong. My parents are the best, but telling them would only put them in danger."

"From a high school student?" Auri asked, astonished.

"You don't understand. His reach is long. And he's about as crazy as they come if that night was any indication."

Auri started to ask her about the kid's reach, but her gut told her not to. She was getting good intel. No need to bring it to a screeching halt just when things were getting good. "Did you see any signs leading up to that night?"

"Besides the kink? No. But the kink was enough. I should've known better. He was like a matador with all the red flags he waved."

"The kink?" Auri lowered her voice. "What kink?"

"Auri," Chloe said with a soft grin, "there are some things you're too young to hear."

"Chloe, my mom is a sheriff. I've heard it all."

"A bit jaded yourself, huh?" she asked almost sadly.

"Maybe a bit."

Chloe took a moment to fill her lungs, then admitted, "He used to give me hickeys when we had sex."

"Oh," Auri said, a bit let down.

"On the insides of my thighs."

"Oh," she repeated, only much more enthusiastically.

"And a couple of times he bit me. Hard enough to leave bruises."

Auri sucked in a soft breath. "I'm sorry. That must've . . . Are you okay?"

"Oh, yeah," Chloe said, waving a dismissive hand. "I mean, that girl in the canyon got it a lot worse than I did. If he had anything to do with it, that is," she quickly added. "Auri, this could all be a horrible coincidence. That's another reason I just can't say who it is. What if I'm wrong?"

Auri leaned in and gave in to her baser urges by taking one of Chloe's hands into both of hers. "What if you're right?"

"I'm sorry, Auri. I've said too much already." She squeezed Auri's hand, then withdrew her own before checking the time on her phone. "And we're going to be late for class."

Auri tried not to be disappointed. "Thanks for meeting with me. Can I share this information with my mom?"

"Yes," Chloe said, raising her chin a notch. "It's important."

"Thank you."

Chloe pointed to Auri's head. "I heard about your concussion. That seems to happen to you a lot."

Auri straightened in her chair, her heart swelling with a triumphant kind of joy. "You remember?"

She laughed softly. "How could I forget? I've envied that coppery hair of yours ever since." When Auri smoothed her hair, basking in warmth of her idol's praise, Chloe smiled graciously, and said, "I'll leave first." She stood, then added, "You're pretty cool, Auri."

Auri felt tiny hearts burst out of her eyes as she watched Chloe leave.

Poetry and Zee walked to her table.

"You did good," Poetry said.

Zee nodded in agreement. "You're a natural. You need a ride to school?"

"My mom's coming. She wants a report."

"Gotcha."

Her phone chimed with a text. "She just pulled up. Thanks for being here," she said, grateful beyond measure.

"You did fantastic," her mom said when she got into the cruiser.

"Thanks," she said, plopping her backpack on the floorboard. "Wait, how do you know?"

She tapped on her phone. "We were listening. We recorded the whole conversation."

Auri gaped at her for a very long time. When her mom pulled into traffic, she asked, "Why would you do that?"

"Not for use in court, if that's what you mean," she said with a suspicious scoff. "I just wanted to hear what she had to say for myself."

"You should've told me. I feel like we violated her trust."

"The fact that we didn't tell either one of you technically makes it illegal to use in court, hon. At least one party of a conversation must be privy to the fact that it is being recorded."

"I still would've liked to know."

"I know. We didn't want to risk you feeling self-conscious and losing her."

Auri sank back into the seat and crossed her arms over her chest to give her mother visual confirmation of just how angry she was. But she wasn't too angry to ask about Cruz. "Can we check on the boy I have wrapped around my finger before school?"

"Only if you want to be really, really late."

"I don't mind."

"I do, so, no."

"Man." She uncrossed then recrossed her arms. That'd show her. Since the drive to school was, like, two minutes, she didn't have a lot of time to pump her mother for info. She needed to work fast. "Since you heard anyway, is he our guy?"

"He is most definitely our guy, and I hate to be the one to break it to you, bug, but if we don't figure out who it is soon, I'm going to have to bring Chloe in and talk to her myself."

Auri straightened in the seat. "Mom, I promised!"

"Auri, people's lives are at stake."

"But no one has died."

Her mom pulled the cruiser up to the school, and said almost reluctantly, "Actually, that may not be true."

Taken aback, Auri stilled and let the words sink in before asking, "For real?"

"For real, bug. At least we suspect. I'll try to keep Chloe out of it, but if it comes down to the wire—"

"I understand. I just hope I haven't gotten someone else hurt."

Sun put the cruiser in park and then turned to offer her a smile like that of a coach whose team had come in dead last but they still won nifty participation trophies. "You said it yourself, that's your specialty."

Auri patted her arm. "Thanks, Mom."

"Just keeping it real, bug."

"And I appreciate it." She didn't, but who was she to argue with statistics?

She bit her lip, wondering if she should tell her mom her latest plan or just give it a shot and, if it bore fruit, present the results to her afterward in a PowerPoint presentation complete with pie charts and sound effects. She decided on the latter. It probably wouldn't work anyway, but if it did, if she could figure out who Chloe went to prom with, her mom would be able to get the scumbag off the vaguely mean streets of Del Sol.

She crossed her fingers as she got out of the cruiser, tossing out a quick, "Love you, bye!"

But she stopped short when she saw Principal Jacobs standing there waiting. She realized the tardy bell had already rung. She groaned. Not, like, aloud. It was more of an inward groan of despair as she waited for the lecture that was sure to come.

"I got your message," he said to her mom instead. "Here you go, Auri." He handed her an excused tardy slip, and Auri resisted the urge to do a fist pump.

"And as to the other thing, go right ahead."

Auri frowned and looked between the principal and her mom. "What other thing?"

"Your mom wants to search my bushes," he said, giving her mother a quick wink.

Auri turned an astonished expression on her mom, leaned back into the cruiser, and asked in a harsh whisper, "Mother, is that a metaphor?"

Her mom's face flatlined. "No, bug."

"Oh, right!" she said when realization dawned. "The world's tiniest boy band. Well, have fun." She gave them a quick wave before hurrying off.

# 17

*If your potted cactus died and you are literally*
*less nurturing than the desert, we can help!*

—SIGN AT DEL SOL NURSERY

After watching the redheaded Tasmanian devil tornado her way
to class, Sun booked it over to Mr. Jacobs's house to rummage
through his bushes. Sure enough, she found not only a sewing
tin—presumably Wanda's—but some official papers, a man's
grooming kit, and an Elvis-shaped bottle opener. Either Mr. Jacobs
was a pig, or those kids did indeed toss half of their take, probably
figuring it wasn't worth anything on the black market they were
surely hooked up with. Them being criminal masterminds and all.

Sun grabbed it all, carefully placing the tin and the grooming kit in evidence bags, and drove back to the station, where she
walked in like she owned the place.

"Thanks for the backup this morning," she said to Rojas and
Zee.

"No problem." Zee handed her a message. "The DNA test results on our Jane Doe are expected this afternoon, but they're just
now running the sample from the brush you got from her dorm
room. That'll take a couple more days. Then we'll know for sure if
she's Whitney Amaia."

"Fantastic," Sun said as she read over the report. "Any change
in her condition?"

"Not yet."

"Thanks, Zee."

"Sure thing, boss."

Before Zee got back to her desk, Sun asked, "Oh, have you talked to Wanda today?"

Zee nodded. "I checked in on her this morning. She's doing better. Just worried."

"Thanks for taking care of her. I should be wrapping that mess up today." She walked to Rojas's desk, which was about two steps away from Zee's, so it wasn't a long journey. "You got anything, Rojas?"

"Besides a caffeine buzz? What do they put in their triple espresso lattes?"

"A triple espresso."

"Oh, yeah, that makes sense. Also, the dogs can't be here until tomorrow."

"What?" Disappointment sank into her like water in sand. She'd blocked out the whole morning. "I've already penciled them in. Now I have to erase." Admittedly, there was a part of her that was afraid their suspect would get to the canyon first and remove whatever evidence he'd left behind before the team got there, especially with them finding their Jane Doe. Criminals were notorious for second-guessing themselves and returning to the crime scene. "Did they give a reason?"

"Got called into an emergency near Capitan. A five-year-old went missing last night."

"Oh, yeah, that definitely takes precedence." She walked to Quince's desk. Again, not a long journey.

He handed her a latte.

"Gracias."

"De nada. Nothing on Chloe Farr's social media so far," he said to her without looking up.

"Were you listening to their conversation?"

"Every word, thus my search. She's not as into posting every aspect of her life like a lot of kids are these days, but look here." He pointed to a pic of Chloe getting chummy with a boy. "She apparently dated this guy for, like, three years, but they broke up long before prom."

She bent for a better look. Clearly a football star, Chloe's guy was a handsome blond with dimples and they'd looked good together. "Maybe they decided to give it another shot and it didn't go well? She could've deleted all the pics of them together just before that night. I damn sure would have."

Quince lifted an unconvinced shoulder. "But why only delete some of them and not all? I mean, if he attacked her . . ."

"No, you're right," she said, nodding. "Keep looking."

"Will do. By the way, I didn't notice anyone suspish watching Auri and Chloe this morning. I know Chloe was worried she was being tailed."

"Okay, thanks."

She started to leave when he asked, "How are you doing?"

"I have a horrible headache." She pressed a palm to her temple. "No idea why."

He ticked off a few suggestions on his fingers. "You don't drink water, you get three hours of sleep a night, and you think coffee is a major food group."

"I know, right?" She took a sip of her latte. "It's a mystery."

He finally spotted the sewing tin in her hands. "Taking up a new hobby?"

"No. And this is none of your business."

He perked up, his interest piqued instantly. "Why isn't it my business?"

"This is a side job."

"You're fighting crime on the side, too? Do you ever sleep?"

She certainly didn't last night. Hiding a grin at the thought, she turned to see Seabright coming into the station.

"Hey, you," she said when he greeted her with a nod.

"Where do you want me?" Seabright asked.

She tilted her head. "Is that a trick question?"

"Sorry, boss," Rojas said. "We were talking, and we think

someone should keep an eye on our possible crime scene until the canine unit can get out there. You know, in case our suspect decides to pay it another visit."

She truly had the best team ever. "Good thinking, guys."

Zee backed him up. "I figure we can take six-hour shifts."

"No need," Seabright said. "I'll keep an eye on it today and camp out tonight. If anyone does show up, what am I authorized to do?"

Sun raised an eyebrow. With his experience, he was certainly qualified to do a lot. "Let me swear you in first, then you can use your best judgment, but it's probably best if you just snap some shots."

He grinned, clearly knowing exactly where her thoughts had landed. "You got it."

"Let's go to my office. Deputies?" she said, calling them to attention. They stood and followed her in, Rojas elbowing Seabright on the way. She turned and motioned for Anita to come record the event.

Her administrative assistant hurried into the bullpen, her face beaming.

The deputies moved chairs out of the way, then formed a half-circle around their new comrade. While they previously used a handheld, phones made the clunky things nigh obsolete. Anita used her phone and would later upload it to their server.

Sun opened the handbook. "Please raise your right hand."

Seabright offered her a lopsided grin and raised his right hand. She couldn't help but think he was enjoying every second of his new life.

She craned her neck to look up at him. "I, state your name . . ."

"I, Keith Lyndsey Seabright . . ."

She leaned forward and whispered, "Lyndsey? Really?"

He laughed softly and nodded.

"I love it." She straightened and continued, ". . . do solemnly swear . . ."

While the swearing-in ceremony was short and sweet, she had a feeling it was much more meaningful to Seabright than he was letting on, and she realized he'd been off-grid for so long, living in the wild, protecting the love of his life's son, that he was probably very ready for a more normal existence. Structure was good. A meaningful life was better. Family was best. And he was getting all three in one fell swoop.

Before she sent him off to the canyon, he took her hand in his. "Thanks for taking me on, *boss*," he said, emphasizing her new role in his life.

"Please," she said with a playful scoff. "I'm pretty sure I now have the best qualified team in the entire state, and that's saying something. Take snacks." She pointed to the break area.

He laughed and went in search of sustenance for his stakeout.

Feeling much better with the canyon about to be in lockdown, she sat at her desk to check out the treasures she'd fished out of Mr. Jacobs's shrubs. She called Wanda, but when she didn't pick up, Sun left her a message with the—hopefully—good news.

After gloving up, she pulled out the tin and opened it. Nothing. So the kids took the contents. Unless the papers *were* the contents. She quickly examined the men's grooming kit. It smelled like leather and old cologne, the shaving tools practically ancient, and Sun suddenly wondered if Wanda had been married before coming to Del Sol. She'd never asked and Wanda had never offered.

She moved on to the papers. An old vaccination record for a Wanda Watkins—clearly Wanda's maiden name—a social security card, a handful of life insurance papers, and an old marriage certificate. So that answered that. Sun stopped when she came to the final page. It was a birth certificate for a boy named Benjamin, born to Wanda Watkins. Sun sucked in a soft breath. She had a child out of wedlock. While that's nothing today, back then it would've been a very big deal. But Wanda had never mentioned having a child. Did she give him up for adoption, as was the most common practice back then? Or perhaps her family forced her to.

She wanted to look into it, but it was none of her business. It certainly didn't pertain to the case, speaking of which. She put everything in order and grabbed her coffee. She would only take fingerprints if necessary, but since she already had the bandits on video—sort of—it probably wouldn't be.

"I'll be back in a few."

"You need backup?" Quince asked.

"Not for this. Keep digging. And call Chief Medina in Farmington. I want everything he has on Misty Sandoval. Including phone records."

"You got it."

"Wait." She looked her BFF up and down and rethought her position. "Maybe I do need you. You can be intimidating, right?"

"Duh," he said, showing his palms as though asking if she were crazy.

"Okay, you come with me. Zee—"

"I'm on it."

She started out the door, but before she got far, she looked back to the bullpen and asked, "Has anyone checked on Doug?"

Doug, as luck would have it, was still alive and kicking and milking his neck injury for all it was worth. Sun and Quince pulled into the Del Sol Elementary parking lot and walked into the school, hoping the principal would be in. She didn't know Mrs. Baca well, but Principal Jacobs said she was a good egg. That worked for Sun.

"Are you going to tell me what this is about?"

"Can't. Just go along with me."

"You can go back, Sheriff," the young admin said, pointing to an office behind her. Then she smiled at Quincy and said, "You, too, Deputy Cooper."

"Thanks."

"Sheriff," Mrs. Baca said, stepping out to greet her. She shook Sun's hand first, then Quincy's. "To what do I owe the pleasure?"

"I have a question about a few of your kids."

"Of course you do." She seemed to wilt with Sun's confession. She gestured for them to sit, then added, "It's always about the kids."

"Well, you do have over a hundred. Two words: birth control."

That got a giggle out of the woman. Josie Baca's head barely reached Sun's chin, and Quincy towered over her like a skyscraper built beside a historical church, her body curvy and her hair a mass of curls. The curls bounced as she led them inside her office.

"I was wondering if you could check out a video and tell me if you recognize the kids in it."

"Oh, sure."

Sun brought the video up on her phone and angled it so Mrs. Baca could see. "Sorry about the lighting. It was the best my technician could do on such short notice, but do you recognize these kids?"

Mrs. Baca pursed her lips. "No worries. I know exactly who those three little troublemakers are."

"Really?" That was easy.

"What did they do now?"

"Well, they may have been involved in a break-in."

Startled, both Mrs. Baca and Quincy asked, "A break-in?"

She scowled at Quince, then asked Mrs. Baca, "Are they here today?"

"As far as I know." She pressed her intercom. "Susan, can you send the troublemakers to the conference room, please?"

"Yes, ma'am."

Sun grinned. "She knows who the troublemakers are?"

"Yeah, well, they have a bit of a rep here at school."

"I can only imagine."

She led them to a small conference room next door, and they chatted for a few minutes about everyday minutiae until three second-grade boys walked in, throwing attitude. They stopped short when they saw Sun and Quincy.

"Boys, this is Sheriff Vicram."

They exchanged glances, the blood draining from their adorable faces, and Sun had to force herself to hold fast under fire. She could not be swayed by their cuteness.

"Sheriff, this is Caleb, Leo, and Duran. Otherwise known as Skillz."

"Ah," Sun said, nodding. "Why Skillz?"

Though Caleb seemed like the shiest of the three, glancing at her from underneath long lashes that sat atop a sprinkling of freckles, he spoke first. He ran his fingers through his short brown hair, then crossed his arms and struck a pose before saying, "That's our band name, Holmes."

Sun had to fight a grin, though not as hard as Quince did. He was in the middle of an all-out war when Mrs. Baca said, "Boys, be nice. I mean it."

They chilled with the attitude under her scrutiny, dropping their gazes and toeing the carpet.

"I'll leave you to it," she said. Then she left them alone with the tiny boy band. They could not have been more than seven years old.

"Would you like to sit down?" she asked them.

They risked a glance at Quince, who stood, again like an angry skyscraper with his arms crossed, glaring down at them. They gave him a wide berth before taking a seat at the round conference table.

Sun sat, too, but Quince remained standing. "Before we start," she said, "I have to tell you, you can call your parents and have them here if you'd like."

All three heads shot up simultaneously.

"That's okay," Caleb said, shaking his head. "We don't have to call them."

She figured as much. "Okay, then I'm going to ask you a few questions about what you were doing two nights ago."

They exchanged glances again, only these were much more furtive than the previous ones.

"Did you, perhaps, break into any houses?"

"Don't say anything," Leo said, leaning back in his chair. "Snitches get stitches."

"That's funny. I told my daughter the same thing right before she was arrested. She's in juvey now, but at least she didn't snitch. Amirite?"

"We don't have nothing to hide," Duran said, eyeing her through black-framed glasses. He pushed them back up his nose.

"Yeah," the others agreed. "We robbed a couple houses. Broke into a couple of cars. We even kicked that perv's butt."

They exchanged fist bumps before refocusing on Sun, chins held high.

"Perv?" Sun asked before realization dawned. "You mean Doug? You're the gang that attacked Doug?"

Leo nodded. "*Vato* flashed my mom."

She looked at Quince in shock, then back to the boys. "You stabbed him in the neck? You're, like, three feet tall."

Duran scoffed. "Hell, no."

"Language," Sun said, crossing her arms over her chest and flashing him a warning glare.

He caved instantly. "Sorry. He was trying to convince us he had a knife. Like I don't got a grandma, too. When Leo kicked him in the shin, he tried to run and fell on it."

"Stabbed himself in the neck," Leo added. "We tried to tell him."

Caleb lifted his chin. "But he wasn't taking us seriously, so we had to step it up. Throw him some shade. Know what I mean?"

She wanted to offer suggestions as to why someone might not take them seriously. For example, the stick-on tattoos did not scream *badass*. In the end, she decided against it. Mostly because she wanted to adopt them all right then and there.

She opened her hand, palm up, and held it out to them.

"What?" Leo asked, his brows sliding together.

"Mrs. Stephanopoulos's coins." Sun ignored the surprised look Quincy cast her way and stayed focused on her prey.

"We don't have any coins."

"I have it on video. You broke into Mrs. Stephanopoulos's house two nights ago and then you threw half your take in the bushes across the street."

"Man," Leo said. "We traded those coins for coke." When she narrowed her eyes at him, he added, "Okay, one Coke." He dug in his pocket and produced five coins. "Only one of them would work in the vending machine."

The fact that they meant an actual soda was almost Sun's undoing, but she held fast under the increasing pressure. "Which vending machine?"

"The one at the high school."

She would call Mr. Jacobs to fetch it. She pulled out her phone and called Zee. "I need a patrol car at the elementary school to arrest three juveniles. Right. Right. Bring three pairs of cuffs. Extra small."

All three faces paled, their worried expressions weakening her steely resolve. She decided to leave the room before she caved.

Caleb spoke up before she walked out. "Hey, you're not gonna call my mom, are you?"

She didn't answer. Let them stew in the cesspool of their own making.

Quincy followed as she called Poetry. "Hey, I need a favor."

"Anything, boss."

"Are you okay revisiting your past?"

"Like a weekend visit type thing?"

Sun chuckled and explained her plan to the only deputy in the state who'd done time in the big house. He had enough tattoos under his uniform to be more than convincing.

Mrs. Baca walked up then. "How'd it go?"

"Is it wrong that I want to kidnap and keep them forever?"

"Yes. Very much so. But they're all yours for a bitcoin and a lifetime supply of Sugar Babies."

Sun gasped. "I love Sugar Babies." She thought back to her childhood longingly when she could eat a bag of Sugar Babies and not wake up four pounds heavier.

Quincy put a heavy hand on her shoulder to get her attention. It worked. She gaped up at him.

"Are you going to tell me what's going on with Wanda and explain why you didn't tell me before?"

"No," she said, slapping his hand away. "C'mon. We have a lot of phone calls to make."

# 18

*If the longest part of your morning routine is*
*summoning the will to live, we can help!*

—SIGN AT CAFFEINE-WAH

Auri saw a distinct drop-off of Chloe's social media presence after the prom incident. She didn't post anything for a few weeks, but she slowly came back online like a deer peeking from behind a tree. Her friends posted a lot after the *accident*, mostly asking for prayers for Chloe, but none of them seemed to know what really happened, either.

"She wouldn't tell you who attacked her?" Sybil asked, whispering behind her. They were back in Coach Love's, working at their desks on their laptops. In other words, filling time until the bell rang. This last week of school was more a formality than anything. It was the teachers who had the most work, grading tests and papers and getting everything entered.

"No, she's too afraid. Especially now, with that girl found in the canyon."

"Maybe we need to protect her. Like bodyguards."

As ridiculous as it sounded, Auri had almost suggested the same thing to Chloe. But them hanging out could do more harm than good. If whoever attacked her realized she was hanging with the sheriff's daughter, Auri could rain down all kinds of trouble on Chloe's head. Then again, that was apparently her thing.

"I wish we'd been here last year," Auri said. That was the problem with being the new kid.

She took out her phone and messaged Chastity to meet her in the bathroom in two.

Chastity messaged back with a thumbs-up.

"Okay, I'm going to ask Chastity. You keep looking."

"Oh, say hey for me."

Auri grinned. "Roger that."

The entire point of Auri's social media quest was not to find out who was in Chloe's pics, but to find out who was *not* in her pics after prom. After all, who would post photos of their attacker?

"What's up?" Chastity asked, her blond ringlets bouncing with each word.

"Thanks for meeting me. This is a what-happens-in scenario."

Chastity nodded, intrigue infusing her cheeks with a soft pink. "Right. Just to be clear, you mean what happens in . . . ?"

"This bathroom."

"Oh." Chastity snorted. "I knew that. What's up?"

Just to be safe, Auri decided to muddy the waters a bit. Chastity tended to blurt out things she shouldn't at the most inopportune time, but she knew everything about everyone in high school, even though she was a freshman, too. But she'd lived here her whole life. She could do a lot of historical referencing.

"I'm working on a . . . project"—she added a wink—"with my mom for a case she's working on."

Chastity shivered with anticipation.

"Do you know who took who to prom last year?"

Chloe could've gone with or without a date, and that date could've been from any grade, technically. Or any town.

"I do. I mean, I've seen all the pictures in yearbook."

"That's right. You're on the yearbook committee." This was perfect. "Okay, do you know who took Amelia Gray?"

"Pfft. Easy. Robert Olivas. Why? Did something happen?"

"What? Oh, no. She's looking into several different couples. What about—"

"Wait a minute," Chastity said, narrowing her lids to fine slits. "Is this about that girl they found and the fact that Chloe Farr was found last year after prom on the same road?"

Crap. She figured it out. "Kind of. I'm sorry."

"Why? It's all good. But what do all the other couples have to do with it?"

Maybe she didn't figure it all out after all. "My mom thinks someone may have seen something and they're scared to come forward."

"Wow. Okay, who else?"

"Auri named as many seniors as she could think of before getting to Chloe herself. Chastity knew every single one of them. Who took who. Who got into fights and ended up splitting after prom. Who got busted for booze. Who brought booze but didn't get busted. The whole shebang. But when it came to Chloe . . .

"I don't think Chloe actually made it to prom. I think she was in that accident on the way."

"Do you know who she was dating at the time?"

"No one that I know of. She was dating Marlin Insinger, but they broke up around Christmas the year before."

"So he wouldn't have been her date?"

"No, he went with April Apodaca."

"Chas, how do you remember all of this stuff?"

"Just blessed, I guess. Anyone else?"

"Wait a minute." Auri couldn't help but wonder if Chloe's *date* went to prom without her after she jumped out of his truck. Maybe to establish an alibi? "Chastity, do you think I could see all the pictures? Even the ones that didn't make it into the yearbook?"

"Sure. They're on the computers in yearbook class. I have it next, and we're just goofing off, if you can finagle your way in. You seem to be really good at that," she said with a cheeky grin.

Auri shrugged. "At least I'm good at something, I suppose."

"Okay, see you in a few if you make it."

"Thanks, Chas." She let Chastity leave first while she checked her phone. Her mom had texted a knock-knock joke, but before she could read it, a female voice jerked her out of her musings.

"What are you doing?"

Auri spun around to see Lynelle in the bathroom. "What are you doing? No one was in here."

"The door was open. Doesn't mean no one was in there."

She grimaced. "You go to the bathroom with the door open?"

"No. I was . . . hiding."

"From who?"

She stepped to the mirror and fluffed her long brown hair. "Mrs. Ontiveros is looking for me to make up my final, but I didn't get to study last night. My mom made me come to school anyway, so I'm pretending to be sick."

"Oh. How's Tim?"

She sneered at her. "What's it to you, freak?"

"Really?" Auri released a long sigh. "Is *freak* the best you got, 'cause it just doesn't bother me like you think it should."

Lynelle leaned in closer to her. "How about *bitch*?"

Despite the fact that she expected nothing less from Lynelle, her words still managed to sting. But Auri feigned otherwise. "Better," she said, nodding her approval. "Is he okay?"

"Why are you so worried about Tim?"

"Because he was beat to hell?" She let her intonation communicate the implied *duh*.

Lynelle shortened the distance between her face and the mirror to reapply her lip gloss. "He wasn't beaten up," she said, smacking her lips. "He was in a car accident."

"Ah. Is that what he told you?"

"As a matter of fact—"

"Because not many cars leave knuckle marks around the eye socket. Just saying."

Lynelle's lids rounded as Auri turned and strode out the door.

The bell rang and ten minutes later Auri had talked her way out of history and into yearbook with Chastity. After getting the okay from the teacher, the two of them sat at a computer and went through prom pics, which steadily got worse as the night wore on. Red eyes. Shiny faces. Random locks of hair falling out of hair clips.

In all honesty, Auri had no clue what she was looking for. Most of the guys there had graduated and moved on before Auri started. And those that she did recognize hardly screamed psycho criminal. Even if Chloe's attacker did show up, it wasn't like he would have any scratches on his face. Chloe said she jumped out. She never said he touched her or gave her the opportunity to injure him.

"Can you tell me which of the guys drives a truck?" she asked Chastity.

"Please." The girl laughed maniacally, making Auri laugh with her. "Who do you think you're talking to?"

Of course, she would know such a thing. Unfortunately, almost every guy in Del Sol with a vehicle drove a truck. Still, by the time she left, Auri had a list of truck connoisseurs from Del Sol High. At least she had a starting point.

Twenty minutes and thirty phone calls later, Zee and Salazar escorted the boy band into the station. Sun had needed their parents' permission to pull off a *Scared Straight!* scenario, but hopefully, this would reboot the little shits and put them on a better path.

She was a little surprised, frankly, that the parents had agreed to such strong tactics, but once they found out the kids were facing some pretty serious charges, they all signed on, for better or worse. They didn't need to know Sun had zero intention of charging them. Despite the seriousness of their crimes, a little TLC went a long way in these situations.

The deputies took the kids through the entire process. They searched and patted them down before booking them, complete with fingerprints and mug shots. Sun was worried the boys were going to be sick. Each of them had turned a putrid shade of green, all bravado vanishing completely.

What they didn't know was that two of their parents were in the control room with her, watching the whole thing on her computer. The third one, Caleb's mom, couldn't get off work to come down, but she gave not only her permission, but her blessing.

"I'm sorry," Duran's father said, leaning close to the monitor. "Is that a raccoon?" He pointed to the panel of the hallway between their tiny jail and the bullpen.

Quincy, who'd been in the control room, too, shot to attention and went to full battle stations. He ran out of the room, sprinting toward the back. Sun didn't know he could move that fast. She prayed the fluffball could move faster.

There were no cameras in the holding cells, but the parents could put a stop to the game at any point if they got nervous for their children. Sun knew she would be if this were Auri.

"All right, losers," Salazar said to the boys, and Sun had to hold back a giggle. "Line up. We're putting you in a holding cell for a few days until the judge gets back from vacation."

"A few days?" Caleb asked.

"She hasn't had a real vacation in years. I'm not calling her back early for the likes of you."

Leo paled. "Don't we get a phone call?"

"You get one. You can use the landline. Do you know the number?"

"N-no. It's in my phone and you took it."

Zee and Salazar feigned a look of utter disappointment.

"Sucks to be you," Zee said. "You have to know the number. Once we take your phone, we can't give it back."

"And what seven-year-old has a phone anyway? Get in there." Salazar opened the holding cell, and the detainee inside, who half lounged on the metal bench that served as a cot when there was a mattress, looked up at them from underneath his lashes. He'd gone all out. He wore a previously white tank that now looked to be splattered with blood. It showed off his plethora of tattoos. The jeans he wore had seen better days as well, and the steel-toed boots were weapons in and of themselves.

"Wait," Duran said, turning back to Salazar, "should he be in here?"

Salazar slammed the metal door shut and locked it. Then she turned and collapsed against it. Looking heavenward, she said to Zee, "We're going to hell."

Sun rubbed her mouth to hide her giggle, but Leo's mom burst out laughing. "This is better than reality TV."

Thrilled they were being such good sports about it, Sun walked over to her deputies and all three of them leaned close to the door to try to hear what was going on. Hearing nothing, Sun dared a peek inside the postage stamp window. She could see in the room, but the boys were too short. Which meant they were plastered against the door.

Rojas started to get up, eyeing them like they were mice and he was a panther. He shot her a warning glare and she ducked, feeling both guilty and tickled. It was an odd combination.

She looked over her shoulder just as Anita let Wanda in.

"What's going on?" Wanda asked as she hurried inside. She dropped her voice and asked, "Did you find the tin?"

"I did. Would you like to meet the criminal masterminds?"

"What?" she asked with a gasp. "Why would I want to meet them?"

"Wanda, they're children. I want to show them that their actions have consequences. Are you okay with that?"

She nodded, not certain at all.

Just as Sun gestured to Salazar to let them out, the boys started pounding on the door and yelling to be released. But what was more telling was the woman laughing from the control room. Sun wasn't sure if she should be grateful or horrified by Leo's mother.

Salazar opened the door and the boys rushed out, falling over each other and landing in a heap at her feet.

Rojas was standing there, legs slightly spread, face pure evil. Sun was almost convinced as well, but she figured he'd had to develop such a look when he was inside.

She stepped over to him as Salazar helped the kids up, and asked under her breath, "What did you say to them?"

He tried not to crack up when he answered, "Not a damned thing, boss. I hadn't even gotten to the good part yet. I just stared."

Sun almost doubled over. Poor kids. "Come on, boys." She took them into her office and sat them at her desk.

Like when they met earlier, Caleb was the first to speak. "That man was going to kill us. I'm not sure you're supposed to put kids in the same cell as hardened criminals."

"Really? Is that a law?"

They looked at each other and decided to just go with it by nodding hysterically.

"Oh, well we only have the one holding cell. The actual jail with the really hardened criminals is in the back, but if you'd prefer that—"

"No, it's okay," Duran said. "Can we just stay here?"

She looked at the booking information and glanced up at the one named Duran. "Your last name is Duran, too?"

He nodded.

"Did you know there's a band—"

"I know," he said, rolling his eyes.

"Well, kids, I thought you might like to meet the woman you robbed."

All three jaws went slack.

"You know, the house you broke into? Yeah, someone lived there, and now she no longer feels safe in her own home thanks to you three."

"We don't want to meet her," Leo said, a tremor in his voice.

"Why? So you won't feel guilty for what you put her through?"

He didn't respond. Instead, he dropped his gaze and his cheeks pinkened.

"Mrs. Stephanopoulos?"

Wanda walked in, almost as reluctant to meet them as they were to meet her.

"Please take my chair." Sun sat her in the chair behind her desk. "Is there anything you'd like to ask them?"

Wanda seemed paler than usual. She didn't speak for a moment, then finally looked up at them. And just like with Sun, her heart melted. Sun saw it the moment it happened. Wanda nodded and said meekly, "Why did you choose my house?"

They had yet to look up, preferring to peek at her every so often.

Finally, Duran said softly, "It was the only house on the block with no lights on outside and it was unlocked."

Visibly shaken, Wanda nodded, unsure of what else to say, and Sun wondered how much of her reaction was a show. That woman once fought off a rattlesnake to protect a baby owl. No way were these three wannabes scaring her this much.

"Boys, do you have anything you'd like to say to her?"

They looked up at last, but it was Caleb who took the lead. "We're sorry. We didn't mean to scare you."

"We won't do it again, either," Leo said. The others agreed. "Never. We've decided to give up on a life of crime and start our band for real instead. If," he said, ducking his head, "if we don't go to prison first."

"Well, that's up to Mrs. Stephanopoulos." She looked at Wanda, already knowing the answer. "Wanda, would you like to press charges?"

Their hopeful faces were silent pleas for leniency.

"Let these babies go, Sunny. They didn't mean any harm." There she was.

All three of the boys jumped up and hugged each other. Then they ran around Sun's desk and actually hugged Wanda.

Wanda laughed and kissed each one of them on the cheek. To their credit, only Caleb wiped the kiss off, but he waited until Wanda wasn't looking.

She motioned for Salazar to take them to their parents. If only all criminals came around so easily. Not that they'd keep their noses clean forever, but she figured they stood a pretty good chance, especially after Poetry got a hold of them.

They went with Salazar, and Wanda waited until they were out of earshot before saying, "I knew it. I'm always forgetting to lock my door. There was a time when I didn't need to."

"I know, hon. Unfortunately, that time has passed. I'm going to have Dad get you some security lights that work on a motion detector, and he'll change your lightbulbs to the kind that come on automatically at night. That way you just leave them on all the time. And I think we should get you a keyless entry that locks automatically every time you close it."

"Oh, that would be nice, Sunshine. But what about my tin?"

She took Wanda's things out of the filing cabinet and handed them to her. "I couldn't help but notice the paperwork."

She ducked her head. "You read them?"

"Just a glance. You don't have to tell me anything, but is the document you were worried about there?"

Wanda thumbed through the paperwork and pulled out the birth certificate. She held it to her breast. "It's here."

Sun pulled up a chair beside her. "Can you tell me why it's so important?"

She shook her head. "It's only important to me, Sunny." And in true Wanda fashion, she looked around the station and changed the subject. "Is Quincy running around here somewhere?"

"Actually, I think that's exactly what he's doing. He's chasing a raccoon."

"That's my boy," she said, slapping her knee.

As though on cue, Quincy ran into her office, out of breath and wheezing slightly. He grabbed hold of the doorframe to catch his breath, then said, "You have to see this."

Sun hurried after him to the hallway where they'd seen Randy. Pretty much the only hall in the building. He handed her a flashlight and told her to get on all fours.

"Quincy, I swear, if you're punking me . . ."

"What, no." He pointed. "Look."

"Fine." She sank all the way down onto her belly, looked in the vent he'd opened, and gasped. She looked back up at him and then back to Randy. "Raccoon babies!"

"It's Randi with an *i*," he said, his excitement infectious. He lay on his belly beside her as the other deputies filed in to see what had Quince so excited. The kids and their parents followed as well.

She looked at him again. "We're grandparents."

"And look." He pointed. "She dragged my shirt out of the trash can and used it for her kits."

"Can we see?" one of the boys asked.

"Of course." She scooted over and let the kids take turns looking at the kits. They oohed and aahed.

"There are five," Duran said, smiling and waving at Randi.

When she hissed, Sun came to her rescue. "I think we're making her nervous."

Duran scrambled back. "I think you're right."

"We need to get her some Raccoon Chow," Quincy said. "She has to keep up her strength if she's going to keep those kits healthy." He wiggled his fingers at her, and said in a high-pitched voice, "Hello, Randi."

"We'll leave you guys to it," Duran's father said. "We have a long talk we need to get to."

Salazar got up off the floor to show them out. She'd been waiting for a turn to visit the new mom and never got the chance.

"I'll show them out, Lieutenant. You say hi."

Salazar's face brightened. "Thanks, boss."

"Then it's my turn," Wanda said.

Quince was lucky she wasn't down there already, what with him being prone and all.

"Okay," Sun said to the boys. Mr. Duran was going to take all the kids back to school as Leo's mom had to get back to work. "What did we learn today?"

"A life of crime doesn't pay," Duran said.

"And that jail is scary," Leo added.

"And that I never want to be arrested again."

"Exactly, Caleb. Then it's been a good day."

"Also," Leo said, "is Auri dating anyone?"

"Out." She opened the security door and shooed them outside.

Sun's phone rang, and she sucked in a sharp breath the minute she saw who it was from. She answered anyway. "Oh, hey. I was just thinking about you."

Rojas's tone turned dubious. "Is someone going to let me out already?"

# 19

*Is "as fuck" your favorite unit of measurement?*
*Then you're in the right place.*

—SIGN AT THE ROADHOUSE

Two hours later, Sun sat at her computer going over the file on Misty Sandoval Chief Medina sent over, paying close attention to the girl's phone records. She'd been texting someone with a blocked number who claimed to be male, from Del Sol, and still in high school. But a catfish can say anything.

The texts turned hot fast. But in no message was his name ever mentioned. He simply went by HotJock. So, ew. And she went by MOW, Mist on Water.

Anita put a call from the chief through. "Hey, Chief," Sun said. "What do you think?"

"Interesting. Why Redding didn't follow up on this is beyond me." Though she had an inkling.

"We can't prove those texts came from a phone in Del Sol. We can't prove anything, really. Just that she was texting someone who claimed to be from there."

"True. What did you think of the Shiprock charm?"

"Sheriff, you would not believe the goose bumps I got when I saw that."

"That makes two of us. Could Misty's family identify it?"

"No, which is odd. I'm wondering if perhaps the man she was

meeting gave it to her, thinking she'd like it since she's from the area. If it was indeed her."

"That's a definite possibility. I have my guys trying to track it down. I'll let you know what we find."

"Thank you. Is there anything I can do?"

"Not at the moment. The dogs will be here tomorrow and I have a man watching the site until then. Did she know anyone from Del Sol? Do you have any idea how she met this guy?"

"I've interviewed everyone in her circle. No one has ever met anyone from Del Sol. Hell, half the kids had never even heard of it."

"That's not surprising," she said sheepishly.

"Sheriff, I feel like we're getting closer. I feel like this is finally coming to a head. The family just wants closure at this point."

"Here's hoping we can give that to them, Chief." Sun hung up and continued poring over Misty Sandoval's case file, looking for anything that stood out as unusual or noteworthy. She scoured her social media as well. Whoever this guy was, he was a ghost. No pictures of him. Not even a mention. Why would a girl drive four hours to meet a total stranger? They never exchanged pictures through texts, so they had to be talking somewhere else.

Quince came into her office bearing gifts. "Your mother brought tamales."

"Sweet." Sun set the paperwork aside and took a plate.

Quince sat across from her with his own. "So, why didn't you tell me about Wanda?"

"Because she asked me not to."

"Not to tell me specifically?"

"No, Quince," she said, trying to put his mind at ease. She thought about the birth certificate and how adamant Wanda was that it be kept secret.

It was none of her business. The case was over. The kids were brought to justice, so to speak. But that birth certificate was gnawing at her. It was from a hospital in Las Cruces. She eyed her computer. It would be so easy.

She set her tamales aside and pulled up the database, typing in the pertinent information. There were two hits. Two babies born in Las Cruces that day. A girl and a boy. The boy, Benjamin Jordy Watkins, was born to one Wanda Watkins at 3:34 a.m. The father was listed as a man named Anthony Barros. And that was that. What was the big secrecy?

"Whatcha doing?"

"Not digging into things I shouldn't be, if that's what you're implying."

"Sorry I asked. Whatcha digging into?"

"Nothing about Wanda." Sun re-created the first conversation she'd had with Wanda about the tin, and how important it was that no one from Del Sol find what was in it. But why? Why Del Sol?

"Can I help?"

"Nope."

"Are you sure? I'm pretty good with a shovel."

"Yeah," she said with a scoff. "Shoveling shit."

"Hey." When she spared him a sideways glance, he conceded. "Fine. But Wanda's okay, right?"

"That's what I'm trying to find out."

On a hunch, one that had gotten drunk somewhere between First and Main, Sun went into the DMV database and typed in the DOB of little Benjamin Watkins. Only one person in all of Del Sol was born on that day of that year and the name stunned her.

"What?" Quince asked. "If you're not going to share with the class, you have to stop."

"Dude," she said, gathering her things, "this town is like *Peyton Place* on crystal meth."

"I could've told you that. Where are we going?"

"You're not going anywhere. I'll be back in a bit," she said, grabbing her keys.

"I hate being left out of the loop!" he called after her.

Ten minutes later, Sun was sitting in Wanda's living room, and she had not exaggerated. It was like a tornado hit it. "How can you find anything?" she asked her.

Wanda chuckled. "It's all a strategy. When your house is a mess, people don't come over as often."

Sun laughed. "Is that my cue to leave?"

"Bite your tongue. You and that little ginger of yours are always welcome."

"Thanks, Wanda. So, I have to be honest with you."

"About?"

"I did a little digging."

Wanda stilled with her coffee cup halfway to her mouth. "Digging?"

"I saw the date on the birth certificate. You had to give a baby up for adoption, didn't you? His adoptive parents changed his name, of course, but his birth date gave it away."

She put her cup down and walked to the picture window overlooking her street.

Sun followed suit. "Wanda, I would never have brought this up if not for one salient thing."

"What's that?"

"I think you're the grandmother of a boy who desperately needs a family right now. Cruz is your biological grandson, isn't he?"

Wanda's shoulders shook instantly as she sobbed into her hands.

Sun put an arm around her. "I'm sorry, hon. I'm not here to upset you, I swear."

"No." She plucked a tissue out of a box nearby and dabbed at her eyes. "It's not your fault, Sunshine. I knew the minute that tin went missing I might have to deal with this at last."

"Deal with it? Wanda, why don't you want him to know?"

She turned to her in surprise. "Sunshine, that's not it. I would love for him to know. I would've loved for his father to know. I've wanted nothing more than to be a part of their lives for years, but I just couldn't work up the nerve to introduce myself. I mean, what would I have said to Chris? 'Oh, hey you. I'm the woman who abandoned you at birth.'"

"He would've loved to have met you."

"It's just not that easy. I moved to Del Sol to be near him and Cruz. And months went by, and then years, and I just watched them from afar. Afraid to introduce myself. After a while, I realized that I would have to explain why I didn't make contact sooner and all of the excuses just seemed so flimsy. I never learned sign language, for one. I tried. It just didn't come easily for me."

"It's not an easy language to learn, especially when you don't have someone to practice with every day." Sun led her back to the sofa and sat beside her.

"And, well, look at me, Sun. I'm a hot mess, and I just didn't think Chris would want that in his life. Or his son's."

"We're going to have to agree to disagree."

She pressed her mouth together with a sniff. "I'd become so comfortable watching them from afar, and then Chris died and my world fell apart." She sobbed into her tissue again. She had lost a son and no one knew. "It's not that I was terribly young, mind you. It's just, I didn't think I could take care of a baby and work and go to school, and my parents had kicked me out when they found out I was pregnant."

Sun rubbed her back. "Wanda, you don't have to explain a thing to me."

"No, I do. I need someone to understand." She took hold of Sun's hand, her frail fingers squeezing her tight. "They told me I could move back home if I gave him up. I felt so guilty for letting my parents push me like that. Funny thing was, I never moved back in with them. We hardly spoke again. But to find out that his adoptive parents surrendered him when they found out he was deaf? Oh, Sunshine, I didn't know he was deaf when he was born. I would never have let him go if I'd known they would give him up. When I found out he grew up in foster care . . . I've never been so devastated in my life." She sobbed uncontrollably for several minutes, and there was nothing Sun could do to ease her pain other than be there for her.

When she started to calm, Sun went to the kitchen to get her a glass of water.

"Thank you, hon," she said, sniffing into a fresh tissue. She took a drink, then drew in a shaky breath to regroup.

Sun gave her another couple of minutes, then asked, "Can I ask how you found them?"

She offered her a sad smile. "It was a bit of an accident, actually. I had a friend who worked for child services. I asked her to find out who'd adopted my son, only to find out the answer to that was no one." Wanda looked at her, a fresh set of tears streaming down her face, the supply seemingly endless. "And now I can never tell him how sorry I am."

Sun drew her closer. "Wanda, there is still a boy out there who would love to meet you."

"No." She stood again and started clearing the cups. "I can't. He'll hate me for not coming forward sooner."

"I'm positive you're wrong. I want you to think about it, okay? Either way, I will not bring this up again. This is your decision and I will respect it."

She nodded, but Sun could tell her mind was made up. She could only hope Wanda would come around. Cruz could really use someone like her in his life right now.

She left Wanda's house and went straight to Doug's crumbling abode. He lived in an ancient RV behind his sister's house, mooching off her water and electricity. She knocked on his door and waited. If she hadn't heard him shuffling around, she would've left.

"I want the story," she said when he opened the door.

He frowned, his Coke-bottle glasses so smudged she wondered how he ever saw a thing. "I told you, I was attacked."

"By a boy band?"

He disappeared inside the RV, holding on to the bandages at his neck and clearly expecting her to follow. She did. Even he wouldn't be stupid enough to flash the county sheriff. She hoped.

"No," he said, his tone that of a petulant child. "They were tall. Really tall. Tall enough to stab me—"

"Save it, Doug." She stepped inside and wrinkled her nose before realizing it wasn't as bad as she'd imagined. It could use a sane person's touch, but the outdated interior was clean and well taken care of. "I know what happened."

Guilt flashed across his face, and he turned his back to her. She'd been so focused on his bandages she'd missed the fact that he was wearing a shirt. An actual shirt. She'd never seen him with a shirt on, even in the middle of winter. He only wore his trench coat come rain or shine.

"Those kids confronted you, and you pulled a knitting needle on them."

"Confronted?" He spun back around. "They attacked me."

She held up a palm to appease him. "One of them kicked you on the shin. I get that. But you did flash his mother. And you fell on the knitting needle after trying to convince them you had a knife."

"That's not how I remember it."

"Filing a false police report is serious, Doug." He didn't reply, so she continued. "I just need to know if someone really did try to stab you with that knitting needle." If Mrs. Fairborn had hunted him down to cause him bodily harm, Sun might need to talk to the elderly woman.

"Someone did try to stab me but I wrestled the needle away from her."

Mrs. Fairborn. "Was it a certain firecracker we all know and love?"

He lifted a shoulder. "I don't know about love, and I wouldn't call her a firecracker. More like a nuclear bomb. You should know."

"Why should I know?"

He hit her with a face that explained why some species eat their young. "Because, Sheriff, she's *your* daughter."

# 20

*Waking up is never easy, but just remember:*
*the world can't revolve around you unless you get out of bed.*
—JOURNAL ENTRY: AURORA VICRAM

Auri lay on her bed, combing through every picture Chloe Farr ever posted. Cruz had been helping her, but Quincy picked him up early. Suspish? Yes. But only because five minutes later her mom called telling her she was bringing pizza and a guest and they needed to talk.

"If this is about the 'worthless' comment, you don't have to worry. You were right. I looked it up. My organs are worth a fortune."

"It's not about that. I'll be home in a bit."

Ruh-roh. A guest. Who could the guest be? She wracked her brain, coming up with all kinds of scenarios. Foreign exchange student. The butler she'd been begging for. The president of the local chess club. Her mind swam with all the possibilities as she scrolled through photos looking for one thing: who had been banished from Chloe's social media after prom.

She went back and forth through Chloe's timeline, studying the before-and-afters, but no one popped out at her. First off, Chloe didn't post that often, which made it difficult to detect who'd magically disappeared. Second, after prom, she posted even more rarely. Then something caught her attention.

A memory she'd posted about a month back from a cookout at her parents' house. She'd captioned it *Happier Times*. It was a pic of her throwing the peace sign at the camera, not realizing a water balloon was rocketing toward the back of her head. The photographer had perfectly captured the initial burst of the balloon, the exploding water creating a halo around her like an angel. Chloe hadn't even reacted to it yet, her expression completely oblivious, which was what made the pic so funny. But it had been cropped. Auri remembered seeing kids in the background, splashing in one of those blow-up kiddie pools in the original.

She saved the pic to her desktop, then scrolled back through Chloe's old photos to find the original post, but before she got too far, she heard the front door open. She bounced off the bed to greet her mom and was instead greeted by Levi Ravinder.

"Levi!" she shouted, running into his open arms. "Are you the mystery guest?"

"Afraid so." He squeezed her to him. "Are you disappointed?"

She leaned back to look up at his handsome face, scruffy and only a little bruised from the ordeal a few days earlier. "No way. I mean, I was kind of hoping Mom had finally hired a butler, but you'll do."

He laughed softly and hugged her again. Auri sank into his warmth. He smelled like expensive men's cologne—and cinnamon candy, for some reason.

"Hey, Levi," her grandma said when Auri finally let him go. She gave him a quick hug and kiss on the cheek.

Her grandpa just shook his hand. It was the manly thing to do.

"I beat your mom here, I take it?" he asked, sitting at the snack bar when her grandma offered him coffee.

"You did." Auri hopped up on the stool beside him, hoping beyond hope Levi and her mom were finally going to hook up for good. There was only so much pining a girl could do before she lost hope entirely, and her mom had been pining a really really *really* long time. Not that Auri could blame her. Levi's eyes sparkled with humor and warmth every time he looked at Auri. She could only imagine how he looked at her mom. And what it did to her.

"How's every little thing?" her grandma asked him as she put down a cup of coffee.

He lifted a shoulder. "Same old."

"I'll take a cup, too," she said to her grandma.

"Firstly, no. And secondly, you can get it yourself."

"See?" she said to Levi, getting up to pour herself a glass of juice. "We totally need a butler. The staff around here is dismal."

He laughed at her, the sound making her smile from the inside out.

"When is your last day of school?" he asked.

Both of her grandparents chuckled at that.

"Not that she's mentioned it every day for the last month," her grandpa said, "but it's tomorrow."

"Oh, wow. One more day."

"Yeah. And it's an all-day field trip."

"To the strip clubs in Albuquerque?"

"Levi," her grandma admonished.

"Nothing nearly that fun. Or illegal. It's to the petroglyphs."

"Nice. They're a bit of a hike, but worth every step."

"I'm sure. I'm just excited it's the last day."

"I'm excited for you, Red."

She squelched a sigh, reveling in the nickname he gave her when she was seven.

The front door opened again and her mom walked in.

"Hey, Mom."

"Hey, bug. Mom. Dad. Levi."

"Sunshine," he said from behind his cup.

Was it just Auri or did her mom seem nervous? "Is everything okay?"

She put two boxes of pizza down. "Super."

"Really? I thought we were cutting back on pizza."

"I know. It just seemed easier for tonight."

Auri grabbed a slice as her grandma handed her a plate. She did the same for Levi and her mom.

"Levi and I would like to talk to you about something, bug."

Her stomach flip-flopped, hope, dreams, and a little bit of anxiety making her suddenly too full to eat. She nodded and waited for whatever they had to say.

"Before we do, though," her mother said, and something in her tone made Auri do a double take, "did you try to stab Doug with a knitting needle?"

Her stomach flip-flopped again, only this time it landed on a pile of sharp rocks, the jagged edges cutting into the lining. "What?" she asked, adding a soft giggle for effect. "No. I would never . . ." When her mother's expression flatlined, she clenched her jaw and rolled her eyes so far back into her head she strained a muscle. "He ratted me out?" She jumped off the stool and started pacing. "Is there no honor left in this one-horse town?"

"Aurora," Sun said, appalled, "you told me he'd never flashed you."

"He hasn't. Not, you know, directly."

"You lied to me."

Auri stopped pacing long enough to cast her mom a questioning frown.

"You told me he's always been nice to you."

"He is." She started pacing again. "Or he was until he ratted me out."

"Auri," she said from between gritted teeth.

"Mom, he wasn't flashing me. He was flashing Mrs. Fairborn. I was just an innocent bystander. I walked up to tell her something and then suddenly it was just . . . out." She made a face at the thought. "Dangling there all . . . exposed and dangly."

"Oh, my god, I am going to kill that man."

"Exactly. I couldn't tell you. Mrs. Fairborn brought out her knitting needle to scare him away but when I came up behind her, I scared her and she dropped it, so I picked it up and waved it at

Doug like a sword so Mrs. Fairborn could get away. She was just trying to protect herself."

"I'm not so sure about that, bug. Then what happened?"

"Mom, I didn't stab him. I swear. I waved it at him and told him to back off, but he grabbed my wrist."

Her mother froze. Worse, Levi froze. He went completely still, his face becoming completely impassive, reminding Auri of the calm before the storm, and she stumbled on her next words. "It wasn't like that."

"Did he hurt you?" her mother asked.

"No. He just grabbed the knitting needle out of my hand and took off. But I knew if you knew that I knew what his man part looked like, you'd arrest him."

"Yes. That is precisely my job."

"In a way, I guess."

"In every way, Auri. You should have told me the moment you learned what happened to Doug."

"I'm sorry. Did you figure out who stabbed him?"

"He did. He lost his balance and fell on it."

"For real? Well, he's not off balance because of his you-know-what. Seriously, Mom. He doesn't have a lot going on down there."

"Auri!" her grandma shouted.

She cringed. "I'm just trying to be honest."

"Levi?" Her grandpa spoke softly to him, as though trying to calm an angry animal. "Sunny will handle this."

Levi cast her mom a glare from underneath his lashes, and Auri realized her mistake. "Levi, it's really okay. I wasn't hurt at all. He's perfectly harmless most of the time."

"That's where you're wrong, Red," he said, turning a softer expression on her. "This should have been dealt with years ago."

"And I'll do the dealing, Levi." Her mom's tone was the one Auri never dared argue with.

Apparently, Levi didn't get that memo. "You have a week."

She stepped closer. "Don't give me ultimatums."

He stood, the snack bar between them suddenly not distance enough. "Don't make me."

"Oh, my god." Auri tossed her hands into the air in helpless frustration. "Are you guys hooking up or what?"

Four gazes shot to her like they'd been fired from a cannon.

"Why else are we having this chat? Not that we'll ever get to it, talking about knitting needles and flashers and Doug's penis." She grabbed her pizza and started toward the living room. "I'm going to eat in here. You can join me when you guys are ready to talk about something that is actually important to the parties present."

"Mom, Dad," her mom said, "can you give us a little time?"

Wow, her mom was dismissing her grandparents. This must be really important. This must be— She gasped when it hit her. They were getting married! They were getting married and Auri was going to be a bridesmaid. She wondered what her mother's colors would be.

*Please pick pink.*

*Please pick pink.*

*Please pick pink.*

"Oh, look at the time," her grandmother said. "We were supposed to go to Wanda's for coffee." She grabbed her husband's hand.

"What?" he said, disappointment setting in. "This is just getting good."

Her grandma grabbed her purse and dragged the man she loved most in the world to the door. "We'll be back in, say, an hour?"

Her mom nodded furtively.

"No," her grandpa protested. "I'm going to miss my show."

"Honey, everything is streaming now. There's no such thing."

"Right, I forgot we aren't in the Stone Age anymore."

When the door closed, the butterflies in Auri's stomach exploded to astronomical proportions. This was it. This was actually it. She tried to slow her racing heart.

"Are you ready?" her mom said softly to Levi.

He nodded. "I am. But, seriously, you have a week."

A soft grin lifted one corner of her mom's mouth. She was so pretty and Auri believed she honestly didn't know. "Levi Ravinder, don't tell me how to do my job."

"Do it and I won't have to."

"You're pushing it."

"Yeah?" They both leaned over the bar until their mouths were a hairsbreadth apart.

"This is getting gross," Auri said from the living room.

They broke apart and walked into the living room hand in hand. It took Auri's breath away. Her mom had been so in love with this man for so many years. To see it finally come to fruition . . .

They took the sofa across from the chair she was sitting in. She'd been pretending to scroll through her phone, taking bites when she got to something she wanted to stop and read.

"Auri," her mom said, her voice shaky, "there's something Levi and I would like to share with you."

Suddenly exuberant, she put her phone and her pizza on the coffee table, leaned onto her elbows, and gave them her full attention.

"First, we want you to know how very much we love you."

"Okay," she said, growing wary. Her mom seemed way more nervous about this than she should be. "I love you, too?"

"Good. Right." She looked at Levi, then back to Auri. "So, knowing how very much we love you—"

"Oh, my god, are you guys sending me off to boarding school so you can start a new family without lugging all this baggage around?"

"No, Auri, it's just—"

"I need to say this," Levi said, interrupting her. He took her hand and squeezed it. "It should be me. I'm the one who's known all this time."

"Guys," she said, blinking in rapid succession. "You're kind of scaring me."

"I'm sorry, Red." He dropped his gaze for a moment before looking at her again. "Auri, I'm your father. Your biological father."

She snorted. "Is this a *Star Wars* thing?" she asked before his words sank in. She scooted back on the sofa, warily putting a few more inches between them. "Did you . . . did you abduct my mom?"

"What?" He sprang forward and sat next to her. "No, Auri. That's not what this is." He looked at her mom helplessly. "I'm screwing this up."

"You're doing fine." Her mom sat on Auri's other side, boxing her in. She squeezed into a ball, wondering where they were going with this. "Auri, you know how you found out when you were seven that . . . well, that I got pregnant with you during my abduction?"

"Yes." She pulled her knees to her chest, growing more uncomfortable by the second.

"And do you remember how I lost my memory? How I couldn't recall anything that happened for about a month beforehand?"

She nodded.

"It turns out that, about a week before the abduction, Levi and I had . . ." She stopped to search for the right words and Auri's jaw fell open.

"You *did it*?"

A startled cough burst from her mother and she choked on air for a solid minute before responding. After recovering, she drew in a deep breath and said, "For lack of a better phrase, yes, we did." When Auri only stared, she added, "In his truck. It was raining."

"And we're getting married," Levi tossed in, clearly hoping that would help.

Auri gaped at her mother. "What was all that talk about the devil's doorbell and the sin cave?"

"The sin cave?" Levi asked, eyeing her mom.

"Auri, I was seventeen. You're twelve."

"I'm fifteen, Mom."

"Really? When did that happen?"

"Wait." She thought back then refocused on Levi. "You said you've known the longest. How . . . how long have you known?"

Regret washed over him. She could see it in every line on his face. The set of his shoulders. The intensity of his gaze. "I figured it out pretty soon after we first met. I didn't know at the time that your mom had lost a month's worth of memories, Red. I just figured she didn't want to have anything to do with me after what Kubrick did, and I didn't want to force my way into your lives. You have to realize, Auri, I thought for a long time she really met and married a man named Samson Vicram. I had no clue it was a cover-up to keep her kidnapper from realizing you may have been his. Your grandparents had the best intentions when coming up with all of that, not knowing that the abductor was already dead. They were just trying to keep you safe, but they had the whole town fooled. Well, most of it. Including me. I had no idea until . . ."

"Until?" she asked, hanging on his every word.

"Until I met you on the cliffs at Del Sol Lake."

Her lids rounded at the memory. "Oh. What gave it away? That I was yours?"

He leaned forward and took her chin in his fingers. "For one, the red hair."

She nodded. "And two?"

"Look into my eyes. Namely this one. It has more." He pointed to his left eye, the one that was still bruised and bloodshot, but she saw it.

She lay a palm on his cheek. "Your irises have tiny green freckles like mine do."

He smiled down at her.

"That's how you figured it out?" she asked.

"That put me on the path. But we need to talk about what's going to happen later."

"We do?"

He nodded. "Later you're going to start thinking much more analytically about all of this."

"I am?"

"And you're going to wonder, despite everything I've just said, why I didn't tell you. Why I didn't become a part of your life sooner."

She dropped her gaze to study her cuticles, but he lifted her chin again, ever so gently.

"I just want you to know, I'm going to do everything in my power to make up for all the time we missed. All three of us." He offered her an apprehensive smile. "And I would be honored, Aurora, if you would consider taking my name."

She sucked in a sharp breath at the exact moment her mom did.

"Don't answer now." He looked at her mom. "Either of you. Take some time to think about it. I don't want to force my way into your lives if you're not ready. When the time comes—"

Auri threw her arms around his neck and hugged the man she'd loved for so long. A thought hit her, and she leaned back to ask, "Do Grandma and Grandpa know?"

"Not yet, bug."

"How do you think they'll take it?"

She didn't miss the exchange of worried glances between her parents.

Parents!

She had parents. Two. Two humans who loved her unconditionally. And one of them clearly felt guilty about his lack of presence in her life. Oh, yeah. She could work this to her advantage on a daily basis.

"I'm sorry, can we back up?"

"Of course, bug."

"Did you say you're getting married?"

Sun beamed at her. "I proposed."

"I proposed first."

"And he said we can't become engaged because we're already engaged and have been for almost sixteen years."

Auri clasped her hands together. "This is so romantic. What are your colors going to be?"

Her mom laughed. "I haven't thought quite that far ahead."

"Please pick pink. Please pick pink."

"I don't know." She narrowed her eyes on Auri. Tugged on a strand of hair. "What about apricot? You look amazing in apricot."

"But, Mom, you look amazing in pink."

She frowned. "I do?" When Auri nodded, she said, "You've never told me that."

Auri gasped as another thought came to mind. "What was playing on the radio?"

"What?"

"When you guys were doing it. What was on the radio?" She clasped her hands together and begged. "Please tell me it was Barry White."

Her mom rubbed her brow, and whispered admonishingly, "Auri."

"Whatever it was, that should be your song. You have to play it at the wedding."

"I don't remember," Levi admitted.

"I do." Her mom seemed embarrassed by that fact. "Or at least the group. It was Lifehouse."

Auri sucked in an audible gasp. "You used to play Lifehouse all the time, Mom! Maybe a part of you remembered."

Her mom shook her head and tucked the strand of hair behind her ear. "Your mind is amazing, bug."

Her heart swelled to three times its normal size as she looked between the two most important people in her life. "Thanks," she said, fighting a telltale sting in the backs of her eyes. "I get it from my parents."

# 21

*I'm the type of person whose sense of humor could be*
*described as inappropriate with a chance of ruining family*
*dinner.*

—JOURNAL ENTRY: AURORA VICRAM

Sun and Levi answered Auri's questions for well over an hour as they waited for her grandparents to get home. She asked everything from the first time they met to what went through Sun's mind when the memories started coming back.

They were sitting on the sofa, Auri in the middle with her head on Sun's shoulder as she asked yet another question. Levi got up to use the bathroom, so Sun took the opportunity to do a wellness check.

"Are you okay with all of this, bug? Really?"

Auri nodded like a bobblehead on a dashboard, but added, "Do you think that's weird? I mean, should I be mad at him for not telling us sooner?"

"Hon, no one can tell you what you should and should not feel. Feelings are intrinsically our own."

"Are you mad at him?"

"Quite often," she said with a grin. "But today? No, I'm not."

"Okay, good. Me neither. But I do have one favor to ask."'

"Anything," Levi said, sitting beside them again.

"Can we keep this to ourselves for a while?"

A look of surprise flashed across Levi's face, but he hid it quickly. "Of course. You take all the time you need."

"No." She sat up to face him. "It's not that. It's just, Cruz lost his dad and I just got one and somehow none of this seems fair."

"It's not, bug. What happened to Cruz will never be fair."

"Do you think it's okay to tell him?"

"If Cruz is the man I think he is," Levi said, "he'll be thrilled for you."

She sank back into her mother's arms. "I hope so."

When the front door opened, Sun drew in a deep breath and whispered to Levi, "You know we're going to have to repeat everything all over again."

"I'm good with that. As long as your dad doesn't shoot me."

"We should hide his guns. Just in case."

"Agreed."

She looked at Auri, then back at him. "Are we ready?"

"No," he said, making Auri giggle.

Sun winced. "Me neither. Here goes nothing."

They stood together as her parents walked in, her mother chittering about a candy dish Wanda had. She hung up her purse and walked to the kitchen. "Okay to come in?"

"Yes," Sun said, waving them forward and gesturing toward the small kitchen table. "Mom, Dad, can you guys sit down a minute?"

"Oh," her mom said, tossing a grin over her shoulder at her father. "This must be serious."

"It is," Auri said, bouncing from one foot to another.

Sun didn't miss the fact that Levi took Auri's hand into his. She squeezed it to her chest as they waited for the Freyrs to settle, and the look he gave her held so much love Sun thought her heart would burst. Or possibly a blood vessel in her brain. It would be just like her to have an aneurysm when she was so close to having everything she'd dreamed of since puberty.

They gathered around the table, Auri taking the seat between Levi and her grandmother while Sun took the one separating him from her father, disappointed they didn't have time to round up the firearms in the house. For now, she'd be the buffer between the two. She could be buff when she needed to be.

"Well?" her mother asked, rubbing her hands together.

"Levi's going to be my dad!" Auri shouted, unable to contain herself any longer.

Sun's lungs turned to concrete and she and Levi sat stock still, waiting for their reaction.

Her mom covered her mouth with both hands and looked between them. Her dad waited for more intel before making a decision.

"Are you two getting married?" her mom asked, hope glittering in her eyes.

"Yes!" Auri shouted again, and that time Levi chuckled.

The bubbling enigma known as Elaine Freyr jumped up to hug them, but Sun formed a T with her hands, signaling a timeout.

Her mom put on a pretty pout and sat back down. "Isn't this a good thing?"

"Yes, Mom, it is, but there's a little more to the story."

"Ah. Well"—she checked with her sidekick—"we're all ears."

Her dad nodded, though he seemed a bit more concerned.

Levi took the lead before Auri could say anything else. "Mr. and Mrs. Freyr, I'm actually Auri's biological father."

Her mom blinked at them like the lightbulb was on but no one was home.

"I have been her whole life," he added, as though unsure about what else to say.

Her mom looked between them, her gaze bouncing back and forth several times. "You were right," she said to her husband. "They didn't know."

"Looks like," he said.

Sun hated gaping. It was so unladylike, but no one had ever, not once in her entire life, accused her of being a lady. "You mean, you've suspected all this time?"

"Frankly, darling, we thought you did, too."

"No, Mother, I did not."

Levi looked at them, his expression as horrified as Sun's. "Did you . . . did you think I abducted her?" he asked, almost unable to get the words out.

"What?" It was her mother's turn to be horrified. "No, Levi. Honey, look at the hospital surveillance tape. It's clearly a young man. A man who loves the girl he's brought in."

"We've known for years you were the one who saved her, son," her dad said. "It just took us a few more to figure out the father part, but it became clear to us around Auri's ninth birthday."

"What happened on my ninth birthday?"

"Auri got a moped," her mother said.

"A moped nobody in the entire town fessed up to getting her," her dad added.

Auri looked at Levi. "That was you? All those anonymous presents?"

"Guys," Sun said, everything clicking into place, "I always thought it was you getting her those things, and you didn't want me to force you to take them back, so you denied getting them."

They both shook their heads.

"If I had known, I would've investigated."

"Which is exactly what we did," her mother said. "Once it became clear Auri had a secret admirer, we did a little investigating of our own."

Levi scowled. "Roe Farkas at the sporting goods store sold me out, didn't he?"

"Like a two-dollar whore," her dad said.

"Dad!" Sun chastised him with her best glare, but Auri was too busy beaming at . . . at her father to notice. Her father. The concept was going to take a while for Sun to wrap her head around completely. But for now, she unleashed her admonishment on Levi. "You got a nine-year-old a moped?"

"And that's why I didn't tell you," he said, lying through his teeth. "She wanted a dirt bike. I figured this was safer."

"Oh, good thinking. Wait, how did you know what she wanted?"

"I asked her."

"You did?" Auri asked.

"When we went for ice cream that summer you fell off your bike."

"Oh, yeah. My knee was bleeding and you cleaned it up and bought me ice cream."

Sun crossed her arms. "Do you tell your secrets to any strange man who buys you ice cream?"

"Duh. Ice cream."

She shook her head and turned to her mom. "Why didn't you guys tell me? Why would you keep this from me all these years?"

"First off," her mother said, "it took us a while to figure out why some strange man was buying our granddaughter gifts."

"But once it clicked into place, everything made sense." Her dad gave Levi a sympathetic nod. "Even Kubrick. We realized later he'd disappeared—a fact few people knew—and we figured Levi may have had something to do with that."

"Wait," Auri said, surprised. "You saved my mom from him?"

"Barely. It almost ended badly for all of us."

She leaned into him and he wrapped his arms around her, kissing her softly on the head.

"Second," her mom continued after taking a moment to enjoy the scene, "you weren't ready."

That got Sun's attention. "What do you mean I wasn't ready?"

"You weren't . . . here. You were still running and we worried that telling you would send you even farther away from us. Farther away from Levi. We wanted you to figure it out on your own."

"But I didn't," she said, her voice cracking.

Her mom patted her hand. "It took you a little while, but you got there in the end."

"With a lot of help," she argued.

"We all need help sometimes, Sunshine."

Sun sat stunned.

After staying up far too late, Sun insisted Auri go to bed. She stayed with her grandparents so Sun and Levi could have some quality time.

And boy was it. Sun lay in Levi's arms, soaking in the warmth wafting off him, and played with his hands.

"Do you read palms now?" he asked as she ran two fingers along his lifeline.

"I wish I were that intuitive."

"You are. It's what makes you a good investigator."

"Yeah. Then how did I miss all of this for so long?"

"Because all the good was wrapped up with all the bad and your mind couldn't separate it. It's hardly your fault. Even the most intuitive people can't see their own destinies. It's a forest-for-the-trees thing."

She propped her head up on an elbow and ran those same fingers over the outline of his full mouth. The sculpted one that had filled many of her deepest, darkest fantasies. "You're much deeper than you appear."

"Thanks?"

She laughed softly and looked over at the nightstand. "You didn't drink your wine."

He followed her gaze, then turned back. "Yeah, I don't drink."

"Since when?"

"For some time now."

She narrowed her gaze. "When you say you don't drink, you mean, other than for work?"

He shook his head. "Not even then."

"But you own a distillery. Your family owns a bar."

"So, surely I drink the inventory?"

"Well, no. But the distillery?"

"That's where my cousin Joshua comes in. You'd never know it by looking at him, but that man has a very sophisticated palate."

"I never thought I'd hear his name and sophisticated anything in the same sentence."

"I rinse."

"You don't swallow?"

"I'm going to pretend you didn't ask me that."

She reached over him and took his glass of wine. "I don't want to interfere with your sobriety."

He took it out of her hands and drank it down in one gulp. "It's not about sobriety. There was just never anyone else I wanted to share a drink with."

"Else?"

"If you'll remember, we almost hooked up at the lake when you were a freshman."

"How could I forget that? You were drunk on your family's moonshine and you kissed me."

"I wasn't that drunk."

She smiled. "You're saying you wanted to kiss me?"

"I wanted to do a lot more than that."

"It wasn't just the booze talking?"

"Booze rarely talks, and when it does, it has nothing interesting to say."

"Rather like televangelists."

"Rather like."

She fell asleep in his arms, her mind swimming in all the unanswered questions and uncertainties they still faced. The logistics of their situation. The complications. How all of this would affect Auri.

Fortunately, they had all summer to figure it out. They might have to actually do that camping thing for some alone time with her . . . *their* daughter.

But he was hers. And that was enough.

She slept approximately twelve seconds before waking up to the call of nature. She lay curled up with an arm wrapped around her. Levi's mouth rested at her ear, his deep breaths fanning across her cheek. She hated to disturb him, but as her mother would say, when you gotta go, you gotta go.

She untangled their limbs and slid under his arms. He protested and pulled her back against him, so she waited until his breathing was even and tried again. Huzzah.

As a career law enforcement officer, when Sun walked to the bathroom wearing a Three Doors Down T-shirt and nothing else, she really should have noticed the man sitting in her living room. More to the point, she should have noticed the man standing in her kitchen holding a gun.

# 22

*If she said she missed you and
normally that would be good
but she's reloading, take cover immediately.*

—PRO TIP FROM DEL SOL SPORTING GOODS

"Dad?" she said, forgetting she had nothing on below her T-shirt. Fortunately, it was long enough to disguise that fact. She opened the refrigerator door and bathed him in light. "Whatcha doin'?"

He stood lounging against her sink, arms crossed, 9 mm at the ready. He gestured toward her living room with a nod.

Her catlike reflexes kicking in—as they were wont to do—she spun around and saw yet another man sitting in her living room. Same chair. Different guy. This intruder was blonder than the one she'd had the night before.

She stepped around the island to glare at the escaped convict who'd invaded her sanctum sanctorum. Levi's uncle Wynn sat staring at her, a charming grin lifting one corner of his mouth. It was odd how he looked nothing like his nephew, but he was just as handsome in a hardened criminal, shot caller kind of way. He wore plain clothes—a T-shirt and jeans—and had a baseball cap resting on one knee. Part of his brilliant disguise, she was sure.

"What is it with you Ravinder men? Do any of you just knock?"

"I would have," he said, raising an unapologetic brow, "but

you and my nephew looked pretty chummy. I thought I'd give you guys some time to catch up."

"So you just let yourself in?"

"I could hardly hang around outside. Not with half the cops in the state looking for me."

"Yeah." She crossed her arms over her chest. "Thanks for that. The US marshal assigned to the case is about ninety percent certain I helped, since I was at the hospital when it happened."

"I saw you. In my defense, I had no idea you'd be there."

"Who was your accomplice?"

"Come on, apple blossom. You know I can't answer that."

She turned on a lamp and gave him a once-over. "You've looked better."

"I've felt better. But you look amazing."

"I'm not wearing pants," she said the second it hit her.

"You won't hear me complaining."

"Excuse me." Not wanting to bring Levi into it just yet, she hurried to the bathroom and threw on her robe which, unfortunately, wasn't one of those thick things that hide body parts. It was a shiny, silky thing that did anything but hide her girl parts, but at least it was something.

He seemed mildly disappointed when she came out wearing it, so clearly it was doing its job.

"Dad, you want to sit down?"

"I'm fine, pumpkin."

She figured as much. He could keep a better eye on the intruder from his current position.

She sat on the sofa catty-cornered across from him. "What are you doing here?"

"We need to coordinate our efforts."

"What efforts?"

"I told you when you came to see me, I needed two weeks to see to Clay."

That was something she had yet to tell Levi. She checked her room. The door was still closed. "You said you needed two weeks to get the evidence to bring him down. Not that you were going to escape from prison."

"Yeah, well, that wasn't going as well as I'd hoped, so I improvised."

"By purposely inducing a heart attack?"

He confirmed by lifting a shoulder.

"Wynn, I have to take you in."

"Sorry, apple. No can do."

"Then why are you here?"

"I told you, we need to coordinate our efforts. And I knew you'd never let me see her."

Sun froze, doing everything in her power to show no reaction.

"The girl," he added in case she didn't understand.

She most definitely understood. "You can't see her."

He pressed his mouth together. "We had a deal."

"That was before you became an escaped convict."

"So you would've brought her to the prison to see me like we agreed?"

After drawing in a deep breath, she answered honestly. "No. I wouldn't have."

"There you go. Not that I can blame you, apple. Maybe when she's older?"

"Maybe. Wynn, I have to ask again, why would you risk an arrest to come here?"

"I have new infor—" He stopped mid-sentence, and Sun followed his gaze to Levi standing at the bedroom door.

He stood barefoot with a half-fastened pair of jeans and a smirk stolen from an archangel. He walked over to Wynn as the escaped convict struggled to his feet, and Sun realized Wynn was in much worse shape than she'd imagined. He straightened and put a hand on the side of Levi's face, taking in every aspect of him, his gaze as loving as a father's.

Sun understood. She did the same thing quite often.

"You've grown up," he said.

"I've gotten old."

Wynn laughed softly. "You were born old. I could see it in your eyes, that old soul you kept safe no matter how hard your dad tried to beat it out of you."

Sun stifled her surprise at his words, struggling to keep her poker face intact. Not that she would put child abuse past Levi's father, but to say it out loud made it more real. More palpable.

Levi let his gaze slide to her dad, who lounged against her sink like he hadn't a care in the world. "Cyrus," he said warily.

Her dad nodded. "Levi."

"So, what's going on?"

Sun decided to explain the ridiculous situation she found herself in. "Your uncle thought it would be a good idea to come for a visit in the middle of his manhunt, because no law enforcement agent in the world would think to look for relatives who might harbor a fugitive."

"No, I meant why are you in a robe?"

"Oh." She tugged the lapels together. "It was either this or a towel."

Wynn laughed and pulled Levi into a bear hug complete with a couple of slaps on the back. When he set his nephew at arm's length, he said, "I take it you two have finally worked out your issues?"

Levi laughed. "We're getting there. But you didn't risk a stopover to see how my love life was faring."

"I didn't. I can't say how I got this information, but whatever Clay is doing, he's doing it soon. And if I had to take an educated guess, his plan is to kill you."

"That's what we thought all along," Sun said. "So why now? Why the hurry?"

"Because Clay suspects he had something to do with Kubrick's death."

"Why should he care?" she asked with a scoff. "It wasn't like Clay and Kubrick were besties."

"No, but family is family. He sees it as his responsibility to retaliate."

"Fine. But again, why now?" Sun asked.

"Because today would have been Kubrick's birthday. From my understanding, he wants to make a big show of it. Let the higher-ups know he can take care of business and make them money in the process."

Sun swept a wary gaze over him. "Wynn, where are you getting your information?"

"Can't say."

"I don't suppose you have any proof? Something I can use to bring him in on?"

"Not a thing, and I wouldn't reveal my source either way. Just arrest the man already."

She stood and started pacing. "Wynn, this isn't a game. This isn't the wild, wild West. I can't just arrest him for breathing my air. I need something."

Wynn nodded as though expecting her to say that very thing. "It's worse than all that, apple."

She stopped and turned toward him.

He bit down and said softly, "Clay knows who Auri is."

Sun's breath caught as she stared at him in absolute disbelief.

He looked at Levi. "He knows the girl is yours, son. He knows you left her a third of everything, and you know he can't let that happen."

Auri tossed and turned more than a roller coaster at full speed. She'd been trying to go to sleep. Trying and failing. All of a sudden, her heart was too big for her chest, her stomach was flooded with butterflies in every color of the rainbow, and her skin tingled with exhilaration. Levi Ravinder. Her dad. A real dad she could talk to and hug. Not the pretend one she'd never met.

She made a mental list of all the questions she wanted to ask him, mostly about the fact that she and Jimmy were technically cousins. She'd never had a cousin before. And she had an aunt, now, too. But what would she call her? What would she call Levi?

Dad just seemed so . . . personal. So perfect. But would he want her to call him that?

Even with her head swimming as it was, she felt the pull of sleep at last when she saw a light go on at her house. She scrambled onto her knees and looked out the window. Someone was in their kitchen. A man, but it wasn't Levi. She squinted and realized it was Grandpa. But why would her grandpa be in their kitchen at—she looked at her alarm clock—5:30 in the morning?

She sank back onto the bed and tried once again to go to sleep, but her curiosity got the better of her. She threw on her shoes and went out the back door. She should have just gone into her house, but there were people in there. Like, a lot. So she snuck to the window to peep inside instead.

Her grandpa was standing at the sink. Just hanging. Her mom and Levi were in the living room with another man. As tall as Levi. Rugged like a cowboy. Or the leader of a motorcycle club. She leaned in closer to see her mom pacing. Then her mom stopped. Stunned. She argued. She sank onto the couch. She argued some more. It was like watching a silent movie, and just as dramatic when everyone stopped what they were doing and all eyes turned to the window. The same one she was looking in from.

Now she had a decision to make. Run, pretend like she was sleepwalking, or go inside and tell them she woke up and was going to get ready for school.

When her mom crooked a finger at her, she had no choice. She stepped inside but stopped short by the front door. "What's going on?"

Her grandpa put his hands behind his back and no one said anything for a really long time, but Auri's attention had been captured by the man standing by her dad. *Her dad!* He was staring at her like he'd never seen a girl before. The man. Not her dad. It was probably her hair.

"Auri," her mom said, gesturing her over. "This is Levi's uncle Wynn."

"Oh, nice to meet you," she said, reveling in the fact that she had an uncle that wasn't Clay. Because ew.

He took her hand and held it. "My god in heaven," he said, his gaze boring into her soul. Which was not awkward at all. "Those eyes. They're exactly like your grandmother's."

"You know my grandma? Wait, aren't you in jail?"

"I . . . got out," he said after tossing a questioning gaze to her mom.

She pulled her hand back. "Well, good for you. Happy . . . release day?"

"Thank you, Auri. I've wanted to meet you for a long time."

Auri could've beat around the bush now and asked questions later, but she figured, what the hey. "You weren't in prison for kiddie porn, were you?"

He laughed, as did Levi, but her mom just stood there like she was in shock. And her grandpa had yet to come out of the kitchen. The dark kitchen casting him in shadows.

"I most definitely was not in prison for kiddie porn. It's just, I knew you'd look like her."

She eyed him doubtfully. "I don't look like my grandma."

"Your father's mom."

Auri gaped at her mom. "He knows? How does he know and I'm just finding out?"

"Oops," he said to her mom. "Sorry, apple."

"We just told Auri about Levi tonight." Sun pulled her close, wrapping an arm around her.

"At least I didn't let the cat out of the bag, right?" He winked at her mom but she didn't take the bait.

"Auri, why don't you go get ready for school. You have that field trip today."

"It's still early. I was thinking coffee and a chocolate croissant."

"Fine. Have your grandma get you one."

"Mom, are you okay?"

She forced a smile. "Of course, bug. Go stay with your grandma, now."

"All right already. Geez. Could you try to get rid of me any harder?" When Wynn breathed a soft laugh, she asked, "Will you still be here when I get back?"

"I hope to be around for a long time."

"Good. Because I want the lowdown on my dad. All the juicy bits." She giggled at Levi as she turned and walked out. This week just got better and better.

Frustration and astonishment bubbled and boiled inside Sun as she watched her daughter bounce out of the house. The wetness pooling between her lashes was just the tip of the iceberg. The edges of her vision darkened and nausea pushed bile up to sting the back of her throat.

"We need to keep her home from school," Levi said.

"He won't touch her," Wynn said. "Not yet. Not until he's taken care of you, Levi. He is the worst kind of coward, son. Always was. She's safe as long as we keep you alive."

"I don't want her to know anything is wrong," Sun said. "We have to act normal."

Her dad stepped closer then, the gun back in plain sight. "I'll go on the field trip with her, today, Sunny. Just as a precaution."

She nodded. "Thanks, Dad. I'll call Mr. Jacobs to make sure it happens. In the meantime, I'm going to have to take you into custody, Wynn."

"Well, you could," he said, casting a furtive glance at Levi, "but I think I'll stay out just a little longer."

"Sorry. I can't allow that."

"But Levi can," he argued. "And so can your dad."

"Why would I do that?" her dad asked.

"I told you. He knows who Auri is."

Sun protested. "You just said he won't make a move until—"

"And he won't," Wynn said, holding up a hand to stop her. "But how long do you want to wait for that day? Unable to breathe, worried with each phone call you'll hear that your daughter was killed in a hit-and-run? Or a break-in? Or a drug overdose?"

"Stop," Sun whispered, her stomach somersaulting.

"You see to Redding, apple, and leave Clay to me."

"Redding?" Levi asked.

"I don't know why or how, but Clay has some pretty big plans for this town, and Redding is somehow involved."

"How do you propose I see to him?" she asked.

"Just keep an eye. If everything goes as planned, we'll know more by the end of the day. Then you can take me in. Pinky swear."

"Fine, what's your plan?"

"Apple, there are some people on this planet who just don't deserve to live on it. Clay happens to be one of them. I plan to see that he leaves it."

She studied him as his meaning sank in. "You're going to kill him?"

"After I extract some information, of course."

Sun laughed and sank onto the sofa. She may not have her duty weapon, but her dad was armed, and Levi could take him should it come to that.

"And you think you can get past all three of us?"

"Nope. Just you." He looked at Levi. "You have to let me go. He'll kill her."

"I'll go with you."

"What?" She jumped up. "Levi, what the hell?"

"We're going, Shine."

Her dad stepped closer and clicked the safety off the gun. "I can't let you do that, son."

Levi dropped his gaze. "I'm sorry, sir. You'll have to shoot me, and I don't think you'll do that."

"No, I won't, but I will shoot him." He gestured toward Wynn.

Levi took a step to block his line of sight. "Sir, my one goal in life at the moment is to keep your granddaughter alive."

"I thought you might say that." He put the safety back on the gun and handed it to Wynn. "You might need this. It's untraceable."

"Dad!" she said, stunned. Not only about his betrayal but about the fact that he had an untraceable gun in his possession.

"What about you, Sheriff?" Levi said, turning to her. "Are you going to shoot me?"

"Levi, don't do this. I have to take him in."

"And I have to make sure my daughter lives a long and healthy life."

Her dad walked around the sofa and stepped between her and Levi. "You go on, Levi. Finish this."

"Dad," she whispered.

Levi nodded and ran to the bedroom for the rest of his attire.

When she started to follow him, her dad took hold of her arm. She looked at the large hand encircling her biceps, then lifted her gaze to her father's resigned face. "You realize I could take you if I really wanted to," she said, praying she wouldn't have to prove it.

"You could try."

He was way more confident about his chances than she would've imagined.

"Apple," Wynn said, gesturing goodbye with a nod.

She could only watch as he left with Levi, who didn't even spare her another glance. Then she turned to the traitor in disbelief. "You are the worst backup ever."

# 23

*If you hate waiting in lines and wish*
*the woman would just pick a suspect already,*
*maybe try not breaking the law next time.*

—PRO TIP FROM THE DEL SOL COUNTY SHERIFF'S STATION

Sun pulled up to the school to drop Auri off for the last time that school year, the realization bittersweet. "Oh, I meant to tell you," she said to her, "Mr. Jacobs asked your grandpa to chaperone the field trip."

Auri brightened. "No way. That's so cool. I wish Cruz was going. And Sybil. But at least I'll have Grandpa."

"Sybil's not going?" she asked in surprise.

"No. Her mom wouldn't sign the permission slip. Blamed it on her allergies. She's been so possessive lately."

"I can't imagine why."

"The bus leaves at nine," Auri said, ignoring her. "Does Grandpa know that?"

"He knows. He just had to run a couple of errands." God only knew what his errands were. He probably went out to get another untraceable gun. They really needed to have a heart-to-heart.

"Meeting Wynn was amazing even though he's been in prison. Or possibly because of it," she added, crinkling her nose in thought.

Sun bit down as she picked at a loose thread on the steering wheel. "Don't get too attached, bug."

"I won't. I just . . ." Her voice softened and she asked, "Are you okay with all of this?"

Sun turned to her. "All of what?"

"You know. You and Levi having a kid together."

She let out a breathy laugh. "Aurora Dawn, I am in heaven right now."

"Right?" Auri clasped her hands at her chest and looked up dreamily. "Me too."

"Although . . ."

"Although?" she asked, sobering.

Sun changed her mind with a shake of her head. "Oh, it's nothing."

"Mom, what?"

"It's just, if we don't make it, you know he and I will fight for custody."

A brilliant smile flashed across her face. "You'd fight for me?"

"What? No. We'll fight over who has to take you. I've had you all to myself for fifteen years. He needs to take a turn at the wheel, if you know what I mean. He has no idea what he's just gotten himself into." She laughed when Auri pursed her lips at her.

"Mother, that's not even funny."

"It's a little funny."

"No, it's not." She started to open the door, and Sun realized she was making a huge mistake. Not only was she lying to her daughter by omission, she was putting her life in danger.

She put a hand on her arm. "Auri, wait."

Auri turned back to her.

"I know we've given you a lot to think about, but can I ask you to do something for me without explaining why?"

"Sure," she said, settling back in her seat.

"I can't give you any details right now, but if you see Clay Ravinder, if he is off in the distance or you see him walking toward you on the street, I need you to run. In the opposite direction. Not walk, bug. Run. Duck into a business or find an adult and tell them what's going on, then dial 911."

"Mom," she said warily, "you're kind of freaking me out."

"I know." Sun pulled her daughter's head onto her shoulder and patted her cheek. "And I'm sorry. I promise to explain later, but just for now, just be very aware of your surroundings."

She acquiesced with a nod. "Is that why Grandpa is going on the field trip?"

This kid. She should've known she'd figure it out. "It is."

Auri straightened and looked at her. "Thanks for telling me. But what about Wynn?"

Sun smiled inwardly. "Wynn you can trust with your life," she said, now more confident in the man than ever.

That brought a satisfied smirk to Auri's lovely face. "I figured as much when I met him."

"Good instincts."

Auri raised her chin a visible notch. "Just like my mom." She opened the door only to be greeted by Del Sol's only tiny boy band.

"Hey, Auri," Leo said. "We're starting a band for real and thought maybe you'd want to be our singer."

Auri turned back to her to hide her grin as she closed the door.

Now Sun just had to figure out how she was going to keep an eye on Redding while helping coordinate the search with the cadaver dogs. Before she got too far into her speculations, however, her phone chimed with a text from Auri.

*There are baby raccoons at the station???*

The boy band must've told her.

*Can we keep them?*

*No. Get to class.*

She sent a dozen sad face emojis as Sun drove to the station.

"Hey, boss," Anita said when she walked in.

"Hey, any word on our Jane Doe?"

"No change, but Bob called. He'll be at the canyon floor with the dogs in about thirty minutes."

"Fantastic, thank you. Now we just need the ATVs."

"Already loaded and ready to go," Quince said, walking up

behind her. "And why do you look like you didn't get any sleep again last night?"

"Because I didn't. I would tell you about it but I don't want to make you an accessory after the fact."

"Oh, hell, no," he said, leading her out the door. "You better be rethinking that. What's going on?"

Sun let a sigh slip through her lips before beginning. "First, we told Auri everything."

"Everything?"

"For the most part. And then I had a visitor." She lowered her voice. "One who may or may not have escaped from a maximum-security prison recently."

He stopped midstride and gaped at her. "And he's not in our holding cell because?"

She patted the air, reminding him to keep his voice down. "Because Levi and my father turned traitor."

"Your dad?" he asked far too loudly. Then he changed his attitude and asked softly, "Do you think your mother will leave him over this?"

She snorted. "No, Quince, and you're dating someone anyway. Speaking of which, how is that going?"

"No time for that now. You have to tell me everything. Start from the beginning."

Honestly, having Quince as a BFF was better than a thousand girls' nights.

While Auri still had a signal, she continued her search for Chloe's prom date from hell, hoping to find the original photo of the one that Chloe had cropped for her memories album.

Sybil sighed from behind Auri, her body draped over her desk in true dramatic fashion. "I can't believe my mom won't let me go. You have asthma and your mom still lets you go. I have a sniffle and my mom calls out the national guard."

"She's a monster," Auri said, trying not to giggle. "I'm just bummed the entire freshman class is going. A reprieve from

Lynelle and her goons would've been nice." She spotted said goons surrounding their queen a few feet away. "I wonder if they have to make regular human sacrifices to her or if it's more of a seasonal thing."

"On the bright side," Sybil said, "we'll have the entire summer without them."

"Except when we see them in town."

"True."

"And at the lake."

"Yep."

"And at the grocery store."

"Auri, you're ruining my summer and it hasn't even started yet."

"Sorry," she said right as she scrolled past the pic she was looking for. "Oh, my god, I found it."

Sybil bounded up and leaned over Auri's shoulder to see for herself. Sure enough, there were children playing in a kiddie pool in the background, but closer up, standing right behind Chloe was . . . "Tim Redding?"

"No way," Sybil said, leaning closer, her lids the size and shape of teacup saucers.

"That can't be. He was . . ." Auri thought back, trying to make sense of it all. "He was beaten up, Sybil. It must not be him, unless . . ." She brought out the list of names she'd taken down of all the guys at prom last year who drove trucks. Since their classes were so small, it wasn't a very long list. Tim was there. "His name is on the list, but this makes no sense."

"Who do you think beat him up?" Sybil asked. "I mean, he's like a super jock. Chastity said the other guys are afraid of him."

Auri turned to her. "Afraid? In what way?"

"I don't know, they say he's a little crazy. Like he purposely hurts the other football players."

"You mean during a game?"

"No, I mean during practice. He'll sweep their legs. Mess up their knees on purpose. At least that's what Chastity told me."

"She didn't say anything to me."

"She didn't really volunteer the information out of the blue. I was wondering about him when he put his number in your phone, so I asked her. Still, he has a full ride to UNM. Whatever he's doing is working."

"You mean injuring his team members to make himself look better?"

She shrugged. "Maybe. Auri, do you really think he could be Chloe's attacker?"

"No." Auri shook her head. "I've heard my mom and I know his dad is crazy, but I just can't see Tim doing something like that."

"My mom says no one knows what people do behind closed doors. You never really understand someone until you live with them. And even then, it's iffy."

"That's true." Auri looked closer at the picture and a scenario began to materialize. "Sybil, does it look like he was the one who threw the water balloon at her?"

"It does. But guys do that crap all the time."

"That's not it. Look at his face. At his expression. It's calculating and vengeful."

"Auri," Sybil said, shaking her head. "It's predatorial."

"And she's at a cookout in the middle of summer with a swimming pool in the backyard." Beside the kiddie pool was an aboveground pool with a few teens swimming who Auri recognized from school.

"Okay, and?"

"Well, look at Chloe. She's slim. Gorgeous. A cheerleader and a volleyball star. And she's wearing a calf-length bathing suit bottom?"

"I'm not following."

"She said she had bruises. Between her legs."

Sybil sank back into her chair.

"If it's him, who beat him up? The girl they found in the canyon?"

"No. No, he was hit hard with a large fist. I don't know who it was, but I need to call my mom." She grabbed her phone and asked for a bathroom pass.

She dialed her mom's number, but she didn't pick up. She may already be at the canyon, so Auri left a message: "Mom, I think it's Tim Redding. Chloe's ex. I think Tim is the one—" She turned to see Lynelle standing behind her.

"Who are you talking to?" Lynelle asked, stepping inside Auri's space bubble, bursting it like she did everything else.

Auri ended the call. "My mom."

"Why are you talking about Tim?"

"Why are you in here?"

"I had to go to the bathroom before the field trip," she said, her tone and glare a perfect match. "Why are you talking about Tim?"

"Lynelle, was your cousin Whitney talking to him? Were they dating?"

"No. What's it to you?"

"Are you certain?"

Surprisingly, she paused to think about Auri's query. "He did have her number in his phone, but only because they met when she came down for spring break. They didn't hook up or anything."

"How long have you been friends with him?"

"We're dating, actually. He asked me out the other day. Jealous?"

A warning siren went off in Auri's head. "Has he ever hurt you?"

"How dare you." Somehow, she managed to get even closer. "He was so nice to you, nicer than you deserve, and now you're going around talking shit about him?"

"Lynelle," she said, sharpening her tone, "has he hurt you?"

Lynelle visibly shook with fury, and Auri honestly thought she was going to hit her. She braced herself for an impact that never came. When Lynelle had no comeback, she said, "I'll take that as a yes," and left the bathroom just as the bell rang. They were due at the bus, so she would have to give up her sleuthing for now. She prayed her mother would get the message soon, though. She packed her things and said goodbye to Sybil. "What are you going to do?" she asked her.

"I have to go to the library and read."

"The horror."

Sybil giggled. "Have fun."

By the time she got to the bus, Lynelle was back to ignoring her. Auri tried to hide her devastation. It was hard. So hard.

"Grandpa!" she said, running toward her bodyguard. She threw her arms around him. "Thanks for coming. I'm sorry you had to."

"I wanted to."

"No, you didn't."

He chuckled. "Peanut, I always want to spend time with you. What did your mom tell you?"

"To run for my life if I see Clay Ravinder."

"So she got straight to the point."

"That's my mom."

They boarded the bus. Auri sat with her grandpa and Chastity took the seat behind them.

"Sweetheart," her grandpa said, "don't sit with me. Sit with your friends."

"I am." She took his arm in hers. "Also, I need deets."

"Ah. So, I'm to be interrogated the entire time?"

"All the way up and all the way back."

He nodded, accepting his fate. "Go for it."

Ignoring the fact that Lynelle looked like she'd been crying—because good—she asked, "First, and I'm asking this only as a concerned citizen, how did Wynn Ravinder get out of prison?"

He rubbed his brow and mumbled, "Your mother's going to kill me."

Forty-seven minutes later, Auri sat staring into space. She had learned more in the last half hour than she had in the last fifteen years from her mother. "So, he saved her?" She felt the sting of tears in her eyes. "He saved Mom from his uncle Kubrick?"

"And he almost died in the process. Multiple stab wounds."

"Just like Cruz when he saved me."

"Yes."

A recalcitrant tear slipped past her lashes as they pulled to a stop.

Mrs. Ontiveros stood up to address the ranks. "All right everyone, your bags will be safe here. We'll walk to the petroglyphs and then come back and have lunch at the picnic tables. We have water bottles, but only take one if you think you can refrain from throwing the bottle on the trail. These images are hundreds of years old. Please respect that."

"Are you coming, Grandpa?"

"Wouldn't miss it. I haven't been to the petroglyphs in decades."

# 24

*If Scooby-Doo taught us nothing else,*
*it's that real monsters are always human.*
—SIGN AT DEL SOL COUNTY SHERIFF'S STATION

"I love these subs," her grandpa said as they finished lunch two hours later.

"Me too," Auri said. "And the petroglyphs were cool. Can you imagine living back then?"

"Right? No cell phones. No Netflix."

Auri laughed. "I can live without technology. I just choose not to."

"Ah. Is your friend okay? She keeps glancing this way." He pointed to Lynelle, and Auri and Chastity exchanged horrified glances.

"She's not a friend, Grandpa."

"What makes you say that?"

"She's psycho."

He wiped his mouth and gathered his trash. "That makes it difficult to develop a lasting relationship."

She laughed. "It does."

They tossed their trash in the public bins and headed back to the bus. When the entire freshman class is only twenty-three students, it's easy to take the whole group on excursions together. Especially when a couple of them stayed behind.

"I may have to take a nap on the way back," her grandpa said as he took a seat in the middle of the bus. "I'm at that age, you know."

Auri sat beside him again and rested her head on his shoulder. "Maybe I'll join you."

Mrs. Ontiveros counted students, then gave the driver the go-ahead. "What did you guys think?" she asked the students when she sat down.

"Beautiful as ever," Bea Morales, a tough girl with a heart of gold, said.

"I loved it," Chastity said. "I want to write a blog on it, except I don't have one because nobody reads them anymore, which is crazy because who doesn't love blogs; also I like fan fiction." She looked up in thought. "I could write a fan fiction piece with it."

Auri laughed as she raised her phone into the air, searching for a signal.

"You'll get one in about ten minutes," Mrs. Ontiveros said, pointing to her phone.

The driver pulled onto the mountain road that would take them back, and Auri pretended not to notice the million-foot drop that the tires of the bus seemed to be skirting. She'd never been afraid of heights. She was, however, afraid of their bus driver, Mr. Davis. The rotund grump seemed a little jaded when it came to high school students.

"You know," her grandpa said, probably picking up on her distress, "you could always ask me about—"

Before he could finish his sentence, a muffled pop sounded and the bus swerved sharply to the right. Auri watched in horror as Mr. Davis struggled to control the massive vehicle, his arms straining under the force. Her grandpa wrapped his arms around her, securing her against him. Mr. Davis tried to slow the bus, but they were going downhill. He pumped the brakes to no avail, letting out a few choice words in the process. After several harrowing seconds, he managed to wrest control over the vehicle the very moment another pop sounded. This time the bus veered in the opposite direction.

The rest happened in slow motion and yet so fast Auri couldn't focus. Gravity gave way as the bus tumbled down the incline. Screams echoed off the glass and metal. For a moment, she was on top of Mrs. Ontiveros, Chastity on top of her. Then everything reversed and went the other direction. They flew into the air, time seeming to stand still until it all came to a stop as quickly as it started. They landed hard and upside down, sliding another thirty feet before skidding to a halt. The screams stopped instantly and an eerie silence filled the cabin. One by one, her classmates tried to sit up. Each one looked around confused and disoriented.

"Grandpa?" Auri said, blinking into the sun-filtered space. She scanned the area and realized he'd landed near the front of the bus. "Grandpa!" She scrambled up and rushed to him, stepping over terrified kids and the scattered backpacks that littered the roof of the bus. She dropped to her knees beside him. "Grandpa, are you okay?"

"Auri, get back. Away from the windows, hon."

She hurried back, confused as her grandpa struggled to push off the door and get deeper into the cabin. She looked over at Mr. Davis, who lay crumpled directly under his upside-down seat. Blood covered one side of his face.

"Grandpa, what happened?"

He held up a finger, asking her to hold that thought, then crouched to scan the area. "Everyone, get down!"

But it was too late. Bullets hit the side of the bus and screams of absolute terror filled the cabin as kids scrambled toward the back.

Her grandpa lunged for her. He covered her with his body until the gunfire stopped.

"It's a shooter, peanut. Someone shot the tires. Look." He pointed out the windshield, but Auri saw the blood soaking his pant leg.

"Grandpa, you're shot."

"No, I'm injured from the wreck," he grunted, trying to sit up. "I think my leg is broken."

"Oh, my god, Grandpa."

He took her by the shoulders and shook softly to focus her. When her gaze met his, he explained, "He's up high, but he's going to come down here. Do you understand?"

She nodded, then glanced over her shoulder as the other kids tried to get the back door open. A couple of them had been knocked out. Backpacks and purses were strewn everywhere. Lynelle looked around in shock, half her face covered by her hair.

"You need to run for the trees, baby." He shook her again. "Do you understand? And then you keep running."

"Auri," Chastity said, crawling to her. She had blood streaming down one side of her face. "What's going on?"

"Auri," he said, insisting she pay attention. "Get these kids away from the bus. Get them to the trees. Hide those who can't run, and then you keep going until you get a signal."

"Mrs. Ontiveros," Auri said when the dazed teacher started for the bus driver.

"No!" her grandpa shouted.

She stopped and looked back at him.

"He's better off where he is and the shooter might see you. Stay away from the window."

"We need to get to the radio."

He shook his head. "It's too late. The shooter has a clean line of sight through the windshield."

"Grandpa," Auri said, a strange kind of calmness overtaking her, "I'm not leaving you here." She grabbed a discarded jacket and pressed it to his leg.

He winced and took it from her. "I'm not bleeding that badly. I'll be okay knowing you've gotten away."

"I'm not leaving you."

"Auri, peanut, you have to." He took hold of her chin and said softly, "Look, sweetheart, look," before gesturing toward the windshield with a nod.

She looked into the distance, up the incline and to the right. A man came down the mountain toward them carrying a military-style rifle like the kind in the movies. His gait was slow, calculated, as he loaded a new magazine and slapped it into place. The world tilted around her as shock sank its teeth a little deeper.

"Peanut," he said to get her attention again. "What do you see?"

"W-what?"

"Tell me what you see."

She shook so hard she could barely talk. Her voice came out in breathy chunks. "Single shooter. Semiautomatic rifle with two—"

"No."

"—three extra magazines. He's . . . young. Probably in high school, taking the statistics into consideration."

"Good. He's already used one magazine and discarded it. Pay attention to when he starts shooting again. He can't hit anything through windows yet from that angle, but he'll hit ground level soon and then all bets are off. When he pauses between reloads, run for the trees."

Before she could argue, another rain of bullets hit the side of the bus. The screams reached a fever pitch as students crawled over each other to try to get out the back and through the windows on the opposite side of the bus.

"Get to the back," her grandpa said above the roar. "The minute the bullets stop, run."

A new determination washed over her. She had to get help. She had to save her grandpa. She grabbed armfuls of backpacks and layered them over him for camouflage. He smiled at her and patted her face. Satisfied with her work, she hurried toward the back just as Raymond Navarro grabbed his best friend Bea's hand and shoved the back door open.

He started to run, but Auri dove over a couple of students and grabbed his arm. When he looked back, his eyes wild with terror, she shook her head. "Not yet." She held up an index finger as though putting him on pause.

He nodded, seeming to understand, and sank onto his knees with Bea, covering her head with his arms as they waited for the bullets to stop. A couple bounced off metal and still managed to ricochet harmlessly into the cabin, but they elicited a new level of panic, even in Auri.

She fought to tamp down her fear and decided humor would work best. "If we make it through this," she said to Bea and Raymond, "you two have got to hook up. You've been in love for months."

The two exchanged surprised glances.

Raymond seemed more terrified of that thought than the shooter. "We're just friends," he insisted, and Bea nodded in agreement.

"Whatever helps you sleep at night," she said, silently begging them to make it. "Stay in teams of at least two and try not to get separated. If you can't run, hide and wait for help. My mom will be here soon with the cavalry." She had faith. Her mom would figure this out. She would come.

The minute the shooting stopped, she looked at Raymond and nodded, saying softly, "Now."

But before he headed out the door, Raymond grabbed Bea and kissed her passionately. Bea kissed back. An appreciative smile flashed across his face before he tore out of there, dragging Bea across the broken glass with him until she could gain her footing. Auri grabbed Chastity and ran for dear life as kids spilled out of the bus, staying low to keep the bus between them and the shooter as they traversed the uneven ground.

It took the shooter mere seconds to reload and for the bullets to start flying again. Students ran in all directions, but from what Auri could tell, none of them were hit.

They crossed into the tree line, and Auri stopped to look back. Mrs. Ontiveros made it into a copse of trees just as a bullet ricocheted off a boulder nearby. Another kid screamed and stumbled. Auri started toward her, but Chastity took hold of her arm as another spray of bullets peppered the treetops overhead. They were like missiles, random and relentless, as though the shooter wasn't even aiming. Which was a good thing, she supposed. But he'd shot the tires with military precision. How was he not hitting anyone?

"Auri," Chastity said, "he's coming. We have to go."

Auri glanced back at the girl who'd stumbled. She'd made it into the trees and Auri lost sight of her. She scanned the area, wondering if they'd have a better chance of getting a signal if they went up instead of down.

"Run, kids," Mrs. Ontiveros said, trying to catch her breath. "We can't stay here."

Auri looked back and watched with dread as the shooter crouched to look inside the back of the bus. She plastered both hands over her mouth to keep from screaming when he fired a single shot inside, but he only shot the radio. She watched through a broken window as the radio splintered. Her trick must have worked, because he didn't shoot again. She almost collapsed with relief when he stood and started for the trees, but he changed direction and seemed to come straight at them.

"Auri," Chastity whispered, and they took off, Mrs. Ontiveros right on their heels.

Students were running through the trees in all directions, branches slashing across faces and rocks twisting ankles, but still they ran. Most of the kids headed downhill toward civilization. Auri split off to the side, running neither up nor down. She didn't get far before she saw Lynelle tumbling down a particularly steep path. She turned and started toward her, but she had to slow her progress substantially as they half ran, half slid down the path.

Lynelle hit a tree stump, its sharp angles cutting into her rib cage, but she caught it and held on with all her might, struggling to get her legs under her. Auri skated to a stop and dropped to her knees beside her. She looked over her shoulder. Chastity and Mrs. O were sliding their way down the incline behind her.

Lynelle was hysterical. Her gaze darted about wildly as she looked for the shooter. "It's him," she said, her face dirty and covered in tears. "I know it's him."

Auri helped her get onto her bottom. "It's who?"

She looked at Auri as though just realizing she was there. Her chin trembled as she started to cry again.

"Auri," Chastity said, sliding to a stop beside her.

"He's so mad, Auri."

Lynelle's words finally sank in. She tore her gaze off the path behind them, off her frantic search for the shooter, and refocused on her. "Who's mad?"

Lynelle covered her mouth with a bloody hand.

"Lynelle, what are you talking about?"

"I . . . I called him." She hiccupped and scanned the area again.

Auri grabbed the collar of her pink blouse and forced her to focus. "You called who?"

"I know it's him. He's so mad."

"Lynelle, look at me."

The girl finally focused on Auri's face. Blinking past the tears, she said, "It's Tim. I called him. Told him what you said in the bathroom."

Auri slammed her lids shut. "You didn't."

A sob wracked through Lynelle's body and she nodded. "He was so mad."

"We have to get you out of sight, Lynelle."

"You don't understand." She reached over and grabbed Auri's shoulders. "He's not after me." Regret—an emotion Auri didn't know Lynelle was capable of—washed over her face. "He's . . . he's after you."

Auri stared at her a long moment before sinking back onto her heels.

"I'm sorry, Auri. I just thought . . . I don't know what I thought. I was in denial, I guess. But you were right. About everything."

"Did you know he was coming here?" she asked, repulsed. "Did you know he was going to do this?"

Stunned, she shook her head. "No. I swear, Auri. He was just so mad. He started cursing and told me you'd regret sticking your nose where it didn't belong."

"I usually do," she said, resigned to the fact that she could die here today. But no one else needed to. She turned, stole another quick glance behind them, and looked at Chastity and Mrs. O. "You guys keep heading down. See that line in the trees right there?"

They followed her line of sight to what looked like miles below them and nodded. "That's the road. It picks up down there. Get on it and run until you get a signal or can flag someone down. Chastity," she said, squeezing the girl's arm, "my grandad is still back there. Please, please, please bring help."

"Where are you going?" she asked, fear constricting her vocal cords. The poor girl shook visibly, and Auri suddenly realized she was shaking just as bad.

"I'm going up. I'll try to get a signal up higher, but I'm not placing a bet on my chances."

"Auri," Mrs. Ontiveros said, "you don't have to do this. We don't know that he's really after you."

"Of course he is, Mrs. O. This is what I do." Her voice cracked, and Mrs. O looked at her confused just as a branch exploded beside her head.

Auri dove behind a fallen log, taking Lynelle with her as the other two tumbled down the path. Without thinking, she grabbed Lynelle and dragged her down the trough on the other side of a crest where they hit slightly more even ground. They glanced at each other and took off at a dead run, adrenaline pushing Lynelle past any pain she may have felt from her collision with the tree stump.

They ran for what seemed like hours, though Auri was sure it was more like ten minutes. She wasn't the athletic type, however, as the muscles in her legs kept reminding her. As did a fiery pain in her side.

"Wait," she said, panting. "I have to stop."

"Me too," Lynelle said.

They ducked behind a thick grouping of trees, both of them doubling over to catch their breaths.

"Your hand is bleeding really bad," Auri said.

Lynelle looked at it, then wiped it on her jeans. It didn't help. "Do you think we lost him?"

"Surely we did." Auri studied their surroundings while gulping handfuls of air. "I'm going to go up, try to get a signal at the top of the crest."

"You're going back?" she screeched rather like a barn owl.

Auri shook her head. "No. I'm going to give him a wide berth and try to get past him. He won't expect it."

"I'm not sure that's a good—"

Auri lunged at her and covered Lynelle's mouth with her hand. She saw movement from somewhere overhead. It could be any of the other students, but she couldn't take that risk.

They sank to the ground and held their breaths as best they could until the kid in black came into view.

"How does he keep finding us?" Auri whispered. She watched as he pulled something from his pocket. It was too big to be a phone. He studied it, then looked through the trees, seemingly straight at them. "Is he tracking us somehow?"

Lynelle gasped when a thought hit her. "Can he be tracking your phone?"

Auri shook her head. "How could he? There's no signal."

"Oh, my god." She tugged a pendant out from under her shirt. "He gave me this necklace. Said it had a tracker so he could keep an eye on me. I thought it was romantic." She stared at it before looking back at Auri. "But I don't understand. There's no signal up here. How can he track me?"

"He doesn't need a signal if it has satellite capabilities."

"What?" she breathed, sinking farther onto the ground.

"That means he's after you, Lynelle. Not me."

She shook her head, the tears starting anew. "No, Auri. He's not. He told me to give you the necklace."

Auri's lungs stopped working a solid minute before they restarted. "What do you mean?" she asked in disbelief. "When?"

"When I called him," she said with a sob. "He said to give you the necklace. I was too jealous to." She raised a quivering hand to cover her eyes, her whole body shaking. "I had no idea he would use it like this."

Auri sank next to her and put a hand on her shoulder. "Give me the necklace."

She lowered her hand. "What?"

"Give me your necklace."

Instead of reaching around her neck and releasing the clasp like Auri thought she would, she grabbed hold of it and ripped it off. "Ow," she said when she handed it to her. "That kind of hurt."

Auri grinned at her. "Okay," she said, peeking back up through the trees, "we leave this here and try to get some distance between it and us."

She nodded in agreement. "We should bury it a little. Make it hard to find."

"Good thinking."

They dropped the pendant and brushed some dirt and leaves over it, nothing that would disrupt the signal. Auri looked back just as he raised the rifle to look through the scope. She quickly ducked back behind the trees, bringing Lynelle with her.

"We need to keep these trees between him and us for as long as we can."

"Shouldn't we go for the road, too? Like Mrs. O?"

She nodded. "That's exactly what I want you to do. Just keep going down until you hit a road."

"Wait, what about you?" she said, her whisper rising an octave.

"I'm sticking to my original plan. Getting to higher ground to try to get a signal."

"You're leaving me?" she asked, digging her nails into Auri's upper arm.

"Lynelle," she said, peeling her hand off her, "he's after me, remember? You'll be safer if we separate."

Lynelle looked at the terrain below them. She swallowed hard and nodded, not entirely convinced but going along with Auri's plan anyway.

Auri risked a peek and her heart capsized in her chest. "He's coming. Let's go. I'll break away from you once we've gotten some distance."

They took the slope slowly at first but gravity soon took hold and they found themselves sliding more than walking. Whatever helped.

As soon as Auri found her footing, she took a sharp left, glancing over her shoulder just once to make sure Lynelle kept going. She prayed someone got a call through, but just in case, she still planned on going up. She had noticed when they were at the petroglyphs she had a single bar, but her mother had yet to call or text her back about Tim. If Tim was really the shooter, he needed more help than Auri could've imagined.

Now for the hard part. It was true, she wanted to get to higher ground for a signal, but more than that, she wanted to get back to her grandfather. The thought of him lying there alone caused a crack down the middle of her heart. She turned back, and though she could see neither the shooter nor Lynelle, he had a definite advantage. He had a scope.

She crouched behind another grove of trees and tried to slow her breathing so she could listen. When she heard nothing, she took out her phone and tried to even the playing field, at least a little, by using her camera as a scope. It certainly didn't have the distance of his, but it would work in a pinch. She zoomed in and studied the area she'd just come from to make sure he wasn't following her. When she didn't see him, an odd type of elation rose inside her, subdued and sprinkled with hope. Maybe they'd really thrown him off their track.

She stuffed her phone in her jeans pocket, drew in a deep breath, and raced uphill as fast as she could. Sadly, it wasn't all that fast. And *raced* was a bit of an overstatement. She grunted and groaned—internally as she didn't want to make a sound—with every burning step she took, and it was a constant tug-of-war, two steps forward and one step back as she slipped and slid on the steep terrain. She clawed at the ground in some parts, digging her fingernails into the dirt, ignoring the branches and bushes tearing at her clothes and scratching her face and arms.

Thirty minutes later, she had no clue where she was or how far she'd come. It wasn't like she had any sense of direction to help guide her. Her only saving grace was the fact that she knew up from down. Surely, she would either come to the road they had been on or she would reach the peak. But the more she hiked, the farther the peak seemed to recede. And then her legs simply quit on her.

Unable to go any farther, she found a grouping of boulders and hid as best she could, not really knowing which direction she wanted to hide from. Why hadn't she hit the road yet? Or found the picnic area where they'd eaten lunch? Had she gone that far across the mountain? Had she simply missed it?

She checked her phone. It was after three now. They would be missed when they didn't show up at school. But hopefully some of the others had already been able to get help. Surely her mom was on the way.

After climbing to her feet and managing to keep her legs underneath her—barely—she started uphill and smelled a campfire. Or perhaps the fire from a cabin. She whirled around, searching for smoke when she found more than she'd bargained for. She sucked in a sharp breath. A wall of smoke was headed straight toward her.

# 25

*If one day you intend to be the little old person in a nursing home who leads the rebellion and puts vodka in all the IV bags, we are having a sale on Absolut. Stock up now!*

—SIGN AT THE ROADHOUSE

Sun sat alone in Seabright's UTV, listening to her stomach growl. Since Seabright knew the area so well and could get her to the canyon floor in record time, she'd ridden down with him. But Quincy had insisted on bringing their only official ATV, mostly because he looked for any excuse to do so. He sat beside her as they ate a late lunch of cold cuts and stale bread.

"Whoever organizes these lunches needs to find a new job," she said, disappointed in the fare.

Quince glanced over at her. "Yeah, that was you."

"Exactly. I am so fired. And I mean it this time."

The incident commander, William Ledbetter, came on the walkies. "Sheriff, we found something."

"Hop on," Quince said to her.

She dropped her food and jumped on the back of the ATV as Quince raced the couple hundred yards to the scene. The search team stood not far from where they found their Jane Doe, in exactly the same place Sun had guessed the suspect dropped Misty Sandoval over the side of the guardrail.

"Female remains," Commander Ledbetter said, pointing to a secluded area beside the boulders.

The dogs were going crazy. Half a woman's foot protruded from the ground where the crew had dug when the dogs alerted them to a body. She wore pink toenail polish that matched the tips of the blond hair they'd found on the guardrail up top.

"Thank you, Bob," the commander said to the wilderness first responders as they wrangled the dogs.

"Yes, thanks, Bob. Cathy." Sun shook the volunteers' hands, noting the embroidered saying on Cathy's shirt, the search-and-rescue motto: THAT OTHERS MAY LIVE.

Touched by their altruism and saddened by their discovery, Sun studied the area. She'd never been so disappointed to be right. The suspect had dumped her over the guardrail, then taken another route down to bury her. He would have done the same with their Jane if she hadn't fought. If she hadn't ruined his plans for her to fall all the way to the bottom.

"You nailed it," Quince said.

"We'll get forensics out here to process the scene." She turned toward the commander. "Thank you."

He took her hand. "Of course, Sheriff." He looked past her. "Looks like your lieutenant may have something as well."

Sun turned to see Salazar running toward them, her thick dark braids bouncing around her shoulders.

Salazar skidded to a stop beside her, breathless, her expression not exactly hiding the concern she clearly felt. They really needed to work on her poker face. "Boss, something's happened," she said, gasping for air.

The last time Salazar ran up to her and uttered those words, Auri had almost been killed. And that was only days ago, so the reaction she had now—the narrowing of her vision, the increasing heart rate, the sound of blood rushing in her ears—could be chalked up to a latent case of PTSD. "What is it, Lieutenant?"

She looked from Sun to Quincy and back. "There's been a shooting."

Sun nodded and looked at Commander Ledbetter.

"I've got this," he said to her.

They stepped to the side. Quince followed and Seabright stayed close, too.

"Where?" Sun asked her.

"At the petroglyphs."

At first Sun thought she misunderstood. She shook her head at Salazar.

"It's a bus full of schoolkids. A group of them flagged down a motorist, who called it in. Boss, there's an active shooter up there."

Quince grabbed Sun's arm before she realized she was swaying. "Bring him," she said to Quincy, pointing at Seabright as she and Salazar sprinted for the man's UTV. Quince and Seabright scrambled onto the ATV so Quince could give him a ride to his UTV, considering Seabright was the only one in the bunch who almost died a few days earlier and shouldn't have been out there at all.

They beat her and Salazar to the vehicle, but the minute she jumped in the four-seater, she asked Seabright, "How fast can you get us to the top?"

He lifted a brow at the challenge. "Let's find out."

Seabright took a lot of risks getting them up to the small access road, but it paid off. The three of them made it to the top in less than fifteen minutes. Quince's ATV wasn't far behind, and his ride was the more dangerous.

Once up top, she ordered Seabright to stand down, and she and Quince jumped in her cruiser. Rojas picked up Salazar and they raced down one mountain pass to go to another one that led up to the petroglyphs. They were met on the way by a convoy of first responders. State police, Fire, and EMS sped up the road until the whole line came to a screeching halt. The EMTs spotted three girls running down the highway. One had blood running down her face. Sun jumped out and sprinted toward them as the EMTs got out.

"Girls, what happened?"

"There's a shooter," one of them said, a curvy Latina she'd seen Auri talk to on several occasions. "He shot at the bus as we were leaving and we tumbled down the side of a hill. It's upside down."

"And the shooter kept shooting," another said, part goth and part book nerd. "We were trying to get out the back, and then Raymond got the door open but Auri told us to wait."

"Auri?" Sun asked, her voice barely a whisper.

An EMT led the third girl, the one with the head wound, away.

"Yes." The goth nodded. "She told us to wait until the shooter paused to reload, and then run for the trees, so we did."

"Did you see her after that?"

The girl looked at Sun, clearly knowing who she was. "No, Sheriff, I didn't. I'm sorry. We just ran and kept running, like she told us to. We didn't stop until we saw you guys."

"Okay." Sun drew in a deep breath and nodded to the EMT.

She put a blanket over the girl's shoulders and led her to the back of an ambulance.

"Sheriff," one of the state cops, an Officer Bucannon, said, "we need to cordon this entire area off and get some more fire trucks in here."

"What? Why?"

He turned and pointed. "There's smoke."

She whirled around to see smoke billowing up the side of the mountain.

"And we have an active shooter on-site," he reminded her.

"I have to get up there. My father and my daughter were on that bus."

"Yes, ma'am. I'll send a couple of my men up there with you and coordinate a search for more survivors. Be careful."

"You too, Officer."

She and Quincy got back into her cruiser, after giving Salazar and Rojas instructions, and hurried up the mountain with two state police units right behind them. They came across more survivors running down the road. Three boys and a girl, but no Auri. No Dad.

Sun let the last state cruiser take care of them. They pulled over to assist the kids as Sun and the other state officers continued on. The higher up they went, the thicker the smoke became, and the more Sun's chest squeezed in panic.

"They're okay, Sun," Quincy said, as though soothing himself as much as her. "They're okay."

Sun's hands tightened on the steering wheel. "This is not happening, Quince. With everything she's gone through, this is not happening."

He didn't answer. Instead, he stared out the window at the wall of fire coming toward them. The smoke became so thick, she had to slow down in case more kids came running down the road.

The cruiser behind them pulled to the side of the road, and Sun realized they'd spotted some students running below them. She and Quince drove another couple of minutes until Quincy pointed.

"There," he said, and she swerved to miss a girl helping a boy down the road. The boy leaned heavily into her and she was struggling to stay upright.

Sun pulled to a stop as the two turned back and walked out of the smoke toward them, the girl swaying from exhaustion and fear, her cheek scratched and bleeding. Sun jumped out of the cruiser and raced to their side.

Quincy grabbed the boy and helped him to the cruiser as Sun took the girl to the other side. They sat them in the back seat and Quincy went to the rear to get the first aid kit.

"We need to get them to medical," he said when she joined him.

"I agree. Get them down the mountain. I'll go up on foot."

He stopped and looked at her. "You can't be serious."

"I am and you know it."

"Then, no."

"Quince—"

"Not just no," he said, easing closer, "but fuck no, Sunny."

"Quincy." She closed the distance between them, pulling rank. "Do your fucking job. Get them to safety."

He bit down and shook his head as though unable to believe what she was asking of him. "You're not doing this to me right now."

"I am, Deputy."

"Fine. I'm going to take them to the officers we just left, and then I'm coming back. After that, *Sheriff*, I quit. So don't try to order me around again."

Her next heartbeat twisted painfully in her chest, but having gotten her way, she gave him a curt nod, then started running. She heard the tires squeal as he put the cruiser in reverse and took the curves far too fast, heedless of the fact that there could be more kids out here. She ignored the stinging in the backs of her eyes. He wouldn't really quit. She knew that. But the mere thought was enough to spike her already skyrocketing anxiety.

It seemed to take days, but Auri finally found her way back to the bus. Back to her grandpa. The smoke became thicker with each step she took, but other than her eyes burning as much as her legs, she was fine. She could still see and breathe thanks to her inhaler. She'd taken several hits on the way up, but the albuterol was running seriously low.

She glanced around for Tim before leaving the cover of the trees. Flames licked along a wall of smoke to her left. She couldn't wait any longer. She turned and made a run for it. Logically she should go down to avoid smoke inhalation, but she had to get to her grandfather. Smoke was already filling the bus.

Ducking inside, she hurried to the backpacks and tore through them. Her grandfather was still there but unconscious. "Grandpa!" she shouted, patting his cheek. It was cold. Too cold for the warm weather. "Grandpa, please," she whispered through a sob. "Please."

"Auri?" he said, his lashes fluttering against his pale cheeks.

"Grandpa!" She lunged at him and showered his face with kisses.

"No, Auri. No." He fought to open his eyes. "Peanut, what are you doing here?"

"There's a fire. I think Tim set it."

"Tim?"

"Tim Redding. He's the shooter. At least I think he is. I haven't actually seen his face. Grandpa, we have to get you to safety."

"No." He tried to push her away. "No, Auri, run."

Her grandpa had always been the strongest person she knew. Seeing him like this tore her apart. "Please, Grandpa. We have to get you out of the smoke. The fire is coming so fast."

But he was out again. He'd been lying to her. His wound must've been worse than he said.

She found a sweatshirt and tried to rip it, but she couldn't quite manage it. Her hands were shaking so bad and her strength had all but abandoned her. She tied it around his leg as tight as she could, finally noticing the pool of blood he lay in. With tears pushing past her lashes in droves, she covered him with the backpacks again before deciding to try the radio, just in case.

The bus driver lay in a pool of blood underneath his seat, one arm thrown over his head, but his chest was moving. He was still alive. Auri slipped on his blood when reaching for the mic.

She put it to her mouth and pressed the button on the side. "Hello?" she said, turning knobs with her free hand. "Is anyone there?" When no one answered, she examined the large hole in the front of the radio. Tim had shot it clean through.

A bout of coughs wracked her shoulders, and she took another hit off her inhaler, only then realizing her hands were covered in blood. She stowed her inhaler and wiped her hands on her jeans before looking up the mountain. She had to get back up to the petroglyphs. She only managed one bar there, but a single bar was better than none. Someone had to know her grandpa was in the bus. He and the bus driver would burn to death if no one knew to look for them.

She scrambled back to her grandpa and pressed her forehead to his. "I'll be right back, Grandpa. I'll get you out, but I want to try to get help first in case . . . in case I can't manage it." She said the words, but her mind was already racing with ideas on how to get him out. They involved making a stretcher by tying backpacks together and dragging him off the bus, but he would need an ambulance either way, and that took precedence. "Please don't leave me," she whispered.

Never feeling more alone in her life, Auri ducked out the back exit. After another quick assessment of the area to make sure Tim hadn't doubled back, she hurried up the slope, following the grooves the bus left when it slid down. The bus had rolled farther than she thought, and it took some time to get back up to the road. From there, she sprinted past the picnic area and took the trail up to the petroglyphs.

She didn't stop to catch her breath. Excitement spurred her forward as she took out her phone, running at breakneck speed until she had a bar. She stopped and clutched the phone to her chest, then texted her mom before trying to call, just in case her calls wouldn't go through.

*Grandpa injured in bus. The fire is close. Please come get him.*

She hit SEND just as a female voice sounded behind her. "See?"

Auri whirled around.

Lynelle stood there, her requisite smirk perfectly placed. "Right where I told you she'd be." She crossed her arms over her chest, and Auri's head spun in disbelief.

Tim Redding walked up behind Lynelle, the gun trained on Auri's torso, when her phone rang. She didn't dare move when he reached over and plucked it out of her hand.

He tossed it onto the ground and stomped on it before retraining his gaze on her. It did a lot of traveling, his gaze, as he studied every inch of her, pausing on her chest and then again at her crotch. "How'd you figure it out?" he asked her.

"Figure what out?"

"C'mon, Auri." He flashed her his superstar smile. "Don't wuss out on me now."

She lifted one corner of her mouth in a halfhearted attempt to feign confidence. "It wasn't that hard, Tim. You're not that smart."

"Damn." He laughed, and the face that Auri once thought handsome became a twisted, deformed thing. "I knew I liked you." He lifted the gun and pointed it at her chest again. "I'm really going to regret this. Such a waste. Any last words?"

She lifted a shoulder. "Duck?"

"What?" he asked, but it was too late. Lynelle had raised a rock and smashed it into the side of his head.

He fell to his knees, stunned as a river of blood flowed down his face, too fast for the wound not to be serious.

Lynelle tried to get around him to Auri, but he caught her ankle and tripped her.

"Lynelle!" Auri cried, hurtling forward, but he had the rifle trained on her with one hand before she took two steps.

He grabbed Lynelle's hair with his free hand, lifted her head, and slammed it into the ground. Blood poured from Lynelle's nose and mouth.

Auri gasped and covered her own with her hands.

"You got a little bit of fight in you after all, don't you? And here I figured you for a spineless cow."

Auri stepped closer. "Tim, please."

But he slammed Lynelle's face into the ground again. She went limp as the bones in Auri's legs dissolved. She sank onto her knees, silently pleading for Lynelle to wake up.

Tim stumbled to his feet, pressing a hand to his temple. "That was a bitch move, Lynelle." He swayed and pointed the rifle at Lynelle's back.

"Tim, no!" Auri lurched forward, but he retrained the gun on her instantly. Her lungs seized as he took the rifle in both hands and slowly took aim, like a sniper zeroing in on his target.

She thought about so many things in that moment. It was weird how quickly the mind could process what would normally be trivial events but now meant the world to her. The time her mother sprained her ankle trying not to step on a lizard. The night her grandparents rushed into her room at midnight to wish her a happy birthday. The way Cruz's eyes sparkled when he grinned at her. The way Levi looked at her mom. Sybil and Chastity and even Lynelle. It was the people most important to her that flashed before her eyes in the end.

Well, that and a second shooter stalking up to them.

# 26

*Some things are better left alone.*
*Like me, for instance.*

—T-SHIRT OFTEN WORN BY SUNSHINE VICRAM

Surprisingly, Sun found the scene before Quince made it back to her, and it was like an abstract painting, tragic and surreal. She had to stop and allow her mind to adjust. To take it in. The bus lay upside down, the back open with items strewn about the ground. The bus driver lay slumped underneath his overturned seat, and adrenaline dumped into her system. Where were her father and Auri? She was just about to head down to check on the driver when she saw blood drops leading to the picnic area across the road. Not a lot, but enough to convince Sun to head to the petroglyphs.

She spotted another vehicle, a silver Dodge Ram, in the grass farther up the mountain and wondered if it belonged to the shooter. She hurried over for a quick assessment. No weapons in the cabin or the bed and the tread pattern was different, so not the same tires that had parked at the pass at Copper Canyon where they found their Jane Doe. These were factory. The tires at the crime scene were aftermarket. She tried the passenger's-side door to check the registration, but it was locked. It could've still been the shooter or a concerned citizen or a hiker who got caught up in the horrific events of the day. There was no way of knowing just yet.

After a quick scan for the owner and finding no one, she eased up the path to the rock formations with the petroglyphs, keeping a lookout for anything unusual. She slowed when she heard voices. Or, more to the point, one specific voice. The voice she'd been searching for.

Fighting the urge to sprint to Auri, she drew her sidearm and crept closer just in time to see the shooter slam a girl's head into the ground.

Auri sank onto her knees, begging him not to shoot the girl, but when he repositioned the rifle—the rifle he had in his left hand—and trained it on Auri instead, a calmness sank into Sun like she'd never felt before. A sense of calling like she'd never known. She raised her sidearm, aimed for the base of the man's skull, and pulled the trigger.

He crumpled instantly, losing all motor skills and falling into a heap all the way to the ground.

She'd taken the only shot she knew would incapacitate him instantly so he couldn't pull the trigger and kill Auri in reflex, but the smoke that was getting thicker by the moment had obstructed her view for a split second. She was afraid she'd missed his spine. She still may have. The fact that he went down didn't mean she'd completely incapacitated him. Her bullet could've grazed his spine instead of severing it, stunning him instead of ending his life as planned.

Keeping her sidearm trained on the shooter, she hurried up and kicked his rifle down the trail. He lay on his left side, eyes open as though in disbelief but unable to move. Before she could search him for other weapons and check his pulse, she was tackle-hugged by her very reason for living.

"Mom!" Auri cried, squeezing the breath from Sun's lungs. Anacondas had nothing on her daughter.

Sun holstered her duty weapon and hugged her back, squeezing with all her might before Auri remembered the other girl and tore away from her.

"Lynelle!" she said, falling to her knees beside her.

Sun knelt to check the girl's pulse, but the poor thing started to come around with a soft moan. "Hang tight, Lynelle," Sun said, trying to keep her immobile with a light hand on her shoulder. "Help is on the way, hon. Don't move."

Lynelle groaned again, and Auri surprised Sun by taking the girl's hand. "It's okay, Lynelle. My mom is here just like I said." Auri sucked in a sob and Sun put both arms around her shoulders. Not for comfort. Not for support. Not because she was startlingly proud of the woman her daughter had grown into. The brave, selfless human she'd become. All those things were true. All those and then some.

But she put her arms around Auri because the shooter had pulled a pistol and was aiming it at Auri.

Too late to draw her sidearm, Sun raised a palm as she slowly nudged Auri behind her.

"What are you—" Auri began, then she saw the gun, too. She froze, so Sun pulled harder at her arm, trying to block the gun's targeted trajectory. Namely, her daughter's head.

The shooter still lay on his side, barely able to lift his head much less the gun, but he was simply too close to miss. The left side of his face hung in shreds from Sun's bullet which had entered the base of his skull and exited through his cheek. Blood poured out of the wound, clumping in his hair and pooling on the ground.

A male voice, cautious and subdued, sounded from behind them. "It's okay, son."

Sun turned ever so slightly and saw Tim's father, former sheriff Baldwin Redding, slowly stalking toward them. He'd picked up the rifle Tim had dropped and trained the tip on the back of Sun's head.

"Dad?" Tim said. "I can't . . . I can't move my left side."

"It's okay, son. I'm here now." He looked at Sun, his face twisted into a mass of hatred and agony. He jerked the rifle he had perched on his left shoulder, motioning for Sun and Auri to get back.

They scrambled back, Sun doing her best to put herself between the firearms and her daughter, but Auri seemed to be doing the same. She kept trying to get in front of her, so Sun had to keep a firm hold on the headstrong girl.

Emergency vehicles sounded in the distance, getting closer by the second and ramping up Redding's anxiety. He rubbed a cheek on his shoulder as he scissor-walked to his son's side. But he kept his aim steady, not daring to take his eyes off Sun.

When Sun slowly inched her hand toward her sidearm, he tilted his head and deadpanned her. "I know how fast you are, Sunny Girl. How about you keep that hand right where it was."

She raised her palms. "I'm just trying to understand all of this, Redding."

"Isn't it obvious?" he asked, a breathy sob escaping him.

"Not from the cheap seats. Is this, like, a bonding experience with your son?"

Tim tried to aim his gun at her but he couldn't quite manage a steady hold, and if Sun was right, he was left-handed like his father, which would make his aim less accurate since he held the gun in his right hand. Even with him unable to keep a steady hold, if he got really lucky and pulled the trigger at just the right moment, he could very well hit one of them. Or both.

"Something you two do in your spare time?" she continued. Auri's fingers clutched at her back, and Sun realized she was having a hard time breathing. Auri clutched at Sun's shirt and coughed as Sun snaked an arm behind her and pulled her closer. She had to get her out of here now. If the Reddings didn't kill her daughter, the smoke would.

Redding wiped his face again, and she realized he was crying. "It's not his fault."

His reaction threw her off, but she recovered quickly while continuing to scan the area for possible escape routes for Auri. "Whose fault is it?"

"He was just . . . born wrong. He doesn't mean to hurt them."

"So, it's all just a big misunderstanding?" she asked, wracking her brain, trying to figure out how to get Auri to safety, and she realized she simply needed to keep him talking. Quince would be here soon.

"He's sick. He needs help."

"He needs more than that," she said, sparing the partially paralyzed teen a quick glance.

"Don't you think I know that?" he asked, jabbing the gun in her direction.

She held up a palm, trying desperately to placate him. Maybe she could get him talking about Clay Ravinder. How did all of this play into their dealings together?

"I've tried everything, Sunshine. I've tried counseling and medication and all the things they said. Hell, I even tried to beat it out of him, but there are just some things that burrow inside too deep. You can't get it out no matter what you do."

That would explain why Tim had been beaten up recently.

"I'm sorry, Dad," Tim said, his arm swaying as he tried to keep aim.

"Don't you worry, son."

"Does this have anything to do with your deal with Clay Ravinder?" Sun asked, trying desperately to keep him talking.

He furrowed his brows as though thrown by her question, then shook his head. "Not in the way that you think."

"Explain it then," she said, catching a glimpse of movement below them. And then she had an epiphany. "Is that why you want your old job back so much? To cover up your son's indiscretions?"

"That's part of it."

"What does that have to do with Clay?"

"We have very similar goals."

She nodded, scanning the horizon. Maybe she'd imagined the movement. Either way, she just needed to keep this man talking. "So, what? Clay kills Levi and you kill me and you two run the kingdom of Del Sol together?"

A wry, bitter laugh escaped him. "Clay can't kill Levi. His family would never let him get away with it. He needed a rock-solid alibi when the deed went down. Something indisputable."

"Ah. And that's where you come in. You kill Levi, and then what? Clay kills me to make sure you get your old job back so that you can clear his name?"

"Not even close," he said, sparing a lightning-quick glance at his son. He wiped his cheek again, keeping an eye on her from underneath soot-covered lashes.

She saw movement again and hope blossomed in her chest. It had to be Quince. If she could cause a stir, make some noise, he could make it close enough to take a shot. She took hold of Auri with the one hand she had behind her back and prepared to push her down the slope. There were enough trees and bushes to give her some semblance of cover as Sun and Quince saw to clan Redding.

She waited a few moments more for Tim to lose his strength again, as he did every few seconds, and lower the gun to take a breath. In the meantime, she kept up the game with Redding. "Then what? What was Clay's part of the deal?"

"Something I couldn't do myself." He pressed his mouth together and began to sob and Sun realized he was stalling as much as she was.

The truth sank into her bones like icy water in a frozen lake. She frowned and looked from Redding to Tim, then back again. "Redding," she whispered, almost afraid to ask, "what are we waiting for?"

Another sob wrenched from his chest as he stared at her from over the barrel. After a moment, he answered, "We're waiting for my son to bleed out."

Sun sat astonished, the air whooshing from her lungs.

Tim's eyes had rolled, turning them completely white for a split second, but he snapped back to life with his father's confession. His brows slid together as he asked weakly, "Dad?"

Redding's shoulders shook, and he started to lower the rifle, but Sun called out to him when Tim raised the gun.

It happened faster than her mind could register. Tim pulled the trigger at the exact moment a second bullet snapped his head back, the impact nearly taking it off. He went limp and Sun finally saw Quincy advancing up the trail, his rifle now trained on Redding senior.

But Tim had succeeded in shooting his father. Redding stumbled back, holding his chest as blood spilled from between his splayed fingers. He looked at Sun and nodded a heartbeat before he lost his footing and slid down the side of the mountain.

Sun grabbed Auri to her, not wanting her to witness the tragic events, but she wasn't having any of it.

She hugged Sun back for a few glorious seconds, then lunged for her friend. "Lynelle!" she cried. Taking Lynelle's hand into her own, Auri ignored the boy lying in a pool of his own blood not five feet from her.

"Is it over?" Lynelle asked. "I tried to stay really still."

Auri brushed her hair off her face. "You did great, Lynelle," she said, before succumbing to a fit of coughs.

Sun patted her jeans. "Where's your inhaler, bug?"

Auri pulled it out and drew in what she could. "It's out," she said, trying not to cough, "but I think I'm okay."

"We'll get you some oxygen." She waited for Quince to check their assailants. The adrenaline coursing through her veins was catching up to her. She started shaking uncontrollably. Not for herself but for Auri. She'd almost lost her. Again. What the actual fuck?

"They're gone, boss," Quince said when he rushed up to them.

Auri threw her arms around his neck and, by the look on her smoke-streaked face, tried desperately to hold back a sob.

He rose to his full height, taking her with him and hugged her for as long as she would stay still.

"Oh, my god, Grandpa!" she said. She slid out of his arms and started sprinting down the path before he could steady her. So she was a tad wobbly.

Sun scrambled after her. "Auri, wait!"

She looked out over the landscape below them and pointed. "Grandpa's in the bus!"

"What?"

"We have to get him, Mom! He's bleeding and he broke his leg!"

And Sun thought she was all out of panic-inducing adrenaline. Emergency vehicles started filing in when they got to the picnic area. A helicopter flew overhead as they ran across the road and slid down the slope to the bus. The flames were only a couple hundred yards out. Far too close for Sun's comfort.

"Grandpa!" Auri cried. She rushed inside and started throwing backpacks around.

Sun didn't realize why until she saw her father lying underneath them. "Dad!" She hurried to him and checked his pulse.

"Mom?" Auri asked, tears streaming down her ashen cheeks.

"He's alive."

"Damn straight, I'm alive," he said with a soft cough. "I'm just resting my eyes."

"Grandpa!" Auri draped herself over him while Sun checked his wound. Wound care was above her pay grade but it looked bad. The large pool of blood underneath him looked worse and she felt the world tilt to the left.

"Auri," he said, his voice hoarse, "I always knew you'd light the world on fire, but this is a bit extreme, even for you."

"Not me, Grandpa."

Sun patted Auri's back. "I'll be right back."

"Don't hurry on my account," he said. His lids sealed shut but there was a sweet smile on his face as he rubbed his granddaughter's head.

Sun gave him a quick kiss on the brow, then went to check on the driver. He was still breathing, but he had a gaping head wound. She sprinted back up the hill.

"Well?" Quince said to her. He was busy organizing emergency services like a maestro.

"He's alive. They both are. We need two stretchers. Where's Lynelle?"

"EMTs are bringing her down now."

"Good," she said, looking for another ambulance.

"They're all at the bottom seeing to the kids," Officer Bucannon said. "All but two have been accounted for."

"There are two here along with the shooter, Tim Redding, and one more . . . victim," she said, categorizing the former sheriff accordingly. "We have to get downwind of this fire."

"I agree. There's another ambulance on the way."

"Can we safely get them out of the bus while they're en route?" Quincy asked her.

"It's safer than them suffocating from smoke inhalation. And Auri needs oxygen."

He nodded and grabbed a portable canister out of the ambulance.

Sun started back down the hill when she heard a commotion. She turned to one of the state cruisers and saw Levi and Seabright in the back. Clearly, Seabright followed orders as well as the rest of her staff did.

"Oh," Officer Bucannon said, "we had to put those two in cuffs. Your partner wanted to assess the situation before letting anyone else up, and they were not fond of his plan."

"Of course they weren't," Sun said. She turned to Quince. "Happy now that you got to put him in cuffs?"

A wicked grin spread across his face. "You have no idea."

Quince and Sun headed down to the bus while Bucannon released the prisoners. She was inside when the pair stormed the gates. Seabright was all business. He helped Quincy get the oxygen on her dad—because Auri had refused it—while Auri ran into Levi's arms. To say that Levi was livid would be the understatement of the Cenozoic era, but she could tell by the look on his face he was also relieved. And possibly even grateful.

"I take it Seabright called you?"

The fury he'd been keeping in check was apparently not all directed at Quincy. "Why didn't you?"

"I'm sorry, Levi. I could hardly focus on driving, much less making my way through the phone tree on the rare occasions we had a signal. Speaking of which, I need to call my mom." She took out her phone only to be once again left with no bars.

"I had Salazar call her," Quincy said.

"We have one stretcher. Waiting on another." One of the EMTs, a young kid from Del Sol named Toby, stood at the opened emergency door.

Sun stood, ducking under one of the seatbacks. "Okay, we need to clear the area."

Despite the cramped space, Levi picked Auri up and carefully carried her, ducking under the floor panel to get out. She'd wrapped her arms and legs around him and held him tight even after they exited. Sun pressed her mouth together and looked away, fighting the blur of tears. Their poor kid would need years of therapy after this. And the smoke billowing around them wasn't helping.

"I'm kind of light-headed," Auri said as they walked uphill. Half a second later, she went limp in his arms.

"We have to get her some oxygen," Sun said, hurrying Levi up the slope to the waiting ambulance while Quince, Seabright, and two EMTs got her dad loaded and up the hill, then went back and made the same trek for the bus driver.

Most of the emergency crews had already gone back down the mountain, surely struggling to see through the ever-thickening smoke, when the second ambulance arrived. They got her dad loaded and Auri on oxygen seconds before the fire jumped the road and headed toward the petroglyphs. Thankfully, two fire trucks had doused the area. That, along with the recent rains, seemed to be doing the trick.

After getting the bus driver into an ambulance, they descended the mountain as quickly as they dared with such limited visibility. Levi still held Auri, and Sun was trying not to fall even further in love with the man, when her phone sounded with an alarm. Levi's went off as well as they'd both received service at the same time, and if Sun had to guess, so did Quincy's. The alarm was their proverbial bat signal. The Dangerous Daughters were calling them in.

"You have got to be kidding me," she said, letting go of her dad's hand long enough to check her phone.

Levi didn't even bother. Auri had regained consciousness and lay nestled in his arms. It was a moment he was not going to sully. He pulled her tighter, and she snuggled against him.

But it wasn't a call to arms. It was a call to Levi's distillery. Apparently, the Double D's had a man—or woman—on the inside and something was happening there. An altercation with at least one death.

"Levi," Sun said, hating to do it, "check your phone."

He pulled out his phone. Auri sat up to give him space, but he kept an arm around her, not willing to let her go just yet. He read the text, then cursed under his breath.

"What's wrong?" Auri said, her voice almost gone, her breathing labored as Toby checked her oxygen level.

"When we get to the bottom, I have to run and take care of something," he said to Auri, "but I'll meet you at the hospital, okay?"

"Okay, but I don't need to go to the hospital. I'm feeling much better."

Sun rubbed her back. "Nice try, bug. I'll tell you what. You go with Toby to keep Grandpa company and maybe let them check you out while you're there?"

"They have a breathing treatment waiting for you the minute we show up," Toby said.

She nodded, acquiescing as her grandfather lifted a finger to her. It was all he could manage under the straps and plastic tubing.

"I'll keep him safe, Mom."

"I'm pretty sure you've already done that, bug."

# 27

*If I'm ever murdered, take comfort in knowing*
*that I ran my mouth until the bitter end.*

—JOURNAL ENTRY: AURORA VICRAM

The ambulance they were in pulled over when they got to the bottom. Emergency vehicles in every color under the sun, each with lights blazing, sat in a semicircle. Beyond that were vehicles filled with parents and school personnel and news crews. Word had definitely spread.

Sun's mother was escorted toward them through the melee of concerned parents and reporters. "Sunshine!" she shouted, waving her arms frantically.

"You don't have to go with me," Levi said when Quincy pulled up with Seabright in the passenger's seat. "Stay with Auri."

"My mom's got this. There's been a death, Levi. I'm going." She gave her panicked mom a quick hug before they hopped in the back seat of the cruiser and emergency personnel cleared an opening for them. Quince turned on the lights and siren to get them through traffic faster.

"How are they?" Quincy asked her.

"Alive."

"Boo-yah," he said softly, paying close attention to the congested road. As soon as they cleared the crowds, Quincy made good time to Levi's distillery.

But they had a good fifteen minutes between point A and point B. Oddly enough, despite all the doubts and the concerns and the questions, no one said anything until they were almost at their destination.

Then Levi said softly, "I'm not mad."

She scoffed. She wasn't angry, either. She just found his statement a tad laughable. "When aren't you mad, Levi?"

"I don't handle uncertainty well. Or fear. When Seabright called me—"

"Instead of me. I know."

"You've been there, Shine. You understand what that's like, only you actually know how to process and deal with those kinds of emotions. I just become an ass."

She hid a smile.

"You don't become an ass," Quincy said, handing the compliment to him almost reluctantly. Then he added, "You become *more* of an ass. There's a difference."

Seabright looked out the window to hide a grin.

"Do you mind?" Levi asked. "We're having a moment."

"Oh. My bad." He raised a hand and shimmied his shoulders, and it was one of the cutest things Sun had ever seen. A grown man, especially one the size of Quincy, shimmying his shoulders was not something one saw every day. Probably for the best.

"We're having a moment?" she asked Levi.

"Yes, damn it. I'm trying to apologize for my lack of social skills. But you have to consider who I was raised by."

He had a point. "But you *were* mad."

"No, Shine, I was frustrated that I didn't get to shoot that fuck in the head myself."

"Oh. Okay. Then what about the last fifteen years? You've been either angry or aloof since I can remember."

He looked out his window, but Sun caught a glimpse of the turmoil glistening in his eyes. "I told you, I don't handle things right. I never have."

"Well, you better learn for our daughter's sake."

He visibly relaxed when she brought up their daughter, and Sun wanted to throw her arms around him. "For our daughter's sake?" he said softly. "Anything."

Sun ignored the warmth that spread inside her with his declaration. They pulled into the distillery's parking lot, the gorgeous building equal parts metal, wood, and rock. As with everything Levi did, it was elegant and robust. "Do you have any idea what's going on? I'd love to know what we're walking into."

"I don't have a clue."

She nodded despite the disappointment, wondering if this was part of the Dangerous Daughters' plan they'd spoken about earlier. She had so many questions and so little time to waterboard people for answers.

With the front of the building teeming with onlookers, they pulled up to yet another shit show. Quincy's words. "'Nother shit show, guys."

"Figures," Sun said.

"Those are my employees." Levi jumped out of the cruiser almost before it stopped.

An entire shift of workers stood outside the main distillery. Sun had only been here once, and she had yet to see the inside, but if it was anywhere near as nice as the outside . . .

"Mrs. Fairborn?" she asked. Looking around, she realized not everyone standing outside the distillery worked for Dark River Shine. Not unless Mrs. Fairborn and two other Dangerous Daughters had changed careers, but Sun couldn't see Myrtle Andrews rejoining the job market at ninety-two. "What's going on?" she asked as Levi and Seabright pushed against the door. It had been barricaded from the inside.

"There was a fight," Mrs. Fairborn said. "We came to kill Clay, but an altercation of some kind broke out before we got here. The workers won't let us in."

Sun pinched the bridge of her nose. "Mrs. Fairborn, you can't tell me stuff like that."

"That the workers won't let us in? Whyever not?"

It was only when she saw what Myrtle had in her hands that she started to believe her. "You literally brought pitchforks?"

Mrs. Fairborn snorted. "No, just Myrtle. She's old-school. I brought this." The tiny woman who'd once been suspected of being a serial killer pulled a Magnum .45 the size of her torso out of her bag.

"Mrs. Fairborn!" Sun said, lunging for it before the woman killed someone. Or herself. She snatched it away and handed it to Quincy. "Stay put. And don't kill anyone."

"I can't make any promises."

She waited for Quincy to lock the gun in the cruiser and get back. Levi and Seabright had pushed past the barrier. All four of them hurried inside but were stopped instantly.

Sun sniffed the air. "I'm not sure what a distillery is supposed to smell like, but I'm pretty sure it's not gasoline."

Levi ran to a control room to check surveillance. A security guard lay unconscious on the floor, a trickle of blood on his temple. Sun knelt to check on him. He groaned as Sun put pressure on the wound.

Levi had a state-of-the-art system that showed the admin area as well as the distillery floor. Massive metal stills took up most of the floor with thick pipelines protruding out in all directions. They looked like the product of an 1800s science-fiction novel, and Levi was the mad scientist who ran it all.

"There," he said, pointing.

Clay appeared on one of the monitors, dousing the entire place with gasoline, which seemed redundant.

"Isn't this entire place flammable as is?" Sun asked Levi.

"Maybe he wants to speed things up a bit," Levi said with a quick shrug. "You need to leave."

"I agree. Quince, get this man out of here and get everyone back. If this place goes up—"

"Aren't you forgetting something, Sunburn?" He stepped closer to her and poked her in the chest. Not hard. Not enough to hurt, but he poked her. In the chest. What the actual fuck? "I quit," he reminded her. "You don't get to order me around anymore."

She exhaled her frustration and poked him back, emphasizing each word with a jab. "Quincy. Now. Is. Not. The. Time."

Quincy slapped her hand away and rubbed his chest as Levi said, "Actually, I was talking to you, Shine." He tried his hand at a death stare. It wasn't bad for a novice.

Still, hers was better. "I'm not leaving. Quince, please take him."

"I'll take him."

They turned to see Joshua Ravinder, one of Levi's cousins and his plant manager, standing at the door, looking like he'd been in a fight with a mountain lion.

"Joshua, are you okay?" Sun asked. She stood as Levi checked out his cousin's most obvious wounds.

"Sorry, cuz. He got the jump on me. He's locked himself in the stillroom."

Levi narrowed his eyes on the screen again. "Yeah, well, he's too much of a narcissist to be suicidal. He has a plan."

"He usually does." Joshua bent to wrap an arm around the security guard and help him stand.

"Joshua," Sun said, making sure he heard her, "you have to make sure everyone gets back. Way, way back. If this thing goes up, it's going to take a lot of real estate with it."

"You got it, Sheriff."

She turned to see Levi glaring at her. "Is this you being frustrated again?"

"No. This is me being mad. Get out of here, Shine."

"You know I can't." She stepped closer, trying to make herself understood. "You know I wouldn't if I could."

He stalked out of the control room. The rest of the crew followed. When they got to the stillroom, Levi used a master key. He opened the door just enough to peek inside, then he turned and tossed the keys to Seabright, motioning for him to go around to the other door. Quince followed Seabright.

"I know he's not suicidal, but surely he wouldn't be stupid enough to light that on fire with him inside?" Sun whispered.

"You don't know my uncle very well," Levi said from between gritted teeth.

She took his arm. "Levi, you need to know, Redding made a deal with Clay. Redding was supposed to kill you in a way that your family couldn't prove Clay had anything to do with. I think maybe Redding couldn't bring himself to pull it off? I'm not sure, but I just want you to know, your uncle definitely wants you dead."

"I assumed as much," he said with a stoic nod. "They're at the door."

Sun looked past him and through the jungle of floor-to-ceiling pipes to an access door on the other side of the huge room. It slid open just enough for Seabright to look inside.

Levi nodded to an old-school fire axe on the wall behind a small glass door. "Can you get that axe for me?"

"Sure," she said. Like an idiot. Like she was born yesterday. When she went to retrieve the axe, Levi slipped inside the stillroom then closed and locked the door behind him.

"Levi!" she half whispered through the observation window. She shoved against the solid metal door to no avail.

He pointed behind her and mouthed the words *get out.*

She shoved again. No way was she getting through that, even with the axe. Certainly not without alerting Clay to their presence. She looked around, unsure of how Seabright and Quince got to the other door, but she had to at least try. She ran back a few yards and took the first hall she came to. After one dead end, two wrong turns, and three halls half the length of a football stadium, she found the unlocked door at last. She burst through it just in time to see Seabright, the only man in the room who'd recently been stabbed, fighting the burly Clay Ravinder.

Quince was cheering him on, wincing occasionally like a spectator at a boxing match when his fighter took one to the kidney. And Levi was playing with a square device of some kind.

She hurried up to him, feeling a little like she'd walked into an episode of *The Twilight Zone.* "What are you doing?"

"Goddammit, Sun," he said, searching the heavens for strength. He refocused on her. "Do you ever listen?"

"Me?" she asked, utterly appalled. "You locked me out!"

His jaw strained under the pressure he was exerting on it. "Exactly."

She started to rail at him some more, but the device in his hands caught her attention. Or at least part of her attention. The rest was taken up by the nearby wrestling match. "First, what is that? And second, shouldn't we be helping?"

Levi looked over his shoulder just as Clay slammed Seabright back into a massive still. The man grunted but kept his arms padlocked around Clay's neck in a vise grip any professional wrestler would be proud of.

"Nah, he's good. And this," he said, holding it up to her, "is a timed incendiary device."

"Ah." She winced as Seabright took an elbow to the ribs. "So, he's not suicidal."

"Nope. He said something about if he can't have the distillery, no one can."

"Bitter much?"

"But I'm thinking his motivation has a lot more to do with the fact that he took out a huge insurance policy on the place several months ago as a backup plan." He gestured toward the timer. "Pour a little gasoline, set this to go off after you leave, and you have a pretty good bomb."

She tried not to be alarmed, but the digital timer was still counting down. "Did you disarm it?"

"No clue."

"Because it's still counting down."

"I can see that."

"It's saying less than two minutes."

He looked at her. "I can also tell time, Shine."

"Well, technically, that's not telling . . . Look," she said, drawing in a deep breath as the two men behind them fell to the ground. Hard. "Shouldn't we get that out of here since it could explode?"

"It won't explode so much as catch fire."

"In a room full of gasoline and corn whiskey. What could go wrong?" She threw her hands into the air and turned to Quince. With a gesture toward Seabright, she asked, "Are you going to help him?"

"Me?" he asked in alarm. "I don't want to get hit. You help."

He was right. She was the sheriff. It was her responsibility. She pulled her sidearm and both Quince and Levi sprang forward to stop her.

"What?" She slapped them away. "I'm not stupid. I'm just going to threaten him."

"No need." Levi tilted his head to study his friend as Seabright struggled to keep his grip. "You got this?" he asked him.

"Yes," Seabright grunted from between clenched teeth, applying more pressure to the burly man's throat. Clay thrashed and fought as hard as he could. He landed another elbow to Seabright's rib cage and Sun winced.

"You sure?" Levi asked. "I can help."

"Fuck off."

Levi shrugged and simply watched as Clay slowly—oh, so slowly—went limp in Seabright's arms.

Seabright filled his lungs and kicked the man off him only to have Levi grab a container and throw liquid in Clay's face. Hopefully it was just water.

Clay sputtered and spit back to life, and Sun raised her sidearm, but Levi simply knelt in front of him and held out the device. Clay's eyes rounded to the size of saucers. He lunged for the box and disarmed it with three whole seconds to spare. Just like in the movies.

Sun hadn't realized she'd been holding her breath. She exhaled and fell back against a still for support. "Holy crap, Levi."

As Quince finally took Clay to the ground and cuffed him, Levi stood. He turned to her and grinned, holding out his palm to show her a small piece of plastic with something that looked like the frayed end of a rope attached to it.

"What's that?"

"The part that would have caught fire."

"The only part that would've caught fire?"

"The only one."

"So it wouldn't have gone off?"

"Nope. Well, I don't think so," he said, studying it.

Sun rubbed her temple. "I quit."

"Hey," Quince said, dragging Clay to his feet. "I quit first. You can't copy me."

"How did you know to take that out of the box?" she asked Levi.

"I didn't." He gestured to his right.

Sun looked and saw Wynn Ravinder standing there, leaning against a still like he hadn't a care in the world. He did, however, have a killer shiner and was apparently covered in gasoline.

Reflexively, Sun raised her duty weapon before catching herself and holstering it. It had been a long day. She walked over to him, sniffed, and crinkled her nose. "Maybe we should get you into a shower."

"I'd like that."

"And see to that shiner."

"Nothing a little corn whiskey won't fix."

"You son of a bitch," Clay said, trying to get to Wynn as Quincy hauled him off.

Wynn raised a brow. "Language, big brother. I'll see you in hell." He turned back to Sun. "Aka, prison."

Sun chuckled, then walked over to a panting Seabright, still on the ground catching his breath, and sank to the ground beside him. "Are you okay?"

"Never better."

She sat cross-legged. "This town is like Smallville only none of the crazy people were infected by meteor rocks."

"Yeah, I don't know what that means."

She patted his head. "Then you've led a sad life, little man."

"Little?" he asked, appalled.

Oh, yeah. He'd be fine.

# 28

*If your body is not a temple but a federation starship*
*with critical hull damage and shields at 0%, we can help.*

—SIGN AT DEL SOL FITNESS AND MORE

Two hours later, Sun watched as her mom paced back and forth in Auri's hospital room. The man she'd been married to for thirty-seven years was still in surgery.

Levi had to stay back and oversee the cleanup of the gasoline before he could get to the hospital lest his life's work actually go up in flames, so she and Quincy brought a curmudgeonly Seabright to the ER no matter how much he insisted he was fine.

Fire and rescue already had the flames by the petroglyphs under control. Thanks to the recent rains, it was more smoke than fire. The bus driver had regained consciousness, which Sun found extraordinary. His prognosis was good.

Auri had to be admitted. They put her on oxygen and a bronchodilator, but nothing seemed to help more than Cruz's visit. She sat up in bed when he walked in, her face full of elation as he pulled her into his arms.

After a moment, he set her back. "This again? Really?"

She lifted a shoulder. "I can't help myself. I love the attention and, quite frankly, bruises look good on me."

He swiped at a lock of hair to get a better look at the bruise on her head. "So do submissive hemogoblins."

"No submissive hemoglobins this time. Just a plain old asthma attack." She coughed lightly as though in confirmation.

"You act like smoke inhalation is bad," he said. She giggled but his expression turned serious. "I should have gone with you."

Auri started to argue when Wanda Stephanopoulos walked in, out of breath and carrying a first aid kit.

"Wanda," Sun said, eyeing the kit.

"Oh, I brought this just in case, but I see they have everything under control."

Sun looked from Cruz to Wanda and back again. "So what did you guys do this afternoon?"

Cruz ducked his head, a charming dimple forming on one corner of his mouth. "Auri, I just found out Wanda is my grandmother. My biological grandmother on my dad's side."

The look of stunned disbelief on Auri's face with a light sprinkling of horror was enough to make the rest of Sun's week. Possibly the whole year.

"You told him?" Sun asked Wanda.

"It's like you said, Sunny. Life's too short to sit on your ass and be stupid."

"Yeah, I don't think I said that."

"Or wear boring clothes."

"Nope."

"Or drink bad coffee."

"Yeah, I may have said that." She leaned in closer to Wanda. "So, how did he take it?"

Wanda's face brightened, but before she could answer, Levi stepped to the door and leaned against the frame, gazing adoringly at his daughter, and it was like the clouds had parted and heaven shone down. At least for Auri. He walked around the other side of the bed and pulled her into his arms, and the strangest thing happened. Auri let go. Finally. All of her bravado crumbled. A sob wrenched from her body and her shoulders shook as she devolved into a mass of tears as he rocked her.

The scene stole Sun's breath. She'd always been surprised at how close they were, but for Auri to feel so at ease, so safe with him near, it was like someone opened a puzzle box and tossed all the pieces into the air only to have them land perfectly assembled.

"I'm here, Red," he said, smoothing her hair as he kissed her head. "I'm not going anywhere."

Sun fought a round of tears herself as she watched them. Her mother did as well. When a doctor knocked on the door and motioned for Sun's mom to step out, she hurried past the crowd. Sun followed.

Once they were all in the hall, he turned to them. "Mrs. Freyr, your husband is going to be fine."

The emotion her mom had been holding inside burst out of her in a cry that was part relief and part elation. They held each other as the doctor explained the intricacies of the operation. How the break was clean and the laceration had probably been obtained when the bus rolled. It had nicked an artery just enough to cause serious blood loss after such a long time without medical attention. He added that Sun's dad was unusually strong for his age, healthy as a horse, and expected to make a full recovery.

"You can see him in about an hour. They'll send someone to get you."

Sun and her mom held each other for a long time. When they stepped back into the room, Auri looked at her with a combination of hope and fear. "He's going to be fine, bug."

Auri started crying again, snuggling deeper into Levi's arms.

He questioned her with a raised brow, asking if Sun wanted to take over as though worried he was overstepping. Sun shook her head. No way would she miss seeing this. Seeing her daughter so adored. Loved so completely. Sun didn't miss the fact that Auri had yet to drop Cruz's hand. He sat on her bed, rubbing his thumb over her palm.

The tender moment came to an end soon enough when Quincy showed up, their prisoner in tow. Freshly showered and wearing some of Quincy's clothes, Wynn Ravinder stepped inside the al-

ready crowded hospital room. Quincy got to Auri first. Cruz stood
so he could get a hug. Then Wynn stepped up to her.

"Uncle Wynn!" she said, like they'd known each other all their
lives.

The hardened criminal, the shot caller from one of the most
notorious gangs in prison history, offered her a sheepish grin and
leaned in for a hug.

US Marshal Deleon walked in and stood beside Sun, unsure of
why he was there. "You called?"

Sun nodded and gestured toward one of Auri's visitors. "He's
all yours, Marshal. If you can untangle him from the spell that little
sprite put on him."

The fact that his fugitive was sitting not ten feet from him sank
in, and the astounded look on his face told her Wynn Ravinder was
the last person he'd expected to see. He looked at Sun and then
back again, and whispered, "Holy shit."

He put a hand on his sidearm.

Sun stopped him by placing her hand on his. "He's turning
himself in, Marshal. There's no need for that."

"Sorry," he said, dropping his hand. "Reflex."

"I understand." She looked up at him, her expression turning
serious, and said, "You owe me."

He huffed out an astonished breath. "Damn straight, I do."

"I'm going to assume any other questions you may or may not
have about anyone in my employ will be dropped?"

After a long moment of consideration where he stared at her
as though trying to see into her soul, he nodded. "As you wish,
Sheriff." It was noble of him. His curiosity would get the better of
him eventually, and Sun might have a few questions to answer, but
Deputy Rojas was in the clear for the time being.

Wynn touched Auri's face and repeated his sentiments after
their first meeting. "My god, those eyes."

Auri beamed at him.

"I'll be gone for a while, but I'd love to get to know you better
when I get back."

"Because you escaped from prison to save my dad from your brother and now you have to finish your sentence?"

Wynn's look of surprise mirrored Sun's. "How did you know that?" she asked, but thought better of it. "Never mind. I don't want to know."

Wynn laughed softly. "She's as smart as you, Sunshine." He gave her another hug, then stood to shake his nephew's hand. "You done good, son. I'm proud of you."

"Thank you, sir." He stepped closer and said softly, "I'm sorry about your brother."

"Clay?" he asked, confused.

"The other one."

Wynn nodded, knowing Levi was talking about Kubrick, the man Levi killed saving Sun. Wynn dropped his gaze for a moment, then said, "I'm sorry about your dad."

It took a second for his meaning to sink in. Levi's poker face was immaculate, but even he showed a minuscule flash of surprise when understanding dawned.

"I loved her," Wynn said. He had to be talking about Levi's mother. The woman who, according to Wynn, Auri most took after. The woman with the eyes that haunted him to this day. "I couldn't let your dad get away with it."

Levi fought hard to keep his expression passive. He nodded in thought. "I knew. Deep down, I think I always knew."

"I'll be closer now. Don't be a stranger." He pulled Levi into a hug, then walked over to Sun.

Her expression was nowhere near as schooled as Levi's. Her shock must've shown through, because he said, "I told you, apple. I've killed before. I'm just in prison for the wrong murder."

She nodded. "I'm still going to look into that."

"I know you will."

He gave her a curt nod, then stalked out into the hall, Deleon right on his heels. To Deleon's credit, he didn't cuff him right then and there. It was a gesture of good faith and Sun knew Wynn would honor the gesture by not being difficult.

The rest of the evening was a parade of well-wishers, but the true pièce de résistance was when Lynelle walked in—*walked*—wearing a hospital gown and connected to an IV, her mother in tow.

"Lynelle!" Auri ripped the oxygen off her face and started toward her new friend, but three pairs of hands pushed her back down.

Lynelle walked to her bed. The poor girl's face had seen better days. She had stitches on her cheek and forehead, and her nose had been broken for sure, but it was all superficial. Surprisingly, she hadn't sustained a single fracture.

Lynelle's mother seemed hesitant about their sudden friendship, perhaps because of all the danger that seemed to follow Auri around like a bad habit. She looked at Sun, her chin raised a notch too high. "She wanted to check on your daughter."

"I wanted to come and apologize," Lynelle explained. "I'm so sorry, Auri."

"Sorry?" She took Lynelle's hand into hers. "You could've left me there and saved yourself, but you didn't."

"You could've done the same thing," Lynelle said with a sly smile that turned appreciative. "But you didn't."

Auri looked up at Lynelle's mom. "Mrs. Amaia, your daughter saved my life."

The woman looked at her in surprise. "Lynelle told me you saved hers."

"Because she did, Mom," Lynelle insisted.

"But you saved mine first," Auri argued.

Lynelle laughed. "We're going to have to agree to disagree."

Her mom cleared her throat, a telltale wetness gathering between her lashes. "Well, that certainly sounds like something you'd do, Lynelle."

"Thanks, Mom."

"Auri," the woman said, pursing her lips, "thank you for everything you did for Lynelle and Whitney."

"Whitney?" Sun asked.

Mrs. Amaia nodded. "Turns out your daughter was right. That is my niece lying down the hall. I finally got a hold of my brother- and sister-in-law. They'd been trying to call Whitney for days. They said the texts just didn't sound like her. When I told them Auri's theory, they flew back immediately. They're with her now."

"I'm so sorry, Mrs. Amaia," Auri said. "Lynelle."

"Thanks, Auri. I just wish I'd listened sooner."

"Is she awake?" Sun asked. She hadn't gotten a call, so she guessed no. She guessed right.

"Not yet, but they're going to reduce her meds now that she's out of danger. She could wake up as early as tomorrow."

Auri pressed a hand to her mouth. "I'm so happy for you, Lynelle."

The look that flashed across Lynelle's face gave Sun hope for humanity. After all the nastiness, for Lynelle to look at Auri like Sun did. Like she hung the moon.

They let Sun's mom into post-op to sit with her dad, but they moved him to a room in the middle of the night. Thus, her daugh- ter's infinite capacity for escape and evasion as she snuck past Sun and Levi to go visit him. They'd both fallen asleep in the room with her, Levi in the chair closest, so it was mostly his fault her escape went unnoticed.

Sun woke up at around two in the morning to a frantic Levi.

"She's gone," he said.

But Sun had been here repeatedly over the last few months. "I know where she is."

Thankfully, Sun was still wearing her uniform. That seemed to keep the charge nurse from stopping them when they sought the fugitive in the one place Sun knew where to find her.

Sure enough, they walked in to see Sun's dad and Auri having a quiet conversation as her mom slept in a recliner.

"Mom!" Auri whispered.

Sun hugged her dad, careful of the IV and monitors. But at least his color had returned. "You look better without all the blue."

He chuckled. "Thanks. Your daughter was filling me in."

Sun was a little jealous. Auri hadn't even filled her in. Not completely. They had yet to get her official statement of what happened. Sun didn't want her to have to go through that just yet.

"How are you, Dad?"

"Pretty wonderful at the moment. They have me on the good stuff."

"Really?" she asked, coming up with a plan. She leaned in and whispered to Auri, "Go with me on this."

Auri nodded and Sun frowned and rubbed her head. "I don't . . . I don't feel well." She collapsed into a chair as Levi looked on, completely unmoved.

Auri fell to her knees beside her. "Mom. Mom, no. Don't go. I need you."

Sun moaned and Auri draped herself over her, fake crying like she was making a bid for an Oscar. "Oh, Mom, what will we do without you?"

Sun's mom woke up just in time for the show. Sun was so happy for her.

"Dad," Sun said. She held out a hand to him. "You can't let me go to the grave without knowing about your stint in the big house."

"Hold on," he said, grabbing the handheld button to dispense more pain meds. "I need more drugs for this."

"Sunshine Blaze," her mom scolded. "You're acting like this after everything that happened today?"

Honestly, it was like her mother didn't know her at all. "I'm not going to make it," she continued, laying it on thick.

Her dad brightened. "Good thing we're in a hospital then, eh?"

"Everything is getting dark."

"Well, it is past midnight."

She looked at Auri. "There's so little time left."

Auri draped herself over her again. "No, Mom. Don't go."

"I was convicted in the summer of '69," he said, telling the story at last.

But Sun kept up the performance just in case. She lay a hand over her forehead like in a Renaissance painting. Auri draped over her added to the illusion as well. Not that she didn't believe her father. She just didn't trust him. Probably because he would've been, like, five in '69.

"I went in as a regular inmate so I could find out what was really happening in the prison. So I could ferret out the rampant corruption. I was really the new warden."

Sun dropped her hand and glared at him. "Was your false identity Robert Redford? Because that's straight out of *Brubaker*."

"Ah, but it was based on a true story." He touched his nose like they were part of some conspiracy.

"Yes, a true story that happened when you were in diapers."

"Excellent point," he said, winking at her. "I was testing your math skills."

Auri got up and sat on the bed with her grandfather. Abandoning Sun in her time of need.

"I guess I'll keep looking. Who knows what I'll uncover in the process?"

"It wasn't a prison," he said, releasing a hapless sigh. "It was a brig. And I really did go in undercover to expose a ring of corruption."

She shot up, her back ramrod straight. "How long?"

He ignored the shocked expression his granddaughter was giving him. "Seven months."

"Holy crap, Dad. That's a long time to be undercover."

"Trust me, it seemed like a lot longer."

"I'm sorry, Grandpa," Auri said.

He brushed back a lock of hair. "It's okay, peanut. It was my job and we took down a man who needed taking down."

"Poetry was right," Sun said, her awe apparent by her vacant expression. "He really does have a superpower." She'd probably have to give him a raise now.

Sun's mom walked over to the bed. She put her arm around Levi, who reciprocated wholeheartedly. "Sun," she said almost reluctantly, "your father and I have changed our minds."

Sun snapped back and looked warily between her mom and her dad. "About?"

"We think maybe you should get your old job in Santa Fe back," her dad said. "Give up this whole sheriffing thing."

Her mom nodded. "Nothing like any of this ever happened when you were a detective. You and Auri were both a lot safer."

"After getting me elected illegally? You want me to turn tail now?"

"We think it would be best. For both of you."

"Maybe, but you have to admit, everything that has happened recently is pretty rare. This town is normally so quiet."

"That's true, but lately it's been one thing after another."

"What do you think, bug?"

"We can't pack it in now," she said, looking at Levi like she wouldn't leave him for the world. "We've come so far. And you guys are here and Cruz is here and . . . and Dad is here." She looked at Levi almost askance, as though calling him Dad might upset him, but it was the surprise in his eyes that had Sun smiling. On the inside because she didn't want to ruin the moment.

"Besides," Auri added, "after all we've been through, what else could possibly go wrong?"

And there went that.

"I think the bigger question should be, is Dad moving in with us or are we moving in with Dad?"

Sun and Levi's gazes met in surprise. Leave it to her daughter to skip ahead.

# Acknowledgments

Thank you, my loverly readers, for picking up this, the final mystery of Sunshine and Auri Vicram! I can't believe their story has come full circle already. I am so in love with these characters and am having a very difficult time letting them go. Alas, on that note, there are so many people who helped with this journey, and I will never be able to express the depths of my gratitude. The following is only a partial list of the heroes who came to my aid.

First, thank you to my incredible agent, Alexandra Machinist. I've never forgotten our first phone call and am still honored to be with you. And to my film agent, Josie Freedman, whose savvy never ceases to amaze me. May the three of us have many more adventures together.

Thank you to my amazing editor, Alexandra Sehulster, who works hard to keep me on my toes. And she puts up with me. That in itself is an achievement worthy of celebration. As always, I am beyond grateful.

Thank you to copy editor Ed Chapman. Or, as we like to call him, Eagle-Eye Ed. (Just kidding. No one calls him that. But they should. He's outstanding.)

Thank you to Trayce Layne, my continuity editor, beta reader, research assistant, shoulder. . . . As always, you somehow manage to see the forest *and* the trees.

Thank you to Jeffe Kennedy for hanging out, brainstorming, commiserating. I cherish our time together.

Thank you to everyone who works so tirelessly behind the scenes at St. Martin's Press, Macmillan Audio, ICM Partners, and Piatkus for everything you do.

And thank you to the invincible Lorelei King! You breathe such gorgeous life into my characters and I am so very, very grateful.

Thank you to my Netters and my Dana. Aka, my everythings.

Thank you to Ursula for lending me your husband, and to Malin for agreeing to be lent. Your insight is simply invaluable.

Thank you to everyone at Portales Writer's Coffee. I look forward to every Saturday because of you. And because of Sweetwater's mocha lattes. But mostly you.

Thank you to my family. You know who you are. You know there is no escape. All hope is lost. Just give up. You are stuck with me. Stop contacting lawyers.

And lastly, thank you to my GRIMLETS!!! You are the best! Second only to BTS, but it's a super close race, so hang in there! Mwah!

Donita Massey

*New York Times* and *USA Today* bestselling author
DARYNDA JONES won a Golden Heart Award and a RITA
Award for her manuscript *First Grave on the Right*. A born
storyteller, she grew up spinning tales of dashing dam-
sels and heroes in distress for any unfortunate soul who
happened by, annoying man and beast alike. Darynda
lives in the Land of Enchantment, also known as New
Mexico, with her husband and two beautiful sons, the
Mighty, Mighty Jones Boys.